VILLAINY
IN
VIENNA

VILLAINY
IN
VIENNA

A FIONA FIG MYSTERY

Kelly Oliver

First published by Level Best Books/Historia 2021

This novel is entirely a work of fiction. The names, characters and incidents portrayed in it are the work of the author's imagination. Any resemblance to actual persons, living or dead, events or localities is entirely coincidental.

Kelly Oliver asserts the moral right to be identified as the author of this work.

Author Photo Credit: Vanderbilt Photo Studio

First edition

ISBN: 978-1-68512-067-2

Cover art by B.&P Design Studio

This book was professionally typeset on Reedsy.
Find out more at reedsy.com

For Dad, my favorite Fiona fan

Praise for the Fiona Figg Mysteries

"I love Fiona Figg! In *Villainy in Vienna*, Oliver delivers a satisfying tale of World War I espionage, rich with historical details from 1917 Vienna, and perfectly laced with humor and high jinks. Brilliant!"—Margaret Mizushima, author of the award-winning Timber Creek K-9 Mysteries

"The Fiona Figg mysteries are a perfect blend of wit, fun, and intrigue."—Debra Goldstein, Author of the Sarah Blair Cozy Mysteries

"A fun diversion with an entertaining female lead."—Kirkus Reviews

Chapter One

The Sacher Hotel

A s I sipped my strong Viennese coffee, the mournful wail of St. Stephen's Pummerin bell echoed through the dining hall. I cringed at the thought of another heroic soul martyred for Britain. The Great War had been dragging on since 1914, three long years now. *Crikey.* And here I was, behind enemy lines with a list of British agents, trying to prevent one—or more—of them from being assassinated. If I wasn't careful, I would be the next in line at the cathedral.

The ringing of the cathedral bells signaled that another Allied collaborator had been found guilty of treason and publicly executed in St. Stephen's Square. I hated to think what happened to English spies. They were probably drawn and quartered. I shuddered. *There but for the grace of God...*

I took another sip and licked the cream off my upper lip. Strictly a tea-drinker back home in London, the bittersweet beverage had been growing on me since I arrived in Vienna a week ago. Like everything else in Vienna, its deceptive surface hid layers of surprises underneath.

Under a light sprinkling of cocoa powder lay a thick layer of cream floating atop the dark black brew below. Although the transparent glass revealed its strata, the effect on the tongue was no less shocking. First, the flavor of chocolate tickled the mouth, then the cream exploded like a balloon, only to be popped soon after by the sharp bite of the coffee. I took another sip.

Glancing around the scarlet dining room of the Sacher Hotel, I felt myself enveloped in the velvety petals of a red rose. As I'd learned from my recent experiences working for British Intelligence, where there were roses, there were thorns.

An odd person caught my eye. At first, I thought it must be a man, due to the stern square jaw and ruddy plain face—at least what I could see of it. But given the lace-collared dress, I decided she must be a woman. Head buried in her notebook, she was frantically writing. Was she a journalist? Or perhaps a novelist? Or a fellow spy?

My curiosity got the best of me. I screwed up my courage to ask if I might join her, seeing as we were two women dining alone. I was about to stand up when two boys joined her. Her sons? The older one must have been a teenager. He had her same pensive eyes and fine hair but wore it short over his ears. The younger one, maybe seven years old, had longer hair, an open face, and was wearing an adorable little sailor's suit. But there was something melancholy, even tragic, about his demeanor.

I felt a hand on my shoulder and turned my head to see Frau Sacher, the hotel's friendly proprietress, standing over me.

"*Mögen sie der Einspänner?*" Frau Sacher smiled down at me.

"*Sehr gut,*" I responded with my deplorable accent. I thought she'd just asked me if I liked my coffee. But "*Sehr gut*" would have been my answer no matter what she'd asked, and not because everything was always *very good*.

Frau Sacher bent closer. "Did you know Einspänner is named for the coachman of a horse-drawn carriage?" she whispered in English. After glancing around the room, she continued. "The whipped cream keeps the coffee hot and prevents it from spilling so the coachman can hold it in one hand and the reins in the other." Like everyone else I'd met at the Sacher Hotel, Frau Sacher could speak perfect English, but usually had the good sense not to... est the bells of St. Stephen's ring for her. "It's the coffee every woman would order if it were a man. Strong but sweet."

Anna Sacher was a formidable woman who'd taken over running the place when her husband died over a decade ago. Her dark hair was neatly pinned in curls on the top of her head. She wore a burgundy dress with a tight-fitting bodice. Perhaps a little too tight for her matronly figure.

Holding a miniature French bulldog in one arm, she used her smoldering cigar to gesture toward the chair across the small table from me and then said something in German.

Since she was pointing to the chair, I assumed she must want to sit down. I smiled and nodded, as I did whenever I was standing on the gangplank of my own limited German.

Puffing on the cigar, she adjusted her skirts and sat down. She leaned so close that her nose brushed against my wig. "We all must take the bitter with the sweet. *Ja?*"

The little dog wiggled out of her arm and stepped up onto the table. *Blimey.* With its considerable tongue, it lapped the cream off the top of my coffee. "*Ja,*" I said, blowing into the little beast's face in hopes it would back off.

Frau Sacher laughed. "Bruno, you naughty boy," she said sternly, as if scolding him in English made her playful reprimand more serious. Instead of removing the animal from the table, she waved at one of the waiters and barked orders at him in German. From what I could make out, she'd instructed him to bring another *Einspänner* for me and something for Bruno.

Seems we would be three for breakfast. One of us had awful breath and appalling table manners. Thankfully, when the waiter returned, he set a bowl of cream on the floor and then removed the stubby black dog from the table and placed him near the bowl at Frau Sacher's feet. With the spartan war rations, some people back home would have given their eyeteeth for that nice bowl of cream.

"*Braver Junge,*" she said, bending down to pat the pup between its batlike ears. "Good boy." As she ascended to human heights once more, she blew out a billow of cigar smoke.

It was bad enough I'd had to endure Clifford's blasted cigarettes all the way from London. Captain Clifford Douglas also worked for the War Office and had recently become a good friend. He'd been ordered to drive me here for my mission. On strictly a need-to-know basis, however, he didn't know all the details.

A foul cloud of cigar smoke ambushed me, and I stifled a cough.

Frau Sacher was rarely seen without a cigar in one hand and a dog in the other. How did she get the cigars? Tobacco was hard to come by these days, which in my opinion was the one advantage of the war.

Anyway, whoever heard of a woman smoking cigars? Either Austrian women were pluckier than British women or Anna Sacher was in a class of her own. From what I'd seen of the elegant sopranos who crossed over Kärntner Strasse from the Hofoper Theater on the arms of dukes or tycoons, I'd say it was the latter.

As if reading my mind, Frau Sacher stubbed out her cigar into a small gold case she carried in a secret pocket. She placed the half-smoked cigar in a matching gold tube and slipped both into her dress. Putting a hand up to hide her mouth, she whispered conspiratorially, "you'd never know I was born a butcher's daughter." Beaming with pride, she made a sweeping gesture with her hand, leading my gaze in a panoramic appreciation of her accomplishments, which were considerable. "Of course, the war has taken its toll...."

Despite the war, the lofty engraved ceilings and marvelous wooden beams gave the dining room an air of dignity. The grand hotel boasted a bright marble lobby soaked in warm golden hues with carved mahogany accents and two striking oriental vases almost my height.

Two hallways led from the lobby in different directions. Off one hallway was the scarlet dining room, and off the other, the emerald dining room. Both were dripping in color—monochromatic color. In the scarlet, everything from serviettes to drapes, and wallpaper to lampshades was, well, red. *Talk about wearing rose-colored glasses.* The emerald was the mirror image, only in a lush green. Both were adorned with paintings of hounds and Kaisers. At the end of the scarlet hallway, near the public lift, was a dark masculine library with rich oak-paneled walls, a stained-glass ceiling, and deep-red satin and velvet chairs and divans. Heavy gilded lamps hung from thick chains overhead.

Nothing at the Sacher Hotel was done by halves. Still, like the rest of the war-torn world, the splendor of its heyday lingered under a melancholy shroud of dust and broken promises.

Frau Sacher called another waiter over. With most men away on the battlefield, her staff was made up of wounded warriors and war widows. After a brief discussion in German, she waved the waiter away and turned back to me. "Let's move to a private room, shall we?" She lifted the dog into her arms. "That way we can talk freely, *Ja?*"

"*Ja.*" I picked up my coffee cup to bring it along.

"Leave that," she said. "Werner will bring you a new one."

"Werner?" That was one of the names on my list. Before I'd left London, Captain Hall had given me a list of agents operating in Vienna. As a newly minted spy, my clearance level wasn't very high, and as such, I was only able to see the code names of low-level operatives. The list contained only three names: Werner Liebermann, Maggie O'Dare, and Oscar Fuchs. After I memorized the names, I burnt the list. If I was caught, I wouldn't have that information on me. And no one could pry it from my brain. Not even with hot pokers or electric wires.

Any or all of them could be Fredrick Fredricks's target in Vienna. Fredrick Fredricks was a South African huntsman working as a spy for the Germans and posing as an American reporter for a New York newspaper. The blackguard got around.

"What is Werner's last name?" *What are the chances?* "I have a cousin whom I haven't seen since childhood. His name is Werner Liebermann. Probably not, but..."

"That's it. Werner Liebermann." Frau Sacher smiled. "Small world. Although it is a common name in Austria. Does he look at all familiar?"

"I need another look."

"How about a piece of cake?" she asked. "To celebrate finding your cousin?"

"You still have cake?" I blurted out. The Sacher Hotel had been famous for its delicious Sacher Torte, invented by Frau Sacher's father-in-law as a special pudding for the prince. *But how can they continue to make it on war rations?* I'd heard that the Central Powers were even worse off for wheat than the Allies.

"Only for special visitors." Frau Sacher leaned closer. "I have friends in Hungary... and other places," she said with a sly smile. "Unless you'd rather have a slice of K-Brot?" She winked. Liberated prisoners of war told stories about the heavy dark German bread made of barley, potatoes, and sometimes even straw.

I shook my head. First thing in the morning seemed a bit early for cake, but I couldn't resist. "*Danke.*" My mouth watered in anticipation. I hadn't had a decent chocolate dessert since before the war broke out.

Frau Sacher led me to a small private dining room off the kitchen. Unlike the monochrome palette of the scarlet or emerald rooms, this had the feel of a private chamber only used by the proprietress. It was windowless, but nonetheless bright and cheerful with ivory wallpaper accented with cerulean flowers. I sat down across from Frau Sacher at a small table covered with a linen tablecloth.

"Better, *Ja?*" She smiled and snuggled the dog. "Now we may do as we like and talk about whatever we please without any prying eyes or pricking ears."

Ja. If Frau Sacher escorted you to one of her famous private salons, you could do whatever you liked in whatever language you chose, and no one was the wiser. Even high-ranking officers in the Austrian army and their German counterparts enjoyed the pleasures of secret assignations in Frau Sacher's back rooms. Her motto, "Discretion over decorum," seemed quietly engraved in invisible ink above the entrance to every private suite. She kept the butlers under strict orders to keep their gobs shut or face the Sacher equivalent of a firing squad.

Rumor had it, on any given night in the back rooms of the Sacher Hotel, generals and revolutionaries plotted coups d'état, politicians brokered peace and war, princes and starlets consummated clandestine liaisons, and unsavory businessmen closed shady deals.

Naturally, I had no firsthand knowledge of any such villainous pursuits nor the participants therein. Unless you counted last night, when I glimpsed Count Manfred, shirt unbuttoned, waving a champagne bottle at a certain lacy lady of the stage, who was decidedly not the princess...or yesterday, when I heard the murmuring of deep voices, accompanied by the rustling of papers, which stopped abruptly at a pause in the clacking of my heels on the hallway floor. Not that I was eavesdropping, mind you.

As a spy for British Intelligence, I had more sophisticated means of gathering information. I didn't need to conveniently drop my hanky and peek through keyholes.

Werner delivered a beautiful piece of toast with melted butter to Frau Sacher and another Einspänner heaped with whipped cream, along with a generous slice of Sacher Torte, to me. I clapped my hands together, positively giddy at the sight of the lovely cake. Obviously pleased with my reaction, Werner bowed.

"Werner," Frau Sacher said. "Mrs. Douglas grew up with someone with your same name." She turned back to me. "Do you think you know each other?"

"Unlikely," Werner said. "I grew up in Ruhr, Germany, ma'am." With that, he turned and limped away.

"Poor man," Frau Sacher said. "Injured in the war."

Suddenly, I lost my appetite. "Both sides have seen their share of causalities," I said and then regretted it. I hoped I hadn't given myself away. "Kind of you to hire the war wounded." If Werner had fought for the Germans, then he wasn't the right Liebermann. Then again, if he'd turned and was now working for the British, he could very well be Fredricks's target. I needed to get Werner alone and question him.

"All of my staff are either war wounded or poor students. I let them eat for free. Otherwise, I dare say they would starve."

"That's very kind of you."

"I wish this war would end. It's bad for business." She kissed Bruno on the head. "Isn't it Bruno, *meine liebe?*"

"Except those for whom war *is* their business." As a defense against the cigar and the dog, I held the cup to my lips and inhaled the bittersweet aroma of cream and coffee.

"Some get fat off others' suffering." She gestured toward my cake. "Aren't you going to try it?"

I half-heartedly picked up my fork. It didn't seem right to eat cake while others went hungry. I pushed the fork tongs through the surprisingly resistant outer layer of chocolate and scooped up a bite. Frau Sacher watched expectantly as I popped the forkful into my mouth. *Oh my word.* Dark-chocolate icing, dense chocolate sponge cake, and a thin layer of apricot jam.

"Do you like it?" she asked, her eyes bright.

I picked up another forkful. "Absolutely scrummy." I closed my eyes so I could savor the sweet treat. "Genius. Apricots and chocolate. Brilliant!" No frills or pastry flowers. Just a simple layer cake. So simple, in fact, it was downright masculine. I imagined crown princes, philosophers, and race car drivers enjoying a slice of Sacher Torte with a good cigar...*if there was such a thing as a good cigar.*

Since I had her ear, I might as well ask about the other on my list. "I have another cousin whom I haven't seen since childhood. By any chance have you ever come across Maggie O'Dare?"

"Pretty redhead?" she asked.

Not knowing what else to do, I nodded.

"Ah, that was a tragedy." She tightened her lips.

"Did something happen to Maggie?"

"She used to come to the hotel with Colonel Schmidt when he visited from Berlin." She waved her cigar. "Sadly, the last time he visited, he told me there was an accident at a lake while they were on holiday, and she drowned. Poor girl."

A German colonel. An accident. More likely he discovered she was a British spy and dispatched her. Poor girl indeed. "Very sad." *Sigh.* I could cross Maggie O'Dare off the list.

"On a happier note, a barn swallow told me you've been invited to His Majesty's birthday party." Frau Sacher had a mischievous twinkle in her eyes.

Is there anything this woman doesn't know? She probably knew the best-kept secrets of the entire city. "I have the honor—"

She cut me off. "Their Majesties won't visit us at the hotel unless they have to." She leaned so close I could smell the acrid cigar on her breath. "They think us decadent."

Speaking of decadent, I took another bite of cake. Holding my hand in front of my mouth, I tried to chew and speak. "Why is that?" As if I didn't know. Cream for dogs. Cake for breakfast. Cigars for women.

Frau Sacher's countenance clouded over as fast as an August thunderstorm. "Our secrets aren't deadly enough for them."

I nearly dropped my fork. *What does she mean? The secrets of the Sacher Hotel aren't deadly enough for the Emperor and Empress?*

There were more layers to Frau Sacher than her father-in-law's famous Sacher Torte. Perhaps at this afternoon's garden party at Schönbrunn Palace, I'd find out what she meant.

Werner appeared in the doorway holding another miniature bulldog. A familiar receding hairline and pair of blue eyes towered over him. *"Ihr Mann ist hier*, Frau Douglas," he said, fiddling with a serviette.

"My man?" I asked.

"Ah, your husband." Frau Sacher nodded at me. "Should we invite him in?"

Blast. I'd forgotten all about my *husband.*

Chapter Two

What to Wear

Clifford joined us at the table. "I say, whose cigar is that?" He spotted the smoldering nub sitting on the edge of an ashtray. Obviously expecting to see some cigar-smoking man appear out of the woodwork, he glanced around the room.

Captain Clifford Douglas was a good sort of chap. The kind of proper upstanding Englishman any woman would be pleased to call her "*Mann.*"

Any woman except me. Clifford was decent and handsome and brave. But he was a bit of a chauvinist, a blabbermouth, and sometimes downright annoying. The War Office had not only made him my personal chauffeur on this mission, but also my bodyguard, working undercover as my husband.

"It's mine," Frau Sacher said, snatching up the nub and taking a puff.

"Good Lord." Clifford's eyes widened. He turned to me. "I say, Fiona, I hope you're not going to take up cigar smoking."

"Why not?" I glared at him. "You smoke."

"That's different. I'm a man and you're my—"

"Frau Sacher, might I have a cigar?" I asked out of spite. Clifford was taking our marital ruse a bit too far.

"Of course, my dear." She smiled and pulled another cigar out of the secret pocket in her frock. Using a special tool, she snipped off one end and then handed it to me.

I held it to my mouth, and she lit it. Hesitantly, I took a puff. *Crikey.* I nearly choked to death. I couldn't stop coughing. And my mouth tasted like my tongue had spent the morning cavorting in a rubbish heap. Just one puff had completely ruined my delightful breakfast. I handed the offensive thing to Clifford.

Frau Sacher laughed.

"See," he said with a smirk, surveying the remnants of my chocolate torte and several empty coffee cups. "And what in heaven's name is going on here?"

"Frau Sacher was telling me about the history of the hotel," I said once I'd caught my breath. "Would you like the last bite of cake?" I asked as a peace offering.

He glanced at his watch and shook his head. "Women smoking. Cake for breakfast. What will be next?"

"Divorce?" I said playfully.

His forehead crinkled and he got that now familiar hurt puppy look. I patted his shoulder. "Now, now, don't pout, Clifford dear."

"Till death do us part," Frau Sacher said wistfully. "In Austria, we mate for life. It's the Catholic way. But I guess you've forgotten that living in England so long."

Clifford took my hand. "I'm sure Fiona was only joking." He gazed over at me so lovingly that I withdrew my hand with a jolt.

Unfortunately, Clifford was serious about marriage. So serious in fact, he'd proposed to no less than three women in the last year. Four if you counted me. A lady didn't dare cry in front of Clifford. He couldn't resist a woman's tears. They brought him to one knee every time.

"Yes," I said, recovering myself. "We have been away too long."

Our cover story was that we were both Austrian by birth, the children of Austrian business partners who'd emigrated to England decades ago, grown up there together, fallen in love, and married. Once the war broke out, the Brits chased us back to Vienna.

"So long in fact," I continued, "I've nearly forgotten my mother tongue."

"Such forgetfulness could cost you your life." When Frau Sacher glanced at me out of the corner of her eye, I got the distinct impression that she

11

knew more than she let on.

My cheeks burned. *Does she suspect me of lying? Have I somehow blown my cover already?* That was precisely why I preferred clever disguises to complicated backstories. A full beard and bushy eyebrows spoke for themselves... not to mention that they could hide the blush of embarrassment over some perfectly innocent faux pas.

"I say, is that a threat?" Clifford asked, his hackles up, always ready to defend his lady.

"Don't be silly," I said. "Frau Sacher is just stating a fact. And you remember your German, don't you, dear?" I feigned a sweet smile.

"Well...I...I suppose...I mean..." Clifford stuttered and stammered. *"Ja. Ich habe hunger..."* He sputtered and stumbled. I didn't think it possible, but his accent was no better than mine.

"Sehr gut," I said.

Frau Sacher raised her eyebrows. "If you want to keep your heads, perhaps you should keep your mouths shut."

"Excellent advice," I said, folding my serviette and placing it on the table next to my empty plate. "But now I must prepare for the royal garden party."

"The gardens at Schönbrunn Palace are magnificent. Even the war can't diminish their splendor." She kissed her dog on the head. "Right, *meine liebe.* Bruno loves a nice garden."

I bet the little beast would love nothing more than digging up the royal daisies. "Thank you for breakfast, Frau Sacher," I said, brushing stray cake crumbs from my lap. "Very kind of you. Now if you'll excuse us." I gestured to Clifford.

He stood and then pulled out my chair. I took his arm. Only for show, mind you. Still, he beamed like a schoolboy just given a sweetie.

"Whatever they offer you, fill your mouths," Frau Sacher said.

"Yes, I imagine they have marvelous food at the palace." I couldn't think of eating another bite after stuffing myself on Sacher Torte and cream.

"No. Their food is not fit for my dogs." Frau Sacher waved her cigar in the air. "But if your mouth is full, your tongue cannot give you away."

She had a point. Not knowing what to say to that, I simply nodded and ushered Clifford out of the dining room.

* * *

Thank goodness Clifford and I had a suite with two bedrooms separated by a living area... and a door.

My room was small but cozy. Compared to what I was used to, it was downright luxurious with its four-poster feather bed, oversized pillows, and the convenience of my own private loo. The décor was tastefully done in soft shades of Argentine jacquard.

Sharing a water closet with Clifford was bad enough. But, for the sake of crown and country, we must keep up our charade.

I was, after all, hot on the trail of the notorious German spy, Fredrick Fredricks, also known as the Black Panther. Originally from South Africa, my nemesis was an expert hunter, skilled marksman, and as stealthy as a panther. This wasn't the first time I'd tangled with Fredricks. But if I had my way, it would be the last.

Bedroom door closed and firmly locked, I stood in front of my wardrobe, asking myself the most important question of the day—of any day.

What should I wear?

Always a difficult question, today it was more vexing than usual. I'd never been to an imperial palace, let alone a royal garden party. Growing up the daughter of a greengrocer, I'd never even had occasion to wear a silk shirt or a cashmere sweater. My wedding to Andrew Cunningham was the first time I'd even worn a fitted gown. *Sigh.* That dress still hung in the back of the closet in our London flat, well, *my* London flat since he'd left me.

Not that I bore him any ill will anymore. Andrew had been dead for almost a year now. I'd been holding his hand when he died. *Bloody Germans.* I shuddered.

Working as a volunteer nurse at the Charing Cross Hospital, I saw too many young men succumb to the horrors of mustard gas. Poor Andrew. He may have cheated on me with his secretary—and then had the cheek to marry her—but even philandering husbands didn't deserve mustard gas. A slow-acting poison perhaps…

I became a spy to get far away from my flat on Warwick Avenue and my memories of Andrew. Perhaps I should have just moved flats. Somehow deadly espionage was easier than leaving behind forever the flat I'd shared with the love of my life for four blissful years. And it was a whole lot more exciting.

As I shifted through my dresses, looking for the perfect outfit for this afternoon's royal garden party, I peeked at the small suitcase in the back corner of the armoire and smiled. I had packed a spare mustache and full beard, along with three very fine wigs, and a couple of clever disguises just in case. *You never know when a good disguise will come in handy.*

Captain Hall, the head of espionage at the War Office, had expressly forbidden me from wearing my "silly getups," as he called them. *What Captain Hall doesn't know won't hurt him.* Somehow, though, he always managed to find out. Blasted spies never could keep a secret.

Even so, before I left London, Captain Hall had given me a modest expense account to purchase some clothing appropriate for espionage at a royal ball. Yes, the garden party was the least of my worries. It was only the appetizer. The royal fancy dress ball to celebrate Emperor Charles I's thirtieth birthday was the main course. Or, as he was known to his friends, Karl Franz Joseph Ludwig Hubert Georg Otto Maria, emperor of Austria, King of Hungary, Croatia, Bohemia, and the head of the house of Habsburg-Lorraine.

No wonder German was so deuced difficult to learn. Officials at the Danube steamboat company were called this mouthful: Donaudampfschifff ahrtselektrizitätenhauptbetriebswerkbauunterbeamtengesellschaft. The way they smashed words together, some of the street signs were a block long. I would hate to see a German word-cross puzzle.

I fingered my new chiffon frock. I adored the delicate ivory ruffles, lilac flowers, and velvet turquoise belt, and the matching smart velvet turban. Just removing the elegant garments from the wardrobe made my heart soar. My first royal garden party. *Imagine. I'll meet princes and dukes and barons.*

I slipped off the plain skirt and blouse I'd worn to breakfast and slid into the airy meringue of chiffon and ruffles. I whirled and waltzed across the room to the dressing table, where I applied a pat of rouge, a bit of eye kohl, and a dab of lipstick.

A glance in the looking glass emptied my head of romantic storybook notions of meeting Prince Charming and eloping to Switzerland. The dress may be beautiful and elegant, but I was not. I looked like a charwoman dressed up in my mistress's finery. This getup felt more like a costume than my Dr. Vogel or Harold the bellboy outfits ever did. Sadly, I looked better with a mustache to cover my thin upper lip, or better yet, a full beard to cover my receding chin.

If only my auburn locks would grow back. My hair always was my nicest feature. I'd cut it off to pose as a man and now it had grown just enough to make me look like a frightened porcupine, which is why I wore a wig these days, even when I wasn't in one of my disguises.

Buck up, Fiona old girl. You're not here to romance a prince. You're here to prevent a murderous spy from killing another one of our agents. Anyway, my heart already belonged to someone. Lieutenant Archie Somersby. I hardly knew the man, but he'd quite swept me off my feet. Of course, for all I knew, he was dead in a ditch somewhere. I shuddered. And even if he wasn't, I'd probably never see him again.

A knock at the door caught me off guard. It was the interior door to my private bedroom, so it could only be Clifford. I glanced at my watch. For once he was early. Fake marriage must agree with him.

I tucked my new spy lipstick and my nail-file set (which was really a lockpicking kit) into my clutch. I couldn't wait to try out the lipstick's tiny mirror for lip-reading or find an enemy's microfilm to tuck into its secret compartment. Of course, picking a lock would be good fun too.

As I closed the clasp, my finger met the hard steel of the only other occupant of my purse. Mata Hari's tiny handgun. The pearl-handled pistol and her jade ring were my only souvenirs of that remarkable woman. Like watching my own husband—ex-husband—die in my arms, witnessing that graceful woman die by firing squad outside Paris was one of the hardest things I've ever done. A chapter I'd just as soon forget.

A quick dab of powder to my nose—for all the good it did—and I was ready to face the enemy emperor… and my sham spouse.

Clifford looked smart in his navy morning suit. The subtle stripes and tailored jacket flattered his trim torso. And his baby-blue tie set off his eyes. He held a ribbon-trimmed boater under his arm. Yes, he'd do. "I say," his countenance brightened. "You look gorgeous. Like a proper lady."

"Do I usually look like an improper lady?"

"Why no… that's not it at all… of course not," Clifford stammered. "You're always a proper lady. Except. It's just that… Really, Fiona, you know what I mean."

Oh, Clifford, if you only knew how improper a lady I am. I laughed. He was always so gullible and sincere. It was great fun to tease him.

"Do you think your old pal Fredrick Fredricks will be at the party?" I asked innocently. Although Captain Hall had assigned Clifford to deliver me from London to Vienna, I wasn't sure how much he knew about my espionage activities or my assignment to report on Fredricks, infamous German spy and one of Clifford's best friends.

Back in Paris, Fredricks told me the Tommies "murdered" his family in Africa during the Boer War, after British soldiers had their way with his sister. Even if it was true—and I sincerely hoped it wasn't—it was no excuse to repay murder with murder. Fredricks was poisoning our agents. More accurately, he was poisoning the double agents, the ones who once worked for the Germans, and therefore knew their secrets. He was making sure they couldn't divulge what they knew to the allies.

According to Freudian psychoanalysis, criminals were made and not born. Biological destiny didn't give birth to the criminal mind, but rather one's childhood circumstances did. If Fredricks was telling the truth when he said he'd witnessed British soldiers killing his family, then it's no wonder he turned to crime.

Unfortunately for me, the War Office had a long list of spies in Austria, which made it impossible to know which one Fredricks was after. Given the sensitive nature of their assignments, and how long it took to embed spies in enemy territory, Captain Hall was not at liberty to give me the full list. Indeed, communications had been cut off for the last several months, and he wasn't even sure how many were still "operative"—as poor Maggie O'Dare's death made clear—or what cover names they were currently using.

If I needed to contact the War Office, I was to telephone a Miss Louise de Bettignies, also known as Alice Dubois, a French spy working for the British, who was in residence at the Holeschau Castle in Hungary.

I had to keep my eyes and ears open. Somehow, I had to stop Fredricks before he murdered another British agent. As a file clerk, the worst that could happen was a misfiled document. But in my new life as a spy, one slip up meant people would die.

"I still can't believe he's working for the Germans." Clifford scowled. "We shot Cape buffalo together in the Serengeti, for God's sake." At least he wasn't completely in the dark. Although I suspected that Clifford still admired his dear friend even after discovering the fiend was a German spy.

"Anyone who can shoot a defenseless animal can shoot a man... or a woman." I tugged on a pair of lace gloves. "Or poison them," I said under my breath. Poisoning was Fredrick Fredricks's trademark. He'd poisoned at least two countesses, both double agents secretly working for the Allies. Fredricks was a woman chaser in the worst sense.

"You say the darndest things." Clifford got a concerned look in his face. "Good Lord. You haven't become one of those vegetable eaters. What are they called? Vegetarians."

"Don't be silly." I took his arm. "With war rations, we're lucky to get porridge, let alone fresh vegetables or meat... or Sacher Torte." The memory of the dark chocolate lingered on my tongue, along with the dregs of that nasty cigar. "We should go. We don't want to keep the royals waiting."

"Imagine," Clifford said with a sigh. "An invitation from the king and queen. How did you wrangle it, old girl?"

"Emperor and empress," I corrected him.

Aha. Clifford didn't know that his dear friend, the Great White Hunter, had invited me for the royal birthday party next Saturday.

The question is why? In a brazen act no doubt designed to humiliate me, he'd sent the invitation to the War Office. Was it some kind of practical joke? Or was he setting a fiendish trap? He did like to toy with me.

Threatening in London. Flirting in Paris. Pretending he didn't recognize me when he did. I truly never knew when the bounder was sincere and when he was having me on. Either way, I'd have to keep my guard up. For all I knew, I was his target and he'd lured me here to murder me on enemy territory.

I'd never been on enemy territory before. And I felt deuced vulnerable wearing this light summer dress instead of a sturdy men's suit. If Captain Hall wouldn't allow my getups because they were "unprofessional," I'd have to resort to my wits. *Too bad.* I'd always found my disguises jolly clever and my wits bloody unreliable.

As we walked down the hallway toward the lift, Clifford nattered on about the time King George V addressed his regiment at the front in France. "He isn't afraid to fight. He was in the navy, you know."

Stepping out of the lift, I almost ran into Frau Sacher. "Oh, pardon me," I said, moving out of her way.

Her face was drawn and pale. She looked like she'd been crying.

"What's wrong?" I whispered. I hoped she hadn't been interrogated by the German army for harboring British spies. My pulse quickened. *She doesn't know I'm a spy, does she?*

When I touched her sleeve, she broke down.

"My babies." She sobbed. "They've been kidnapped."

Chapter Three

The Kidnapping

Even adult children are still babies to their mums, especially if they've just been kidnapped.

"Your daughter or one of your sons?" I asked, holding Frau Sacher by both shoulders. She had one daughter and two sons. Had one of them been kidnapped?

She gave me an odd look. "Bruno and Jana."

I returned her queer look. *Who in the world are Bruno and Jana?* Bruno, wasn't that the name of one of her dogs?

"My beloved hounds." She wrung her hands. "Max was hit over the head from behind and my babies were stolen during their walk."

Max was one of Frau Sacher's employees. He worked in the dining room and apparently also walked her dogs. I'd seen him this morning when he'd served my coffee. He was a clean-cut, fit young man with a permanent frown on his sour face.

"Good Lord," Clifford exclaimed. "Why would anyone want to steal dogs?"

To eat. The morbid thought crossed my mind, but I didn't dare give it voice. In times of war, starving people in Europe had been known to eat dogs. My stomach turned. I prayed nothing like that was going on with these two little dumplings.

"Maybe they want the dogs for themselves, as pets." Frau Sacher wiped tears from her eyes. "Or maybe they want money for them."

"Have you received a ransom note or telephone call asking for money?" I asked.

She shook her head. "Nothing."

"Have you called the police?"

Frau Sacher regained her composure. "Even with my standing in the community, the police won't take it seriously. Not with so many officers fighting on the borders."

"And the dog-walking chap?" Clifford asked. "Is he okay?"

"He has a nasty bump on his head. He's in the dining room having a piece of cake." She sniffled. The poor woman looked like she'd aged a decade since breakfast. I felt so sorry for her that I resolved to help. *And if she does know all the secrets of Vienna, it won't hurt to be in her good graces.*

"Show me where they were taken," I said. "If the police won't look into it for you, perhaps we can find clues ourselves." I'd been known to solve a case or two in the past. The royals would have to wait. "To the scene of the crime and then to the dining room," I said, poking the air with my finger for emphasis.

"But the emperor and empress," Clifford said.

"What is a garden party when lives are at stake?" I asked.

"They're only dogs," he said.

"They may be only dogs, but they mean the whole world to Frau Sacher."

"Yes." She sniffed. "I love them like my own babies."

* * *

Frau Sacher led us outside and across a side street to the opera house.

Unlike London with its crooked uneven streets snaking in all directions, Vienna's streets were level and square, laid out in an orderly grid. Perhaps this said something about the English versus the Germanic mind. In London, most of the buildings were made of red brick. In Vienna, they were gray stone. Like the buildings, the Viennese were bland compared to Londoners. Whereas London was loud, dirty, and stank, Vienna was quiet, clean, and the air was fresh.

In the bright August sun, the façade of the opera house's loggia was bathed in gold, and the green roof sparkled. Marble muses on horseback looked down at us mortals as we passed in front of the triumphal arch flanked by two eagles and the Habsburg-Lorraine coat of arms, topped by the Austrian imperial crown.

"Here," Frau Sacher said, crossing onto the grass. She pointed to the skirt of a fountain with a water sprite perched atop a pedestal in the center and three scantily clothed stone women beneath her. According to the guidebook that I'd glanced at the night before, the stone beauty was Lorelei, a siren whose song caused sailors to crash their ships into the rocks. And her three companions were Love, Grief, and Revenge.

As my grandmother used to say: "Every great love is followed by paralyzing grief or murderous revenge." That was certainly true of my marriage to Andrew.

Her hand shaking, Frau Sacher continued pointing at the fountain's stone skirt. "They found Max lying here, bleeding from his head, cradling Mozart."

"Mozart?" Clifford asked.

"My new puppy." Frau Sacher sighed. "Poor brave Max risked his life to save Mozart."

Adjusting my frock, I carefully squatted next to a bloodstain on the base of the fountain. "Very brave."

By the looks of it, Max was lucky the thief hadn't cracked his skull open. I scanned the area for clues. The dognapper had to have been in a hurry. Perhaps he—or she—had dropped something in the scuffle.

Drat. Except the blood, I saw nothing out of the ordinary. Grass that had seen better days, a few leaves, bird droppings, and a crust of bread. *Wait!* A crust of bread. That shouldn't be here.

"Anyone have a hanky?" I asked.

Always chivalrous, Clifford offered me his. As I reached, I tipped forward and landed on my knees. Oh bother. My purse bounced off the fountain and landed in the grass. On hands and knees, I gathered it up. Righting myself, I brushed the grass off my tea dress and gave up any hope of making a good impression on the Austrian royalty. I picked up the toasted crust between my gloved forefinger and thumb and wrapped it in the handkerchief.

"Why are you collecting trash from the lawn?" Clifford asked.

"It's a crust of bread."

"Disgusting." Clifford wrinkled his nose. "You can't be that desperate for something to eat."

"Don't be ridiculous." I stood up. "This bread shouldn't be here."

"Why not?" Frau Sacher asked.

"First, when is the last time you saw bread? Real white bread?"

They both stood staring at me. I knew the answer, of course. They'd both seen beautiful white bread earlier that morning at the Sacher Hotel, one of the only places bread was still served, thanks to the war.

"Second, this couldn't have been here for long." I tucked the evidence into my clutch purse.

"Why not?" Frau Sacher asked again.

"A bird would have eaten it by now if it had." The bread crust was my first clue. Like Hansel and Gretel, I hoped it would lead me to some answers. Since the bread wasn't Max's—he'd been walking dogs, not on a picnic—it must belong to whoever took Frau Sacher's dogs, and that person must be connected to the hotel, either as a guest or a worker. I scanned the ground for more clues. Sigh. Nothing. Not counting the dog poo, which I planned to leave right where it was.

If only the attacker had left some kind of calling card. "Let's go talk to Max."

"What about the garden party?" Clifford asked.

I guess I was more of a sucker for a woman in distress than he was. "It will wait." I wanted to see Max while his memory and wounds were fresh. Still, Clifford was right. We shouldn't be late for a royal party. *Sigh*. A few more minutes wouldn't matter.

Then again, my mission did matter. Captain Hall wouldn't approve of me playing Sherlock Holmes to a dognapping—even if it was in the service of getting into Frau Sacher's good graces to get more information out of her. *Let's hope the Captain doesn't find out.*

* * *

His head wrapped in a white bandage, Max was sitting in Frau Sacher's private dining room finishing the last bite of Sacher Torte. Max was a young man in his twenties with floppy brown hair and an air of indifference. He wore his hotel uniform like a snake in the process of sloughing off its skin. *Frau Sacher must be having trouble getting reliable help.*

Like a furry centerpiece, Mozart was standing on the table, lapping up porridge from a bowl, his stubby corkscrew tail whirling in delight. He obviously didn't care if his siblings had been dognapped. Unlike his siblings, Mozart was sable with a white tummy and brown mask. I had to admit, he was an adorable little chap.

Frau Sacher said something to Max in German. He smiled and nodded. "*Ja, ja.*"

"Might Max tell us exactly what happened? Did he see his attacker?" I asked.

"No. Did not see," Max said in halting English, which, I'm sorry to say, was worlds better than my German. "Hit head. Behind. Fell down. Dogs gone." His eyes watered, and he looked like he might cry. "Mozart. *Sehr* lucky."

"Yes. Mozart is very lucky." The creature was licking whipped cream off the cake plate. I hoped they would wash that dish in strong disinfectant before using it again. "Did you see anyone eating bread when you were walking the dogs? A crust of bread fell at the scene of the crime." I carefully opened the handkerchief to reveal the bread.

"Is mine." He blushed. "I was eating *brot.*"

"It's okay, Max," Frau Sacher said. "You were very brave. *Sehr mutig.*" She patted his hand. "You saved my baby." Cooing, she picked up the puppy and hugged it to her ample bosom.

Drat. The crust wasn't a clue, which meant there were no clues. I folded the hanky around the *brot* and put it into my new clutch purse—one of the trophies from my expense-account shopping trip before I left London.

"Don't you think we should be going, Fiona dearest," Clifford said, glancing at his watch. "We're so late already. It's just not cricket."

"You're right as always," I said, snapping my clutch shut. "Lead the way, *husband.*"

Clifford beamed, oblivious to the sarcasm in my voice.

* * *

An hour later, Clifford pulled up in front of Schönbrunn Palace. I didn't realize it would take so long to get there, or I might have forsaken Frau Sacher and her missing dogs. Hopefully, the garden party was still in full swing.

Schönbrunn Palace was on the outskirts of town, practically in the country. Indeed, as the buildings grew sparser and the trees more plentiful, I felt as if I'd left the city behind entirely. I'd heard the forest around the palace was full of wild game planted there for the royals to hunt. It was beyond me how blood sports could appeal to anyone, especially during a bloody war.

The cobblestone entrance to the palace rivaled the widest street, and the palace glowed yellow in the afternoon sun. The whole of Vienna was proving itself to be a golden city, blessed with an almost divine halo.

The palace was no exception. It stood before us, layers of white and yellow stone, like a grand wedding cake, topped with guardian statues, each holding a shield and a sheath of arrows. Perhaps the fan of arrows behind each figure served the practical purpose of keeping birds from perching.

As a butler escorted us through the palace to the back gardens, I walked with my mouth hanging open.

"I say," Clifford exclaimed. "Look at that." He pointed to the gilded ceiling fresco and lavish gold chandelier. "Puts Buckingham Palace to shame."

"I wouldn't know," I whispered, afraid to make too much noise in a sacred place.

We exited the great hall into the back gardens. *Oh my word.*

The magnificent hedgerows, statues, and fountains took my breath away. I'd never seen anything so glorious... or orderly. Like everything else in Vienna, the entire garden was planned out on a grid. I clapped my hands together in approval.

Dark swirls in the lawns hinted at better days when those beds were presumably filled with colorful flowers. With the bloody war on, it was a miracle they could keep the hedges trimmed. Then again, the Hapsburgs were the most powerful family in Austria. The Hapsburg dynasty had summered at Schönbrunn Palace for centuries. Why stop now just because of a bothersome little war?

Aha! There he was, my quarry. As usual, Fredrick Fredricks was surrounded by beautiful women fawning over him. With his flowing black curls, muscular build, and dancing brown eyes, he was a rather handsome fellow. But he was also a blackguard, a murderer, and a fiend.

After I'd followed him from Ravenswick Abbey to Paris—where he stole my nun's habit and escaped, *again*—the cheeky fellow had the gall to invite me to the emperor's birthday party. And Captain Hall had insisted I accept so I could discern his purpose in Vienna. Given his modus operandi was assassinating double agents, I was to find out who was his target and warn them before he could carry out his murderous plan.

Through no fault of my own, I seemed to have developed a special rapport with the criminal.

To see without being seen, I ducked behind Clifford, which was like trying to hide behind an arrow that said, "over here."

"Fredricks, old man," Clifford bellowed. "Jolly good to see you again."

Good heavens. I sincerely hope Clifford is acting. Because if he isn't, he's already fallen under the spell of the Great White Hunter. Men and women alike fell all over themselves in Fredricks's presence. It was sickening.

Fredricks ambled toward us with an affable smile. "Clifford, old friend." He extended his hand and Clifford took it. Fredricks clapped him on the back. "I see you've brought the delightful Miss Figg," he said with a spark in his eyes as he stepped around Clifford and came toward me.

Of course, he brought me. Fredricks had summoned me here. What did he expect?

"You're looking lovely Miss Figg," Fredricks said, sweeping up my hand to his lips and kissing it. Thankfully, I was wearing gloves. "And you smell as sweet as peace." He smiled at me.

It must have been the heat of the August afternoon. Overcome with a dizzy spell, I felt I might faint. I fanned myself with my clutch and took hold of Clifford's elbow.

"Fiona is Mrs. Douglas now," Clifford said, grinning from ear to ear. When he put his hand on mine, I pulled away.

"Mrs. Douglas, eh?" Fredricks raised one eyebrow. "Clifford was brave on the battlefield. I hope he's as brave in the marital chamber." He chuckled.

"Good Lord." Clifford blushed. "There's no need to be crass."

I glanced from Clifford to Fredricks and back again. If looks could kill, mine would have burned a hole in Fredricks's muscular chest where his heart should have been, had he had one.

"And what of the dashing Lieutenant Somersby?" Fredricks asked, a mischievous glint in his eyes. "Won't he be disappointed?"

My cheeks flushed. I hated Fredricks knowing I was smitten.

To hide my embarrassment, I turned to examine the closest of the dozen statues lined up along the lane. The marble lady's breasts were bare, of course. I never understood why painters and sculptures insisted on nudity. Wouldn't a clothed goddess do just as well? At least the marble woman had a sheet wrapped round her torso. She also had a lion's head draped over her head, and she was holding some sort of club.

"Omphale." Fredricks's deep voice startled me. "Queen of Lydia."

I stared at Omphale's bare feet. I couldn't come right out and ask him who was his target, after all.

"After her husband was gored by a bull, she took over his reign." He moved so close that I could feel the warmth of his body. "She bought Hercules as her sex slave," he whispered in my ear. "She made him scrub floors, hold her knitting, and dress in women's clothes." He smelled of mint and rum. "Remind you of anyone?"

I turned and glared at him. Impertinent man, reminding me of when he stole my clothes and escaped from prison disguised as a nun. "Have you scrubbed any floors lately?" I asked.

He got a sly glint in his eyes. "I would be only too happy to be your

Hercules."

"Yes, well, I'm not Omphale."

"More's the pity."

"I say, what are you two whispering about over here?" Clifford asked, planting himself next to me. He smelled of cigarettes.

"I was just asking Fiona how she keeps her floors so shiny." Fredricks flashed an obscene smile.

Clifford gave me a confused look. "What's that supposed to mean?"

Yes, what did he mean? The cad. Given the lascivious look on his face, I didn't want to know.

"Come on," I said, taking Clifford's arm. "Let's mingle." To discern what the scoundrel was doing in Vienna and why he'd invited me along, I had to determine who would be his next victim. Surveying the guests at the garden party just might give me a clue. If Fredricks was here, it meant his target might be too. I was on the lookout for Mr. Oscar Fuchs, the remaining name on my list.

I scanned the party of well-dressed Austrians. Women wore large hats adorned with flowers and lace. Men wore uniforms or morning suits. All in all, they were smart but not flamboyant. Was one of these gentlefolk his target?

If Fredricks was sent to Vienna to dispose of a double agent before they could deliver German secrets to the Allies, who in this crowd could be a double agent? Perhaps this secret agent would recognize me or Clifford as British operatives and try to arrange an assignation to deliver information, hoping we'd transport it back to the British brass.

Perhaps that's why Fredricks invited me here. To use me as bait to lure the double agent out into the open so he could dispose of him...or, more likely, her, given Fredricks's penchant for killing countesses who acted as double agents.

Chapter Four

The Emperor and Empress

Given how late we'd arrived, I hadn't had time to mingle before the luncheon as I'd hoped. And I still hadn't found Mr. Oscar Fuchs. So far, I'd learned Maggie O'Dare was dead. And I'd met a Werner Liebermann, an unassuming porter at the Sacher Hotel. If he was a spy, he must be a jolly good one, either that or he was a terrible spy. Not in a million years would I have guessed he worked in espionage. The most daring thing I'd seen him do was put an extra dollop of whipped cream on my coffee. That left the mysterious Oscar Fuchs…unless there was another Werner Liebermann at this party.

As I filled my plate, I tried to discern who else might be secretly working for the Allies. It was deuced difficult to determine who was a spy just by looking. After all, who would suspect me of working in espionage for the War Office? Hopefully no one.

To my surprise—and disappointment—the royal garden party was rather spartan in the food department. After Sacher Tortes and fluffy bread at the hotel, I'd expected a sumptuous banquet at the palace. Instead, we were offered a simple dish of boiled potatoes with parsley and a plate of venison and wild boar shot by the royal household. And in lieu of pudding, we were served coffee with cream. Thank goodness for the cream. The coffee was as thick as mud.

The food was set out buffet-style on a long table. So much empty space on either end of the table made the fare look even more meager. Still, Clifford and I both tucked into the luncheon with gusto. With the war on, you couldn't take your next meal for granted.

As I ate, I watched and listened to those around me, on the lookout for anyone suspicious, or anyone who might be a government operative so I could protect them against the assassin Fredrick Fredricks. I took a bite and surveyed the crowd.

The meat was tender and savory. And the potatoes were better than any English boiled potatoes. *The secret must be parsley*. Herbs were precious these days too. Although I was tempted to go for a second helping, I restrained myself in the line of duty. I was here to gather information, not expand my waistline.

After lunch, I left Clifford engaged in deep conversation with a beautiful woman in pink and took the opportunity to perambulate. Eager to get a glimpse of their majesties, I tried not to trip as I weaved in and out between the guests. Perhaps they were waiting to make a grand entrance. Maybe the potatoes and venison were merely appetizers. *Here's hoping. Who knows how they do things in Austria?* As someone who'd barely made it out of Hertfordshire, I was hardly a woman of the world.

Sipping a cup of sludge, I stood next to a lovely young woman in a wicker chair wearing a plain black frock with a broad white collar. Without a speck of makeup or an ounce of pretense, she played fetch with a wirehaired terrier.

"*Sehr klug hund,*" I said, striking up a conversation in my best German, which was not *sehr gut*.

"Yes, he's very clever," she said, smiling up at me. "Won't you join me?" she asked in perfect English.

"How in the world did you know I speak English?" Keeping a low profile in Austria was going to be impossible given my limited language skills.

"You have that pretty pale complexion of the English rose…and of course, your accent."

"I'm afraid my accent is the thorn," I said, taking the wicker chair next to her.

"You should be careful that you don't become overwrought by our Austrian sun." Her intelligent eyes suddenly seemed steely cold.

Was that a threat? "Yes. Of course."

I launched into my cover story. *Our parents were Austrian diplomats, so we were both raised in London, where we met. Once the war started, the British kicked us out. Blah. Blah. Blah. That's why my German is appalling and his isn't much better.*

"No need to apologize," she said, waving away my excuses. "Ours is a multicultural country with seven national languages," she said proudly. "My husband says he speaks Spanish to God, Italian to women, French to men, and German to his horse." She leaned closer. "But don't tell the Kaiser," she whispered.

"Good thing I don't have a horse." I laughed.

"It's all part of our job."

"You and your husband are translators?"

"No." She laughed and extended her gloved hand. "I'm Empress Zita."

My cheeks caught fire. I was mortified. I'd mistaken her for a member of her court and had been nattering on and on. *What is the protocol? Do I stand up and curtsy? Should I take her hand?*

Empress Zita leaned closer and whispered, "My father fancied himself a French prince reigning in Italy, which doesn't go down well these days."

I should say not. France and Italy were the enemies of Austria, which had unfortunately sided with Germany.

The empress continued holding her hand out like she expected me to take it. Either that or kiss it.

Flustered, I extended my own. As I did, my cup slid off its saucer and landed on the paving stones. *Blast.* I wasn't making a very good impression on Her Majesty. The cup was in pieces on the ground. My lovely lilac skirt was stained brown. I grimaced, and with much trepidation, glanced over to assess the damage.

Blimey. I'd splashed coffee on the empress of Austria-Hungary.

"Fortunately, I'm wearing a black dress," she said, bending to brush droplets off the hem.

"I'm so sorry." I picked up shards of porcelain. "And the cup."

"That old thing." She laughed. "It belonged to my husband's great-great-aunt Marie Antoinette."

"Golly." *Ouch!* I cut myself on a sharp edge of my broken cup. I pinched my finger, hoping to stench the flow of blood. Bad enough I had coffee stains on my new dress, but blood stains too.

"You're hurt." Empress Zita stood up and waved to a young woman who was playing with a group of children not far from the rest of the party. The young woman gathered up a baby and held out her hand to a toddler. The oldest boy, who was still quite small, trailed behind as the woman and three small children all dashed across the lawn.

The young woman stopped short in front of us and curtsied. "Yes, Your Majesty." Probably in her twenties, she had lively eyes, loose chestnut curls, and a pretty figure.

"Please take...our guest inside and bandage her hand." The empress kneeled, and the oldest boy, who couldn't have been more than five, put his arm around her shoulders and kissed her cheek. She hugged him back before rising. "I'm sorry I didn't catch your name," the empress said to me.

"Fiona Figg, Your Majesty." *Crikey.* I completely forgot my cover story. I was supposed to be married to Clifford Douglas. "Fiona *Douglas*, wife of Captain Clifford Douglas."

"Elsie, take Mrs. Douglas to the nursery and bandage her hand. Take the children with you." Empress Zita kissed the little boy's forehead and gently pushed him away. "Be a good boy, Otto, and take your little brother and sister inside."

"Yes, Mamma," Otto replied dutifully.

The empress turned to me. "Mrs. Douglas, kindly go with Elsie and she will doctor your hand."

Not wanting to leave behind a mess, I bent down to gather more shards of cup.

"Leave that and go," the empress said forcefully. It was obvious she was a woman used to giving orders and getting obedience.

"Yes, Your Majesty." I made a feeble attempt at a curtsy and then followed

Elsie toward the palace. "Thank you."

Elsie had the same bright intelligent eyes as the empress. I wondered if they were related. Perhaps a younger sister or a cousin acting as nanny?

The children and Elsie moved so quickly, I had trouble keeping up. I was still taking stock of the guests as we brushed past small groups here and there on the lawn. An older woman in gray. Was she related to the empress or emperor? A tall man with a handlebar mustache that bobbed as he talked. Could he be a secret agent? A group of younger women chatting gaily near a sycamore tree. Surely, they weren't spies, were they?

Squeezing my clutch under my arm, I wrapped my good hand around my dripping finger. My beautiful dress was now polka-dotted with red blotches. By the time we crossed the enormous grounds, I'd look like a murder victim.

Although it was obvious the garden had seen better times, even a few weeds here and there didn't distract from the summer glory of greenery and flowering shrubs. Compared to the obsessively manicured English gardens, even the orderly Viennese gardens seemed wild and haphazard. And the dour Viennese people were even more orderly than their gardens, while the boisterous English people were decidedly more chaotic than theirs.

We'd nearly reached the back entrance of the palace when I noticed the same strange woman I'd seen earlier at breakfast. She was sitting on one end of a bench, still scribbling in that confounded notebook. Who was she?

What could be so important that she'd forsaken the royal party for her writing? Indeed, why was she here? Perhaps she was a journalist reporting on the luncheon... or a novelist who'd just overheard a juicy tidbit she had to record to plagiarize later. Whatever she was doing was so absorbing, she didn't even look up as the little princes and princess dashed past laughing and shrieking.

Surely writing in a diary didn't make her a double agent. Indeed, she'd set herself apart from the rest of the party in a most suspicious way. A spy would be trying to blend in, not isolate herself. With the exception of Fredrick Fredricks, of course. Even the clanging of the heavy doors as they opened didn't get her attention.

Once inside, I had to curb my temptation to gawk at the opulence—given the war, one might even say decadence. The children skated across the marble floor. Babe in arms, Elsie hurried after them while I trailed behind, trying not to trip over my own feet as I looked around in awe. The fifty-foot domed entrance had a gilded ceiling painted with frescos. Statues of Hapsburg ancestors stood guard around the perimeter of the grand foyer. Natural light flooded in through huge windows. And everything sparkled. Obviously, the royals had an excellent housekeeping staff.

The clacking of my heels echoed through the chamber. Out of deference, I switched to tiptoe.

Children in tow, Elsie led me out of the great hall and into the private quarters of the family. Their living spaces were modest compared to the public entrance. Instead of grand portraits of Hapsburg ancestors such as those that adorned the gilded walls of the foyer, the family home displayed religious art. Italian Renaissance paintings in the sitting room and icons of the Virgin with child in the nursery.

The nursery was a large cheerful room at the top of a private staircase. Three small beds neatly made, each with a white rosary laying upon its pillow, sat in a row, next to a crib. The oldest boy and his little sister set to work stacking blocks in the corner of the room reserved for playing. Elsie laid the baby in the crib and then sat in a rocking chair, cradling the smallest boy, who must have been about two.

Three small desks formed a triangle in the other corner of the room. I stopped short when I noticed the magazine on top of a stack of books on one of the desks. I picked it up.

Strand Magazine, boasting the latest Sherlock Holmes story. My mum and I both loved those stories. She'd read them and then passed the magazines down to me. "I love Sherlock Holmes," I said.

"Me too," came a small voice from the corner. Otto ran over to me. "Do you know him, *Fraulein*?"

I smiled. "I know of his adventures."

"Will you tell me about them?"

"Of course, dear." I patted his head, and he looked up at me with big dark eyes. He was a gorgeous child with long blond hair.

"The empress insists the boys learn English and French," Elsie said with a heavy accent. "She says if everyone learned the language of their neighbors, there would not be wars."

The empress is a smart woman. "Learn a language, avoid a war, I always say."

Elsie pointed to a water closet. Inside, I found a small sink. Given the floral soap and the feminine smalls hanging above the bathtub, I ventured that this was Elsie's washroom.

I turned on the faucet, and I washed my bloody hand.

With a light rap on the doorframe, Elsie joined. I glanced out into the nursery and saw the boys playing tug-o-war with the blocks. Their sister intervened and offered them each their own building blocks. If only world peace were as simple. Perhaps if women were in charge.

Elsie opened a cabinet. I craned my head to get a look inside. What in heaven's name? One shelf held the usual small clothes, toiletries, and a few medical supplies. But the rest of the cabinet was full of sweeties and treats. I thought I even spotted a plate of half-eaten Sacher Torte. Tucked away on the bottom shelf was an ornate box. I was dying to know what was inside.

"How long have you worked at the palace?" I asked. "Elsie…I'm sorry I don't know your surname."

"Two months," she answered. "And it's Müller. Elsie Müller."

"Where did you grow up?" Something about her accent made me want to know more about her.

She gave me a curious look. "Berlin."

"Do you have any siblings?"

"Only a brother, Kurt." Elsie closed the cabinet and returned with a strip of cloth. I held out my hand. She dried it with one cloth, then wrapped another around my injured finger, and tied the ends together. "There," she said, triumphantly.

"Only two months. How do you get on at the palace then?" I asked. She seemed to have a good relationship with the empress and the children.

"Very well. Except for the children, I keep myself to myself."

A knock on the nursery door sent her flying toward it.

I took the opportunity to peek in the box. *Crikey.* It was full of German banknotes. Either Elsie was extremely well paid for her services as a nanny, or she'd been saving for a rainy day... *or should I say downpour?*

Hearing a male voice from the other room, I quickly closed the box and the cabinet and went to see who was visiting the nursery.

Elsie was standing at the door, which she'd opened just a crack. She whispered in German. I couldn't see the man on the other side of the door. Elsie's skirts fluttered as she lifted one foot and leaned her head out the door. Although I could barely hear what they were saying, let alone understand it, the whispered tone suggested intimacy.

"Who was it?" I asked when Elsie closed the door.

"The count," she said, blushing. She was concealing an envelope behind her back, but I'd seen it in her hand.

Her rosy countenance suggested I was right. "Count?" I asked innocently. *Perhaps he is a secret admirer giving Elsie gifts of sweets and dosh?*

"Count Czernin." She rushed to the lav.

I followed her, but she closed the door partway. Still, through the crack, I saw her place the envelope in the pretty box. Was Count Czernin giving her money?

She returned to the room, all smiles, and then practically skipped to the corner where the children were playing. "Come now children, time for your lessons."

"Count Czernin," I said. "That name is familiar."

"He is the foreign minister," Elsie said.

The nanny and the foreign minister. Intriguing.

"He does not approve of my teaching the children English, or French. He does not approve of Mr. Holmes."

I narrowed my brows. "Mr. Holmes?"

"The Englishman." Elsie took the smallest boy by the hand, led him to a desk, and lifted him onto the seat. When the boy started fussing, she pulled a sweetie from her pocket. I recognized it as a Mozart Bonbon, like the ones laid on my pillow at the hotel. She distributed sweeties to all the children. *Hmmm.* Chocolates and treats. The palace wasn't as austere as it seemed from the meager luncheon spread. "Mr. Holmes," she repeated.

"He doesn't approve of Sherlock Holmes." So, Count Czernin spent time in the nursery. How interesting.

"The foul language of our enemies in our mouths," Elsie hissed in heavily accented English, "will turn to swords in our hands."

Shivers ran up my spine. *There is more to Elsie than meets the eye.* "Is that what Count Czernin says?"

Elsie nodded.

I resolved to tail this Count Czernin. "Perhaps I should leave you to the children and get back to the party," I said, making my excuses to hurry after the count.

Elsie gave another approving nod.

I tucked my now useless gloves into my purse. "Thank you." I waved my bandaged finger as I left the room.

Of course, the hallway was deserted, and the count was long gone. I scurried up the corridor and made my way to the top of the stairs. The grand staircase led in both directions. *Should I look upstairs or down?* Indeed, the palace was enormous. I had no idea where to start. In fact, I didn't even know what exactly I was looking for. Whatever Fredricks was up to, involved the palace. Were the emperor and empress at risk? Fredricks usually went after double agents, but I'd put nothing past the scoundrel. The spartan lunch sunk to the pit of my stomach.

Now was my chance to do some sleuthing. I had to discover Fredricks's target—surely someone now working for us, who once worked for them—and warn him or her. A double agent, the most useful and the most dangerous. For they know the secrets of the enemy.

Voices from down the stairs made me stop in my tracks. I pressed my body to the wall and listened. Men's voices. One of them sounded like Count Czernin. The other had an accent that didn't sound quite German.

Count Czernin could be the double agent Fredricks was sent to dispatch. *Disparaging Sherlock Holmes. Baush.* He sounded too much like a German patriot. Then again, maybe he was just acting the part. If he was a double agent, he wouldn't advertise it.

A disturbing thought crossed my mind. *What if Elsie is the double agent?* If so, she was in great danger.

Lifting the hem of my skirt, I gingerly crept down the steps one by one. As a guest, I couldn't be expected to know my way around the palace. And if I happened to take a detour on my way back to the party, who would be the wiser? I thought of the cathedral's *Pummerin* bell and shuddered.

The voices were coming from inside a room beneath the stairs. I put my ear to the door. *Dash it.* If only my German was better. Aha. *Das Brief. That means letter.* Was the accented man asking Count Czernin to deliver a letter? Judging by Czernin's angry voice, whatever it was, he didn't like it. The accented man's tone was also distressed, but not nearly as violent as Czernin's. The conversation was heated and passionate. After a crescendo that climaxed with a thump, the conversation stopped.

I jumped away from the door and scurried into the foyer. There, I pretended to admire a painting of a stern woman with a double chin, piercing crystal blue eyes, and a strangely asymmetrical tiara atop her head. I glanced back to see the two men exit the room. I recognized Emperor Charles from his photograph. He had thick chestnut hair, sad blue eyes, a dimpled chin, and a mustache. *Why do men wear those vile caterpillars on their upper lips?*

In the emperor's case, I suspected it was to make him appear older. Without it, his youth combined with his baby face would make it difficult for anyone to take him seriously. A mere boy dressing up in a soldier's uniform. For someone so young, he had an awful lot of medals hanging from his breast.

The man with him must be Count Czernin, his foreign minister and Elsie's secret visitor. Count Czernin also wore a mustache. But whereas it softened the emperor's appearance, it hardened his minister's. Bulging eyes, a receding hairline, and a face as long as a horse's made Count Czernin appear as menacing as the emperor seemed benevolent. The count towered over the emperor as they said their strained goodbyes.

I turned back to the painting, held my bandaged hand in front of me, and kept my gaze glued to the white bosom of the stern Hapsburg lady. Empress Maria Theresa. Next to the portrait of the imposing old woman was another of her as a young woman wearing a gorgeous deep-turquoise gown with a severe V-shaped pearl belt and gold embroidery. In both paintings, she had the same piercing gaze, as if she could see right through me.

Count Czernin passed behind me, and I got a whiff of strong tobacco. Solid pipe tobacco. Not that cheap stuff given to British soldiers, who each received a packet of Three Castles Cigarettes along with a pocket New Testament. It smelled sweet like the Buckingham Cut Plug my father used to smoke.

What would my father think if he saw me now? Hard to believe, the daughter of an ordinary greengrocer, once a wife and a file clerk, had become a spy for British Intelligence. If my mum knew, she'd roll over in her grave. I'm sure she'd think espionage was not a fit occupation for a proper young lady, or a divorced adult one—mum's secret fascination with the stories of Sir Arthur Conan Doyle to the contrary.

I heard a door close and turned in time to see the emperor disappear back into the room under the stairs. Blast. I was hoping he would leave, and I could make use of my lockpick. Glancing around, I unclasped my purse, took out the lipstick, and applied a dab, using the mirror to get a glimpse behind me. The coast was clear.

Aside from Count Czernin, who paid me no mind, no one had seen me lurking about the staircase. *At least I hope no one saw me.* Being a plain-looking woman over twenty had its advantages. Being invisible was one of them.

Snapping my clutch shut, I turned on my heels. *Shame really. Who knows when I'll get another chance to explore the private quarters of the royal family.* And who knows what secrets I might find. It certainly was possible the emperor or empress was Fredricks's target, and if so, I needed to find out which one and why. And what about Czernin and Elsie?

I'd just started down the long hallway when I heard the door shut again. My heart was racing as I slid to a stop behind a large potted plant. Peeking through the fern fronds, I saw Emperor Charles lock the door to the room under the stairs. Was it his private study or perhaps some kind of clandestine government planning room?

The emperor put the keys away in his trouser pocket and then bounded up the stairs. With a war on, he didn't have time for parties. He didn't seem to give a fig that he had a dozen guests waiting for him in the back garden.

There were enough pretty young women among them that I hoped Clifford was well occupied.

I slid out from behind the plant and tiptoed toward the emperor's private room. Perhaps the letter that Czernin refused to deliver would give me a clue to why Fredricks was in Vienna and what he was planning. I took a deep breath and held it.

Now is my chance. I may not get another.

Chapter Five

The Secret Room

I glanced down the hallway in both directions and then ran on my tiptoes to the door under the stairs. My bandaged finger made it deuced difficult to remove the lockpicking kit from my purse. The small leather pouch contained a tension wrench, a pick, and a rake, all neatly tucked into their individual slots. Just fingering the tools was a thrill.

I slid the tension wrench, then the pick out of the pouch, and laid my purse and the pouch on the floor—quietly. I couldn't risk attracting attention from anyone who might be nearby.

Practically panting from the adrenaline rushing through my veins, my hands trembled as I slid the thin metal tension wrench into the lock. Applying pressure in one direction and then the other, I determined that the key to this lock turned clockwise. My two-week crash course in espionage was paying off. Imagine how much better I'd do if they'd had more time to train me.

Holding the wrench in place, keeping pressure on the right spot, I slid the metal pick in under the wrench and carefully felt for the pins. Every lock has pins inside that keep it securely closed. To open the lock, I had to essentially unlock each pin, "setting them," to use lockpick parlance, one by one. I had to be careful not to use too much force. In lockpicking, a gentle touch was key—no pun intended. I closed my eyes and imagined the internal workings of the lock. I needed to identify the binding pin, the one with the most resistance, and set it first.

Aha! I had it. Lightly pressing, I felt the spring of the pin give way and then removed the pick. One down. By the feel of it, seven to go. I repeated the process releasing another pin. Two down.

Tiny beads of perspiration were forming on my brow. *Another reason my mum would say spying isn't ladylike. A lady doesn't sweat... unless, of course, she's risking the firing squad by picking a lock in an enemy palace.*

My wig slipped. I wanted to rip it off my head. Instead, I ran my forearm across my forehead, wiping off sweat and brushing the hair out of my eyes. Practicing back at the War Office hadn't prepared me for the anxiety of fieldwork. In fact, back at the office, I'd been jolly good at lockpicking, best in the class. That didn't go down well with my classmates, who were all men.

Holding pressure on the tension wrench with my left hand, I felt my way through the pins using the pick with my right. *Yes!* Three down. I glanced around. No one. Thank goodness.

Fourth pin. Only three left.

Time seemed to go in slow motion. Minutes seemed to stretch into a lifetime, as if I were a sheep tick awakened after a year's slumber by the smell of blood and jolted into action.

The glorious click and give of the pick told me the next pin had retracted. I was nearly there.

My breath caught. Footfalls came from upstairs. *Good grief, Fiona. Hurry up. Or this really will be the summation of your entire life.* Unfortunately, lockpicking was an art form that couldn't be rushed. I held my breath and manipulated the wrench and the pick. One pin to go.

The sound of the footsteps was getting closer. Probably the emperor coming back. Click. The last pin. *Voilà.* The door popped open. I snatched my purse off the floor and ducked inside. *What if the emperor is coming back?* I was in. I'd have to take my chances. Of course, if I was caught, the Pummerin bell would be ringing for me.

My back to the door, I took in the chamber. Unlike the rest of the palace, which was light and gilded, this room was dark and masculine. The wood-paneled walls had absorbed centuries of cigar smoke and royal intrigue. *If these walls could talk.* A large mahogany desk sat in front of a built-in bookcase, which was stuffed to overflowing with dusty leatherbound books. An armoire stood in one corner, guarded by a suit of armor.

Luckily, the emperor had left the overhead light on. Unluckily, that probably meant he was coming back soon.

I rushed to the desk and stood staring down at messy piles of papers. *Why can't people be orderly? How difficult is it to file papers?* I'd done it for over two years at the War Office. I'd nearly perfected my filing system when I was recruited for espionage.

I put on my gloves and lifted a folder from the top of one pile. It was thick with telegrams in German. I scanned the latest missives in the hopes that I could recreate them later, even if I couldn't fully understand them. Someone in the War Office could translate. If only Captain Hall had given me one of those nifty little spy cameras. He expected me to get the job done with my photographic memory and little else, except my special "attributes" as a lady spy.

My photographic memory may not be as reliable as a camera, but at least I couldn't misplace it. Obviously, I couldn't memorize everything on this desk, let alone this whole file. It didn't help that most of the papers were in a language that I didn't read well. It was hard enough to know what was important to the war effort even in my mother tongue.

Then again, if these papers were just sitting on the top of the desk, they couldn't be as important as what I might find hidden inside. I opened the top drawer. Rosary beads and a small prayer book. I'd heard that the emperor was pious. Some even considered him a saint. The prince of peace. Then again, others considered him a traitor because his wife was Italian, and his brothers-in-law were fighting against Germany.

Good heavens. Fredricks must be planning to assassinate the emperor. The whole bloody war had started after some nationalist zealot assassinated the emperor's uncle in Sarajevo.

I tugged the handle on another drawer. Locked. *Aha.* What top secrets did the emperor have hidden inside? With my handy lockpick, I was about to find out. Thankfully, desk locks are easier to pick than those on doors.

In no time, the drawer popped open so fast I nearly fell backward. Inside was a stack of letters. On top was an ivory envelope addressed to *Prince Sixtus, Paris, France.* Why would the emperor of Austria-Hungary be writing to a prince in France?

I lifted the letter and examined it. The heavy paper was very fine, much nicer than anything I ever purchased from Woolworth. I turned it over in my hands. Interesting. No stamps.

This must be the letter the emperor had asked Count Czernin to deliver. He must have expected Count Czernin to hand-deliver it. Had he refused? I needed to get a look at its contents. *Drat.* It bore the emperor's wax seal. Both my lockpicking kit and my photographic memory were useless. What I needed was X-ray vision.

Do I dare tamper with the seal?

As if in answer to my question, there was a clattering outside the door. Frantic, I scanned the room for a place to hide. On the chance that the emperor had just written the letter, I grabbed the blotter paper from the top of the desk. Perhaps I could trace the words and discover the letter's contents—if I got out of this room alive.

It was either dive under the desk, or hope I fit in the armoire. I gritted my teeth and dashed across the room. Throwing open the door of the armoire, I took a deep breath and stepped inside, wedging myself between a throng of dress uniforms. Then I quickly tucked the piece of blotter paper into my clutch purse and tried to close the armoire door. But with one hand injured and occupied with my clutch, closing the door with my other hand was a struggle. The harder I tried, the more the door swung open. I gave up and dug my fingernails into the inside lock mechanism and held the door as nearly closed as I could manage.

The door to the room creaked open. The resinous scent of smoky cypress signaled a male presence. Given the rosary and spartan luncheon buffet, I hadn't figured the emperor for extravagant colognes. The rustling of papers reminded me that I hadn't closed the desk drawer. I sucked in air. My fingernail felt as though it might be ripped off from the weight of the armoire door. I didn't know how much longer I could hold it shut.

The smell of smoke and melting wax overpowered the cologne. What was the emperor burning? It wasn't tobacco.

"Prince Sixtus of Bourbon-Parma, eh?" a man's voice said. "Zita's brother. Just as I suspected."

I narrowed my brows. That voice was familiar. And it definitely was not the emperor.

"They are planning a secret meeting, and by hook or by crook, I aim to be there. Conspiring with the French." When the man chuckled, I knew.

I flew out of the armoire. "What in heaven's name are you doing?" I asked.

"Why Fiona. What a pleasant surprise." As ever unflappable, Fredrick Fredricks smiled over at me and continued resealing the letter with melted wax.

"What are you doing with that letter?" I demanded.

"I could ask you the same thing." He beamed.

Irritating man.

"You've learned some new tricks since Paris," he said, holding the ring on his finger over the puddle of red wax. His Black Panther insignia. How brazen.

"I'm going to report you," I said. To whom, I didn't know. After all, I was incognito in enemy territory.

"Again, I could say the same thing." He seemed to think better of leaving his calling card. Instead, he rifled in the desk drawer until he found the emperor's seal. He pressed it into the wax, and then slid the envelope back into the drawer and closed it. "Remember where you are, *ma chérie.*"

"Yes, and why is that?" I still didn't understand why he'd invited me to the royal ball.

"You are a princess and belong in a palace."

I scoffed. "You are a prig and belong in a prison."

"We tried that already, didn't we?"

It still galled me that he'd engineered his escape from a French prison by tricking me.

He stared at my bandaged hand. "But you've been injured." He came around the desk. When he reached for my hand, I jerked it away. "Now, now. Don't be like that. Not after all we've been through. We're like two peas in a pod, *ma chérie.*"

"Pshh." I let out an exasperated breath.

The mischievous spark in his eyes told me he was enjoying this. *Cheeky devil.* He was right that we'd been through a lot. I'd followed him from Ravenswick Abbey in the English countryside to Paris, shared strawberries with him, and visited him in prison. Still, I was determined to catch him in the act of sabotage or murder and bring the fiend to justice.

"Well, what did it say?" I asked.

"See, we're more alike than you'll admit."

I rolled my eyes. "I'm nothing like you."

"Two sides of the same coin," he said playfully. "Two halves of one whole… the thorn and the rose."

"You're obscene."

"Your ire just makes you more irresistible, Miss Figg…or should I say Mrs. Douglas?" He laughed. "Clifford would have no idea what to do with a woman like you."

"Oh, and you would?"

"Try me." He gazed down at me and took me by the shoulders.

A shiver ran up my spine. I averted my eyes and took a step backward, nearly tripping over my own feet.

"Admit it. You like me." He teased.

"I do not."

"Just a little bit?" He brushed a lock of wig out of my face.

"I loathe you."

"Admit it and I'll tell you what the letter says."

Argh. "You're insufferable." My cheeks were burning. I was tempted to plunge my lockpick into his chest.

He took a step closer. I took another step backward. This dance continued until I hit the armoire and dropped my clutch purse. It hit the carpet, bounced, and ejected some of its contents onto his shoes. Luckily, Mata Hari's gun didn't come flying out. I bent down to pick up my kit. I thought better of it when I came face-to-face with the front of his trousers.

"Let me," he said with exaggerated gallantry and a wave of his hand. "Oh dear," he said, unwrapping the napkin.

Dash it. I'd forgotten all about the corner of toast I'd stuffed into my clutch.

"What have we here?" He stared down at the toast. "Have you taken to pilfering the famous Sacher Torte from your hotel? Come to my hotel and we will feast on strawberries and champagne."

I furrowed my brows. War rations had made both bread and pudding scarce, but surely the annoying man could tell the difference between toast and cake. I snatched the napkin out of his hand. "It's evidence."

"Exhibit A in the trial of a rat? Have you no cheese to complement your toast?" So, he did know it was toast.

"If you must know, someone kid— er, dognapped Frau Sacher's bulldogs." If he knew I was staying at Frau Sacher's hotel, surely he knew who she was too.

"Someone who eats cake on toast?"

What was he on about? I examined the crust of bread lying in the palm of my hand. Good heavens. He was right. There were dark bits of chocolate stuck to the edges of the toast.

Now that I studied it again, I noticed that the toast had been cut and not bitten. The toast was merely an implement used to smuggle the torte. It must have been smuggled, since Frau Sacher only served Sacher Torte to her guests in the hotel's dining room.

Why didn't I see this before? "A thief who takes cake and dogs," I said under my breath. "What does it mean?" Max admitted he was eating bread when he was hit on the head. But where did the cake come from?

"It means Frau Sacher needs to sack one of her employees." He smirked. "Or should I say sacher?"

"Very funny."

Fredricks grabbed me and shoved me.

"Unhand me!"

He clasped his hand over my mouth. "Shhh… Listen. Someone's coming." He lifted me into the armoire, climbed in after me, and pulled the door shut.

How in blazes did he shut the door from inside?

"*Ouch!*" Something poked me in the head.

"Be quiet," he hissed.

I tucked myself into the far corner of the closet. In the tight quarters, there was no getting away from Fredricks. As we huddled in the dark amongst the uniforms, someone entered the room. A man and a woman in tense conversation. I recognized the man's as the strangely accented voice of the emperor. The woman's voice was also familiar. They were speaking German.

I thought of the crude, if amusing, American author Mark Twain joking that German should be a dead language because only the dead have time to learn it.

Wait. They'd switched to French. *Now that's interesting.* Why would the Austrian emperor be speaking French? And with whom?

Thankful for my French lessons as a teenager at the North London Collegiate School for girls, and my recent "refresher course" while working undercover in Paris, I listened intently.

The emperor was asking the woman to have her brother deliver a letter, a top-secret letter, a dangerous mission. It was of the utmost importance that the letter reached Prince Sixtus, Empress Zita's brother, in Paris. Could the woman arrange it?

From the gist of the conversation, I got the impression that this woman's brother, Kurt, was a jack-of-all-trades, especially the dodgy black-market sort.

Good heavens. Kurt Müller. I knew I recognized her voice.

Yes, her brother could deliver the letter…for a price.

Of course, the emperor would pay half now and half upon delivery.

A deal was made.

I felt Fredricks's warm breath on my neck. I'd almost forgotten about the blackguard. Too bad he was hearing this too, an enemy spy.

I heard the desk drawer rattle.

"Someone has unlocked my desk," the emperor said in French. "Was the door locked when we entered? I know I locked it when I left. Someone has been in here. And in the last few minutes."

"*Mon Dieu*," the emperor exclaimed. "If the Kaiser finds out what I'm up to, he'll have my head."

For such an experienced spy, Fredricks hadn't done a very good job of covering his tracks. But perhaps he'd covered mine.

The emperor and the woman were speaking so fast, I had trouble keeping up. I made out "danger," "agent double," and... *good heavens*... my name. Fiona Figg. Did Elsie think *I* was a double agent? Or was she reporting me as a single agent? And agent for their enemy.

I gasped.

Fredricks grabbed me around the waist and clasped his giant hand over my mouth. Again! He pressed me up against his torso and held me tight.

My pulse quickened...from my fear of facing a firing squad—certainly not from the heady smell of his cologne.

Chapter Six

The Ransom Note

Once I was satisfied that the emperor and his accomplice, Elsie Müller, had left the room, Fredricks and I exited the armoire. Thank goodness I didn't have to spend another minute locked up with that fiend.

Yes. I'd recognized the voice. It was Elsie. And her brother Kurt would be engaged to deliver the letter.

Fredricks insisted on escorting me back to the garden party. In other words, he took my arm and dragged me through the palace.

"Why are you here?" I asked.

"For the emperor's birthday bash," he said.

"Why am I here?"

"Because I'm irresistible?" He raised his eyebrows.

"Seriously, why me?" I hurried to keep up with his long strides. "Why did you invite me to the royal ball?" *And why did you send the invitation to the War Office?* He had to know I'd be sent with orders to find out what the infamous saboteur and German spy was doing in Vienna.

His expression turned serious. "You know why." He stopped.

"No really, I don't." I pulled out of his grip. "Tell me."

"I'm in need of a dancing partner." He was on the move again.

"Obviously, you've never seen me dance." I started after him.

When I caught him up, he laughed. "Didn't you learn anything from Mata

49

Hari's dance of the seven veils?"

"How dare—"

"Now, now, Fiona. We mustn't judge." He clucked his tongue at me.

"Not even a traitor and a murderer?" I wasn't thinking of Mata Hari.

"One man's enemy is another man's savior." He stopped and turned to me. "It's not just beauty that's in the eye of the beholder."

My cheeks burned and I averted his gaze. "What evil plan do you have this time?" Fredricks already knew I was working as a spy for the War Office, so I had no reason to beat around the bush with him.

"Why, Fiona, I thought we were friends." He smiled. "The truth is…" He stopped again and turned to face me. "I invited you here to help me to negotiate a peace treaty."

"A peace treaty?" I stared up at him, dumbfounded. How could I help negotiate a peace treaty? More to the point, why did he think he could?

"The question you should be asking is what is Emperor Charles up to."

That was precisely what I was trying to find out. What was the emperor up to? And why did Elsie mention me to him? *She must have somehow sussed out that I'm a British spy.* Blast. If so, my life was in grave danger.

"I did ask, but you didn't tell me. So, what's in the letter?"

"I'm hurt that you won't meet my terms." He started walking again, pulling me along.

The man was insufferable. As if he thinks I'd say I like him just to gather intelligence.

"If you're such good mates with the emperor, why doesn't he know you're the Black Panther?" I glared over at him.

"Black Panther?" He chuckled. "Wherever did you get that idea?"

I dug in my heels and skidded to a stop. Spinning around to face him, I grabbed his hand.

"Why Fiona," he whispered. "How charming. Holding hands."

Grrrr. I bared my teeth. "Your ring. It is obvious."

"Not everyone is as observant as you are, *ma chérie.*" He started pulling me along again.

As we hurried along, I wondered what I could figure out on my own. The blotter paper. Did it hold the secret to the letter's contents? Was the emperor himself a double agent? Could he be secretly working for the French? He was speaking French, writing letters in French, and contacting his French relatives. Fredricks had said the emperor was conspiring with the French, but that meant little since Fredricks lied as easily as he breathed. Still, surely that would all look extremely suspicious to the emperor's German allies if they found out about it. Would Fredricks spill the beans to them? I bit my lip. Or would Fredricks just dispatch the emperor?

My mind was racing. Would he actually assassinate an emperor? One who ostensibly was an ally of Germany?

Of course, no one had ever caught Fredricks in the act. Still, I was as sure he was a spy-killer as I was certain his grip on my arm would leave nasty purple bruises.

The trick would be to catch him in the act *and* save one of our agents from becoming his next victim. No easy feat.

"Fine, I admit it," I said as we crossed the threshold to the outside world. The afternoon sun was blinding. I shielded my eyes and squinted. *Where is Clifford?* I didn't see anyone. Was the party over already?

"Admit what?"

"You promised." I tried to jerk away from him. "If I agreed that you and I are like two peas and all that blather, then you'd tell me the contents of the letter." I would not admit I liked him.

"Why, you are a curious little pussycat, aren't you?" He tightened his grip. "I'm upping the ante."

"What do you mean?" I glared up at him and yanked my arm away.

"Sit with me at dinner tonight and I'll tell you all about the emperor's plans." He smiled.

"I can't," I said. "I'm married to Clifford." I took off across the lawn toward the open area where I hoped the garden party was still going on.

"Clifford's a fool."

"Clifford is my husband and your best friend." I picked up my pace.

"That only proves my point." He dashed to keep up with me. "Anyway, he's your *fake* husband. As for my friend—"

I really should put aside my personal feelings and accept his invitation and pump him for more information. Not that he'd ever tell me what he was up to anyway. "Yes. Fine. Where are you staying?"

"I say, there you are." Clifford appeared out of nowhere and intercepted us. The man had terrible timing.

"Speak of the devil," Fredricks said with a wry smile.

"Where have you been?" Clifford ran his hand through his hair. A sure sign he was agitated. "I was about to send out a search party."

"Your *wife* and I were just having a *petite tête-à-tête*." Fredricks winked at me.

I jabbed him with my elbow and then turned to Clifford. "We should probably be going."

"I'd say so." Clifford looked indignant. "The party broke up half an hour ago while you two were off... off... doing whatever it was you were doing."

At that moment, a strange thought crossed my mind. I wondered if Clifford had ever... done what we were definitely not doing. My mum would be having an otherworldly conniption if she knew I had such unladylike thoughts. But I had been a married woman once, after all.

The lack of oxygen in that armoire must have gone to my head. Instead of my former husband in the marital bed of my mind's eye, I saw Archie Somersby, the handsome soldier I'd met last summer at Charing Cross Hospital. Archie Somersby, whose acquaintance I'd had the pleasure to renew last month in Paris. Archie, whose lips had touched mine for one brief—but oh so memorable—kiss.

I blanched. In Paris, he'd kissed me when I was disguised as Harold the mustachioed bellboy. I didn't realize he knew who I was until he kissed me—and frankly, I wasn't even sure then. *Will I ever see him again?*

"Come on, old girl." Clifford's voice brought me back to my senses. "Let's get back to the hotel before they give us the boot."

"Good idea," Fredricks said. "I'll call for my motor and give you a lift."

Clifford huffed. "I have my own car."

"Thank you," I said, glaring at Clifford. Now was my chance to continue my conversation with Fredricks... alone. "Clifford, you don't mind if I ride back with Fredrick, do you?"

Clifford sputtered.

"Good." I patted his arm. "I'll see you back at the hotel."

* * *

Never one to do anything by halves, Fredricks's automobile was as ostentatious as his driver. The huge two-toned contraption was driven by an oversized man who made the motor look like a toy. The man was wearing a navy-blue uniform that was bursting at the seams under the strain of his bulging muscles.

In preparation for my first mission posing as Dr. Vogel, I'd done some bodybuilding and read some books about it, but I'd never seen as muscular a man as Fredricks's chauffeur.

"You seem to have a keen interest in Ivan," Fredricks said.

I hadn't realized I'd been staring. Lashes fluttering, I looked away.

"I pulled him out of a Russian katorga, and he's been very loyal ever since."

"Katorga?"

"Labor camp." Fredricks opened the back door of the automobile. "After you, *ma chérie*."

Once we were comfortably seated on opposite sides in the back seat of the car, I recommenced my interview. "You never answered my question."

"Which one? You asked so many." He smiled over at me.

"For starters, why don't you tell me how you know the emperor?" *And do you plan to kill him?*

"I met emperor Charles at Franzenbad when we were both there taking the healing waters. That was almost ten years ago now. His aunt lived there." He gazed out the window. "Before he and Zita got married." As if coming out of a trance, he started and turned back to me. "Next question."

"What was the emperor saying to Elsie about her brother Kurt Müller?"

"Elsie? Who is Elsie?"

"The nanny."

"Are you telling me that Kurt Müller's sister works in the palace?"

53

I felt the blood draining from my face. What had I done? I was giving up more information than I was gaining. How did the fiend always get the upper hand? Not knowing what to do now, but determined to keep my gob shut, I just nodded.

Fredricks countenance became deadly serious. No more smiles or flirtation. No more teasing. "You know what this means?" he said more to himself than to me.

"No. What?"

"What you don't know won't hurt you." He leaned forward. "Ivan, can you go any faster?"

"Of course, sir," Ivan replied.

Why in the world was Fredricks suddenly in such a hurry? Who was Kurt Müller? Obviously, Fredricks knew him. Or knew of him. Could Elsie's brother Kurt be his target in Vienna? Elsie made it sound as if her brother knew his way around the dodgy parts of Europe. Maybe this Kurt Müller was the double agent. "Do you know Mr. Müller?" I asked nonchalantly.

"If I'm the black panther, Kurt Müller is a snake in the grass." Fredricks's steely eyes sparked.

"What do you mean?"

Fredricks went back to staring out the window. We rode back to the hotel in silence, the blackguard refusing to answer any more of my questions.

As soon as the motor stopped in front of the hotel, I hopped out and marched inside before he could offer his hand to help me out of the car, assuming he wasn't too distracted by news of Elsie's brother. No sooner had I set foot on the sidewalk than the motorcar took off. Whatever I'd inadvertently told Fredricks must have been of great importance. Blast. And I never found out where the devil was staying.

I gathered my key at the front desk and headed for the lift.

Waiting for the lift to arrive, I contemplated what I'd overheard. How did Fredricks know Kurt Müller but not his sister Elsie?

Perhaps the emperor's secret letter would give me a clue. I wondered what I might learn from the blotter paper. I took it out of my purse and examined it. Sure enough. It was covered with indentations where the emperor had used it under his stationary. But would it tell me what I needed to know? I'd need to trace over it with a pencil to see what it said. Where in blazes was the blooming lift?

I heard soft crying coming from down the hall. On instinct, I followed the sobs to the door of Frau Sacher's private dining room. The soft crying turned into outright sobbing and then wailing. Good heavens. Had something happened? Had someone found the bodies of her beloved dogs. I shuddered to think. I stashed the blotter paper back in my clutch, opened the door a crack, and peeked inside.

Her head in one hand and a hanky wadded up in the other, Frau Sacher was sitting alone at a table puffing on a cigar.

I ventured inside. "Frau Sacher. Is everything okay?"

"*Nein.*" She lifted her head. "*Meine Hunde.* My dogs. They are still missing."

"You haven't received a ransom note?" I sat down across from her.

"*Nein.*" She shook her head and blew her nose. "My poor babies. They will be missing their dinner." She patted little Mozart, who was curled up in her lap. At least she wasn't alone.

"If someone took them for money, they have every reason to take good care of them," I said, hoping it was true.

"You think so?" Her voice brightened.

A knock on the door caught our attention. Werner, his leathery face pale, entered.

Confound it. Clifford was right behind him, waving at me from the doorway.

"Frau Sacher," Werner said. "This was delivered with the post." He held out a letter. Talk about timing.

I jumped up, fetched the letter, and examined it. No postmark. Someone had dropped it off. The ransom note, at last.

"Who delivered this?" I asked.

"I don't know, ma'am," Werner said, looking at his shoes. "It was mixed in with the regular post."

"Did you see anyone suspicious around the hotel this afternoon?" I handed the letter to Frau Sacher, who snatched it like a hungry beggar grabbing a piece of bread. "Was it delivered with the post or snuck into it later? Who delivers your mail? Where do you keep it?"

"Fiona, darling, why are you interrogating the poor man?" Clifford asked, joining me.

Werner was visibly flustered by my rapid-fire questions. Was it my imagination, or was he trying to hide something? I couldn't come right out and ask whether he was working for the British. Given my limited intel, I was more likely to give myself away and end up with my head on the block than save his.

"Let's take them one by one, shall we?" I gave him a reassuring smile. "Did you see anyone suspicious?"

"No, ma'am." He glanced up at me and then promptly fixed his gaze on his shoes again.

"No one out of the ordinary? Maybe someone who came into the hotel and then left again without checking in or going to the café?"

He shook his head. "Wait." His weary eyes turned bright. "There was a woman."

"Tell me about her." I opened my clutch, hoping to find a paper and pencil. All I found was Clifford's handkerchief wrapped around the crust of bread… along with my spy gadgets, of course, and the blotter paper.

"She was a war widow, dressed in black and wearing a veil."

"Go on." I nodded encouragingly.

She came into the lobby and sat down. Just staring at the entrance as if she expected her dead husband to come through the doors.

"I say, I saw her too," Clifford said. "I was reading the newspaper, mind you, when I saw a very attractive young woman dressed all in black. Poor thing."

I ignored him and turned back to Werner. "And then what?"

"Nothing." He stared at his feet again. "I went about my business and when I came back, she was gone."

Clifford was stammering, trying to get my attention.

I relented. "Yes, Clifford. Can you describe her?"

"She was very attractive and young."

"You've said that already." I shook my head. Clifford thought anything in a skirt was attractive.

"Listen to this." Frau Sacher's hands trembled as she read from the letter. "Have Max deliver thirty thousand kronen to the Lorelei Fountain at precisely six o'clock this evening. Put it in a plain paper sack and have him set it at the base of the fountain. No funny business or the pooches will give away the spoon." She gasped.

"Give away the spoon?" I asked.

"Death," Frau Sacher said. "You don't have that saying in English?"

"Kick the bucket," Clifford chimed in. "Buy the farm. Hop the twig. Push up daisies. Give up the ghost—"

"Thank you, Clifford." I glared at him. "Thirty thousand kronen. Is that a lot?" Currency exchange was not my strong suit.

"Over a thousand pounds sterling," Clifford said. He did come in handy sometimes.

"Geez. That's steep for a couple of dogs." I immediately regretted saying it. "Of course, Bruno and Jana are worth it." I hoped I'd remembered the little pups' names correctly. "Do you have that much? Do you plan to pay it?"

Frau Sacher gave me an incredulous look. "Why, of course. What else can I do? The police have no interest in finding stolen dogs."

"May I?" I held out my hand. Frau Sacher passed me the letter. It was typed on heavy paper like that I'd seen at the palace. Did everyone in Vienna use such fine stationery? I doubted this note originated at Schönbrunn Palace. Judging by the typeset, it was typed on the ubiquitous Corona 3, the same typewriter I used back at the War Office. I sniffed the letter. The faint scent of apricot. I'd smelled that fragrance before, but where? Wait. Was I imagining it? Or did I also get a slight whiff of chocolate? *Sacher Torte!* I'd almost forgotten about the evidence wrapped inside the handkerchief.

I handed the letter back to Frau Sacher. "Do you mind if I sit down?"

"Please." She blew out a plume of smoke that persuaded me to seek a seat farther away from her smelly cigar… not to mention the stinky little beast in her lap. Perhaps that's why she smoked. To camouflage the smell of dog breath. What did she feed them to make them so odiferous? Certainly not Sacher Torte? I put my hand to my mouth in case I suffered the same fate.

Clifford pulled out a chair for me, and I had no choice but to sit down next to the cigar. I adjusted my skirts. *Crikey*. What a mess I was. I'd forgotten my dress was splattered with blood. I must be quite a sight. Frau Sacher was so forlorn, she must not have noticed. No time to worry about my appearance now. I was hot on the trail of a dognapper.

If I recovered the pups, Frau Sacher would tell me whatever I need to know about the emperor, Kurt Müller, Elsie, and that strange little woman with the notebook. Frau Sacher had a virtual ledger of who went behind closed doors into her private rooms, the rich and powerful Viennese men cheating on their wives or plotting to overthrow some government. If I helped save Frau Sacher's dogs, she'd be so grateful that no doubt I could glean all sorts of useful information for the War Office.

Right Fiona, old girl. Go ahead and rationalize how finding a couple of missing dogs is a clever act of espionage.

Although we'd hit it off straight away, Frau Sacher wasn't forthcoming about the secret meetings that took place in her private rooms. No doubt, Captain Hall would be pleased if I got the gen on any liaisons involving German officers that the Allies could use to their advantage to catch them with their pants down, so to speak.

With Clifford still standing behind my chair, breathing down my neck—annoying man—I laid my purse on the table and opened the clasp. "I suspect our dognapper has been smuggling food from the hotel," I said, removing the handkerchief and unwrapping the corner of toast. "There are bits of Sacher Torte on this piece of bread, which suggests our culprit is someone who works here or is a frequent visitor." I glanced around to make sure no one was eavesdropping. "How well do you know Max?"

"Max is a good boy." Frau Sacher leaned down to kiss her puppy. "Isn't he, Mozart darling?" She glanced over at me, her brow furrowed. "Surely, you don't think Max hit himself on the head?"

"He could have an accomplice," I said. Maybe Max smuggled the Sacher Torte to his accomplice, who then hit him on the head. And when I asked

Max about the bread, he said it was his to throw me off the track.

"An accomplice who cracked his head open?" She shook her head. "And why leave little Mozart behind?" She caressed the puppy.

"To make it seem real?" She did have a point. If Max was in on it, he'd made a great sacrifice to his skull.

"Max admitted he was eating a piece of bread. That is not a crime," she said through a cloud of smoke. "At least not yet."

"True." *Although if the bloody Germans have their way...* "But why didn't he mention the cake? It feels like he must have sneaked it out on the bread to give to someone. If he'd eaten it himself, he would have mentioned it."

"Maybe he would have if you'd asked about it."

Maybe. What would he have said if I'd noticed the crumbs immediately and asked about them? Had Max innocently eaten the cake on the bread? Or had he given it to someone else, a coconspirator? If he was involved in the dognapping and I'd asked him about the cake, he probably would have said he ate the cake on the bread. So, asking him would have done no good. In the end, Frau Sacher trusted Max. I wasn't so sure. "Why ask for Max to deliver the ransom? Why him in particular?"

"So, the thief will recognize him?" Frau Sacher's eyes widened.

"But how did the thief know his name?" Clifford asked.

"Exactly." I rewrapped the evidence and put it back in my clutch. "I will watch Max when he delivers the ransom."

"Good Lord, Fiona. It...it...could be dangerous." Clifford's face turned red. "I should be the one to follow him."

"Why?" I glared up at him. "Because you are a man?"

"Yes, now that you mention it." He put his hand on my shoulder.

The annoying man was taking his husband-protector role too far again. I shrugged his hand away.

"I don't want you to get hurt...or..." Clifford stammered.

"Give away the spoon?" I winked.

"Why, Fiona, that's not at all funny." Clifford had that priggish tone I knew so well.

"Okay. We will both follow him." I knew Clifford wouldn't give up, so I might as well give in.

"No!" Frau Sacher said. "The letter says no funny business." She was wringing her hands. "I won't allow it. What if the kidnapper recognizes you from the hotel?" She tugged little Mozart to her breast like a woman lost at sea clinging to a life preserver.

Chapter Seven

Paying the Ransom

G iven the reasons I'd come to Vienna in the first place—to save a double agent and catch the Black Panther red-handed—I'd known it would be hectic. But not *this* hectic. Dognappers, royal secrets, and mysterious women scribbling in journals. What a day. And it wasn't over yet. I'd gotten myself entangled in spying on Max the bellboy as he drops off the ransom when I should be spying on Fredricks the blackguard as he prepares to bump off another one of our agents.

I still didn't know where Fredricks was staying, let alone who he was after. If I could get into his room and have a look around, perhaps I would find out who would be his next victim. If my hunch was right, he would pounce at the royal ball. And unless I uncovered the double agent before then, I'd merely be a spectator while the Great White Hunter disposed of his prey.

I dropped into a chair next to my dressing table, where there was a little pile of Mozart Bonbons I'd been collecting from when the turndown service left them on my pillow. I remembered how Fredricks's invitation to Vienna had been wrapped in a Mozart Bonbon, the cheeky cad. The wily criminal was in for a surprise. I planned to beat him at his own game for once.

I pulled a tiny key from my purse. Unlocking the top drawer of the dressing table, I removed a bottle of invisible ink, some paper, and a charcoal pencil. In their place, I hid the contents of my purse, pushing Mata Hari's gun to the back of the drawer before twisting the little key to lock it again. I dropped the key back into my clutch purse.

After Clifford's incessant nattering, I enjoyed the peace and quiet of the room, if not my thoughts. I could still hear the commotion of carriages, motor cars, and paper vendors in the street below. But from the fifth floor, the clamor was muffled and mingled into a reassuring concerto. I treasured these few private moments back in my hotel room...alone.

I smoothed out the emperor's blotter paper on top of my dressing table. Carefully, I laid a piece of paper over it. Taking up the pencil, I gently rubbed the charcoal across the paper. A jumble of words and letters appeared. I made out the words Sixtus, Rax, *urgente*, and *paix*.

Sixtus was the name of empress Zita's brother. *Urgente* was urgent. And *paix* was French for peace. But what was Rax? A German word perhaps? In English, rax meant to stretch. But why was it capitalized? And why would the emperor be using an English word?

What was it Fredricks had said to himself when he read the letter? *Prince Sixtus of Bourbon-Parma, Zita's brother. Just as I suspected. They are planning a secret meeting, and by hook or by crook, I aim to be there. Conspiring with the French.*

I picked up the guidebook from the top of my dressing table and flipped to the index. Aha! *Reichenau an der Rax* was a village in the Austrian Alps. I flipped back to read about it. Goodness. According to the guidebook, the royals spend summers at their alpine palace, Villa Wartholz.

If I was right, the emperor was planning a secret meeting with Prince Sixtus that would take place in Rax. But what was Fredricks's role in this meeting? By hook or by crook, I aimed to find out.

First things first. Change out of my garden party clothes into something more practical for sleuthing. I removed my blond bob and placed it on its stand. It was always a shock to see my shorn reflection in the looking glass. I looked like a child whose mother, upon the discovery of head lice, had gone after it with the clippers.

My own mother had been fond of wigs. She'd introduced me to the artifice of feminine disguise early on. We'd spent many a lazy Saturday morning trying on costumes at Angels Fancy Dress Shop. Those were some of my best memories of my mum. Fancy dresses lifted her otherwise melancholy spirits... that and locking herself away with a strong cup of tea and the latest edition of *Strand Magazine*. I missed the conspiratorial way she passed the magazines on to me, hiding them from my father. He did not approve of such frivolous pastimes as spending afternoons matching wits with Sherlock Holmes or puzzling over Henry Dudeney's "Perplexities."

Captain Hall had ordered me to accompany Fredricks to royal luncheons and dinner parties, culminating in the emperor's birthday gala, a fancy-dress ball. I couldn't resist a good costume. Obviously, I could not use one of my usual disguises. Dr. Vogel the expert of female maladies or Harold the helpful bellboy would be inappropriate... although I did have Harold's evening suit.

As luck would have it, I'd planned to go as Marie Antoinette—before she was beheaded, of course. I had an exquisite, powdered wig that was as tall as a layer cake. And the gown was a replica of one she'd worn in a famous portrait by some French artist. Now my costume would be a constant reminder of my clumsiness. How was I to know she was the emperor's great-aunt?

Still, it was a jolly good outfit. I'd purchased it at Angels Fancy Dress Shop in London before I left, and I couldn't wait to try it out on Saturday.

In the meantime, I had two French bulldogs to recover, a killer of double agents to catch, and a dinner party to attend at the hotel this evening. Of the three, the dinner party was not only the least appealing, but also the most vexing. Partying while all those poor boys were dying on the battlefield just seemed wrong.

I went to the wardrobe and peered inside. I stood there staring—as if gazing into the darkness long enough would make the answers flash onto the back of my closet like the titles of a motion picture onto a screen. What does one wear to a dinner party hosted by the most prominent hotelier in Austria for her emperor and empress?

From what I'd heard about the royal couple, it was a wonder they'd accepted the invitation. I'd gotten the impression that the royal couple didn't approve of the kind of dangerous liaisons carried out at the Sacher hotel, even if, as Frau Sacher claimed, her secrets weren't dangerous enough for them.

Considering the meager spread at the royal luncheon, perhaps even the royals secretly longed for a slice of rich chocolate cake with sweet apricot filling. My mouth watered just thinking about it.

I glanced at my watch. My mouth would have to wait. Half five. Two hours until dinnertime. And half an hour until the ransom drop-off. After what happened to my luncheon party dress, I'd learned that I couldn't wear my dinner gown to catch a thief. Most certainly I could not wear my one Paul Poiret hobble-skirt gown. *Why on earth would a man design a dress to restrict women's walking?* No. I needed more practical clothes for chasing down dognappers... and assassins.

I quickly changed into a plain loose-fitting cotton skirt and matching tunic, and then slipped on my flat-heeled oxfords. *I can't be running after villains in heels.* I was halfway out the door when I remembered my porcupine hair. *Drat.* I ran back inside and tugged on my wig. Just in time too.

Clifford was knocking on the interior door to our suite. At least I hoped it was him. I smiled to myself. *Will miracles never cease.* He was on time, again.

I opened the door. "What in heaven's name?" I snickered.

Clifford was the spitting image of Sherlock Holmes, complete with a plaid deerstalker cap, calf-length Inverness cape, and freshly polished spats.

"What?" he asked, clenching a calabash pipe in his teeth. His face fell.

He really does fancy himself a detective. "You look marvelous." I put my hand to my mouth and pretended to cough to stifle another fit of giggles. "But won't you be sweltering in that getup?" I realized I'd used Captain Hall's derogatory term for my own disguises. "Outfit?" I corrected myself.

"I thought you admired Sherlock—"

"I do," I interrupted. "But there's a difference between fiction and reality." I had to admit, with his aquiline nose and long neck, he did resemble Sidney Paget's illustrations for the *Strand*.

I took his elbow and led him into my room. "I doubt even Mr. Holmes could solve a mystery under the Austrian August sun wearing a wool cap and full-length wool cape." I gestured toward the chair in front of my dressing table. "Leave them here, why don't you?" After all, our goal was to blend in and follow Max, not announce his arrival.

Clifford scowled.

"I insist." I pointed to the chair. "Take them off now."

Clifford dragged his feet.

I glared at him and tapped my watch for effect.

"And the pipe," I said after he dropped his cape and hat on the chair.

He frowned but reluctantly obliged.

"Much better." Indeed, he looked quite handsome in his taupe linen suit. I took his arm. "Let's go retrieve Frau Sacher's hounds."

* * *

I took up my hiding place. From behind the large column under the opera house arch, I had a view of the Lorelei Fountain... or at least one side of it. Only from the roof could I have seen the entire fountain. Unfortunately, I had neither the means of getting up there nor the stomach for trying. *Just as well*. How could I run after the thief if I was stationed on the roof?

The sun was low in the sky, casting long shadows. Shopkeepers were closing up for the evening, while restaurants were just getting busy.

Clifford was parked across the street on a bench in front of the hotel. From that vantage, he could see the other side of the fountain. So, we had it covered from two angles. He held a newspaper up in front of his face, pretending to read. At least, I hoped he was pretending. He was supposed to be watching the fountain. Alas, Clifford was easily distracted, especially by pretty girls.

I held my wrist up, trying to see the hour and watch the fountain at the same time. Five minutes until six o'clock. I glanced across the street. Clifford was still at his post. The door of the hotel opened, and Max walked through wearing his uniform. I had been wondering why he was wearing a hotel uniform instead of a soldier's uniform. Maybe Frau Sacher had enough pull to keep her favorite dog walker from fighting at the front.

Max stood in front of the hotel, holding a brown paper bag and looking at his watch. *Good boy, Max*. The ransom note said six o'clock sharp. He stood like a statue between the potted scrubs at the hotel entrance. At six on the dot, he made his move.

I kept my eyes glued to him as he crossed the street. The mix of determination and fear was palpable even from a distance. He reached the fountain, looked around, and then set the sack on a ledge. He did a three-sixty-degree turn and glanced across the street. I hoped he didn't spot Clifford, or he'd know we were spying on him. I bit my lip.

Max took off running, crossed the street, and disappeared into the hotel. My heart took off running too. I leaned into the column for support. With just enough of me poking around the column to see the paper bag, I held my gaze on the spot. *Come on, thief. Where are you?* I resisted the urge to look at Clifford. *I just hope he is still on the job.*

The Pummerin bell clanked and scared me half out of my wits. The church bell was announcing six o'clock mass. *Where is our dognapper?*

The August sun was low in the sky and seemed to be aiming right at me with its fierce rays. I pushed myself even closer to the cool column, trying to get into the shade. If the thief didn't appear soon, I would melt into a puddle at the base of this column. *Oh, for a drink of water...or a fan.*

My eyes were stinging from sweat. Yes. I was full-on sweating. I'd never been one for sunbathing. Empress Zita was right about the heat. The English rose was wilting.

As the church bells struck their last note, a trolley car passed in front of the hotel. I couldn't help but glance at it out of the corner of my eye.

A woman's scream made my heart leap into my throat. My head jerked in the direction of the shrieking. *Oh dear God in heaven*. A woman was lying in the middle of the street. She'd been hit by the streetcar. My hand flew to my mouth.

Torn between helping the poor woman and catching our thief, my eyes raced back and forth between the street and the fountain.

When I fixed my gaze back on the fountain. "No!" I couldn't believe it. The paper sack was gone. How on earth could anyone be that fast?

I hoped Clifford had seen what happened. *Dash it.* The trolley must have cut off his view entirely. That must be why the thief insisted on six o'clock sharp. Bloody Austrians. In London, the trolleys wouldn't run like clockwork.

Trying not to get hit myself, I dashed across the road. A crowd gathered around the woman—a maid, based on her outfit—who was lying motionless in a heap, a streak of blood across her cheek. It didn't look good. As I got closer, I could see that the woman was still breathing. Thank God. "Someone call an ambulance," I shouted in my best German accent.

No one moved. The folks gathered round seemed transfixed by the injured woman. I sucked in air and held my breath. The street noises seemed to increase in volume. Sprinting into action, I made my way to the bench where Clifford was still sitting, gaping over his newspaper at the scene of the accident.

"Go into the hotel and call an ambulance," I said. "I'm going to inspect the scene of the crime."

"It was an accident," Clifford said. "Good Lord. You don't think someone attempted to kill the wretched thing?"

I scowled. No woman was a wretched *thing*. Not even a poor maid lying in the street. "Go call an ambulance," I said sternly.

Clifford stood up, stepped over to the curb, and peered down at the woman. "I say, she looks familiar."

"Go call an ambulance," I repeated, this time pointing toward the hotel entrance.

As if kicked in the behind, Clifford jumped up and hurried inside the hotel.

I pushed my way through the crowd, which was growing with every passing minute. A man was trying to lift the woman off the street. The woman coughed and opened her eyes.

"Don't move her," I barked and then knelt down next to her. "It's okay. Don't move. An ambulance is on its way." At least I hoped it was on its way. Strange. There was a patch of pebbles strewn around the woman's body. *Perhaps that's why she fell.* But why were the pebbles here and nowhere else?

The injured woman stared up at me with startling green eyes. Even with her hair strewn across her face and dirt on her cheeks, she was a remarkably pretty girl. The maid's outfit suggested that she worked at the hotel. Maybe Frau Sacher could identify her. Was she on her way to work? Or her way home? Was it just an accident? Or something more? *Wait.* Hotel Imperial was embroidered on the pocket of her uniform. She must work there.

"What happened?" I asked.

Her mouth opened and closed like a fish out of water, and then she went limp. *Good heavens.* I felt her neck for a pulse. *Thank goodness.* She was still alive. A small envelope fell out of her clenched fist. Just as I reached to pick it up, the woman groaned. Was she regaining consciousness?

I scooped up the envelope and glanced at it. It was addressed to a Mileva Einstein at the Sacher Hotel. I tucked it in my pocket, and then knelt cradling the woman's head until the ambulance arrived.

Could it be just a coincidence that a woman was screaming at the very moment our thief collected the ransom? Was the injured maid in cahoots with the dognapper? Or, had the dognapper staged the accident to distract us from the ransom pickup? Surely, no one would volunteer to be hit by a trolley, not even for thirty thousand kronen.

Chapter Eight

The Dinner Party

Laying out my dress for dinner, I was distracted by this evening's turn of events. The dognapper had gotten away with the ransom. If Max was in on it, we didn't know. Still no word on when or how the bulldogs would be returned. Needless to say, Frau Sacher was beside herself.

The poor unfortunate maid had been carted off to hospital in an ambulance. She still hadn't regained consciousness when they loaded her up. What a tragedy, especially if she had been pushed in front of the trolley to throw us off the scent of the dognapper.

Her scream echoed through my head, and I shuddered. "Stiff upper lip," as my father always said. Nothing I could do but wait. *First thing tomorrow, I'll visit her at hospital.*

Clifford seemed to recognize her. Yet, Frau Sacher reported no maids missing. So, who was this woman who worked at Hotel Imperial? Or was the maid's uniform a ruse?

I had been known to wear a maid's outfit now and then, and I was no maid. Could the woman have been wearing a disguise? Perhaps she was paid to distract us from the thief snatching up the paper sack. In that case, why was she willing to risk for her life for this dognapper?

My mind was whirling with questions. So many in fact, I fetched a notebook from my suitcase and began to write them down. As I did, I thought of that funny little woman with her head in her book, scribbling away not saying a word to anyone. Who was she? Could she be involved in today's strange happenings? I wrote down these questions too, and then, on the next line, wrote: "Fredrick Fredricks. How did he fit in?" He was in Vienna for a reason—no doubt a nefarious one. Surely, he wasn't desperate enough to steal pets to collect ransom.

Insufferable fellow always seemed to have plenty of money. And yet, he was supposedly just a war correspondent working for a New York newspaper...unless of course he was being paid by the German government. After all, I was being paid—such as it was—by the British government. Come to think of it, I was still operating on the wages of a file clerk. I would have to talk to Captain Hall about that. It seemed reasonable that risking my life every day was worth more than risking a paper cut. Yet I felt lucky to get a few new outfits and a tin of dry bully-beef rations—*bloody war*—except, of course, when I was on assignment at the Sacher Hotel.

As I removed my skirt, I felt the sharp corner of the note I'd taken from the injured woman. I pulled it out of my pocket and examined it. The paper was heavy, and the handwriting looked familiar. Mileva Einstein, Sacher Hotel. I didn't remember meeting anyone by that name.

Curiosity piqued, I slowly and painstakingly unsealed the envelope. *Good heavens.* The note was from Fredrick Fredricks to this Mileva Einstein person. Unfortunately, it was in German. Fortunately, Clifford was fluent. But did I really want to involve Clifford? The answer was a resounding no.

I fetched my German dictionary from my suitcase and studied the letter. After a half-hour of flipping through the dictionary and translating one word at a time—an entirely ridiculous exercise—I was beginning to get the gist of the note.

Fredricks was imploring Mileva Einstein to recruit her husband, along with some physicist friend of hers named Lise Meitner. Apparently, the latter discovered a new element, and the former discovered a formula that could be useful to Germany. *I hate to think how.* Fredricks's note seemed to imply it was their patriotic duty to support Germany's war efforts.

I glanced at my watch. *Crikey.* The dinner party started in less than twenty minutes. Mileva Einstein would have to wait. I quickly slipped into my gown and slippers and tugged on a pair of white lace gloves.

I checked the looking glass and adjusted the long gold lapels on my royal-blue silk gown. They drooped over the bust like lazy lily petals. The gown also had a matching silk sash and oversized embroidered pockets—handy for stashing my spy lipstick and nail file lockpick set. Not that I'd need them at dinner. Still, best to be prepared.

I applied a last pat of powder to my nose. Not much I could do about my plain face. But at least my dress was lovely.

When I knocked on Clifford's door, he opened it with enthusiasm, bolstered by his appreciation for my evening gown. "Fiona, you look smashing, old girl."

"So do you." I smiled. He did look fine in his black evening suit and starched white collar. I took his arm and we headed down to the dining room for what promised to be an elegant feast in honor of the emperor's birthday. Distracted as I was, I tried to put on a brave face.

The dining room was already bustling with guests standing around holding small plates of hors d'oeuvres and champagne flutes. And a string quartet was tucked into one corner, playing a lovely Haydn tune.

The table was set with fine china and crystal, and each place setting had a name card. Excellent. Now was my chance to see if Oscar Fuchs, the last name on my list from the War Office, was in attendance. I circled the table, reading the place cards as I went. Drat. He was not among the guests for the royal dinner. No Mileva Einstein either.

After my trip around the table, I approached the empress. "Good evening, Your Majesty." I curtsied.

"Mrs. Douglas." Her smile was radiant. "How good to see you again. May I introduce my husband, Emperor Charles." She took her husband's arm. "Darling, this is the charming woman I was telling you about."

Emperor Charles nodded but there was absolutely no sign of recognition in his face or his countenance. Even if Elsie had told him I was a spy, he wasn't letting on.

A gong rang and two women dressed up like footmen escorted the guests to their seats at the long rectangular table.

Frau Sacher sat at one end of the table, using her cigar like a wand to give the staff directions. Brushed and polished, Werner and Max were delivering cocktails and wine round the table, which was covered in a lace cloth.

Besides Clifford and me, there were two smartly dressed couples and another woman in a long ivory satin gown, who was wearing a tiara. Perhaps she was Empress Zita's sister. Her flaming auburn hair alone would have Clifford proposing before the pudding course was served.

The room was illuminated by candlelight, which gave it a warm romantic glow. Heavy drapes blocked the light from the street and dampened the noise as well. I felt as if I was in a cocoon of wealth and privilege, protected from the realities of war, hunger, and poverty.

The female footmen asked our names and led Clifford and me to our seats. Gallant as ever, Clifford held out my chair for me.

Werner asked if he'd like a cocktail.

"I say so," he said, his blue eyes sparkling. "I'll take a sidecar."

"I'm sorry, sir." Werner's lips wrinkled into a prune. "What is a sidecar, sir?"

"It's a divine elixir of brandy, orange liqueur, and lemon juice invented by my superior when I was stationed in Paris." Clifford chuckled. "It's a funny story, really. It's named after the motorcycle sidecar I used to drive the Captain in when we went to a little French bistro. What was its name—"

I kicked him under the table. *Really. Mentioning that he was stationed in Paris? Talking about French cocktails?* He'd be lucky to survive the night. I glanced around quickly to see if any of our tablemates had overheard.

"Why did you do that?" he asked, obviously crestfallen.

"Remember where we are," I said under my breath, flashing a saccharin smile at Werner.

"And for the lady?" Like a well-trained waiter—or a deuced clever spy—Werner ignored our scuffle.

"*Milk* tea, please." I removed my gloves and laid them in my lap.

"Excuse me, Madame," Werner said. "What is milk tea?"

Clifford poked me in the ribs with his sharp finger. "Who's forgotten where we are now?"

"Phff." *For a country that loves cream, how can they not know milk tea?* "Black tea, please. With a splash of milk."

"Yes, madame." Werner departed, whispering to himself. No doubt trying to remember the two odd orders from the suspicious English-speaking "Austrians"...unless he was planning a way to make contact with us. Could unassuming Werner Liebermann be the double agent and Fredricks's target?

The musicians played a lively Austrian fanfare, and all the guests stood up. I followed suit. The emperor and empress stood at the head of the table next to Frau Sacher. Count Czernin and a matronly woman I took to be his wife flanked the proprietress on her other side. After that, the dinner party began without much ceremony...*unless you count Frau Sacher extinguishing her cigar.*

The royals were not as gay as the rest of the party. In fact, compared to the rest of the guests, me included, the royal party was rather subdued. The emperor's eyes were heavy, and he looked like he carried the weight of the world on his slim shoulders. Most young men his age wouldn't know what to do with half the responsibility he bore.

The emperor and his foreign minister, the dodgy Mr. Czernin, were both in full dress uniform, complete with gold sashes, lots of ribbons and medals, and high embroidered collars.

Empress Zita had on a plain black gown adorned by one small strand of pearls around her neck. Did she always wear black? I was beginning to wonder if she was in mourning. Even the royals were not immune to heart-wrenching losses from this interminable war. I'd heard that several of her brothers were fighting—and on opposite sides.

Frau Sacher was putting on a brave face considering Bruno and Jana were still missing and the culprit had absconded with her money. Yet her smiles and pleasantries were betrayed by the occasional sigh and the trembling of her upper lip. Her brave face was clearly haunted by the specter of more heartbreak. She loved those pups as much as—perhaps more than—her own children.

I'd never had any pets. So, I couldn't understand the attachment. Childless and alone, perhaps I should consider getting a dog... or maybe a cat. Yes, I think a cat might suit me better. I valued independence over loyalty. And that was the very reason I couldn't get a pet. A spy can't very well take care of dependents and carry out international espionage.

Speaking of espionage. The Great White Hunter, Fredrick Fredricks, made a grand entrance. He was decked out in the traditional Austrian loden jacket with bone buttons and a mandarin-style collar, carrying a riding crop, a top hat atop his head. What kind of spy wore such an extravagant ensemble? How he always managed to blend in by standing out was beyond me.

Everyone at the table seemed acquainted with the bothersome fellow. From hotel guests to hotel workers, from Austrian royalty to Austrian apparatchiks, to the person, he was greeted with flirtatious smiles by the women and hearty slaps on the back by the men. Ever the lady's man and the man's man, Fredricks circled the table kissing cheeks and shaking hands.

Frau Sacher went a bit overboard with her welcome, fawning over him like he was a prince...when a real princess—one of the empress's sisters—sat ignored at the other end of the table. How did he manage to charm everyone he met?

Clifford and Fredricks were pumping hands and laughing, no doubt at some witty comment made by the hunter cum spy.

Brilliant. It was my turn. I got a heady whiff of lavender soap mixed with juniper cologne as Fredricks bent down to kiss my cheek.

"Fiona, you're the most beautiful woman at this table," he whispered in my ear. Of course, it was a bald-faced lie. But I enjoyed the compliment, nonetheless. His warm breath in my ear sent a shiver down my spine, and I felt my face flush. He probably said the same to every woman here. Cheeky cad.

He sat down next to me. "Do you like how I arranged to sit next to you?" He asked with a smirk and then leaned closer. "You know," he whispered again. "Since you are supposed to be my date for these events, it's dashed inconsiderate of you to bring your husband along."

"Given your reputation, any upstanding woman would bring a chaperone."

"*Moi?*" He flashed a sly smile. "I have a reputation? You mean as a great hunter."

"Exactly. And I don't want to be your next trophy."

"Shame. What a trophy you'd be."

I glared at him and gave my napkin a good flick in his direction before dropping it in my lap.

"Who are you hunting these days?" I figured it was worth a try. He thought he was so clever…he just might say something coded or present me with a riddle. The bounder loved to play games with me. He obviously enjoyed the chase. I was especially keen to see his interactions with Werner Liebermann since his name was on the list from the War Office.

Fredricks didn't seem to be paying attention to anyone but me, and certainly not Werner. Then again, Fredricks was a cagey cat.

The sound of a knife on crystal silenced the table. Frau Sacher was standing at one end, a wine glass in her hand. She gave a lengthy toast in German, most of which I did not understand. But I did discern that it was a toast in honor of His Majesty's birthday. At the word "*Prost,*" I knew enough to lift my glass.

"Cheers," Clifford said as he clinked glasses with me. "What a lovely tribute."

Mr. Twain's remarks about German came to mind again. I took a sip of my wine. *Crikey.* I tried not to grimace. Never much of a drinker, I found the stuff simultaneously sweet and cloying and bitter and acidic… and generally foul. I hastily washed it down with a drink of water.

"Splendid wine," Clifford said, obviously enjoying the horrid stuff.

When his wine glass was empty, I glanced up and down the table and quickly switched glasses with him.

Clifford continued drinking, oblivious as he chatted up Empress Zita's pretty sister, who I'd learned was Princess Francesca. Poor boy didn't know she was visiting before taking her vows to become a Benedictine nun at St. Cecilia's Abbey. Ah well, as one of twenty-four children, no doubt the empress had plenty of other pretty sisters.

I turned to Fredricks, who seemed to be listening intently to the conversation between the emperor and his foreign minister, who had their heads together at the other end of the table.

I tried to hear what they were saying. It must be important if Fredricks was so rapt. Unfortunately, their voices were too low and hushed, but there was tension between them. That much was obvious. The emperor and his minister, Count Czernin, were not getting along.

Keen to interrupt Fredricks's eavesdropping before he learned more state secrets, I tapped him on the shoulder.

"What's captured your interest?" I asked.

"It's my job to report on the war." His intense gaze made me uneasy. "What better way to get information than from the men in charge?"

"Whose side are you on?" I whispered.

"The same as you." He raised his eyebrows. "The side of peace."

Werner and Max delivered the first course. A white soup. Max held the tureen while Werner ladled. When I asked what it was, Werner called it "roux soup." *As in flour and butter?* To my surprise, the soup had a delicate texture and wasn't heavy at all.

"Where are you staying while in Vienna?" I asked Fredricks.

"Why?" He chuckled. "Are you fed up with Clifford already?"

I scowled at him. Indeed, I was rather fed up with Clifford, but that was beside the point.

The next course arrived. I hoped it tasted better than it looked. Whole fried fish on a platter. Max held the platter while Werner served each of us a portion of fish and potatoes. Blimey. When it came my turn, I looked away. Having my dinner staring back at me was deuced unsettling.

Hesitantly, I picked up a tiny piece on my fork and popped it into my mouth. *Ummm.* Delicious.

"Do you know many people in Vienna?" I asked innocently. Did I dare ask if he knew Mrs. Einstein? The recipient of the letter I'd intercepted.

"Doctor Freud claims we don't even know ourselves let alone anyone else." Fredricks smirked and then took a sip of wine.

"So now you're a disciple of Freud? I thought you considered him a sham."

"He's very persuasive in person." He balanced a bit of fish on his fork.

"You should attend one of his informal meetings at Café Korb. You might benefit from his insights into sexual repression."

Blasted man. I decided to take a different tack. "Are you looking forward to seeing old friends at the ball?" *And dispatching one of them?*

"I'm ablaze with anticipation of our first dance." He winked at me, the cad.

I scoffed.

Werner and Max delivered the main course, roasted goose stuffed with red cabbage. I tucked in. The tart flavor of the cabbage perfectly complemented the fatty bird. Almost as good as the pork and apple stuffing my grandmother would make at Christmas. If only she could see me now. Dining with royalty. And behind enemy lines too, working as a spy.

"Take off their finery and royalty aren't as grand as they seem," my grandmother would say. "Give a parlor maid a tiara and she's as good as a princess."

With all due respect, Granny, this royal dinner is grand...and a far cry from the toad-in-the-hole and suet pudding they serve in the canteen at the War Office. I hadn't eaten this well since before the war.

Judging by his obscene moaning, Clifford seemed to be enjoying it too. "I say." He smiled over at me. "This is the life, isn't it, old girl?"

Of course, the pudding course was the hotel's famous Sacher Torte served with a small glass of Eiswein. After the first wine, I'd managed to exchange my full glasses with Clifford's empty ones all through dinner.

The Eiswein was the gorgeous color of a deep-hued sunset and looked more appealing than the others. I took a sip. *Oh my.* A delicate fruity taste of plums and cherries hit my tongue, followed by a hint of orange. Scrummy. It was especially nice with the chocolate torte.

A lady's scream interrupted my Eiswein rapture. The tiny glass slipped from my hand and wine splashed onto my frock. As the glass shattered on the floor, I clasped my hand to my heart. The last time I heard a lady scream was when the poor woman got hit by the trolley. What in heaven's name was going on now? I glanced around to ascertain where the screams originated.

The odd little woman I'd seen scribbling in her notebooks stood in the doorway, her face flushed and her eyes wild. She kept repeating the words "*gestohlen*" and "*notizbuch*."

"Good Lord," Clifford said. "Why is she making such a fuss over a bloody notebook?"

Why, indeed?

Chapter Nine

The Notebook

F rau Sacher led the distraught woman out of the banquet room and down the hall toward her private dining room. The woman had a slight limp that I hadn't noticed until now because I'd only seen her sitting down.

I followed on their heels. Clifford was right behind me.

"No need for you to come along," I said.

"And no need for you to chase after them, yet here you are. Besides, I'm keeping my eye on you," Clifford said, nearly running into me. "You're prone to trouble."

I turned around and gave him a dirty look. *Prone to trouble. Horsefeathers. Can I help it if I'm in the right place at the right time?* I didn't know why this woman was so alarmed, but it felt important that I find out.

When I reached the threshold, I stopped. The distraught woman was sitting at a table. She was facing the door but seemed too distracted to notice us. Frau Sacher stood facing the woman and poured water from a pitcher. She put her hand on the woman's shoulder and said something softly in German.

Dash it! If only I could hear what she was saying. Even if I could hear, there was no guarantee I would understand. I'd had only a few days to prepare for this assignment. I'd studied German grammar books all the way from London to Vienna—it had been a good excuse to ignore Clifford's nattering on. With my photographic memory, I could reproduce lists of conjugated verbs, but that didn't help me understand this crying woman. Still, my German was coming along.

The woman wiped her eyes with a checkered handkerchief and then took a drink. Frau Sacher sat down across from her. She reached over and patted the woman's hand. Her back to the door, Frau Sacher hadn't noticed us yet either.

I hated to ask Clifford for help, but he *was* here. "What are they saying?" I whispered to him.

"She's complaining that someone nicked her notebook." He was looking over my shoulder. "Why one earth would someone take a notebook."

"Perhaps it contains valuable information," I said, still peering into the room. "And keep your voice down."

"I say, you may be right," he whispered. "The notebook contains some mathematical formula or something belonging to her husband, Albert, who is apparently a renowned physicist at Berlin University."

"Physics?" *Why would anyone want to steal a notebook full of mathematical formulas?*

The tearful woman was talking a mile a minute... in bloody German. She was wearing a plain cotton dress, a bit tight across the bosom, and troubling her hanky something fierce.

"What is she saying?" I turned to Clifford.

"Darned if I know." He shrugged. "Something about special and general relativity."

"What's that?"

"No clue." His eyes lit up. "I say, the old boy is poised to win the Nobel Prize in a few years."

How in blazes does she know he'll win a Nobel Prize? Does she have a crystal ball? I wondered if the woman was delusional.

Clifford grabbed my arm. "Good Lord. She's set to get the prize money. But only so long as no one ever lays eyes on that notebook."

No one lays eyes on the notebook. How odd. *How much is the Nobel Prize worth?* Probably more than a couple of French bulldogs. *Are the two thefts related? What do dogs and physics have in common?* Ransom, of course.

I stepped into the room. "Excuse me," I said in my best German and waved. "I couldn't help but overhear about the Nobel Prize money associated with this missing notebook." I smiled what I hoped was a sympathetic smile to compensate for my horrible German. "Is it a lot?"

The woman glared at me. "Who are you?"

Thank goodness. *She speaks English.*

"I'm Fiona Figg... er, Douglas." I extended my hand.

Still gaping at me, her intense eyes full of doubt, she took my hand. Her chestnut hair sat like a skein of yarn atop her square head. Her face was flat, like a Persian cat's.

"I'm a bit of an amateur detective." I raised my eyebrows and gestured toward a chair. "May I?" I took their silence as acquiescence and sat down.

"Captain Douglas at your service," Clifford said, bowing. "I too am a detective."

If I hadn't already sat down, I would have kicked him. *Captain.* He might as well have told them he was in the British Army sent here by the War Office. *I too am a detective.* I rolled my mind's eye. When he glanced over at me, I scowled at him. He quietly took the seat next to me.

"*Mr.* Douglas." He corrected with a sheepish smile. "Fiona's husband."

I nodded my approval.

"A detective?" The woman wadded up her handkerchief into a tight little ball and looked over at me with hope in her gray eyes. "Can you help me find my notebook?"

"Fiona is jolly clever." Clifford beamed. "She solved a marvelous murder at Ravenswick Abbey—"

I gave his shin a swift kick with my pointy-toed pump.

"Ouch." He yelped like a puppy and then rubbed his leg.

"Clifford dear." I forced a smile. "Let's not bore the ladies with my adventures." *Shut your gob before you blow our cover.* "Can't you see Mrs.... Mrs....is in distress."

"I must retrieve my notebook," she said, her face red and blotchy. "My husband stipulated in the letter that I would get the prize money as long as

I kept that notebook to myself." Her shoulders shook and she broke down again. "He left me four years ago. Now he is divorcing me to marry his pretty cousin, Elsa." Tears streaming down her face, she glanced over at me. "For the sake of our sons, you must find it." She laid her head on the table and sobbed. "For Hans Albert and little Eduard."

"I'll go fetch some tea," Frau Sacher said, making a hasty departure.

"Should we call a doctor?" Clifford asked. "The poor woman is simply overcome—"

I cleared my throat. He took the hint and shut it.

"What she—Mrs....Mrs....needs is someone to find her notebook, and that is just what we're going to do."

She lifted her soggy face. "Mrs. Einstein. Mileva Einstein." She sniffled. "Really? You'll do that for me?"

My sainted aunt. Mileva Einstein. Of course, all the talk of physics should have given it away. So, this was the woman Fredricks wanted to help him recruit scientists for the Germans.

"Of course we will," Clifford said. I'm surprised he didn't drop to one knee and propose on the spot, given his penchant for damsels in distress... although Mrs. Einstein was not the fair-haired beauty he typically favored.

"We'll need more information, if you're up to it." I snapped my purse open and felt around. I didn't need a spy lipstick or lockpick. I needed my own bloody notebook. "What's in your notebook, if I may ask?"

"Nothing really." Mrs. Einstein turned as red as a beet. Her lashes fluttered. "Only my silly notes."

"Why would someone steal your sill—your notes?" There was something she wasn't telling us. Something vital to understanding the importance of her notebook.

She shrugged.

"We can't find out who took it until we find a motive. And we can't speculate about a motive until we know what's in the notebook."

"I can't say." She sniffed.

Frau Sacher returned with a tea tray. She laid out the cups and then poured from a beautiful china teapot. I nodded in appreciation when she filled my cup. If we weren't in the middle of an important investigation, I would have asked for a splash of milk. Bother. I'd have to drink it black. And black it was too.

"We can't help you if you don't tell us." *What is so important that her husband wants it hidden? How is it connected to the Nobel Prize? And who else knows about it?* Fredrick Fredricks came to mind.

"How do I know I can trust you?" Her voice was hard.

"Why Fiona is practically a tomb of silence," Clifford said. "The very definition of confidant."

"Thank you," I whispered. I was genuinely touched by his trust in me. I took a sip of tea. My nose wrinkled involuntarily. Stout was an understatement.

"And I…why I'm the very epitome of discretion." Clifford smiled.

I nearly spit out a mouthful of tea. *The antinomy of discretion, more like.* The man was a downright blabbermouth.

"If I tell you, you'll find my notebook?" She dabbed at her eyes.

"We will do our very best." I patted her hand.

"If I tell you…" She glanced around and lowered her voice. "You must promise not to tell another living soul."

"Promise," I said, putting my hand to my heart.

"You must swear," she said solemnly. "On a bible."

"Good lord," Clifford exclaimed. "A bible."

"Frau Sacher, might you be good enough to fetch us a bible?" I asked.

"*Ja*, of course." She left the room again, her skirts rustling as she went.

"So, what is so important that you make us swear on a bible and your husband threatens to revoke the prize money?" I said, more to myself than to her.

"The bible," she demanded.

We sat in silence until Frau Sacher returned carrying a leatherbound bible in both hands. She kicked the door closed with her foot. "My family bible," she said as she laid it on the table.

We took turns swearing on our eternal souls to keep the woman's secret. She even made Frau Sacher swear in English and then again in German.

"How dramatic," Clifford said, obviously pleased.

The woman's distress and her insistence on absolute secrecy, combined with Fredricks's interest in her, made me suspect that whatever was in that notebook could be important to the outcome of the war.

As if in slow motion, the woman took a long sip of tea, replaced the cup on the saucer, and then folded her hands in her lap. She sat there staring into space for what seemed like several minutes. *Come on, woman.*

Finally, she took a deep breath. "I was twenty years old, and he was seventeen." She glanced around the table like a woman on trial for her life. "His mother called me a crippled old hag. His parents forbid...I was too old and too foreign...and my limp." She touched her leg.

Her voice was soft but steady as she told her story. A prodigy at mathematics, she obtained special permission to attend an all-boys school in Zagreb and was the only woman in her class at Zurich Polytechnic. There, she met a talented young physicist named Albert Einstein.

My impatient side wanted her to get to the point, to what was in the notebook. But she wasn't the first person I'd met who told things in roundabout ways. I glanced at Clifford, who was rapt. And she was compelling, so I forced myself to listen patiently.

"I was very shy and hardly spoke to anyone." She fingered the edge of the tablecloth. "Albert was the opposite. The class clown. Brilliant but... undisciplined...constantly skipping class and asking for my notes." She gave a weak smile. "He was a very bad boy. So, of course, I couldn't resist."

What is it about bad boys? I thought of Archie Somersby. I didn't know if he was bad, but I was pretty sure he wasn't entirely good. Then there was good old reliable Clifford. Too good.

"I helped Albert with mathematics and applied physics." Mrs. Einstein's hand trembled as she took a sip of water. "The other boys just made fun of me and called me *Der Hamster*." She closed her eyes. "Albert and I were inseparable, doing our homework together and having heated discussions about physics over dinner."

Passionate debates over physics were not my idea of romance. Then again, neither were posies and white weddings. As my father used to say, "one man's—or woman's—toffee is another man's toothache."

"Albert was like a fledgling hawk, so enamored with flying he would forget to land." Mrs. Einstein folded her handkerchief. "I kept him grounded and focused." She stared at me without seeing me. "We were a team." She sighed. "After I got pregnant—"

"Good Lord," Clifford exclaimed.

I kicked him again. He glared at me and rubbed his shin. But really, he was such a prude.

Mrs. Einstein seemed oblivious. "Things changed. He didn't have a job, so we couldn't get married, and I had to leave school. But when the baby died…" Her voice trailed off.

"Heavens." My hand flew to my mouth. Her story was downright tragic.

Mrs. Einstein cleared her throat and then continued. "After years of collaboration, a few years ago, we finally submitted our first article on capillarity." Her face lit up as if someone had flipped a switch.

Capillarity? Is that the theory that Fredricks thinks could help the Germans?

Mrs. Einstein bit her lip. "I insisted we leave my name off—"

"What? Why?" I interrupted.

"Who would take seriously a scientific article written by a woman?" Her face fell.

"What about Marie Curie?" I asked. "She's won the Nobel Prize. Twice."

"Yes, Marie and I are friends. But Albert is not like Pierre.…" Again, her voice trailed off.

Her husband sounded like a pillock, if you asked me. I wondered if Fredricks knew Mrs. Einstein was her husband's collaborator. Given that his note asked her to help him recruit her husband and the other lady physicist, I doubted it. But if he found out, and given Mrs. Einstein's impoverished state, and the blackguard's natural charm… I shuddered to think.

"You were equal partners and yet your… er, he got all the credit?" I asked.

"She's right, you know," Clifford said. "Who would believe a woman could be a mathematical mastermind?"

"What?" I felt like kicking him again. "Are you saying a woman can't be as clever as a man?"

"Well, no...but mathematics...surely..." Clifford stammered. "Surely that's a man's field."

"My notebook proves that I am the co-author of all of his early theories," Mrs. Einstein said. "That's why you absolutely must find it. Albert will win the Nobel Prize for our work on relative motion. But no one must find out about our collaboration."

"Why not?" I demanded. I was tempted to find this notebook just to show the world that this woman was as deserving as her husband of any prize.

"He needs the adoration. I need the money."

I must have had a shocked look on my face. She immediately added, "not for me, mind you. For our two sons."

"At least you have your children," Frau Sacher said. She had been sitting, silently taking it all in.

"New life is not the only thing of importance we women can create," Mrs. Einstein said.

"Indeed." I nodded approvingly.

"My notebook contains my true firstborn. The theory of relative motion." Her piercing gaze scared me.

"Was the notebook stolen from your room?"

"Yes."

"May I see your room?" I needed to examine the locks to determine how the thief got in. "Do you have another notebook like the one that was lost? And I'd like to see a sample of your handwriting." My mind kicked into high gear.

"I'm afraid my sons are asleep now," she said apologetically. "Can you come to my room tomorrow morning? I have an identical notebook and then I can show you my handwriting."

"Was anything else taken from your room?"

"No. Not that I noticed."

"Who else knew about the importance of the notebooks?" I asked. I doubted that any of the staff would know their value. The staff had opportunity, but not motive. Who else had motive and opportunity?

"Only me and Albert." She thought a minute. "Maybe another physicist. We've worked with many. But none of them would ever..."

I may not have understood Mrs. Einstein's motivations, but I understood why this Albert Einstein fellow would not want that notebook to come into the light of day. In fact, he probably preferred they didn't exist at all. *I hope he doesn't feel the same way about his wife.*

"Could this theory of relative motion of yours be used as a weapon somehow?" I asked.

"I say, Fiona, what are you thinking?" Clifford asked.

The blood drained from Mrs. Einstein's face. "I never thought of that."

Unfortunately, I had.

And no doubt, Fredricks had too.

Chapter Ten

Love Letters

The next morning, I woke up early. Too early. I'd tossed and turned all night, fretting about Frau Sacher's pups, Mrs. Einstein's notebook, and of course the dastardly Fredrick Fredricks, who was now in possession of some dangerous formulas that he would no doubt share with the bloody Germans.

Dawn was just breaking when I looked out the window of my fifth-floor room. Vienna was bathed in a soft violet glow. The dome of the opera house reflected the first rays of sunshine on what promised to be another scorcher. A boy swept the cobblestones while women opened their shops since most of the men were away fighting.

Crikey. They're up early. Down below on the street, Max led Mozart on a leash—at least I assumed that tiny speck was the puppy. Obviously, the dog had different ideas about where they were going. The puppy insisted on sniffing around the entrance to a public telephone station across from the hotel. Max was struggling to get the little chap to follow him. But he was not yet leash trained.

That was one advantage of dogs. Unlike men, they could be trained.

Poor Frau Sacher still hadn't recovered her beloved Bruno and Jana, tiny Mozart's older siblings. Yet, she carried on taking care of her guests and even hosting a lavish royal banquet. She kept a stiff upper lip, for which I admired her all the more. Although, she did seem to be smoking more cigars than usual. My gown from last night positively reeked.

As I prepared my toilette, I couldn't stop thinking about the shocking revelations that had disrupted the royal dinner party. The theft of Mrs. Einstein's notebook and her tragic love story, which was all too similar to my own. *Unfaithful husband. Prettier woman. Messy divorce.* The memories still made me queasy.

Poor Mrs. Einstein had helped her husband with physics equations for which she thinks he'll eventually win the Nobel Prize, yet her part in their work would be relegated to the dustbin of history. Of course, if the world discovered those notebooks, then all that would change...and that bounder Albert Einstein would have to share the glory with his wife.

Part of me wanted to find the notebook and share it with the world so she'd get her due. But I'd promised her I'd find it and keep my mouth shut, so that was what I was going to do. I was especially keen to get it out of the hands of Fredricks.

After my toilette, I dressed quickly in a practical skirt, blouse, and my oxford lace-ups, and then tugged on my favorite wig.

I had a very busy morning ahead. First, I would examine Mrs. Einstein's room, looking for clues to who stole her notebook. Next, I would question the staff about both the missing dogs and the missing notebook. They all had the means and opportunity, but did any of them have a motive? And then I would go visit that poor injured woman in hospital. Of course, I had an ulterior motive, which was to confirm that she worked at the Imperial Hotel and how she came to be delivering a note for Fredricks. My guess was that if she worked there, then he was staying there too, and that like so many other parlor maids, he had charmed her into doing his bidding.

If Fredricks did steal the notebook, then why? I had to ask Mrs. Einstein more questions about the contents of her notebook.

I glanced at my watch. It had just gone half six. I was dying for a nice cuppa with a splash of milk. I'd settle for a cup of strong Viennese coffee made palatable by a large dollop of cream and sugar. *Hmmmm...is dawn too early for a slice of Sacher Torte?* My mouth positively watered just thinking about that scrummy apricot filling.

If only I could remedy the tea situation, I could imagine staying the rest of my life as a pampered guest at the Sacher Hotel.

Sitting at the dressing table, I dumped out the contents of my purse. My spy lipstick, lockpicking kit, the handkerchief wrapped around the evidence, and Mata Hari's tiny gun. Unfortunately, I couldn't save her. On my last assignment, I'd tried. *Mata Hari. The woman whose crime was loving too much.*

I unwrapped the cloth and stared down at the crust of bread. Too bad it was impossible to collect fingerprints from foodstuffs.

Were the two thefts from the hotel related? If they were, what did dogs have to do with Mrs. Einstein's notebook? Other things may have been stolen too. Not just dogs held for ransom. Or notebooks. But bread and cakes, and who knew what else. Things of value.

The thief had to be someone who knew about the people and items in the hotel. An employee—or someone who had regular access to the hotel. A delivery person perhaps? I made a mental note to ask around and find out who regularly visits the hotel in addition to its employees...after I had a cup of tea... or if necessary, coffee. And I would ask if any of the staff had seen Fredricks lurking about the hotel. He stood out in a crowd, and no one would forget him once they'd seen him.

The sun had risen above the horizon. I finished dressing, scooped my spy gear off the dresser and into a handbag, and then picked up my Vienna guidebook. Since the birthday ball wasn't until tomorrow evening, I had all day to sleuth. I'd best set out before Clifford woke up and came calling.

Armed with everything I needed for a day of espionage, I headed down the stairs.

I didn't pass another living soul. Even the dust mites were still asleep as they floated past on beams of morning light.

The closer I got to the kitchen, the stronger the smell of fresh-baked bread. The bakers were already up at least. They'd probably gotten several black-market deliveries already this morning. There was no way Frau Sacher could supply her guests with chocolate cake and full-course gourmet meals without dealing with the black market. With war rations, it just wasn't possible.

Did she seek out the black market? Or did she merely turn a blind eye while one of her kitchen staff did? She said she had friends across the country. Friends with farms. Vegetables, butter, and the occasional goose, yes. But what farm in Austria-Hungary grew cocoa beans? Given they only grew in tropical climates, the answer was none.

Maybe the doggies' disappearance had something to do with the black market. When you got involved with criminals, you were asking for trouble.

A large silver coffee urn had already been placed in the public dining room. The blue-orange flame underneath indicated that it had been filled and was awaiting the early risers. I picked up a cup and set it under the spigot. I glanced around in search of warm milk or cream. None. Indeed, there was nothing laid out yet except the urn and the cups. And no one in sight, not even a waiter. *I'll pop next door for my cuppa to fortify myself to question Mrs. Einstein and the staff.*

On my way out of the dining room, I bumped into Mrs. Einstein. Literally. Head on. "How fortuitous," I said rubbing my forehead. "Is this a convenient time to see your room?"

"*Ja,*" she said in a whisper, glancing around like she thought she was being followed. "Come with me." Mrs. Einstein led me back up the stairs to her room.

My goodness. Her room was a cluttered mess of books, papers, and clothes strewn all over. It was a wonder she could find anything at all. I wouldn't doubt that her precious notebook was simply hiding under one of the piles. *What is that smell?* Dirty laundry mixed with rose petals and dust. "Are you sure the notebook is missing?"

The older son was sketching in a notebook. The younger was quietly reading a book. *What a sweet child.*

A pain in my side made me flinch. I thought of Andrew and his new wife and their son. Again, I wondered if that's why he left me. Because I couldn't have children.

"Oh yes," Mrs. Einstein said, running the gauntlet of stacks to a particularly precarious-looking pile in the far corner. "I know exactly where everything is. It doesn't look like it, but I'm really very organized." She ignored the pile of books that just came crashing down around her eldest son.

"Indeed." I instinctively took a step backward and nearly tripped over a pair of boots.

"How long have you been staying at the hotel?" I asked, wondering if she'd been holed up in this stuffy room for months.

"Frau Sacher has been good enough to let us stay. She is a family friend and has been so kind to us." Her voice trailed off.

Aha. Frau Sacher must be letting them stay for free. That explains why the poor woman can afford to stay at such a posh hotel.

With the skill of a magician, she plucked a thick notebook from the bottom of a pile. *Amazing the whole stack didn't come tumbling down.*

"Here is its mate." She held up the large leatherbound book. "My missing notebook looks exactly like this one." She zigzagged back across the room and then handed it to me.

It was surprisingly heavy. When I opened it, a colorful woolen bookmark fell to the floor. I bent to pick it up. The book was plain brown leather with blank white pages. But the bookmark was fine embroidered tapestry like a miniature Persian rug. "Gorgeous."

"My younger sister, Zorka, makes those." Mrs. Einstein fetched a briefcase off the bed, opened it, and pulled out a packet of beautiful handmade bookmarks. "She's a genius at textiles." She pulled a purple patterned ribbon from the pack. "For you."

"Oh, that's not necessary." It was lovely.

She held it out. "Please. The color suits you."

"You're too kind." I took the bookmark and admired it. It really was beautiful needlework. "What does it say?" I pointed to Cyrillic lettering along one edge.

Mrs. Einstein chuckled. "Zorka loves nursery rhymes and children's songs." She fingered the end of the bookmark. "'My sister sits under a tree, and I sit next to her,'" she read in a singsong voice. She pulled another from the pack. "'The daughter has working hands.'" And another. "'Sister come again and lead the dance.'" She ruffled through the deck of bookmarks. "She embroiders little sayings for me."

"How delightful. You and your sister must be very close." As an only child, I'd always wished I had a sister.

"Two boots make a pair," she said with a wistful smile.

"Indeed." I returned her smile. "Do you happen to have any other notebooks with mathematical equations in them?"

She gave me an odd look.

"Just so I can see what it looks like and so I'll recognize your handwriting, mind you." Why was she so hesitant? I couldn't understand her formulas no matter how hard I tried. And I doubt that she'd heard about my photographic memory.

Reluctantly, she pulled a smaller notebook from her briefcase. "My latest work." She held it out and I took it.

The small leather notebook was chock-full of bookmarks hanging out like colorful tongues.

"Who might want to steal your notebook?" I asked, glancing up from the pages.

"I have no idea."

Inside, the pages held line after line of tight script consisting of letters, numbers, and symbols, none of which I understood. One page had only $E=mc2$ written on it. "And the missing notebook has formulas like this? And bookmarks too?"

She nodded. "And letters," she said softly. "From Albert." Her voice trembled. "My insurance policy." Her face went red and blotchy, and I thought she might start crying.

Love letters? "Insurance policy?" I squinted at her. *What did she mean? Insurance against what? Was she in danger?*

"Love letters—"

Aha. I was right.

"Love letters to our work." She hesitated. "The physics papers we wrote together. I wrote them out myself and put them in the post for review. They were as much mine as his."

I was really starting to despise this Albert character. What a rotter.

"I must find the notebook." She wrung her hands. "To save Albert's reputation and make sure I get the money." Tears welled up in her eyes. "He owes it to me."

Oh dear. "Now, now," I said, taking one of her hands in mine. "Look here." I waited for her gaze to meet mine. "I will find your notebook if it's the last thing I do." Of course, I had no clue where to look or how to find the blasted thing. But it seemed like the right thing to say. Not only that. If Fredricks was involved in this business, then it was my job to find the notebook and retrieve it before he could turn it over to our enemies.

"Thank you, Mrs. Douglas."

I cringed at the sound of the name.

"You can't think of anyone who would want to steal your work?" I was tempted to say, "besides your husband," but I held my tongue.

"It is very important work. But Albert has already published most of it."

"But not all of it?"

She shook her head.

"Do you think your husband might have had someone take it to destroy the evidence of your collaboration?"

"No. No. Albert would never do that." Her cheeks flamed. "Never."

I went to the door and examined the lock. It hadn't been broken. Indeed, there was no sign of a break-in. Whoever took the notebook had a key or access to a key. Someone on the inside had to be involved. But why would one of the staff want a mathematical formula? No. What the staff wanted would be money. Whoever wanted the notebook must have paid one of them to get it. Maybe I would get the staff to confess when I interviewed them.

"Last night, when I asked if anything in the notebook could be used to make a weapon, you didn't answer." I watched Mrs. Einstein's face fall.

"It's too terrible to even consider the possibility." She stared down at her well-worn oxfords. "In theory, it is possible…" Her voice trailed off.

"The possibility of what? Done what?"

Her eyes got wide. "Destruction beyond your worst nightmare."

Good grief. Fredricks. He wouldn't have had to pay anyone to break in or help him do it. He could've done it himself without leaving a clue.

I touched my pocket. Should I deliver Fredricks's note? The one I'd taken from the fallen maid. It might be helpful to see Mrs. Einstein's reaction. For all I knew, she was the double agent.

"This note arrived for you," I said, pulling the small envelope from my pocket and handing it to her.

She narrowed her eyes and took it. Glancing over at me, she slipped the note out of the envelope and then read it. "Never," she said emphatically.

"What does it say," I asked innocently.

"Some German wants us to help the Kaiser." She shook her head. "Albert and I are pacificists. We won't help anyone wage war."

Although I worked for the War Office, and I loved my country, witnessing so many atrocities at the Charing Cross Hospital had almost turned me into a pacificist too.

"Who is this, Fredrick Fredricks?" Mrs. Einstein asked. "Do you know?"

"A very dangerous man. I advise you to stay away from him." I, on the other hand, had to find out where he was staying, search his room, and retrieve the notebook before he passed it on to the bloody Germans.

My cuppa would have to wait... and so would interviewing the staff. Fredricks was the most likely culprit anyway. Besides, I was running out of time to determine Fredricks's target before the royal ball. Now I had two reasons to find him *tout de suite*.

Chapter Eleven

The Haberdashery

It had almost gone eight, and I was "burning daylight" as my father would say. The royal ball was tomorrow, and I was no closer to discovering who Fredricks's intended victim was. Now that he had the notebook, he wouldn't kill Mrs. Einstein, would he? She couldn't be the double agent. Anyway, I very much doubted she was invited to the ball. Then again, she had been at the garden party. Her husband must be deuced important indeed.

I had to visit the injured maid in hospital and convince her to help me gain access to Fredricks's room.

I hurried down the stairs, and across the lobby to the entrance. After Mrs. Einstein's stifling room, I was dying to get some air and clear my head.

Outside, the air was fresh with the promise of a new day. With not a cloud in the sky, the sharpness of the blue was startling. I was used to dreary grays or overcast whites. I leaned against a column at the hotel entrance and opened my guidebook. *Where is the closest hospital?* I would confirm that the fallen maid worked at the Imperial Hotel, and find out what she knew about Fredricks, and persuade her to help me locate him… if she was still there…and still alive.

I held my breath as I flipped through the pages. Cafés, hotels, restaurants… hospitals. *Wait! Cafés.* Lightning struck my brain. I had an idea. What was the name of that café Fredricks mentioned? Café Korb. I flipped through the guidebook until I found the listing for Café Korb.

My, my. Even the guidebook describes the café's claim to fame as the famous doctor Freud's meeting place. Every Friday morning like clockwork, it said.

If I hopped it, I could get to the café before nine. If Fredricks had become such a convert to Freudianism, he most certainly would be there. I had to try. Then I could follow him.

Of course, unless I went in disguise, Fredricks would recognize me immediately. I rubbed my hands together. Now was the perfect opportunity to use my new costume. Before I'd left London, a quick stop at Angels Fancy Dress Shop provided the chance of a new look.

I dashed back inside and rushed up the stairs. If I hurried, I could get to the café before Freud—and Fredricks—and stake out the place. Then I could follow the blackguard, and he would lead me back to his hotel. Yes, it just might work.

Completely winded by the time I arrived on the fifth floor, I was nearly panting as I withdrew the disguise from my wardrobe. I didn't have time to take the care it deserved or required, but I needed some camouflage to succeed in trailing Fredricks.

I ripped off my skirt and blouse. I replaced them with baggy trousers, a tight-fitting jacket (after binding my chest, such as it was), a starched collared shirt, and a loose necktie. The outfit came complete with oversized shoes, a bowler hat, a toothbrush mustache, and a short curly wig. Quickly, I applied spirit gum to my upper lip and pressed on the crumb catcher. I tore off my blond bob and tugged on the dark wig.

Glancing in the looking glass, I was pleased with my transformation. Not quite as handsome as Charlie Chaplin's Little Tramp, still the disguise turned me into a passable man. And hopefully, one that Fredricks wouldn't recognize. After all, he already knew my Harold the bellboy and Dr. Vogel.

The oversized shoes, however, proved too much for me. I tripped over my own feet twice just getting to the door of my room. *This won't do.* I exchanged the unwieldy monsters for my own practical oxfords. After all, what good was a disguise if I couldn't keep up with the criminal?

I snatched my purse off the dressing table and was off. I was halfway down the hall before I realized that the Little Tramp would not carry a purse. I dashed back to my room, emptied my purse onto the dressing table, and then stuffed the necessary equipment into the pockets of my trousers and jacket. Lockpick set, guidebook, and Mata Hari's gun just in case.

I breathed in excitement as I set out on my adventure. Until recently, I'd never even been out of England, let alone worked in two major capitals of continental Europe. *Paris. Now Vienna. War espionage was jolly exhilarating.*

After a brisk fifteen-minute walk, I was standing in the *Stephanplatz* in front of the glorious St. Stephen's Cathedral. It looked like a fairy-tale castle, complete with the Austrian Empire's menacing double-headed eagle formed from colorful tiles on the steep roof. As I was gazing up at the dazzling roof, the church bells boomed, calling the faithful to morning mass. The vibrations reverberated through my body and nearly reached my soul.

Lest I be drawn inside, I hurried past, recalling my mission. To spy on Fredricks at Café Korb where he was hopefully meeting Doctor Freud. If memory served—which it always did—the guidebook said take a left on Schulerstraße, and Café Korb would be only another five-minute walk. I don't know why I bothered carrying the blasted book. I had it all in my head.

According to the guidebook, Café Korb was the weekly meeting spot for Sigmund Freud's Vienna Psychoanalytic Society. Surely, I'd get a glimpse of the man. I glanced at my watch. Almost quarter to nine. Only fifteen more minutes and they'd be open.

The café was on a smart-looking corner in the center of town. When I arrived, two young women were carrying small tables and chairs outside. I was delighted to see them setting up umbrellas. Even this early, the Austrian sun was brutal, especially dressed in a man's woolen suit. Perhaps I should have purchased the Mark Twain costume instead. At least it had a linen suit.

I found a shady spot under an awning and fanned myself with the guidebook. Blasted book was good for something after all.

A few minutes later, a waitress waved me over to one of the small tables. As I sat down, I asked for a cup of strong tea.

The waitress gave me a strange look and then a light went off in her eyes as she must have registered what I'd said in my appalling German. Either that or she'd mistaken me for the real Charlie Chaplin. She smiled and nodded. *"Ja, tee."*

As I waited for my tea, I watched soldiers traveling in packs along the storefronts or rumbling up the streets on lorries. Their red-and-blue uniforms were more colorful than our Tommies' drab khaki. But underneath the cloth, they looked the same. Weary boys joking or smoking or just tuning out to avoid thoughts of war. Boys who should be courting sweethearts and dreaming of promising futures. Boys who would come home broken and battered…if they came home at all.

And what was the point? Why did so many young men have to die? Honor? Glory? After three long years of war rations, suffering, and death, I don't think anyone knew why we were fighting anymore.

What's honorable about mustard gas or amputated limbs? Other animals may kill for fun, but human beings are the only animals who wage war and massacre their own. We are the true beasts.

I shook off my gloomy thoughts and willed myself to savor the moment. It felt good to sit in the shade in the heart of a city vibrant with the start of a new day. And one of these days, we would wake up and the war would be over. *Wouldn't that be grand?*

Today was not that day. And I had work to do. I wasn't in Vienna on holiday after all. I was here to gather intelligence on Fredricks and report back to the War Office via Miss Louise de Bettignies, aka Alice Dubois, at Holeschaus Castle, Hungary.

Captain Hall would be none too pleased to learn that I'd become embroiled in not just one, but two mysteries. The missing bulldogs and the missing notebook.

Still, I wasn't one to sit idly by if I could help it. In the words of Charles Dickens, "No one is useless in this world who lightens the burdens of others." And my gut told me Fredricks was involved in all of this, the dogs, the notebook, everything.

Anyway, I may not be beautiful, talented, or a genius at physics, but I was determined to make myself useful.

99

The waitress returned carrying a tray laden with a teapot, a pretty china cup, and a tiny pitcher of steaming milk. *"Wunderbar!"*

I peeked in the teapot and was pleased to see a dark brew. I poured a splash of warm milk into the cup, swirled it around, and then filled it with piping hot tea. I gave it a quick stir with a tiny spoon.

Ahhh. The first sip was heavenly. It may not have been the best cuppa I'd ever had, but it was more than adequate and certainly the best I'd had in Austria.

After I enjoyed the first cup in quiet meditation and complete peace of mind, I poured a second to fortify me in my pursuit of Fredricks, if he ever arrived.

I asked the waitress to borrow a pen to make some notes. I'd just taken up the pen when a dapper man with a neatly trimmed white beard and pensive gaze sat down at the largest of the outdoor tables. He crossed his legs, lit a cigar, and peered at me over his little round glasses. Was it him? Could that be the famous doctor? It must be. My heart was aflutter. Now, if only Fredricks would show up.

"Sigmund." A booming voice came from behind me. A familiar booming voice. *Think of the devil and he shall appear.*

I slid down in my chair and buried my nose in a menu.

Fredricks and the doctor greeted each other like old friends. Luckily, the Great White Hunter was so enamored of the good doctor that he didn't notice me. After all, a good disguise should always allow one to hide in plain sight.

I'd seen books by Freud in Fredricks's rooms at Ravenswick and then again at his bedside in that nasty Paris prison. He'd probably studied Freud's writings to learn how to better manipulate people. But Fredricks wasn't the only one who'd studied psychoanalysis. I'd taken to reading Freud myself, in hopes of learning how the criminal mastermind worked. Fredricks wasn't going to get the better of me this time.

Over the top of the menu, I watched as Fredricks conversed with the doctor. After a few minutes, the two men stood up and shook hands. Fredricks donned his hat and took off toward St. Stephens square.

Never letting him out of my sight, I fished in my pocket for enough coins to pay for the pot of tea and then dropped them on the table. At least I hoped it was enough. I took off after Fredricks.

Walking as fast as I could—good thing I didn't wear those oversized banana peels—I trailed Fredricks from a safe distance. The peacock stopped in front of every storefront window, preening. He stopped so often, I didn't dare get too close to him or he'd realize I was following him. Then again, I was in disguise, so at least he wouldn't recognize me.

Graben Street in central Vienna was lined with bespoke tailor's shops. It reminded me of Savile Row in Mayfair. Some of the shops displayed military uniforms instead of fine men's suits. *I suppose that is how they stay in business during this bloody war.* War or not, I imagine the aristocracy still have to have their handmade suits.

Fredricks stopped in front of a shoe shop called Scheer. Instead of entering through the front door, Fredricks rang a bell and was buzzed into a second door nearby. *Could this be his lodging?*

Once he was inside and out of sight, I hurried to examine the door he'd just entered. Above the bell was a sign for Scheer. *The second door must be a private entrance, for deliveries, perhaps. Or special customers. Dash it.* How could I follow Fredricks into the back of the shoe shop?

I hid around the corner and waited for him to reappear. The sun was beating on my back, and I longed for a cool lemonade, a bit of shade, and a light sundress instead of this bloody hot woolen suit. Dabbing at my forehead with a handkerchief, I peered around the corner.

A few minutes later, Fredricks reappeared carrying a shoebox under his arm. He must have ordered a pair of shoes. Perhaps he was preparing for the royal ball. He walked up the Graben at a jaunty pace.

The Graben was a wide avenue with shops on either side. Streetlamps dotted the walkways, and sporadic bright awnings offered limited shade. The far side of the street boasted statues, fountains, and beerhouses. Just four years ago, this must have been a bustling street, full of life. Now, the occasional horse-drawn carriage was flanked by military lorries transporting soldiers. The walkways were empty but for groups of soldiers and a few shopgirls outside smoking or sweeping.

I wondered if the bespoke tailors had to hire women, too? I doubted any man would trust a woman tailor.

Fredricks stopped again. This time in front of a haberdashery called Knize. He popped inside. I sauntered up to the window and nonchalantly looked inside. A well-dressed older man was leading Fredricks up a staircase. I took the plunge and went inside.

I held my breath as I tiptoed up the stairs after them. The second floor was a grand open space with plenty of natural light streaming through giant windows. Shelves of fabric lined three of the walls and large mirrors hung on the fourth. Alongside the mirrors were two doors, which I assumed led to fitting rooms.

The well-dressed man had a tape measure hanging around his neck. He was showing Fredricks some fabrics and talking a mile a minute. Fredricks had his back to me, and the tailor was too busy to pay me any mind.

With my ears pricked, I strolled around the shop, admiring the fabrics.

"Can I help you?" A man's voice startled me.

I spun around.

The young man looked me up and down. "Perhaps you're looking for ready-to-wear?" He pursed his lips and gestured toward the stairs. Obviously, I looked more ready-to-wear than custom-made.

Afraid to draw attention to myself, I let the young man shepherd me down the stairs. When we reached the bottom, he waved his hand toward the entrance. "You might want to try the shops in the outer ring," he said. "They are less expensive." He wrinkled his nose as if he'd smelled something foul. I took the hint and went back outside.

I hid in the shade under an awning across the street from Knize, watching for Fredricks to come out. After what seemed like hours, but turned out to be only twenty-seven minutes, he emerged carrying another parcel. Whistling, he strode down the avenue and disappeared around the corner.

I rushed to catch up. In his jodhpurs, tall black boots, and slouch hat, he was easy to spot. He was walking at a good clip, and I struggled to keep up. He stopped again in Albertinaplatz, which was a lovely treelined plaza just behind the opera house. Glancing in my direction, he opened the door to yet another shop. *Good heavens. The man is a clothes horse.*

Minutes later, I followed him inside. Jungmann & Neffe was even more ornate and luxurious than Knize. From the entrance all the way to the back of the shop, every wall was lined with carved wooden shelves stacked with fine fabrics. The ceiling alone was worth the trip. Colorful frescos displayed the history of the textile trade.

To my surprise, the shop catered to women as well as men. Indeed, most of the shoppers were wealthy women attended by their lady's maids.

Fredricks was huddled in one corner chatting up a well-dressed woman, whom I could only see from behind. He was jolly attentive to the lady, obsequious even, which made it easier to spy on them unnoticed. I stood a few feet away, fingering a bolt of magenta silk.

The woman's voice was familiar. Unintentionally, my head jerked around when I realized that Fredricks was talking to the empress. Had he arranged a secret meeting with Empress Zita at this dress shop? Or had he simply run into her by accident? Perhaps she was buying a new dress?

I strained to hear their conversation. Heads together, they were whispering. The only words I made out were "Rax," and "brothers."

Fredricks lifted a square of fabric from a shelf nearby. "How about we get another man's opinion?" he said louder than need be.

My sainted aunt. He approached me holding out the fabric. "Do you mind if I ask what you think of this pattern?"

I gulped.

"I couldn't help but notice you too were taking a sartorial tour of Vienna." He chuckled. "And why not? The city is known for its fine haberdashery."

"Indeed," I said in my lowest tenor.

The empress joined us and smiled sweetly.

"Good sir," Fredricks said, holding the swatch near Zita's face. "Don't you think this color would look lovely on my friend?"

"Indeed," I repeated. I was afraid to say too much for fear the blackguard—or the empress—would recognize my voice.

"Where are you from?" the empress asked. "I don't recognize your accent and I'm usually very good with such things."

"Indeed." I sounded like a blooming parrot, repeating myself. "So I've been told." I cleared my throat. "Philadelphia in America."

"The city of fraternal love," Fredricks said. "What a coincidence." He held out his hand. "Fredrick Fredricks. I'm a reporter for the New York Herald."

I shook his hand with as firm a grip as I could muster. Unfortunately, that only encouraged him. I gritted my teeth so as not to yelp in pain. "A fellow American. What are the chances?" I forced a chuckle.

"I'm actually South African," Fredricks said.

At least he was sticking to the same story.

"Why don't you join us for lunch?" he asked.

"Oh no. I couldn't." When I shook my head, my blasted bowler toppled to the floor. I bent to pick it up and cracked heads with Fredricks, who'd also gone for my hat. It was as if the man had set out to maim me.

He got to it first, dusted it off, and handed to me. "Fine hat," he said with a smirk. "Don't see many bowlers these days."

Rubbing my forehead where I'd banged into his, I grabbed my hat. "I should be going." I replaced the hat on top of my wig.

"I insist that you join us," Fredricks said. "I want to hear all about Philadelphia. Mr…. Mr…. I'm sorry, I didn't catch your name."

That's what I was afraid of. I'd never been to Philadelphia in my life… or anywhere in America for that matter. "Chap… Chapmann." I stammered trying to come up with a name. *Dash it.* I really must come up with my backstory before I go out in disguise.

"Like Mr. Charlie Chaplin the film star," the empress said.

"I believe it was Chapmann," Fredricks said. "Am I right?"

I nodded.

Fredricks took me by the elbow. "Mr. Chapmann, you must let me treat you to lunch at the Imperial Hotel."

I flinched. *Come on, Fiona. Pull yourself together.* The Imperial Hotel. That must be where he was staying. The hotel where the injured maid worked. And she was delivering a note from Fredricks to Mrs. Einstein when she was hit. The pieces were falling into place.

104

CHAPTER ELEVEN

I swallowed hard. Overcoming my instinct to run, I accepted his invitation, hoping I could confirm that the scoundrel was lodging at the Imperial Hotel and find out which room he was in without him finding out who I really was.

Chapter Twelve

The Bloodhound

N o sooner had we taken a table outside under a scalloped awning in front of the grand Imperial Hotel, than I felt something brush against my ankle. "Goodness. You startled me," I said in English before realizing my mistake.

A little black-and-white schnauzer was sniffing my shoe. *"Es tut mir Leid,"* the owner of the dog said, pulling at its leash. *"Britta. Nein. Britta. Sitz."* The woman gave me an apologetic smile and continued pulling on the leash. Britta, the little beast, was pawing at my leg and barking.

Did it think I had a treat? Poor thing must be hungry. I returned the owner's smile and shrugged. Even the dogs were getting thin on war rations. I watched as the woman and her pup continued down the street, stopping every few feet so the dog could sniff and snort.

"Don't you like dogs, Mr. Chapmann?" the empress asked.

"I suppose I'm more of a bird man," I said, wishing I could take flight myself.

"Yes, I can see that." Fredricks narrowed his brows. "A great predatory bird." He held out his arms like wings. "An eagle or a hawk." His gaze was piercing. "I'm more of a cat man, myself." He smirked. "Big cats."

"Like panthers," I said. I really couldn't resist.

He tilted his head and smiled. "Exactly. A dog on a scent is determined. A cat on a scent is ruthless." His dark eyes danced as he gazed at me.

A shiver ran up my spine. I never should have mentioned the panther. I was becoming as brazen as he was. "A dog on a scent," I repeated. An idea flashed through my brain. *A dog on a scent. Mozart...of course.* Why didn't I think of that before? As soon as we finished dining, I had to get back to the Sacher Hotel and find little Mozart.

All through luncheon, whenever Fredricks looked at me, I felt as though he could see right through me. I had to stay on my guard and make sure this time I got more information out of him than he got out of me. Not an easy feat when it came to Fredricks, the sly devil.

The empress and Fredricks seemed to be best mates. "How do you two know each other?" I asked, taking a bite of my salad and trying not to get lettuce stuck in my mustache.

"Charles...the emperor...and I have known each other for ages," Fredricks said. "And I was lucky enough to meet lovely Zita at Villa Wartholz." He smiled wistfully. "You'd love it there, *ma chérie.*" He paused, straightened his ascot tie, and then cleared his throat. "Excuse me, Mr. Chapmann."

Ma chérie? Oh no. That's what he always called me. Good heavens. Had he made me? I troubled the edge of my napkin. *Now what?*

He quickly took a sip of water. "I was lost in my thoughts for a moment. Daydreaming about my fiancé, Fiona."

"I didn't know you were engaged," the empress said.

"You'll meet her at the ball," he said, grinning from ear to ear. "She's a lovely creature."

My cheeks got warm. I wanted to kick him under the table. No doubt about it. He was on to me. *When did he recognize me?* All this time, had he been leading me on a wild goose chase across Vienna? The cad.

I laughed. I had to admit, it was dashed amusing.

"What's funny?" the empress asked.

"Mr. Fredricks is a hopeless romantic."

"What's wrong with romance?" she asked.

"Our brains continue to develop from the time we are born until we fall in love," I said, shaking my head. "No, romance is not for me."

"You obviously haven't met the right woman yet," the empress said playfully.

"Obviously not." *And I doubt I ever will.*

After lunch, I left Fredricks and the empress sipping coffee. I couldn't get away fast enough. Being there was a waste of time. He'd never reveal anything since he knew who I was. And I had a dognapper to find.

When I was out of sight of the restaurant, I sprinted back to the hotel. Oxfords pounding on the sidewalk, weaving in and out of soldiers and shopgirls, I zipped past shops and churches, trollies and carriages. Finally, the opera house was in view. Breathless, I crossed the street.

By the time I got back to the hotel, I was panting faster than little Mozart. Dashing from room to room, I went hunting for the pooch. I searched the burgundy room, the emerald room, and the indigo room. I peeked into the library and the dining room.

With the war on, there weren't many guests about. Even the lobby was empty. I took the liberty of making my way down the hall to Frau Sacher's office. The door was shut. I knocked but no answer. *Drat. Where is a French bulldog when I need one?*

I dashed back to the lobby and then to the grand staircase. On my way up the stairs, I ran into Max with the little beastie in his arms. He was taking Mozart out for his afternoon constitutional.

"May I join you?" I asked.

He gave me a queer look, as if I'd just asked him if we might take a quick trip to the moon. He glanced around looking for an escape route. Given I was standing on the stairs in front of him, the only option was retreat. He stepped backwards up one step.

I mounted the next stair and patted the little dog on the head. "I think Mozart might help us find his siblings."

Max narrowed his brows.

"Mozart can follow the scent..."

He stood there blinking at me.

Come on, man. What are you waiting for? Ah. In my excitement, I was speaking too fast and in English. "Bluthund," I said. "Bluthund." Not knowing what else to do, I just kept repeating "bloodhound" in German while pointing at

Mozart.

A grin cracked his face. "Mrs. Douglas?" Max asked in heavily accented English. "Is that you? Why are you wearing a mustache and men's clothes?"

Good heavens! In my haste to find the missing pups, I'd forgotten about my Little Tramp disguise. "Ahh…er…a dress rehearsal for the royal costume ball?"

His eye got wide. "You're wearing *that* to the palace?"

"Maybe." I pulled on the hem of my jacket. "Enough about my costume. We've got to find Frau Sacher's missing bulldogs. And Mozart is just the bloodhound to lead us to them." I waved him down the stairs. "We have no time to waste."

Or at least I had no time to waste. I still had to get to hospital and interview the injured maid about that note Fredricks had given her and enlist her help getting into his room. Fredricks might have been able to pick a hotel room lock fast enough to not be spotted by other guests in the hallway, but I couldn't count on being that quick myself. And with the ball only a day away, I couldn't wait until the coast was clear.

I moved aside, let Max pass me on the stairs, and then followed him down. Once outside, he put Mozart on the ground. The little dog took off running up the sidewalk and came up short when he reached the end of his tether.

It took me several minutes and a game of charades to persuade Max to let the dog lead us instead of the other way round. The idea was to see if Mozart could lead us to Bruno and Jana.

Before we left, we probably should have had the little fellow sniff an article of their clothing or a collar or something. Too bad I didn't think of that earlier. *I admit, I don't know anything about dogs. But it's worth a try.*

Mozart was on the move. I had to rush to keep up. He was a fast little thing. Amazing since his legs were a tiny fraction of the length of my own. Then again, he did have four of them.

The dog led us to a trash bin. He spent a while circling around it, sniffing as he went. Next, he strained at the leash, wanting to cross the street. Max prevented him from crossing until it was safe. The three of us ran across the street and headed toward the grass in front of the opera house.

Yes. Now he's near where his siblings were dognapped. I was chuffed that my idea just might be working. Mozart ran in circles smelling different places on the grass. What he did next was not helpful to our investigation, but at least he got it out of the way. After having done his business, he was on the run again. Max let him have free run off the leash and I trailed after them.

Hardly slowing down, the little dog smelled every column and every corner of the opera house. He ran us clear around the perimeter. I was having serious doubts about his commitment to finding his siblings. His tongue was hanging out. His tail was up. He seemed to be having a jolly good time.

As for me, I was melting. The afternoon sun was high in the sky and hot as blazes. My eyes hurt from its brilliance. And my shirt was soaked with sweat. Yes, I was sweating like a sportsman. I must have looked a sight, wet with perspiration and my mustache wilting.

Our little bloodhound was more interested in caterpillars and squirrels than finding clues to the whereabouts of his mates. I was beginning to suspect he was in on the kidnapping. The cheeky devil.

By the time we made it back to the spot in front of the opera house where the other dogs were taken, we'd been at it for nearly an hour.

Even young Max was wiping sweat from his brow. "I really must get back to work," he said in halting English. He clipped the leash back onto Mozart's collar.

Mozart finally sat down, his tongue hanging out. With what looked like a big smile on his face, he gazed up at us. I had to admit, he was a cute little thing. Too bad he wasn't a better bloodhound.

Using my best German, I tried to persuade Max to continue the search. He just shook his head and pulled at Mozart's leash. The pup trotted after Max as he crossed the street toward the hotel. I threw in the towel and headed back with them.

We'd just reached the entrance when Mozart lunged at a butterfly and yanked the leash out of Max's hand. The little blighter ran full bore up the sidewalk. Max and I sprinted after him.

"Mozart," Max yelled in desperation.

My stomach knotted any time the tiny dog approached the street. "No," I shouted.

At the end of the block, Mozart disappeared down into a stairwell. I slid to a stop at the top of the stairs. Max did the same. We did our best to block the little beast's path. Hopefully, we had him trapped. But we would have to be quick to snatch him up when he ran back up the stairs.

Oblivious to our panic, the rascal explored the bottom landing of the stairwell. The only thing on that level was a metal door that must have led under the butcher shop. A sign said *Fleischerei Fuchs. Fleisch* meant flesh or meat. No wonder the dog landed here. He was probably hoping for a scrap of meat. *Fuchs. That's also the last name on my list from the War Office.* I'd passed this shop several times in the past week, yet I'd never noticed the name. *You must pay more attention, Fiona. Some spy you are.*

The little fellow came bounding up the stairs. My instincts kicked in, and I lunged at Mozart and snatched him up. I held him tightly to my chest as he wiggled and kicked. No matter what the damage to my blouse or my person, I was determined to hold on.

Max grabbed the leash, and when I was sure the dog was secure, I set him on the walkway. What a scare. My heart was racing faster than Mozart's little legs.

What in heaven's name? The dog had what looked like a second tongue hanging out of his mouth. I reached down and pulled. *Disgusting.* A colorful ribbon emerged from his maw covered in slime and bite marks. That decided it. No dogs for me.

I held the edge of cloth between my thumb and forefinger and examined it. *Blimey.* Even covered in dog slobber, there was no mistaking it. One of Mrs. Einstein's bookmarks.

Mozart may not have found his siblings, but he just might have gotten me one step closer to finding Mrs. Einstein's notebook.

"You go ahead," I said to Max. "I'm going to look around."

Max shrugged. He picked up Mozart and carried the pup down the block toward the hotel.

I glanced around and then descended the stairs. The landing was filthy with food scraps and litter. No wonder Mozart had such a grand time down here. Unwilling to touch anything, I scanned the ground for more clues. How had one of Mrs. Einstein's bookmarks ended up down here? Was it blown by the wind? Or was this the thief's hideout? And what did this have to do with Mr. Oscar Fuchs, the name on my list from the War Office?

The corner of a piece of ivory paper caught my eye. It was sticking out from under a tobacco packet. I moved the packet with the toe of my shoe. Careful not to touch any of the debris around it, I lifted the fine cotton paper from the ground. It was a letter, in German, addressed to *Mein Liebling Mileva.*

Aha! One of Mrs. Einstein's missing letters. I would have to get Clifford to translate it for me. *Not because I'm nosey, mind—although I'm dying to know what it says—but because it might give me a clue as to why Fredricks is so interested in Mrs. Einstein's husband. All I have right now are guesses.*

I dropped the letter into one of my pockets, and then made my way back to the hotel. Blast. Clifford wasn't in his room. I headed back to the lobby to inquire as to his whereabouts. Double blast. My disguise. I dashed back to my room, ripped off my mustache, threw off my jacket and trousers, tossed the bowler onto the bed, and slid back into my skirt. No time to adjust my makeup, I hurried to the lift.

I found Clifford in the dining room chatting up Frau Sacher. *My heavens.* Frau Sacher was beaming, puffing on a cigar, and holding one bulldog on each knee. *How on earth...* Bruno and Jana had been returned. Their little brother Mozart was standing on the table lapping up cream from a small bowl.

I hurried to join them. Out of breath and still perspiring from my morning's jaunt, I plopped down into the nearest chair.

"Good Lord," Clifford said. "What happened to you? You look like something the cat dragged in."

"Try dog," I replied. "Mozart has been dragging me around the block for the last hour." I patted the little beastie on the head, and he smiled up at me.

"I say, what's with your hair?"

My hair? What's wrong with my hair. I patted my wig. Heavens. I was still wearing the short black men's haircut. "Trying on wigs for the costume ball." Flustered, I turned to Frau Sacher. "Who found Bruno and Jana?"

"This morning, when I opened the door to my private quarters, they were waiting in the hallway, like nothing had happened." She hugged them both. "Right, my darlings?"

"Did anyone see who returned them?" I asked.

"No. Someone must have brought them into the hotel in the night, and they found their way home." She kissed the brown dog on its head and then stroked the muzzle of the gray one. Not to be outdone, Mozart butted her hand with his head. "The main thing is they're home safe."

So, I was chasing that blooming puppy around the opera house all afternoon for nothing? Bruno and Jana had already been returned, presumably even before Max and I went out. *Sigh.* At least I'd found the bookmark... and the letter!

"Clifford dear," I said. "Might you help me with something?"

"Of course." He smiled like a schoolboy who had just been given a lolly. "What is it?"

"I want to show you something." *Should I show him here in the dining room in plain sight of Frau Sacher and anyone else who wanders in? Probably not.* "It's in our suite."

"Excuse us, Frau Sacher," Clifford said, standing and giving the proprietor a slight bow.

I wasn't keen on involving Clifford. He could be such a blabbermouth. But if I wanted to discern what the Einsteins had to do with Fredricks, I'd best find out what the letter said before returning it to Mrs. Einstein. After all, the whole notebook theft might be a ruse. How did I know she too wasn't a German agent? My German wasn't good enough for a thorough translation. And I didn't want to report inaccurate information to the War Office. Anyway, Clifford loved to feel useful.

Once we were back in our suite and behind closed doors, I showed Clifford the letter.

"I say, aren't you clever," he said. "Where did you get it?"

"I'll tell all later. Can you translate it?" I thrust the letter in his direction.

He took it and studied it. "Well, I'll be..."

"What?" I glared at him. "What does it say?"

"'My dearest Mileva,'" Clifford read from the letter. The gist was that all of Albert's early work was indeed a collaboration with Mileva.

"I miss having you nearby to inhibit my shape. Yours always, Albert," he said, scratching his head.

"Inhibit my shape?" I squinted at him.

"That can't be right, can it?" Clifford sighed. "Do you have a German-English dictionary?"

I did have one. Not that it did me much good. I fetched it from the night table. Every night before bed, I'd tried reading it in hopes that my photographic memory would somehow import the words straight into my vocabulary. Unfortunately, learning a language was much more than learning to string together random words in alphabetical order. I handed the book to Clifford.

He ruffled through the pages, repeating *"männderförmig"* under his breath. He settled on a page and then jabbed it with his finger. "Meandering," he said triumphantly. "To prevent me from meandering."

"Philandering, more like." I paced the length of the room. "This letter proves they collaborated on the relative motion stuff Mrs. Einstein got so excited about."

"If what Mrs. E. said is true." Clifford joined my pacing. "Her husband is a rising star who will be world-famous soon."

I stopped in front of the window and looked out. The blazing blue sky had given way to angry gray clouds.

In any marriage with notoriety, the man gets the pearl, and the woman gets the shell. I had half a mind to make the letter public myself so Mileva Einstein would receive the credit she deserved. *Why can't he share the pearl? And still support his children?*

"Fancy a drink?" Clifford asked, standing right in my path. "I'm parched."

I glanced at my watch. "It's not even three o'clock. Isn't it a bit early for spirits?"

"It's five o'clock somewhere."

"That may be, but not here," I said sternly, staring up into his face.

"A coffee, then?" His voice was so full of hope that I could hardly resist. A pick-me-up would be just the ticket. But I still planned to visit the fallen maid in the hospital and learn what she knew about Fredricks. *Blasted man. How in the world did he recognize me in my Little Tramp disguise?*

And now I had the added task of visiting the butcher's shop again to find out why the bookmark and letter were in their stairwell...and if they know the whereabouts of one Oscar Fuchs. No, I couldn't make time for coffee.

"I would love to, but I have some errands to run before the ball. If you'll excuse me."

"The ball isn't until tomorrow. Surely we have time to do some scouting." Clifford looked at me with pleading eyes. "To see if we can find more letters or Mrs. E's notebook?" He did love to play detective. But I could tell, he was grasping at ways to keep me nearby.

"We?" I shook my head.

"I could be your translator." He got that sad hound-dog look. "Surely we should continue the search while the trail is hot. You can spare an hour." It's true. He could speak German much better than I. Perhaps he could interview the butcher about the letter I'd found in his stairwell. Anyway, he was like a dog with a bone, I'd might as well give in. I wasn't going to shake him anytime soon.

I glanced at my watch. It would be nice to avoid another long walk in the hot sun. I supposed I did have time to search the butcher shop for Mrs. Einstein's notebook and then interview the hotel staff about who might have broken into her room, before visiting the fallen maid.

"Oh, alright." But first, Clifford could help me interview the staff.

Chapter Thirteen

A Second Letter

I had to admit, Clifford's facility with German came in handy when interviewing the staff. During a lull before dinner, we interviewed the cook and her assistant, a shy teenaged girl. The cook was a pleasantly round woman with two small children circling about her skirts like planets around their sun. They seemed as much a part of her as her spoons and knives, which she used so gracefully they could have been her own arms.

Unfortunately, neither the cook nor her assistant knew anything about the no-longer missing dogs or the still-missing notebook, or so they said. And they didn't know of any suspicious delivery people either. Although the cook did mention that she always invited children staying at the hotel into the kitchen for sugar biscuits. And as a result, there were always several children hanging around.

We found Max manning the front desk. He was contrite about losing the pups, but he knew nothing except that he was hit from behind, delivered the ransom as instructed, and the dogs were now recovered. "No harm, no foul." He denied any knowledge of Mrs. Einstein's notebook. And he insisted he hadn't seen anyone suspicious around the hotel. If you asked me, he had been acting suspicious from the time I met him. Leading me all over the place when he knew the dogs had been returned already.

We caught up to Werner in the dining room where he was setting out utensils for dinner. He refused to look me in the eye when I asked him about the dogs or the notebook. Although he denied knowing anything about any thefts from the hotel, his shifty eyes suggested otherwise. *What is he up to?*

Now I wished I hadn't invited Clifford along. I was dying to ask Werner if he was secretly working for the British. Then again, if he wasn't—if he was the wrong Werner Liebermann—my goose would be cooked. I would just have to watch him and wait for some sign and an opportunity.

After a few minutes of questioning, Werner clammed up. "Sorry ma'am," he said. "I must put down the table settings."

What else has he put down? We left Werner to his task and went to find the maids. We asked them about the guests, the notebook, the dogs, but their answers were always the same. "I don't know. I can't say." Frau Sacher had trained them well. If discretion was their motto, they were true to it. Finally, we gave up questioning and made our way back to the lobby.

"What about the notebook and the letter?" Clifford asked. "Shouldn't we go back to where you found them and investigate?"

Of course, *I* should go back and investigate. But the afternoon was slipping away. And I still had matters of life and death to attend to before supper. *The hospital. The maid. Fredrick's room.*

"It's just up the block," Clifford said. "It won't take long." He was aglow with excitement.

"Oh, alright." I relented. I did need to talk to the butcher and find out if he was Oscar Fuchs... or knew an Oscar Fuchs. After all, this Mr. Fuchs could very well be Fredricks's target.

Together, we combed the walkways from in front of the hotel up the block to the butcher shop where I'd found the bookmark and letter. Clifford followed me talking a mile a minute, nattering on about some hunt in Africa with Fredricks. As usual, singing the Great White Hunter's praises. *Fredricks is a spy...for the bloody Germans. How can Clifford still admire him so?* I tried not to let his chatter distract me from my mission.

"It's a rare conversationalist who can compete with silence," I said.

Clifford didn't take the hint. He just kept on blathering.

Truth be told, in an odd way, Clifford was reminding me of my mission. My true mission. Which was to get more dirt on Fredricks. It was certainly not to descend every sticky stairwell in Vienna looking for scraps of paper or clues to the identity of local dognappers. As much as I thought Fredricks might be involved with the thefts, especially that of the notebook, I also recognized I could be dead wrong. Dead being the key word if I didn't find out who his target was before he killed again.

"We were hunting lions in the Serengeti. It was pitch dark and we had only our torches," Clifford said excitedly. "I knew it was a cheetah and not a lion. But Fredricks shot it anyway."

"So, the Great White Hunter makes mistakes after all," I said distractedly, still scanning the ground as we walked.

"A cheetah is even harder to track than a lion, you see." Clifford went on and on about the difficulty of tracking big cats. I found the whole conversation disgusting. *Animals aren't trophies. They're living beings like us.*

"Poor defenseless cats."

"They're not so defenseless. Many a hunter has been mauled or killed. It's actually quite dangerous."

"For them more than you. You seem to enjoy killing for sport. Well, I'm rooting for the cats."

"You would take their side," Clifford said, playfully, ignoring my point. "I say, look at this." He picked up the front page of a newspaper as it blew past. "China has declared war on Germany and Austria-Hungary."

"China? When?"

Clifford examined the paper, which, of course, was in German. "Four days ago." He straightened the paper. "Good Lord. The bloody Germans sunk the HMS Prize." His face went pale. "William Sanders commanded that ship. I met him a few years ago when I was hunting wild pigs in New Zealand." He looked at me with sad eyes. "Damn fine fellow. Jolly good shot too."

"What does it mean?"

"Bloody German submarines keep blowing up our ships." He folded the newspaper. "Remember the God-awful explosion last February that killed over five hundred Chinese workers on a French passenger ship?" He shook his head. "Bloody Germans."

"Careful," I whispered, glancing around. "Remember where we are."

He looked so forlorn that I took his arm. We continued up the block. I stopped in front of the stairwell where I'd found the letter. *Might as well dive back in and see if I missed anything.*

I gingerly set foot on the bottom landing. When I did, something rustled amongst the papers on the ground. I let out a gasp. A pair of beady red eyes stared up at me from a dark corner. It bared its fangs. "Kill it!" I screamed, pointing at the filthy creature. "Kill it. Those fangs."

Clifford rushed down the stairs. "Why, it's only a little rat." He chuckled. "Rats don't have fangs."

"Kill it!" *Only a little rat.* "Disgusting vile thing."

"I thought you were against killing poor defenseless animals." He kicked at the pile of papers. "Shoo. Scat." The rat scurried between two bricks and then disappeared. "My word, Fiona. You'd think you'd seen a murderer."

I huffed.

He put his arm around my shoulder. "I didn't think you were afraid of anything, old girl."

"Rats carry diseases. The doctors at Charing Cross were adamant about the dangers of rats."

"The plague of the Philistines," Clifford said. "The mice that marred the land."

"That proves it," I said. "If science and religion agree, then it must be true." I brushed imaginary crumbs from my skirt.

"Rats, the common enemy of both doctors and priests." Clifford laughed.

"Thank you for saving me from being mauled by a rat." Just saying the word *rat* made my skin crawl.

"My pleasure." Clifford smiled down at me. "I say." He bent down and plucked up a piece of paper. It was plastered up against the bottom stair, stuck in a crack. "I say, what have we here?"

"What is it?"

"Good gracious. It's another letter."

"It must be one of Mrs. Einstein's." I reached for the letter, but Clifford was too fast. A lot of good it would do me anyway. Blasted thing was probably in German.

Clifford scanned the letter. "Good Lord. This Einstein chap is a rather bad sort."

"Read it." I reached for it again, but he snatched it away. "What does it say?"

"Mrs. Einstein's husband, the bounder, is threatening her if she spills the beans about their collaboration."

A loud clanking from the other side of the metal door made me scurry back up the stairs. Clifford did the same. A heavy metal door opened and a burly fellow in his fifties wearing a bloodstained apron emerged. He looked up the stairs at us and barked something in German, his round face red and dripping with sweat.

Clifford tipped his hat and responded. The man seemed appeased by whatever Clifford had said.

"Let's ask him about the notebook," I whispered. "Maybe he knows something." And maybe he knows Mr. Oscar Fuchs.

"You mean interrogate the fellow?" Hat in hand, Clifford glanced at me out of the corner of his eye, still smiling down at the butcher.

"Excuse me, sir," I said in my best German. "Can we ask you a few questions?" At least that was what I intended to say.

The man stared at me like I was from Mars.

Clifford spoke to him in German with more success. The man gestured us in.

I cringed at the thought of joining the rat in the bowels of the butcher shop. But like a bloodhound, I was on a scent. I offered Clifford my hand and he led me down the staircase and into the basement of the shop.

The smell of animal carcasses reminded me of my one and only disastrous deer-hunting adventure with my father. If he didn't wish I'd been born male before then, he certainly did after.

The stone floors and walls of the cavernous cellar were stained with blood. I clutched at Clifford's elbow to steady myself. The dampness and darkness made me queasy. So much so, I was unsure as to whether I could carry out my investigation. The language barrier was stifling enough without the walls closing in on me too.

Clifford waved his free hand as he spoke to the butcher, who carried on with his work as if we weren't there. Truly, I wished I weren't.

Wielding a giant blade, the butcher hacked away at the back end of a hog, all the while mucking about with Clifford. *What in blazes is so funny? They're probably bonding over tall tales of their favorite blood sports.*

I tugged at Clifford's sleeve to get his attention. "Ask him about the notebook."

Clifford ignored me and went on chatting in German.

"Ask him if they deliver to the Sacher Hotel," I whispered. *Why am I whispering? To take in as little of this fetid air as possible.* "Who delivers to the Sacher Hotel?" I asked in a mixture of English and German.

The butcher held his knife in mid-swing and glared at me.

Clifford took over again. Soon, the butcher was back to hacking away, and the two of them were guffawing like a couple of drunken schoolboys. It was really too much to bear, especially since I couldn't understand a word of what they were saying.

"Sorry to interrupt," I said. Although I wasn't sorry. "Who makes your deliveries to the Sacher Hotel?"

The butcher simply ignored me and went on chatting up Clifford. I might as well have been invisible. Sometimes men were deuced annoying.

The butcher tossed his butcher's knife into his wooden cutting board, where it landed with a thud that made me jump back.

"I have work to do," the butcher said. "I can't spend all day chatting."

"Yes, of course. Apologies. Yes, we must be going." Clifford sputtered. "*Entschuldigung. Es tut mir Leid. Danke.*" He repeated his stammered apologies in German. He tapped his hat onto his head and then turned to me. "Shall we?"

As soon as we were above ground again and out of earshot of the butcher, I pounced. "What did the butcher say?"

"You must admit, old girl, I was brilliant. Complimenting him on the goose and the game delivered to the hotel. Buttering him up, you see, to get him talking." He rubbed his palms together. He was rather too proud of himself.

"Yes, you were brilliant," I said to humor him, as if I'd been able to follow his conversation with the butcher. "What did he say?"

"We make a good team, don't we, old thing." He smiled down at me. "What do you say we tie the knot for real?"

I stopped in my tracks. Not again. Sigh. Clifford proposed to me at least once a month.

"Very flattered, *old thing*," I said. "But right now, I'm dying to know what the butcher said."

"So you'll consider it?" He looked hopeful. "Then we wouldn't have to pretend."

Pretending to be his wife was taxing enough. "The butcher." I tightened my lips.

"Yes. Right. Sorry." He stuttered. "Well, you won't believe what he told me. You see, his brother-in-law has a farm in—"

"The point?"

"Of course. Yes. The point." He adjusted his waistcoat and loosened his tie. "Bloody hot in Austria."

"What did the butcher say about the notebook?"

"I was getting to that." He scowled.

"Could you perhaps take a less circuitous route?"

"Right. He hasn't seen any notebook."

"The letters?"

"Knows nothing about them."

"Deliveries to the hotel?"

"His own son, blind in one eye from mustard gas."

"Mustard gas? You mean the blooming Germans gassed one of their own?"

"They're not the only ones using gas, Fiona," he said in a low voice.

I stood there for a moment blinking up at him. I couldn't believe it. "Scandalous," I hissed. My face burned with indignation. "You mean we use it too?"

I'd seen the gruesome effects of mustard gas when I volunteered at Charing Cross Hospital. Andrew died of mustard gas exposure. The devil's breath, he'd called it. It ate through a man from the inside out. I took out my hanky and dabbed my eyes.

"Let's get you a cup of tea," Clifford said, taking my elbow.

I nodded.

"A nice cuppa. That's what you need."

"I need to know what else the butcher told you." I sniffed.

"And you shall, old bean." He took my hand. "As soon as we get you inside."

I allowed him to lead me back to the hotel. He was right. After the filthy rodent, the bloodstained apron, the incessant hacking, and the realization that my own beloved country used mustard gas, I needed a reparative. Perhaps something stronger than tea.

Clifford returned, followed by a waitress who delivered two snifters of brandy, two small glasses of water, and a plate of biscuits. Jolly good thing too. I was feeling quite overcome. I took a sip of brandy and selected a tea biscuit. Scrummy. Vanilla crescent shortbread.

After the waitress was gone, I leaned across the table and whispered. "I'm dying to know what that letter says. And what the blasted butcher told you."

"Yes, quite." Clifford slipped the letter out of his jacket pocket. He unfolded it and then smoothed it out on the table. The fine paper was stained with God-knows-what, and its edges were frayed. "Listen to this." He glanced up at me and then proceeded to read from the letter. The gist was that Mr. Albert Einstein threatened Mileva that no one would ever believe she'd collaborated with him because she was an insignificant woman.

"How awful." I bit the end off a biscuit. "Is it dated? It must be a recent letter."

"Last month." Clifford refolded the letter. "Dreadful, isn't it?"

"Yes, but it proves Mr. Einstein's motive to destroy the notebook, even if she thinks he wouldn't do it." I really would have to sit on my hands to keep from revealing Einstein's secret. *Just because she is a woman. That's no reason she shouldn't get credit for her brilliance. What an infuriating world. I was bloody tempted to join the suffragettes.*

"Why leave these letters lying about?" Clifford asked.

"Why indeed?" I nibbled on a biscuit and pondered his question. "It looks as though our thief was in a hurry. He—or she—ducked into that stairwell, perhaps not even noticing that the letters fell out of the notebook. Either that or they work at the butcher's shop." I really did need to get back there and interview the butcher and his staff myself. I made a mental note to question Frau Sacher too.

"Maybe he—"

"Or she," I added. Although I still suspected our notebook thief was Fredricks. But what did he have to do with the butcher shop?

"Or she... didn't know the letters were tucked into the notebook." Clifford tipped up his snifter and polished off his brandy. "Would you like another?"

I shook my head. I'd barely made a dent in the one I had. I pushed my snifter across the table. Clifford smiled and traded his empty glass for my full one.

"Or whoever took the notebook purposely stole the letters too. Whoever it was knew they were valuable." I drained my water glass. Clifford passed me his and we exchanged glasses again.

With all the drink swapping, if Fredricks is going to poison me, poor Clifford will get the dose instead.

I continued, saying, "And the only person who knew their true value was the estranged husband, Albert Einstein." *And Fredrick Fredricks.*

"Yes, but would a renowned physicist break into a hotel room and steal a notebook like a common thief?" He shook his head. "Preposterous."

"He could have hired someone to do his dirty work," I said. "Someone who works for the butcher or the butcher himself. The stairwell leads only to the basement of the butcher shop, so the only people who'd go down there are people who work there, right? Or maybe people who deliver to there."

"Mrs. E. claims he's buying her off with the award money, so why go to all the trouble of stealing her notebook?"

"Hedging his bets?"

"In that case, her life may be in danger." Clifford finished my brandy. He waved for the waitress.

"How far will a man go to protect his reputation?" I snagged the last of the biscuits. *If I stayed here much longer, I'll develop a terrible sweet tooth.*

"I did good, didn't I?"

"Yes, dear." I reached across the table and patted his hand. In truth, Clifford's excitement outstripped his prowess. The only thing he'd learned from questioning the butcher was that the butcher's son delivered meat to the hotel. But it's not like I had done much better. I'd forgotten to ask the butcher about Oscar Fuchs. And I had to admit, Clifford was proving himself jolly useful as a translator. "We'd better keep an eye on Mrs. E.," Clifford said.

"Agreed." I glanced at my watch. "Good heavens. Look at the time. I really must attend to my errands." The afternoon was slipping away, and I hadn't gone to hospital yet to question the injured maid.

The royal ball was tomorrow night, which meant I had only twenty-four hours to retrieve the notebook, determine Fredricks's target, and stop the assassination of one of our agents.

Chapter Fourteen

The List

I left Clifford sputtering about coming with me and then headed for the trolley. My plan was to visit the closest hospital. Hopefully, that's where the ambulance took the injured maid. After forty minutes navigating the railway, trolleys, and foot traffic, I arrived at Vienna General Hospital.

Perspiring and already exhausted, I entered the institution through the heavy front doors. *I hope to heaven she's here.* Even so, how in the world would I find her? I didn't know her name.

Despite the war, it was relatively quiet. Four uniformed men sat in the lobby. Their faces were haggard. One of them was on crutches, another had a patch covering one eye, and a third was missing a leg. Poor men. Presumably, they were on their way home now. For some of them, readjusting to domestic life was even more difficult than taking a bullet for their county.

I stopped at a nurse's station near the entrance. "Excuse me," I said to a fresh-faced young nurse who was reading a magazine. "I'm from the Imperial Hotel, here to see if our poor maid is okay. She was hit by a trolley yesterday—"

"Christina. Poor girl. She's on the second floor."

"Yes, Christina." *Thank heavens.* "Is she okay?"

"She's on the second floor." The young nurse pointed toward the lift and then went back to her magazine.

"Thank you." If I only knew Christina's family name.

I exited the lift on the second floor. Here goes. I steeled myself for more prevaricating and headed for the nurses' desk.

"Excuse me," I said. "I'm looking for my… cousin Christina's room. She was in a trolley accident yesterday."

A prune-faced nurse gave me the once over. "Christina Hermann?"

"Yes, I'm… Gertrude Hermann, her cousin."

"The women's ward." She gestured in the direction of the hallway. "Room two-twelve, bed eight."

Golly. If she was the right Christina, finding her had been a doodle. If only everything in the spying business worked out so well.

I tiptoed down the hall until I reached room 212. The door was open, so I went in. Small beds were lined up on both sides of the room, maybe twenty in all. About half of them were occupied. Not like the men's wards, which were overflowing with war wounded. The room smelled of cleaning compound and sickness. Combined with the lack of windows and dim lights, it felt close and sultry.

As I crept past the beds, checking their numbers, a woman's voice stopped me. "Nurse," the woman said weakly. "May I have a drink of water?"

Poor thing. Just speaking those few words appeared to be a tremendous effort. I refilled the cup on her side table from a sink near the entrance. After I helped her drink, I continued my mission.

Bed eight was at the far end of the room. The occupant was wearing a hospital gown and had a large white bandage wrapped around her head, which made it difficult to tell if she was indeed the injured maid from the trolley. But it made sense she would have a head injury after her fall and getting hit. I ventured to her bedside.

She was sitting up, staring down at playing cards arranged on her bedtable. I took this as a good sign that she was recovering. When she looked up at me, I recognized her gray eyes and thin lips. *It's her.* I couldn't believe it. I'd found her.

"What are you playing?" I asked with a smile, admiring the pretty daisies on her side table. She must have someone who cared about her. If I were in hospital, would anyone bring me flowers?

"I'm practicing my addition," she said. "You're not wearing a uniform."

"No." I glanced around the room. "I'm not a nurse."

"Oh," she said. "I didn't think so. You look too clever."

What did she mean by that? I gestured to a chair next to the bed. "May I sit down?"

She nodded.

"Might I ask you a few questions about the accident?" I asked.

Her mouth twisted into a worried grimace. "Okay, I guess."

"Did you fall or were you pushed?" I got right to the point.

"Pushed?" She adjusted her pillow and sat up straighter. "No. I'm accident-prone. Always tripping, you know. Or dropping things. Or so I've been told."

"Did you slip on the pebbles then?"

"I guess I must have done." She fingered the white blanket covering her legs.

"Do you know a man called Fredrick Fredricks?" I didn't have time to waste. The afternoon was slipping away, and I had to locate Fredricks's room and search it before tomorrow night.

"That's an odd name. Why two of the same?"

"Why indeed."

"Would he be the nice man who brought me flowers yesterday?"

I squinted at her. "Fredricks brought you flowers?"

"Is he a baker's son?"

Finding Christina was easy. But making any sense out of this conversation was deuced difficult.

"Or was it a butcher's son?" she said thoughtfully.

The prune-faced nurse appeared at the foot of the bed. "Christina, are you having a nice visit with your cousin?"

I cringed, caught in a lie.

Christina's face brightened. "Why didn't you tell me you were my cousin?"

Blimey.

"When Christina hit her head," the nurse said. "She lost much of her memory. Amnesia, I'm afraid."

Good heavens.

"I don't even remember the accident." Christina touched the bandage on her head. "And the only person I remember is my husband."

"That's a blessing," I said, hoping this husband didn't appear and reveal my lie.

"He died at the hands of those barbaric English," Christina said.

"Poor girl is a war widow at the age of twenty," the nurse added. "The only thing she remembers is wearing widow's weeds and going into the Sacher Hotel once a week to have a slice of cake in his honor."

Widow's weeds. The Sacher Hotel. Could she be the widow who may have delivered the ransom note? The one both Hans and Clifford saw the day it was delivered? "I'm so sorry." In spite of the fact that she'd called my countrymen barbaric, I was indeed sorry for the poor woman. No husband, no memory, and who knows what future. If only I could get selective amnesia and forget about my philandering husband and his war widow—the curvaceous, husband-stealing Nancy.

Since Christina wasn't going to be much help to me without any memory of Fredricks, I bid her good day. She made me promise to come back again tomorrow.

My visit to hospital wasn't a complete waste. I'd learned the maid's name. And the receptionist had all but confirmed that she worked at the Imperial Hotel, which I'd already deduced from the uniform. Since she was delivering notes for Fredricks, he must be staying there. *And chances are she's the war widow who brought the ransom note.*

Next stop. Imperial Hotel...right after an all-important detour to my disguise case.

I'd just crossed the threshold to the women's ward and was about to step into the hallway when I had an idea. Maybe I wouldn't need my maid's costume after all. I zipped back to Christina's bedside.

"Christina, dear," I said softly.

She looked up at me from her playing cards.

"Why don't I take your uniform and clean it for you?" I smiled. "It must be dirty from your fall. I'll bring it back when I visit tomorrow."

Her eyes lit up. "Cousin, that's so kind of you. I think they put it in a tray under my bed." She leaned over the bed even though there was no way she could see under from her vantage.

I crouched next to the bed. Sure enough. I pulled the tray out from under the bed. Christina's Imperial Hotel maid's uniform and cap, along with her underwear, and stockings, were neatly stacked with her shoes standing next to them. I tucked my clutch purse under my arm, gathered up the clothes, and stood up. "Tomorrow I'll bring them back all clean and fresh."

"Lovely." Christina smiled. "I hope I can go home soon... I wonder where I live." She looked at me expectantly.

"See you tomorrow, then." Feeling guilty about lying to her, I nipped off before she could ask me any questions about her forgotten life.

Clutching Christina's clothes, I exited the tram at Schwarzenbergplatz, which according to my guidebook was the closest railway station to the Imperial Hotel. The interior of the station was grand with enormous arched ceilings, and travelers bustled to and fro. I found the closest lav and quickly changed into Christina's uniform. It hung off me in places where obviously she was more developed than I. After a good brush-off, and the proper placement of the cap, I looked the part of a proper Austrian maid.

My own garments balled up and tucked under my arm—along with Christina's smalls, which I wasn't about to try—I located a day locker and stuffed my clothes inside. I removed my lockpick set from my purse and slid it into the front pocket on the uniform, then I stuffed my purse under my clothes and shut the locker, dropping the little key into the other front pocket. I would return for them later.

Quite pleased with my plan, I exited the station. Now all I had to do was determine which room was Fredricks's... *and hope he's not in the room and I can get into it without being caught.*

Like everything else in Vienna, the station and plaza were majestic and clean. In the distance, the Imperial Hotel shone, surrounded by a pinkish glow from the setting sun. I hastened my pace and headed for the hotel.

My stomach growled, reminding me that I'd missed dinner. I really should start carrying emergency rations. Perhaps Captain Hall could send some with me on my next mission...if there was a next mission.

The inside of the hotel looked like a palace. Indeed, the guidebook said it was built for Duke Phillip of Württemberg, which is why the top of the building sported a stone balustrade featuring heraldic animals from the Württemberg coat of arms. Bathed in a golden light, the lobby was huge but still warm and welcoming. Colorful Italian marble floors and monstrous crystal chandeliers screamed opulence. The walls were adorned with royal portraits. Its luxury rivaled Schönbrunn palace.

My head held high and, as confidently as I could muster, I walked across the regal lobby toward the registration desk. Luckily, I'd studied acting back at North London Collegiate School for girls.

"Excuse me," I said to the old woman manning the desk. "I'm supposed to deliver a message to Mr. Fredrick Fredricks, but I've forgotten his room number."

She eyed me suspiciously. "I haven't seen you before. Are you new?"

"Yes. I'm taking Christina's place while she's in hospital."

"Oh. Poor girl."

I nodded in agreement.

"Let me check with the manager," she said. "Mr. Fredricks doesn't like to be disturbed."

Drat! My scheme wasn't going as planned. "Perhaps I'll check back later then." I didn't want the manager to come and throw me out on my ear.

Now what? I couldn't very well go door to door. I had to come up with a backup plan. Wait. I had another idea. I'd seen a newsstand just outside the entrance to the hotel. I dashed back out and bought a newspaper.

Back in the lobby, I looked for someone else who worked in the hotel, someone who might know which room was Fredricks's. Scanning the open space, I spotted a one-armed man wearing a suit, one sleeve pinned up. He had a nameplate pinned to the breast of his jacket. I intercepted him on the way to the lift.

"I'm just delivering this newspaper to Mr. Fredrick Fredricks," I said.

"Very well," he said.

131

I followed him into the lift. *Here goes.* I pressed one of the buttons...and waited.

He scowled. "Shouldn't you be going to the penthouse first? Mr. Fredricks doesn't like to be kept waiting."

"Yes sir," I said. "Of course. How silly of me. You're right."

He used a special key to unlock the button for the penthouse and then pressed it. *Bingo!* "Hurry along then," he said. "Don't dillydally."

"No sir." My heart was racing. It was a relief when he exited on the ninth floor. I rode alone up to the penthouse. *I hope Fredricks is out. What will I do if he's not?* I didn't have a mustache or beard covering my face this time. Not that it did much good.

The lift opened and I was presented with two doors. One to my right and one to my left. I had a fifty-fifty chance of choosing the right one. Quietly, I crept to the door on the right. I leaned my head close and listened. Nothing. I lightly rapped on the door. Rustling came from inside...then tapping. *Dash it.* Someone was in there. Was it Fredricks? I held my breath and stared down at the floor in hopes that by some miracle he wouldn't recognize me.

A woman wearing nothing but a flimsy pink robe and feathery slippers answered the door. A scantily dressed woman by no means ruled out the possibility that this was indeed Fredricks's room.

"Yes," she said. Her voice as smooth as silk. "Is that paper for me?"

"Actually, it's for Mr. Fredrick Fredricks," I said. "I must have the wrong room?" It came out as a question.

She flashed a sly smile. "Freddie is out at the moment."

Dash it. How was I going to search his room with this creature lounging about inside?

"You might just slip it under his door." She pointed a long bloodred fingernail across the foyer. "He said he'd be back soon."

Not too soon, I hope. "Thank you." I waited until she'd shut her door to cross the foyer.

Listening to make sure she didn't come back... or the lift wasn't on its way up... I tucked the paper under my arm and pulled the lockpick set out of my apron pocket. I inserted two slender metal picks into the lock and felt my way around the pins. Compared to the emperor's study, this was a piece of cake.

One try and the lock popped open. I slipped inside and shut the door behind me. Leaning against the door, I gave myself a moment to catch my breath and survey the room.

The room was tidy with hardly a trace of its occupant, except for the lingering scent of his Juniper cologne. Quickly, I crossed the room to the writing desk. Opening each drawer and feeling inside, I searched for hidden documents or other clues. I found a writing pad and a pencil, along with a concert program from two nights ago. Otherwise, the drawers were empty. I searched the drawers of the tall wooden chest in the corner of the room. All empty. It was as if the man wasn't actually staying here. With Fredricks, you never could tell.

I went to the closet and peeked inside. Two starched white shirts hung side by side. An evening suit hung next to them. Behind it was a woolen riding jacket. And at the bottom of the closet sat the parcels he'd picked up earlier this morning, along with a pair of tall black boots.

I examined the parcels. Did I dare unwrap them? One of them was surely a shoebox. But were there really shoes inside? The other felt like cloth wrapped inside the paper.

I decided to keep searching and save tearing open the packages for last. I felt inside the pockets of the evening suit. Nothing but a small box of wooden matches from the Grand Hotel in Paris.

I knelt down and shook out the boots one by one, and then felt inside them. Nothing but the smell of worn leather. Stuffing my hands in the pockets of his riding jacket, I felt around for anything that might help me identify his target.

Aha! Inside the righthand pocket, I found a folded piece of paper. I unfolded it. Blimey. A list of seven names:

Empress Zita and Emperor Charles (Austria)
Princes Sixtus and Xavier of Bourbon-Parma (France)
Jane Addams (America)
Archie Somersby (England)

Fiona Figg (England)

My heart skipped a beat when I read my own name, and that of Archie Somersby. *What did it mean? And why the countries next to the names?* The only name I didn't recognize was Jane Addams. *Perhaps she is the double-agent.* I should keep an eye out for her at the ball. And what about Archie? Was he a double agent, too? Fredricks claimed he was. No, I refused to believe it. Anyway, not everyone on that list could be a spy. It must be a list of something else... but what?

I committed the names to memory, refolded the paper, and returned it to the pocket.

Next, I went to the night table. Three books were stacked atop each other like a pyramid from largest to smallest. Atop the pile was a book by Sigmund Freud, *Das Unbewusste*. If I remembered correctly, that meant unconscious. Doctor Freud believed we are all motivated by unconscious desires and fears. *So, none of us really knows why we do anything we do?*

The sound of a key in the lock sent me flying under the bed. Blast it all.

Aha. And what's this? A small metal lockbox sat under the bed.

Voices approached. I lay stock still. Staring up at a cobweb on the bottom of the bed frame, I saw what looked like a big black spider staring back at me. My hands flew to cover my face and I closed my eyes.

"Do you smell peaches?" An all too familiar voice asked. "And lemons?"

"Why no," a woman answered.

"Must be my overactive hunter's sense of smell," Fredrick's said with a chuckle.

As the voices got closer, I held my breath.

"You know, I forgot about an appointment," Fredricks said.

I saw his boots standing next to the night table. A woman's slippered feet stood close to his. I recognized those pink feathery slippers. The woman next door. A romantic tryst? A meeting of spies?

I heard the pages of a book turning. He must be looking through one of the books on the nightstand. He couldn't tell just by looking that I touched them, could he?

"Can I take a rain check on our supper *ensuite*?" he asked.

"But Freddie, I was so looking forward to it," the woman purred.

His feet moved to face hers. "Soon, darling, very soon." His boots moved out of view and with them the slippers.

I heard the door to the penthouse open again... and hushed whispering. I couldn't make out what they were saying. At least they were leaving. Thank goodness. I could get out from under this dusty bed. *But not before I open that lockbox.*

I strained to hear. Dash it. Someone was still in the room. Presumably, Fredricks was back again to prepare for his forgotten appointment.

I craned my head to get a better view from under the bed. Fredricks boots were next to the legs of the writing desk chair. He must be working on something there. Another list of possible victims?

"Dear Miss Figg," he said.

I froze. *How did he know I was here?*

"No that's too formal," he said. A crumpled piece of paper flew into the bin next to the desk.

"My Darling Fiona."

What in the world?

"That's too familiar." Paper rustled. Another crumbled piece of paper landed in the bin.

Is he writing a letter? To me?

"Dear Fiona. We really must put our heads together to stop this tragic war. Together, we are invincible."

What is he on about? Put our heads together? He thinks we can stop the war? How? I was half tempted to pop out from under the bed and ask him.

"P.S. You're like a tall glass of lemonade on a hot afternoon."

Good heavens. The man has lost his mind. I hoped to God he wasn't writing that to me.

More paper rustling. The boots were on the move again. They disappeared from view. What was he up to?

The closet door squeaked open and shut. The sound of hangers shifting. *Bang.* The door to the penthouse slammed shut. *Ouch.* I'd hit my head on the bedframe. Blasted man. Going around slamming doors and scaring me.

Ears cocked, I listened. Was he really gone this time? Silence. I waited another minute. Nothing. Yes. He must be gone. Thank goodness. I let out a big sigh of relief.

I slid out from under the bed, bringing the lockbox with me. Kneeling by the bed, I sat the box on the bed. Then I took my lockpick kit from my pocket and popped the lock open. Easy.

Quickly, I sifted through the contents. *Blimey.* Four passports. I examined them each in turn.

An American passport for Fredrick Fredricks sporting a photograph of a younger Fredricks.

A South African passport. *What the...*The name on the passport was Fritz Duquesne, but the picture was the same.

I dropped that one and snatched up the British passport. *Good heavens.* Captain Claude Soughton. A Captain in the British Army. In the picture, Fredricks was wearing a British captain's uniform. Had Fredricks—or whatever his real name was—infiltrated the British Army? Did the War Office know? I had to get word to the War Office as soon as possible. It was time to telephone Louise de Bettignies, aka Alice Dubois, in Hungary.

I shook my head in disbelief and picked up the fourth passport. Russian. Duke Boris Zakrevsky. Fredricks was posing as a Russian Duke? My heavens. *The big cat really does have nine lives.*

I put the passports back into the box and examined a couple of photographs that were laying in the bottom of the box. The first was a safari picture of Fredricks and the former American president Teddy Roosevelt, big smiles, holding rifles, and kneeling next to a lion. *Disgusting.*

The second was a family portrait of a dark-haired beauty holding a baby, standing behind twin boys who looked to be around eight years old. I'd seen this photograph before at Ravenswick. Originally, I thought Fredricks had a wife and children tucked away somewhere. Later, I learned he was one of the twin boys and the rest of his family was dead, killed by the British during the Boer War.

Staring down at the picture, I wondered which of the sad-eyed boys was Fredricks. I slid the photographs back under the passports, relocked the box, and placed it back under the bed.

I'd best hop to it before Fredricks comes back.

I glanced around the room. What else should I search for? I saw a letter on the writing desk. I rushed over and grabbed it. My heart raced as I read it.

Dear Fiona, my sweet peach. We really must put our heads together to stop this tragic war. Together, we are invincible. Next time you want to come to my bed, just ask. I guarantee laying on top will be more comfortable. Yours always, Fredrick.

The cad. I crumpled the paper and tossed it into the bin. He knew I was under the bed all the time. Sweet peach. Lemonade. Did I really smell of peaches and lemons? He had an imposing nose. And it must be deuced powerful too.

I did another quick search of his room. If he did have Mrs. Einstein's notebook, he'd done a jolly good job of hiding it. *I'd best get out of here before he comes back.*

Slowly, I opened the door to the penthouse. I hoped Fredricks wasn't waiting for me in the foyer. I peeked out. The coast was clear. I dashed to the lift, pushed the button, and counted the seconds until the bloody thing appeared. Without looking back, I hurried out of the Imperial Hotel and back onto the streets of Vienna.

The sun had long set. Very few shops were illuminated. With the war on, like London, Vienna was under a curfew… except for royal balls. Luckily, the clear sky and bright crescent moon provided enough light for me to make my way back to my hotel.

I didn't slow down until I reached the opera house. Careful not to slip on the pebbles in the street in front of my hotel, I made my way to the walkway and then to the hotel entrance. Sigh. I was bloody happy to be home. Blast. I'd left my clothes in the locker. I'd have to retrieve them later.

What a day. I couldn't wait to get back to my room and have a hot bath. But first, I must inform the War Office via my contact in Hungary.

Clifford was waiting for me in the lobby. He stood up when he saw me. "Fiona, where have you been? I've been worried sick."

"So sorry, Clifford dear." I plopped down into an overstuffed chair next to his. "It's a long story."

He wrinkled his nose like he smelled something foul. "Why are you wearing that maid's uniform?" He cocked his head. "What are you up to, old girl?"

"I'll tell you later." I waved away his questions. "Right now, I need something to calm my nerves."

"Shall I get us a brandy?" He already smelled like a distillery. He'd obviously been sitting here drinking for quite a while now, judging by the three empty brandy snifters lined up on the table.

"Actually, I fancy a cup of warm milk."

"Of course." He jumped up and trotted off toward the bar. I closed my eyes and took a few deep breaths. What an ordeal. I thought I'd never get out from under that bed.

A few minutes later, Clifford returned with a brandy snifter in one hand and a cup in the other. He set both down on the small table that was wedged between our chairs.

"I say. You just missed Mrs. E," he said, as he dropped back into his chair. "She's been looking for you."

"At this time of night?" I gingerly picked up the cup.

"I told her what we found," he said excitedly.

"You told her about the letter?" I sat the cup back on its saucer a bit too hard. Warm milk sloshed out onto the table. I dabbed at it with my handkerchief.

"Of course, I did, old girl." He smiled.

I knew I shouldn't have confided in Clifford.

"How is your milk?" he asked. "Just the way my mummy made it for me when I was in short pants." He chuckled.

"Yes, well, some things you never outgrow." *Short or long pants, Clifford can't keep a secret.*

Not like me. I'd been tight-lipped even as a child. Sometimes my mum couldn't get an answer out of me in spite of threats to withhold my pudding.

Once after school, I sat across the table from her for almost two hours while she tried to bribe me with tea biscuits to tell her the name of the boy she'd seen me talking to—and kicking in the shin—at the bus stop. *William Baxter*. She never got it out of me. In a game of wills, I always won.

Clifford looked indignant. "It's her letter. She has a right to know we found it."

"*We*... you mean me. I found it." I took a sip of my milk.

"Well, yes." He ran his fingers through his hair. "But I read it."

"True." He had a point...two points. *My conscience and my translator.* "What would I do without you?" I sipped my milk. "Now I really do need to get some beauty sleep. The royal ball is tomorrow."

"Oh, come now, old thing. You're lovely even without sleep."

I couldn't help but smile. *There are some reasons to keep Clifford around, even if he calls me 'old thing.'* I finished the last drop of milk and left him drinking brandy. *If he doesn't let up, he'll be hungover tomorrow.*

Before going back to my room, I made a detour to the front desk. Max was on duty. I knew it was risky, but I had to notify the War Office via my contact in Hungary.

"May I use the telephone?" I asked, leaning my elbows on the counter.

The taciturn Max blinked a few times and then pushed the phone across the counter toward me. One by one, I inserted my finger into the hole for each number. Of course, I'd memorized the number.

On the other end, the telephone rang and rang. No answer. I glanced at my watch. No wonder. It was half eleven. I'd have to try again first thing tomorrow morning... from one of those newfangled public telephone boxes.

Back in the solitude of my room, I ran a nice hot bath and slipped out of my soiled clothes. While waiting for the bath to fill, I laid out my dress for the ball.

Just touching its purple satin and ivory lace gave me goosebumps. The gown had a tight-fitting V-shaped bodice, a little too low-cut for my taste, but gorgeous. Intricately embroidered flowers adorned the skirt. The half-length sleeves were elegant lace with large purple satin bows at each elbow. I couldn't wait to put it on tomorrow evening.

The warm bath was a tonic for my nerves. I inhaled the scent of the rose petal soap. Much nicer than the smell of the rat-infested butcher or the dusty floor under Fredricks's bed.

Ahhh. I closed my eyes. I hadn't realized how tight my muscles were until I melted into the bathwater. As I drifted into a dreamy state of relaxation, my thoughts turned to Archie. Where was he? Would I never see him again?

By the time the water had gone tepid, I'd chased all thought of Archie from my mind and resolved to get on with my mission.

I stepped out of the bath and reached for a towel. Even the warm summer heat felt cool on my wet skin. I gave myself an extra vigorous rub to remove any lingering miasma from the butcher shop.

Tomorrow was the night of the royal ball. The climax of my assignment in Vienna.

Chapter Fifteen

The Royal Ball

After a fitful night, I awoke feeling dreadful, like I'd been hit by a trolley. What the dickens was wrong with me. In a stupor, I felt like I'd been drugged. Was that possible? What did I eat or drink yesterday?

I hardly ate anything. Anyway, I'd felt fine all day. Aha. The warm milk last night with Clifford. But no one else was around. I shook the cobwebs out of my head and got up. I staggered into the lav and splashed water on my face.

Dash it. The sun was already streaming through the window, which suggested it was late. The information from Fredricks's room. I must get it to the War Office.

I hurriedly dressed and then headed out to the public telephone station. I had no time to waste. The War Office needed the information about Fredricks. And I needed to see if this Louise de Bettignies, aka Alice Dubois, could give me advice. As a seasoned spy, perhaps she would know the meaning of that list of names and countries I'd found in Fredricks's pocket.

The telephone station was a small structure with several telephone machines sitting on tables separated by partitions. A cashier sat at a desk collecting the fee to use one of the telephones. I paid the cashier twenty heller and she pointed to cubicle two. Luckily, no one else was placing a telephone call, so I had the place to myself...except for the cashier.

I hoped someone would answer so I could get word to the War Office with what I'd learned. A man answered and I asked for Louise de Bettignies. "Who?" he asked.

"How about Alice Dubois? Is she there?"

"One moment please."

I tapped my toe and glanced around at the cashier, who was filing her fingernails.

"*Qui*, this is Alice Dubois."

"My name is Fiona Figg." *Why didn't the War Office give me an alias?* "I'm in Vienna on assignment for Captain Hall." I paused.

Silence on the other end. Heavens. Had I done the right thing? What if I'd just given myself up?

"Yes, go on," she said finally.

"Please inform Captain Hall that I found a list of names and countries in Fredrick Fredricks's room."

"Go on," she said.

I told her the names and countries, including my name and Archie's. "Do you know what it means?"

"The princes are Zita's brothers. Jane Addams is an American peace activist. I've never heard of the others... apart from yourself just now."

"A peace activist," I repeated. Why was an American peace activist on Fredricks's hit list? "Do you know what it means?"

"I couldn't say." She couldn't or wouldn't? I was beginning to wonder about this Louise de Bettignies, aka Alice Dubois. "I also found several passports with various aliases."

"Go on," she said.

I explained the names and countries.

Silence.

"Anything else?" she asked. Alice Dubois was a woman of few words.

"Do you know what I should do next?"

"Follow your instructions from Captain Hall."

"Of course," I said. "You will make sure he gets this information as soon as possible?"

"*Qui.*" She hung up.

I scowled. If I wasn't a spy, I might ask for a refund. I'd hardly gotten twenty hellers worth out of Alice Dubois. I hoped she was trustworthy. *Faith, Fiona. You must have faith.*

Working in espionage made me suspicious of everyone. If I was a secret agent, anyone could be a spy.

I crossed the street and went back into the hotel. Heading for the dining hall, I started plotting my next steps.

Tonight, was the night. Although the emperor's birthday was yesterday on August seventeenth, the party was tonight at eight o'clock at the palace. I needed to allow enough time to get ready. I didn't want to scrimp on my bath and toilette... or my espionage preparations. And because it was a masquerade ball, I had to prepare my costume.

Then again, all my preparations would be in vain if I didn't locate the people on Fredricks's list and prevent him from killing them.

I needed to prepare my strategy for tonight. Locate everyone on Fredricks's list at the ball. Determine which ones were double agents. *Or are Zita's brothers and Jane Addams triple agents?* The spy business could be deuced confusing.

Since Fredricks's favorite means of dispatching double agents was poison, I planned to keep a close eye on any food or drink served at the ball.

In the meantime, I would try to locate everyone on Fredricks's list. The emperor and empress were either at Schönnbrun Palace or in town at Hofburg Palace, where the ball would take place. I assumed that Zita's brothers were in France since the emperor had addressed the letter to Prince Sixtus in Paris. I had no clue where Archie was. Indeed, I didn't expect to ever see him again. Was it possible he was in Vienna?

And what about Miss Jane Addams? Or was it Mrs. Addams? In either case, why would an American peace activist be in Vienna? Was she a friend of the emperor and empress invited to the royal birthday ball?

I reasoned that if the princes were not in Vienna, then they were not Fredricks's targets, at least not immediately. That left me, Archie, the emperor and empress, and this Jane Addams person. The only person on my shortlist that I didn't know by sight was Jane Addams. I would start my search with her.

Having arrived at the dining hall, I made a beeline to the coffee urn. I filled a cup with coffee so it barely covered the bottom, and then filled it the rest of the way with warm milk from a small pitcher. Three spoonfuls of sugar would make it drinkable. Famished, I took a plate and snagged the last bread roll, scooped out some marmalade, and then went to a small table in the corner of the room so as not to be disturbed.

Moments later, Max and Werner arrived and cleared the breakfast away. I'd made it just in the nick of time. I glanced at my watch. *Crikey*. It had gone half ten already.

Despite my rush, the coffee and bread with marmalade hit the spot. Fortified, I began my search for Jane Addams. First stop, Frau Sacher's office. If anyone in Vienna could help me locate Miss Addams, it was her.

I found Frau Sacher sitting on the floor of her office, surrounded by bulldogs. Bruno was lapping up cream from a dish. Jana was growling, playing with a ball. And little Mozart was on Frau Sacher's lap, squeaking, eager to join his sister.

"Mrs. Douglas, what a pleasant surprise," she said, standing up. "I was just playing with my babies." She smiled, obviously delighted to be reunited with the little creatures. She smoothed her dress. "How can I help you?"

"Do you know Jane Addams?"

She furrowed her brows. "Jane Addams," she repeated. After a few seconds, she shook her head. "No, I don't think so."

Drat. Now what? Frau Sacher was my best lead. How would I find Jane Addams? "What do you know about Empress Zita's family? Does she have many siblings?"

"Oh, now there's a story for you." Frau Sacher pulled on a cord and a few moments later Werner appeared. "Can you bring us some tea and toast, please?"

Werner bowed like she was the bloody queen. "Yes, ma'am"

"Bring the good stuff from my secret stash."

"Very well." He bowed again and disappeared.

The good stuff. Perhaps I would finally get a nice cuppa after all.

For the next two and a half hours, Frau Sacher regaled me with stories about Empress Zita's family. Seems she was one of twenty-four children and had quite a cosmopolitan upbringing. Princes Sixtus and Xavier were fighting for the Belgians. "The enemy," Frau Sacher said. "And that's why the people don't trust the Empress."

Could Empress Zita be working for the Allies? Was she the double agent? She was on Fredricks's list. I would have to keep a special eye on her at the ball tonight.

By the time Frau Sacher finished giving me the life story of all twenty-four siblings, it was lunchtime. She insisted on ordering lunch for us. Since I had no idea how to locate Jane Addams, I agreed to join her. She was a lovely woman and knew so much about the history of the royal family and the history of Vienna… although I'm not sure how learning that Zita's family took a special railway with sixteen couches to accommodate them all, or that three of Zita's sisters became nuns, helped me figure what Fredricks was up to.

Finally, at half three, I liberated myself from Frau Sacher's hospitality. On my way back to my room, I met Clifford just coming out of the lift.

"There you are, old girl." He kissed my cheek. "Would you like to join me for a brandy?"

"Isn't it a little early for brandy?"

"It's not like I'm having a whiskey." He scoffed. "Or one of those newfangled American cocktail drinks."

I tutted my tongue.

He tightened his lips and pouted. "You really are a prude, Fiona."

"Me?" I laughed. "*I'm* a prude." Clifford was by far the prudier of the pair of us.

"Well, if you won't join me for a brandy, then how about a glass of warm milk?" He raised his eyebrows and tried to smirk, which really didn't become him.

Frau Sacher had stuffed me so full of food and drink, I couldn't take another bite even if I wanted to. "Thank you, Clifford dear." I patted his arm. "But I should get ready for the royal ball."

He looked at his watch. "Good Lord, Fiona. Surely you don't need all afternoon to prepare yourself?" He smirked. "That's a little extreme, even for you."

What did he mean by that? I glared at him.

"I suppose you need to paint yourself up like the Mona Lisa." He shrugged. "What women have to go through to make themselves presentable."

I narrowed my brows. "Are you suggesting, without face paint, women aren't presentable?"

"I say, Fiona." He shook his head. "Why must you always twist my words around?"

"I'm sorry, Clifford, dear." I patted his hand. "By the way, when you went to get my warm milk last night, was anyone else in the bar?"

"Why how did you know?"

A drug-induced hangover told me. Why would he do that to me? Just because he could? Or was there another reason he wanted me to sleep late?

"Fredricks was there having a nightcap with the most beautiful woman. She really was a looker."

"Fredricks, you say?" Could the beautiful woman have been Jane Addams? Is that why Fredricks spiked my drink? He didn't want me to find her?

"Yes, and his date was—"

"Did you catch her name?"

"No."

"Did Fredricks touch my drink?"

Clifford got a sour look on his face. "Why are you so interested in Fredricks? Do you fancy him?"

Sigh.

"Can you describe the woman to me? Fredricks's date?"

"Gorgeous. Nice figure. Lovely face... a real looker." He beamed.

"Never mind." With that description, I would have to interview half the ladies in Vienna. "Now I really must go get ready for the royal ball." It wasn't exactly a fib. My search for Jane Addams, the only person on Fredricks's hit list unknown to me, was indeed preparation for the ball.

My first stop was Fuchs butcher shop. It was too much of a coincidence. Of course, both the butcher and his son insisted they'd never heard of an Oscar Fuchs. What else could I do? I couldn't force them to tell the truth.

For the rest of the afternoon, I wandered from café to café asking after Miss Jane Addams and Mr. Oscar Fuchs. I must have walked the whole length of Vienna. My feet were killing me. Even my practical Oxfords weren't cut out for miles of pavement.

No one had ever heard of Jane Addams. A banker having a brew in a pub behind the opera house thought the name Oscar Fuchs sounded familiar, but that was as far as we got. It didn't help that I couldn't describe either of them.

On my way back to the hotel, I stopped at the railway station to retrieve my belongings.

After a fruitless afternoon, I arrived back at my hotel room exhausted and discouraged. Only two hours until the ball and I was no closer to discerning Fredricks's target... or finding Mrs. Einstein's notebook. Not to mention the dognapper.

I would have to be on my toes tonight if I was going to stop a murder.

First things first. I'd promised Christina that I'd return her uniform. I took it off its hanger, gave it a good brushing with my shoe brush, folded it neatly, and then wrapped it in some paper I had from packing my costumes. Not exactly clean and fresh as I'd promised, but the best I could do in a pinch.

I was in a hurry. So, my trip to hospital would have to be quick. Of course, Christina wanted to chat. She had so many questions. And I had exactly zero answers. Finally, after twenty minutes, she let me go with the promise that I'd be back tomorrow.

Only twenty minutes until the royal ball and I was sticky with sweat and covered with the dust of a wasted day. As soon as I got back to my room, I tore off my dirty clothes and ran a bath.

I had just enough time to wash the street dirt from my person and get dressed.

As I ran my bath, I wracked my brain to figure out what the names on

Fredricks's list might have in common. Archie and I worked for the War Office. The Emperor, Empress, and her brothers were all part of the same family. And there was the mysterious American, Jane Addams. How did she fit in? And then there was Oscar Fuchs. With so many Fuchs in Vienna, surely someone knew Oscar.

I slipped into the warm bath and closed my eyes. I didn't have time to relax and enjoy the smell of rose petal soap and the sound of water dripping from the facet.

Mine was an important assignment. Lives were at stake. But whose? One of the seven people on Fredricks's list, myself included. Unless his target is not on that list. Was Fredricks trying to kill me with whatever drug he put in my warm milk? Or was he just trying to put me out of commission? Then again, he might have been punishing me for snooping around his room.

With the towel wrapped around my torso, I went to retrieve my smalls from my traveling case. Plain cotton seemed too drab for my royal costume. Then again, no one was going to see my underwear.

Blooming costume required a petticoat and a special corset. I'd always hated wearing a regular corset. This low-cut number was murder. And it was bloody difficult to get into by oneself. Too bad I didn't have a ladies' maid. The original lady to wear this design must have had several, along with ladies-in-waiting, handsome footmen, and a butler to oversee them all. *Must be nice.* With my middle-class upbringing, we were lucky to get an ice boy.

After losing the battle with the corset, I tackled the petticoat. In the end, I tied the corset strings around the doorknob and used it for leverage. Yes. I won the war with the corset. I slipped the gown over my head and tugged. I tried to fasten the tiny silk buttons running down the back of the bodice. *Dashed impossible. Curse it.* I was going to have to enlist Clifford's help. *Even fake husbands come in handy sometimes.*

I knocked on the adjoining door. When Clifford opened it, I clapped my hands in delight. "You look smashing."

"I feel ridiculous," he said, tugging at his wig. "Do I have to wear this bloody wig? It itches something fierce." He held a blue tricornered hat. He was dressed in a matching blue uniform with long tails and red piping and had on tall shiny black boots. With the chin-length dark wig, he looked younger and more attractive.

"I bought it new so it shouldn't have lice," I said playfully. I'd purchased the Napoleon costume for him at Angels Fancy Dress shop before leaving London. With his aquiline nose, the costume suited him.

"Lice!" He huffed. "What happened to your hair?"

I touched my bristly scalp. "You've seen me without a wig before." I turned and gave him my back. "Can you button me up?"

His countenance brightened like winter giving way to spring. "Happy to, old girl." He tossed his hat onto my bed. "Why do women have such tiny buttons?" he asked as he fumbled with them.

"Why do men have such big fingers?"

"You say the darndest things." Eventually, he got me buttoned up. "There. You're all set."

"I have to put on my wig and makeup." I crossed over to my dressing table and picked up my Marie Antoinette wig. The tall swirl of hair looked like silky-white candy floss. I pulled it over my too-short auburn hair.

I glanced in the mirror and frowned. I looked like a grumpy judge in a tall, powdered wig. Nothing like the beautiful Marie Antoinette. *Sigh*. Maybe some makeup would help. I set to work transforming my plain countenance into that of a queen.

"You don't need all that paint," Clifford said. "Why cover your lovely face?" He was leaning against the wall, smoking a cigarette.

The foul smoke was contaminating my bedroom. If he hadn't just called my face lovely, I'd make him extinguish the blasted thing at once.

I applied rouge, kohl, and lipstick. *Yes. A bit better.* At least I looked like a woman instead of a man in a wig.

"I say. You look marvelous." Clifford glanced around the room. "You don't have an ashtray?"

I glared at him.

"No, I suppose not." He popped back into his room to put out his cigarette.

I checked my clutch purse for all my spy essentials. Lipstick mirror.

Lockpick set. Mata Hari's gun. Checking my reflection one last time, I patted my wig, grabbed our masks from my dressing table, and then joined Clifford at the door. "Your mask." I handed him a small black eye mask.

"What the devil is this?" He held the mask by its ribbon.

"A mask. It is a masked ball."

"Don't you think you're taking this costume thing a bit too far?" Clifford didn't appreciate my penchant for disguises.

"It's exciting," I said, taking his arm.

"I say. We should get a photograph taken." He put his other hand inside his waistcoat and smiled down at me as if overseeing a newly conquered empire.

∗ ∗ ∗

Although the Hapsburgs were summering outside Vienna at the Schönbrunn Palace, the ball was in town at the Hofburg Palace, which was also the seat of government. Perhaps the emperor wanted to be able to conduct government business between waltzes.

Fredricks sent a car for us—actually it was for me, but I insisted Clifford come along. I didn't want to be alone with that blackguard Fredricks in a car. He may fancy this a date, but I didn't. After all, not so long ago, he kidnapped me, hog-tied me, and stole my nun's habit.

Crikey. It's a different automobile from last time. How many cars does he own? Fredricks was sitting in the backseat of the open carriage. The automobile was a stunning ivory color with red leather seats and gold headlamps. I'd never seen anything like it. Ivan the chauffeur wore goggles and a leather cap strapped under his solid chin.

"An Austro-Fiat Dolomit C Three." Clifford whistled. "What a beaut."

I looked at him like he was speaking Russian.

Fredricks hopped over the side of the vehicle and offered his gloved hand. "You look radiant, *ma chérie.*" He cut a striking figure in his ruffled white shirt and black evening suit.

"You too," I said without thinking. My face was hot with embarrassment.

Something about that man got under my skin.

"I trust you slept well last night?" He grinned, still holding out his hand.

Classic narcissist. He'd wanted to make sure to get credit for his brilliance, even if it meant getting caught. Yes, I too had been reading Sigmund Freud.

The blackguard really was brazen. Vowing not to let him get the better of me, I pretended not to know what he was talking about and held my head high. I took his hand. He opened the door to the car and helped me onto the running board. It was a bit of a thrill. I'd never ridden in a motorcar with the top off.

Fredricks gave Clifford's hand a good pump and then ran around the car and hopped over the other side. I scooted out of the way in the nick of time, or he might have ended up on my lap.

Squeezed in between the two men, I held onto my wig the entire journey, which thankfully was only a few minutes. In fact, the palace was so close, we could have walked. But obviously, Fredricks wanted to make a grand entrance.

"He's not wearing a mask," Clifford whispered in a sulky voice.

"He's always wearing a mask," I whispered back.

The sun had just dropped over the horizon and the palace was lit from within, glowing like the white-hot center of the Viennese universe.

Inside, the ballroom had enormous crystal chandeliers that looked like inverted glass Christmas trees hanging from the ceiling. An orchestra was playing from a balcony overlooking the ballroom. Men and women in fancy dress costumes and masks milled around drinking from champagne flutes. Some of the women held bejeweled eye masks in front of their faces. I glanced around, looking for the emperor and empress, but they must not have arrived yet.

A butler in evening kit took the card from Fredricks and announced us. I asked Clifford to bring me a glass of champagne while I lingered near the entrance, hoping to hear the names Miss Jane Addams or Mr. Oscar Fuchs. It would be blessed convenient if they arrived together.

Dresses sparkled, shadows danced, faces glowed. The scene was mesmerizing. My first royal ball. And luckily, I was the only Marie Antoinette, which pleased me to no end. I only hoped my costume would not remind the empress that I'd broken her ancestor's beautiful teacup.

After one glass of champagne, Fredricks took me by the hand and whisked me onto the dance floor. "Keep your eyes and ears open," he said as he twirled me around.

I was keeping my eyes and ears open. On the lookout for Jane Addams or Oscar Fuchs. They were the only names I didn't know by sight. And I was keeping a close watch on those not already crossed off from Fredricks's list or my own.

"What do you mean?" I asked, struggling to keep up with him.

He danced as if he were floating on air. I danced as if I were sinking in mud. Soon he was lifting me ever so slightly and my feet barely touched the floor. The Viennese waltz was exhilarating.

"This may be our chance to end the war," Fredricks whispered into my ear. "Together, we can change history." He sounded like a madman.

"What are you on about?"

"The emperor," he said.

The music stopped and Clifford—aka Napoleon—appeared out of nowhere. Before Fredricks could finish what he was saying, the music started up again and Clifford pulled me into the center of the ballroom.

The emperor what? Eyes and ears open for what? Confound it, Clifford. I was just getting somewhere with Fredricks. I couldn't very well make a scene. Reluctantly, I let Clifford lead me around the dance floor, all the while keeping my eye on Fredricks.

Clifford and I were evenly matched in the dancing department. We sank in the mud together. While other couples twirled and glided across the floor, we tripped and stumbled. "Ouch!" It wasn't the first time Clifford had trod on my slippered foot. To be fair, I'd trod on his a few times too.

How bold would it be for me to ask Fredricks? What in blazes did he mean? *This may be our chance to end the war.* I sincerely hoped he didn't think that by killing someone tonight, he could end the war. *Our chance?* Why did he keep saying that somehow, he and I could end the war?

I led Clifford around the floor, trying to keep up with Fredricks, who was dancing with one of Empress Zita's pretty sisters—not the one going to the convent.

When the music ended again, the emperor and empress appeared at the top of a grand staircase. They both looked splendid, wearing golden glittering masks tied around their eyes and dressed as two of their Hapsburg ancestors. I recognized Empress Zita's deep-turquoise gown as the same one worn by the young Maria Theresa in the portrait of her as a young woman. As their guests looked on, they descended the staircase hand in hand. The orchestra played their national anthem, the regal "Kaiserhymne."

When they reached the bottom landing, the emperor said a prayer, asking God to bless the Austria-Hungarian Empire and its people. *Or at least that's what I thought he said.* He looked too young for someone so serious. If I understood correctly, he said it pained him to host a party while so many were suffering, and he asked his guests to pray for those brave men and women risking their lives on both sides of the border. *"Für den Frieden zu beten,"* he said. Pray for peace.

"They call him the prince of peace," Clifford whispered.

Someone from the back of the room yelled, "Even the Serbs? They killed your uncle!"

Without missing a beat, the emperor responded, "A father has no favorite among his children. Serbia, Hungary, Austria. We are all part of the same family."

More like a family feud. I had to admit, the call for peace wasn't what I expected from our enemy.

When the emperor finished his speech, the orchestra struck up the "Vienna Waltz." The emperor and empress danced in the center of the grand ballroom. Soon their guests joined them. Skirts whirled and suit tails flew as couples moved across the floor, Clifford and I among them. So much energy. So much life.

It was hard to believe that miles away men were killing each other in muddy trenches. The emperor had a point. I too felt guilty about enjoying myself while others suffered. Then again, I was on duty for the War Office.

I kept my eye on Fredricks as he took turns around the dance floor with every beautiful woman at the party, including the empress herself. Ever popular, Fredricks had half the ladies at the ball fawning over him. Half of the men looked as if they'd like to feed him to the lions.

There was one woman in particular whom he favored. A tall dark beauty. Could that be Miss Jane Addams? I planned to stay close to her in any case. If she was the object of Fredricks's attention, she was most likely in danger.

If I hadn't been so intent on preventing Fredricks from killing someone, the music would have been intoxicating. The air was heavy with laughter, joy, and bodies. So many perspiring bodies. For better or worse, most of the women and half of the men were well-doused in perfume.

Whenever Fredricks floated by, I got a whiff of juniper cologne mixed with lavender soap. And I could tell when Count Czernin was nearby from the smell of strong tobacco that clung to his person. Wherever the empress was, so were they, both. Along with being smart and charming, Empress Zita was a very pretty woman. The emperor was a lucky man.

After an hour of dancing with some awfully handsome men and a few homely ones, my feet were sore, and my forehead was perspiring. It was sweltering despite the three-story ceilings and open windows and doors.

Moonlight streamed in from the windows. And overhead, the chandeliers twinkled, creating what could have been a jolly romantic scene if my nerves weren't frayed from waiting for Fredricks to pounce on his target. I hadn't taken my eyes off the tall dark beauty…and neither had Fredricks.

Speak of the devil. Clifford and I had just finished a quickstep—or should I say just survived a quickstep—when Fredricks showed up. The orchestra was taking a short break, and waiters took the opportunity to deliver more champagne and hors d'oeuvres, tiny pastry puffs on silver trays.

"Have you finished attending to the empress then?" I asked, taking a sip. *I really shouldn't be drinking so much.* But dancing made me deuced thirsty.

"Poor dear isn't feeling well," he said. "She may go up soon."

The emperor had left the party long ago. Just as I suspected, he was too serious a soul for masquerade balls, even if they were in honor of his birthday.

A strange cry like a bird shrieking echoed through the ballroom. All eyes flew to the empress, who had collapsed in a heap in the center of the dance floor.

"Good Lord," Clifford exclaimed.

She must have fainted from the heat. Making my way through the crowd, I rushed to her side. "I'm a nurse," I said, pushing past the partiers. Well, I was a volunteer nurse. And I had worked at a hospital.

When I reached Her Majesty, my breath caught. I'd seen that otherworldly stare before. She was lying in an unnatural position, with one foot turned backward, muscles convulsing. I knelt down next to her and lifted her head. As I did, her wig fell off and with it, an embroidered hair ribbon. I'd seen a ribbon like that before. I picked it up.

What the dickens? It was one of Mrs. Einstein's bookmarks.

Chapter Sixteen

Poison... Again

Empress Zita's beautiful dress twisted around her body as it convulsed in violent spasms. Her lips had gone blue.

"Call a doctor," I shouted. The adrenaline coursing through my veins improved my German considerably.

The crowd closed in around me. I wanted to bat them away. "Please move back," I pleaded. "Give her some air." I needed air too.

Suddenly, the spasms stopped, and Zita's body went limp.

I put two fingers to her neck, checking for a pulse. Nothing. My heart sank. I picked up her limp hand and felt her wrist. Nothing.

"It's too late," I whispered. "She's dead."

Onlookers gasped and murmured.

"Good Lord." I recognized Clifford's voice in the crowd.

My head was spinning. I hoped I wouldn't swoon. Of course, I'd seen a dead body before. But encircled by the thick throng of partiers, along with the August heat, I was quite overwhelmed.

I glanced around for Fredricks. He'd been with the empress before she collapsed. Had she been his target all along? I wiped my forehead with the back of my hand. Tears of rage filled my eyes. I'd failed. I hadn't prevented the demon Fredricks from carrying out his evil plan.

If only I'd been paying more attention instead of enjoying myself. I'd have given anything to go back in time.

Judging by the color of her skin and lips, I suspected the empress had been poisoned. One advantage of my assignment last spring at Ravenswick Abbey, posing as Dr. Vogel, was my crash course in toxicology. Poison was Fredricks's weapon of choice. He'd poisoned at least two countesses who were double agents. And now he'd poisoned the empress. Was she too a double agent? What other explanation could there be, since Austria was allied with Germany?

Where in the devil had the blackguard gone? Why did he bring me here to witness this horrible scene? So many questions swirled in my mind. "Was the empress drinking champagne?" I asked no one in particular.

Obviously stunned, the crowd murmured, but no one answered. I scanned the area around the empress for a glass or some other evidence of how the poison could have been administered. Nothing.

On hands and knees, I crawled around the circumference of the body looking for clues. Anything that might help me determine how the empress was poisoned. The convulsions and bluing complexion suggested a fast-acting poison. Strychnine could be fast-acting in large enough doses. But it was bitter. How would someone, even Fredricks, get the empress to drink an entire glass of the stuff?

The doctor should arrive soon, along with the police. I'd better make myself scarce. Otherwise, I'd blow my cover…and be executed at dawn in St. Stephen's Square. I shuddered. The palace guards were already clearing away the crowd.

Blooding—too late. One of the uniformed men approached me, shouting in German. They took long enough to get here. Probably off smoking instead of guarding the empress.

"Ja, Ja," I said. "Eine Minute."

The guard grabbed my arm and yanked me to my feet. Obviously, he thought I'd killed the empress. Wait until he found out I was a British spy. The Pummerin bells echoed through my head.

"Wait," I said. "Look there." I pointed to a spot on one of the pearls in Empress Zita's belt. The fabric of the dress was dark enough that a tiny spot of blood would be hard to see, especially with a palace guard tugging at me.

But the tiniest red streak on the ivory pearl stood out like a rosebud against a spring snow.

The guard loosened his grip as he stared down at the body, presumably trying to see what I was pointing at.

"*Blut*," I said. Now I knew how the poison was administered. Someone had injected the empress with the poison…or perhaps stabbed her with a poisoned dart? Someone who was dancing with her. Fredrick Fredricks.

I glanced up at the balcony. A dart shot from above? But then, where was it? I'd searched around the body…unless the empress was laying on it.

An injection of poison from a syringe or a dart. When injected, strychnine acted faster and was more lethal than when ingested.

The guard released me and knelt next to the body. The rest of the guards joined him. Now was my chance. Where was Clifford? We had to make our escape before we ended up in jail… and then on the wrong end of a noose.

My mind was abuzz. What were some other fast-acting poisons? Belladonna. Only the juice of a few berries would be needed, especially if injected. Or Cyanide?

A lady's maid appeared out of nowhere. She straightened Zita's legs and dress. She fussed around her mistress and then removed Zita's mask.

Oh, my sainted aunt. The ashen face that appeared from under the mask did not belong to Empress Zita. The dead eyes staring up at me were not Zita's but Elsie's.

The lady's maid gasped and fell backward. Murmurs rippled through the crowd.

What in heaven's name? Where was the empress? What was Elsie doing at the ball dressed as a Hapsburg?

I fingered Elsie's hair ribbon, which I still had in my hand. Why was Elsie wearing one of Mrs. Einstein's bookmarks as a hair ribbon? I surreptitiously tucked the ribbon into my clutch and then tiptoed away from the body and into the crowd.

"I say. What's going on?" I nearly ran into Clifford in the crowd.

"Thank goodness."

"Where's Fredricks?" I asked.

"Deuced if I know." Clifford shrugged. "He stepped out to get some air and never returned."

"I bet."

The Black Panther had struck again and gotten away with it. Captain Hall would not be pleased, although I had informed my contact about Fredricks's fake passports. I should at least get credit for that bit of gen.

I surmised that his target had been the empress, not Elsie, and that the empress must be a double agent. First chance I got, I would try to confirm that with the War Office. Surely, Captain Hall would know if the empress was secretly working for the British. Her brothers were fighting for our side after all.

My heart was racing as I dragged Clifford away from the scene. If Fredricks was after the empress, he very well may strike again.

Clifford, who fancied himself a bit of a detective, wanted to stay and question the staff. I might as well announce that I was an English spy. That I was here to stop a political assassination… a failed spy since I didn't manage to stop it.

Why did the empress send a surrogate to the ball? Did she know her life was in danger?

In shock, Clifford and I walked back to the hotel. A warm breeze at our backs carried us along. After the nightmare at the palace, there was something dreamlike about the twinkling lights and late-night carriages. With the adrenaline wearing off and exhaustion setting in, I took Clifford's arm.

"At least it wasn't the empress," Clifford said. "Imagine the international scandal. Archduke Ferdinand and his wife three years ago—"

"The assassinations that set off this bloody war," I interrupted. "I suppose you're right. Who will care about the death of a poor innocent servant girl?" Shaking my head, I said, "I didn't mean… of course, her death is important. It's just that the empress—" I tightened my grip on his arm. "I'll wager we don't see your friend Fredricks again." *Unless he comes back to try again.*

"Why ever not?" Clifford asked. I always wondered how much the War Office had told him about the operations of the notorious Black Panther.

Clifford seemed quite in the dark. "Fredricks is a good sort. I don't believe all that rot about him killing people."

"Just animals then? Your Great White Hunter."

"That's different." He stopped and turned to face me. "You enjoy a good meat pie as much as the next person."

"*Touché*. But I wouldn't kill for sport."

"And you think Fredricks kills people for sport?" Clifford used a sharp tone I'd never heard from him. "Really, Fiona. Sometimes I think you have an overactive imagination."

"What about Paris?" My lashes were blinking like a sail flapping in the wind. "He was imprisoned for sabotage and escaped." I didn't mention the part about Fredricks tying me up and stealing my nun's costume to make his escape. That was a low point of my budding espionage career. Laying there in my smalls on that lice-infested mattress. I shuddered just thinking about it.

"A French prison is practically a badge of honor," Clifford said indignantly. "As I recall, I had to bail you out of a French jail too."

Touché again. "Let's quit bickering and go in." I pulled at his arm. "I'm completely knackered." It had been quite a day...but it wasn't over yet.

The night staff was on duty at the hotel, and I planned to question them about the butcher's son and his deliveries...and anything they knew about Elsie, the royal nanny. Tomorrow, I would question the day staff and Frau Sacher.

My gut told me there was a connection between the dognapping, the missing notebook, and the attempt on Zita's life. The dogs and the notebook both were stolen from the hotel. The attempted assassination was a completely different animal, and it happened at a completely different place. But the bookmark in Elsie's hair connected the missing notebook and the assassination. And if Fredricks stole the notebook and killed Elsie, then he was the missing link. But what about the dogs? How did they fit in?

Poor Elsie had been in the wrong place at the wrong time. *Did she know what a dangerous job impersonating the empress would turn out to be?*

Clifford walked me to our suite. I entered through my door and bid him good night. Once inside my room, I listened through the wall. I could hear Clifford on the other side running water and tramping about. When all noise ceased, I took the chance to sneak back out of the room and make my way downstairs into the lobby.

Max was behind the registration desk reading a book. *Did the boy ever sleep?* Too bad it wasn't Werner or really anyone else besides Max. The boy was as reticent as a monk sworn to silence. Even after we'd spent an afternoon together following little Mozart from tree to tree, the boy had hardly uttered one word to me.

Still, I had to try. I approached the desk and cleared my throat.

Max looked up from his book, his eyes wide.

If I didn't know better, I'd think the boy was afraid of me. "Excuse me, *bitte*," I said in broken German. "Can I ask you something?"

He just stared at me like I was an apparition.

"Do you know the butcher's son? The boy who makes deliveries?" I asked.

Max got a quizzical look on his face and closed his book.

I leaned in to get a look at the book, taking note of the title, *Die Verwandlung, The Transformation*, by someone called Franz Kafka. "Did you hear what happened at the royal ball?" I asked.

When he stood up, the book fell from his hand onto the floor. *Probably a book about vampires or werewolves. The Transformation indeed.* He didn't bother to pick it up. He just stood there gaping at me.

Now I had his attention.

"Did you hear about Elsie, the palace nanny?" If he did know Elsie, I hated to be the bearer of the terrible news. Then again, if he knew her, he might know why someone would want to kill her... or her mistress.

Max ran both hands through his thick hair. His face went blotchy.

Yes. He knew her.

He put his hands on the desk and leaned closer. "I heard she was poisoned," he whispered.

How does he know about the poison? Word certainly travels fast. I nodded. "She was dressed as the empress. I suspect Empress Zita was the killer's true target."

"The empress?" He dropped into a chair behind the desk. "Why would someone want to kill our empress?"

"Why, indeed." I glanced around. The lobby was deserted except for us. "Do you mind if I sit?"

He shrugged.

I took the liberty of sitting on the corner of the desk. That's when I realized I was still wearing the blooming Marie Antoinette costume. No wonder the poor boy looked bewildered. I removed my mask.

"Did you know Elsie?"

His countenance darkened.

I take that as a yes. "Tell me about Elsie."

"Elsie is a super girl… was." His voice broke. "And so pretty." Max blushed. "She had such nice hair." He sniffled and then bent over to retrieve his book. Or at least that's what I assumed he was doing. But when he didn't come up again, I began to wonder. *Dear me. I hope he isn't crying.*

"She seemed like a very nice girl." I peered behind the desk. "Did you see her much?"

Finally, he stood up. He had been crying. *Poor boy.* "Not since she got engaged to Oswald." He tightened his lips.

I got the distinct impression that this Oswald fellow wasn't the only young man in love with Elsie. *And what about Count Czernin? Elsie and the count seemed jolly good friends the other afternoon in the nursery.* For someone only in town for two months, she had a lot of admirers. "Oswald?" The pointy edge of the desk gouged my backside, and I shifted my weight. "Who's Oswald?"

"Oswald Fuchs." *Is he any relation to Oscar Fuchs, the last person on my list from the War Office?*

"Go on," I said encouragingly.

"Oswald Fuchs?" He narrowed his eyes and smirked like I should know who he meant. "The butcher's son."

Chapter Seventeen

Elsie's Fiancé

fter my enlightening conversation with Max, I returned to my room. Although it was quite late, and earlier I was completely knackered, now I was wide awake. The revelation of the relationship between the dead girl and the delivery boy was like a shot of adrenaline.

I yanked the wig off my head and threw it on the dressing table. *Blasted buttons! How was I going to get out of this bloody dress?* I couldn't very well wake Clifford in the middle of the night to unbutton me. *Could I?* No. He was indulgent, but that would be going too far.

With all the excitement, I hadn't thought of the corset in hours. But now that I had, I wanted the bloody thing off and *tout de suite*. I reached both arms behind my back like a contortionist, grasping at the satin buttons. *Argggh.* If the cursed costume hadn't cost me so much, I'd rip the bloody things off.

Fiona. Come on old girl. Keep your head. What had come over me? Why was I so agitated? Had someone slipped something into my champagne flute? Throwing things and stomping around. It was quite unlike me. I took a deep breath and went to my dressing table. I picked up the wig and placed it on a wig stand and smooth it out. Then I sat down slowly, trying to get a grip on myself. *Breathe. Just breathe.*

Dash it. That was the problem. In this bloody corset, I couldn't breathe,

163

let alone think. I reached around my back and declared war against the bloody buttons. I knew better. Nothing good ever comes from rash action. In the words of Leo Tolstoy, "The two most powerful warriors are patience and time."

I closed my eyes and forced myself to concentrate on carefully and methodically unbuttoning my gown. One button at a time. Starting at the top. And working my way down. Next, I ripped off the corset. *Aaaaahhh.* Once I was free, I slumped over the dressing table in relief.

My brain no longer deprived of oxygen, I could cogitate on the murder and facts at hand. I made a mental list of what I knew so far.

Max was in love with Elsie. Count Czernin was in love with Elsie. Oswald Fuchs was in love with Elsie. Was there any man in Vienna who was not in love with the dead girl? If it was a crime of passion, then the poison was intended for Elsie after all. But how would the killer have known it was her under that costume, especially after she'd made a grand entrance with the emperor? Unless the emperor had a stand-in too. He did give a speech. Still, how could I know it was really him?

I stood up and wriggled out of the dress and then slipped off my shoes. In my stockings and smalls, I paced the room. The thick carpet was a balm to my aching feet after dancing all night in those blooming heels. *Sigh.* There was nothing quite so liberating as taking off tight clothing and breathing freely again. Now I could think straight.

Elsie, the deceased royal nanny, was engaged to Oswald Fuchs, the butcher's son. As a delivery boy, Oswald made regular trips to the hotel. He had access to the kitchen... and therefore was in close proximity to the Sacher Tortes and Mozart Bonbons. *Gracious me.* Elsie had a stash of treats hidden in her bathroom at the palace. Were they illicit presents from Oswald? Or were they from her secret lover, Count Czernin? I intended to find out.

There were chocolate cake crumbs on the toast found at the scene of the dognapping. *Could that mean Oswald is the dognapper?* And what about Mrs. Einstein's bookmarks littered in the stairwell of the butcher shop? Elsie was using one of them as a hair ribbon when she was killed. Did she get it from Oswald? Maybe Oswald was giving her stolen cakes, candies, and ribbons as presents. He could be the dognapper, the notebook thief, and the murderer. Unless, of course, Fredricks was the culprit.

Then again, perhaps Oswald Fuchs was also Oscar Fuchs. The names were similar.

I glanced at my watch. *Crikey. Two in the morning.* My visit to Fuchs Butcher Shop would have to wait. I'd best get some rest. I had to be at my sharpest when I interviewed Mr. Oswald Fuchs tomorrow…especially if he turned out to be the mysterious Oscar Fuchs.

* * *

After a short night, I woke up before dawn. Usually, the stillness of the early morning was my favorite time of day. Today, I just wanted everyone to get out of bed already.

I went to the wardrobe, opened it, and stood staring at my clothes. *What is the proper attire for a murder investigation?* My practical flats, of course. And a cotton blouse and sensible loose-fitting skirt. I settled on a blue gingham blouse with a baby-doll collar, a pleated navy skirt, and a brown leather belt with a heavy silver buckle that could double as a cudgel if need be. I tugged my favorite auburn bobbed wig over my own bristles.

By the time I'd put myself together, it had gone half six. Frau Sacher would have coffee and breakfast laid out by seven. Having skipped dinner last night, and with only a few nibbles at the party, I was famished. I couldn't just spin my wheels. So, I decided to make a to-do list while waiting for breakfast. It was never a good idea to start a murder investigation on an empty stomach—especially since Frau Sacher served real toasted bread with thick-cut marmalade.

I opened my notebook and wrote out a list:

1. Find out who nicked Frau Sacher's dogs… and who brought them back.
2. Find out who nicked Mrs. Einstein's notebook and retrieve it.
3. Find out why Mrs. Einstein's bookmark and letters were in the

stairwell at Fuchs Butcher Shop. Is Oswald related to Oscar?

4. Find out who murdered Elsie, and how, and whether the empress was the intended victim.

5. Find out why someone would want to kill the empress.

6. Last but not least, find Fredrick Fredricks and confront him about the notebook and Elsie's murder.

* * *

At seven o'clock right on the dot, I stepped across the threshold and into the dining room. The smell of coffee whetted my appetite. I was growing jolly fond of the strong, sweet brew. I made a beeline for the coffee urn, lifted the spigot, and watched the dark beverage spill into a cup. I'd learned to leave enough room for lots of warm milk and sugar. Half coffee and half milk with two heaping teaspoons of sugar was perfect. Vienna might turn me into a coffee drinker yet.

I slid two slices of bread into the toaster and magically they appeared out the other side delightfully golden brown. Then I dropped a big dollop of marmalade onto my plate. With my mouth watering, I sat down at one of the tables just as Frau Sacher appeared in the doorway wearing a flowing robe.

A cigar in one hand and a bulldog in the other, she glided across the room until she reached my table. "*Guten Morgen*, Mrs. Douglas. May I join you?"

"Of course." I gestured for her to sit down.

"I heard about poor Elsie," she said, adjusting the dog on her lap. "It must have been horrific." She puffed her cigar and then let out a plume of smoke.

Too bad. I was just tucking into my toast when the disgusting smell quite ruined my appetite. I dropped the toast back onto the plate and hoped the strong coffee might be a better match for her cigar.

"You saw it all?" she asked, cocking her head to the side. "The whole gruesome affair?"

I squinted at her, wondering if we were running up against our linguistic limits. By *gruesome affair*, I assumed she meant Elsie's death. "Did you know Elsie?"

"She was engaged to my nephew." She tapped the ash of her cigar onto a saucer. "Poor boy is taking it rather hard." Seemingly disturbed by the movement, the little dog jumped off her lap and onto the table.

I cringed. "Oswald Fuchs is your nephew?"

"One day he will inherit my father's butcher shop," she said proudly.

Blimey. I'd forgotten Frau Sacher's father was a butcher.

"What can you tell me about your nephew?"

"He's a good boy, if somewhat easily distracted."

"Distracted?"

"By a pretty face."

Yes, like most men. Maybe Frau Sacher knew Mr. Oscar Fuchs. No one else seemed to know him. "Are you by chance related to an Oscar Fuchs?"

"Oscar?" She squinted at me and shook her head. "Not that I know of." She took a puff from her cigar and blew out a cloud of foul smoke. "Not to speak ill of the dead, but it's for the best." Frau Sacher reached over and gave her pup a pat. "Elsie was not the right girl for him."

"Why not?" Elsie seemed like a perfectly respectable young woman. What could Frau Sacher have against her?

"Discretion is my motto," she said leaning closer. "Let's just say the girl was very popular."

"With whom?"

"Men." She stubbed out her cigar. "Princes, generals, bankers—powerful men."

So much for discretion. Perhaps Frau Sacher's secrets were deadly after all.

Frau Sacher stood up and brushed imaginary crumbs from her skirt. "Frankly, I don't think she actually accepted Oswald's proposal. The engagement was a fanciful rumor started by my brother, who considered the girl an ambassador for the imperial court." She shook her head. "My brother is a good man, but he's a fool... and a terrible businessman. If it weren't for me, the butcher shop would be closed by now."

So, Frau Sacher had bailed out her brother. He and his son were in her debt.

"Tell me, how did the poor girl die?" She tilted her head in anticipation. "She was too young to have had a heart attack."

"I'm afraid she was murdered."

"Who would want to kill Elsie?"

"Who indeed." I rotated the cup on the saucer. "You seem to know a lot about the girl. Who might want her dead?"

She shook her head. Judging from the sparks in her eyes, I suspected she knew more than she was saying.

"A jealous wife perhaps?" I asked. "Or blackmail?"

"How was she killed?" Frau Sacher took another puff.

"I suspect she was poisoned."

"Poisoned? At the royal ball? How?" She pressed me for more information.

"I don't know." It was true. I had my suspicions. I'd seen the tiny hole in her belt and a pinhead-sized spot of blood, suggesting someone injected her with poison, probably while dancing with her. Although trying to imagine how someone could stab a needle into her while dancing without anyone else noticing seemed unlikely. So, I truly didn't know.

"If you hear any more, let me know," she said. "And if I hear anything, I'll do the same." With that, she scooped up her pup and turned on her heels.

I took a bite of toast, but it was cold and hard. No time to make a fresh one. I had to head out to find Oswald Fuchs and his father. Maybe just a bit more coffee to get me through the morning. I grabbed a fresh piece of bread on the way out. After all, as my grandmother used to say, "empty stomach, empty mind."

Frau Sacher's swishing skirts stilled when she reached the threshold. She turned around and looked at me with a penetrating gaze. "Discretion, dear lady. Discretion," she said and then disappeared.

The butcher shop where I'd found Mrs. Einstein's letter was owned by Frau Sacher's family. The delivery boy, Oswald Fuchs, was Frau Sacher's nephew. And Elsie the nanny was a tart...that is if Frau Sacher was telling the truth.

I removed my notebook from my handbag and added:

1. Find out about Elsie's romantic liaisons.

I suspected Elsie's popularity played out right here in the hotel. My guidebook said that in his youth, Frau Sacher's husband worked at a tavern in Paris. When he opened the hotel in Vienna, he imported the best French wines and the idea of *Chambre separées,* discrete rooms where aristocrats and royalty could indulge their private pleasures. The guidebook called them "remnants of naughty Paris."

Naughty. Try appalling. Places where wealthy old men preyed on innocent young girls, more like.

Still, whatever her morals, Elsie did not deserve to be murdered. *The question is, does Frau Sacher's relationship with the butcher or the victim change the equation?*

I refilled my coffee cup with warm milk, a splash of coffee, and a generous spoonful of sugar. As I made a few more notes, I enjoyed sipping my "*Milchkaffee,*" as the Austrians called it.

Perhaps Elsie threatened to expose her affair with a powerful man. That would be motive enough for murder. There were a lot of powerful men at the royal ball. How many of them had been engaged in intrigues with the royal nanny?

Count Czernin came to mind. With his long face and hard eyes, he looked capable of murder. Had she thrown him over for Oswald and he killed her in a jealous rage… enabled by a syringe of strychnine he just happened to have in his vest pocket? *Not likely.* This murder was premeditated. Which doesn't rule out the count.

What if Oswald discovered that his sweetheart was as generous with her love as he was with his aunt's Sacher Torte? Could that have driven him to kill her? If so, how did he get into the royal ball? Surely, he wasn't invited, was he? Then again, it was a costume ball. He could have dressed up as a duke and delivered the poisoned prick on the dance floor in plain sight of everyone.

Obviously, Frau Sacher did not approve of the match between Elsie and her nephew. She was a commanding woman in charge of her domain, but was she capable of murder? No. I suspected Frau Sacher had other equally effective and less deadly means of dispatching an unwanted niece.

Of course, this assumes that Elsie was the intended victim. I needed to find out, because if she wasn't, then my first supposition was correct, and Empress Zita was the real target. Who would want to kill the empress? Maybe someone who had discovered she was a double agent?

Or was she not a spy at all? Just married to the wrong person? From Empress Elisabeth twenty years ago to Archduke Franz Ferdinand and his wife Sophie—whose murders started this bloody war—royal assassinations seemed all the rage in Europe.

If only the War Office could tell me if the empress was spying for our side, I wouldn't need to look into Elsie's death. But my clearance wasn't high enough.

Weighing all the evidence at my disposal so far, I still maintained that Empress Zita was the intended victim and Fredricks was the killer. If I was right, then the empress must be a double agent and Fredricks would strike again. But I couldn't ask her that. So, I had to look into Elsie's death and hope I could figure out who the killer had been after.

I jotted down Black Panther and then closed my notebook. Fredricks was probably halfway to Berlin by now…or maybe he was on his way back to South Africa. *You never know where the sneaky devil is off to next.*

I drained my coffee cup, put my notebook back into my handbag, wiped crumbs from my lap, and prepared to begin the investigation in earnest.

"Well, my sainted aunt," I said, dropping back into my chair. *Speak of the devil and he shall appear.*

"Fiona, *ma chérie*." Fredricks swaggered into the room. "I was hoping I'd find you here." He lifted my limp hand and kissed it, all the while gazing into my eyes with a mischievous glint in his. *Impudent cad.*

"Did you try to assassinate the empress," I asked, dispensing with any pleasantries.

"May I?" Without waiting for an answer, Fredricks pulled up a chair and sat next to me at the breakfast table…too close for comfort.

My word. Did the man douse himself in juniper cologne?

"You're looking lovely as always. I especially like your hat." He touched his own, which he was holding in one hand.

Given my mission was investigation, I'd worn a very sensible large-brimmed light straw hat with a ring of flowers around the crown and a bright yellow bow in back.

Don't let the blackguard distract you with his foolish flattery. I leaned as far away from him and his cologne as possible without falling off my chair. "Are you here to kill the empress?"

"No." His mustache twitched.

"Why should I believe you?"

"You shouldn't." He grinned.

Infuriating man.

"If you did it, I aim to find out." Just how, I wasn't sure. Could I make a citizen's arrest? I couldn't let Fredricks get away. Perhaps I could lure him back to my room and incapacitate him. Captain Hall was clear that I was only to watch Fredricks and report his movements. But that wasn't enough. Did Captain Hall expect me to just sit back and watch Fredricks kill the empress?

"I'm sure you will." He smirked. He stood up and dropped his napkin on the table.

Confound it. Is he leaving? How can I detain him? I had to think of something before he got away.

But he didn't leave. He came around behind my chair and bent down. I could feel his breath on my neck. "I know a secret," he whispered playfully. "You're going to want to hear it."

Dash him. I shivered but didn't turn around.

"The empress has invited me to join the royal party for a mountain retreat in Reichenau an der Rax." His lips were next to my ear. "For a secret meeting," he whispered.

I shuddered from the vibrations echoing down my spine.

"Would you like to come along?"

When I spun around in my chair, the top of my head grazed his chin. I jerked backward and nearly fell off my chair.

Fredricks reached out to steady me. "*Sans* Clifford Douglas," he said smiling.

Clifford won't like cooling his heels in Vienna while I go off to the mountains with his best friend. Why would I go to Rax with a killer? To stop him, of course... before he kills again. Anyway, if he'd wanted to dispose of me, he would have done so by now. He enjoyed tormenting me too much to kill me... even if he did slip a mickey into my milk coffee.

"Together, *ma chérie*, we can help stop this tragic war."

"How?" I wished I could believe him. I would like nothing more than to stop this bloody war.

"Come to Rax and I'll show you." With that, he kissed my cheek, turned on his heels, and left the dining room. "*À très bientôt*," his deep voice echoed through the hallway. He poked his head back into the room. "I'll pick you up here this afternoon at one o'clock sharp. Unless you want to join me for luncheon first?"

I sat there dumbfounded. I shook my head. Fredricks had just invited me to join him in the mountains. He said together we could stop the war. We may be on opposite sides, but we had our desire for peace in common. Was he really proposing that we work together? Set aside our differences and work for peace? As much as I despised the blackguard, I had to respect him. He truly believed he was doing the right thing.

Doctor Freud might have attributed Fredricks's murderous streak to his tragic childhood. Maybe the criminal was not beyond redemption. Perhaps it was a matter of healing. After all, the only way to nourish the hope that we could end this bloody war was to maintain faith in the possibility of healing.

Chapter Eighteen

Frau Sacher's Nephew

The summer sun was as hot and oppressive as my mood. Luckily, the brim of my hat shaded my eyes. Otherwise, the glare would be insufferable. I was actually starting to miss dreary old Blighty. A cool gully washer or a chilly peasouper of a day would be jolly welcome.

I took a roundabout route to the butcher shop via the Hofburg Palace. Hopefully the royal party was still there and hadn't yet headed back to Schönbrunn. A guard posted at the entrance pointed me in the direction of a desk where an administrator could help me get a message to the empress. Wandering the foyer, looking for the administrator, I passed Count Czernin, stern-faced and leaving in a bit of a huff. As usual, he didn't seem to notice me—unless that swatting motion was meant for me.

At one end of the cavernous lobby, a little man sat at a big desk. He assured me that he could get a message to Her Majesty. Satisfied he was telling the truth, I left a note for the empress, indicating that I'd stop back by in an hour or so, and if she had the time and inclination, might she see me then? Or leave a message for me indicating when it would be possible to see her again? Yes, it was a rather long-winded message. After all, who was I to call on the empress of Austria-Hungary? Still, I would love the chance to ask her some questions about last night…and find a way to confirm the royal excursion to the mountains.

Now on to Fuchs Butcher Shop and Oswald Fuchs. The working class was more my speed.

Even walking the few blocks back to the butcher shop, I couldn't help but notice that the few couples strolling the boulevard were so well-dressed... and so cosmopolitan. I heard at least seven different languages spoken in as many minutes. Everything so clean and bright. So orderly and just so.

If it weren't for the perspiration dripping from my brow, I'd have thought the city heavenly. At the very least, Vienna was the beating heart of Europe. Too bad they were on the wrong side of this war...*although, truth be told, I'm no longer sure there is a right side.*

I gladly entered through the front door this time, instead of the rat-infested subterranean access. The shop was as clean and sparkling as a doctor's surgery. Indeed, using a giant knife, the butcher was performing an operation on a side of pork with the precision of a surgeon. I kept my gaze on the butcher, trying to avoid the gruesome sight of carcasses hanging all around the shop. At least it offered respite from the blaring sun.

"Herr Fuchs?" I asked.

"*Ja,*" the burly man answered. When he glanced up from his work, I saw the family resemblance. I should have noticed it when we first met. Dark curly hair, dancing brown eyes, and a charming smile. Yet, like his formidable sister, he had a commanding no-nonsense air about him...perhaps because he was wielding a giant meat cleaver.

"Are you any relation to Oscar Fuchs?" I asked.

"No." He scowled at me. "And who are you?"

"I'm Fiona Figg. We met two days ago." I dug in my purse for my notebook. "I'm investigating the mur—er, death, of Miss Elsie Müller. She was the palace nanny. Did you know her?" I was hoping like most Viennese businessmen, he spoke some English, despite that Clifford had resorted to German in their conversation yesterday. I had to find out whether Elsie or the empress was the intended target. If the empress was the real target, then she was still in grave danger, especially since she was about to embark on a trip with Fredricks. All the more reason for me to go along.

"A lady journalist?" He flipped the butcher's knife so its tip stuck into his cutting board and the terrifying instrument stood straight up.

"No, sir," I said, adjusting my collar. *Is it me? Or is it bloody hot in here?*

"You're not a lady policeman," he said, looking me up and down. "Palace sent you?"

When I tried to speak, no words came out. I cleared my throat. Not in the habit of lying—*unless you count espionage*—I merely nodded.

Herr Fuchs narrowed his bushy brows. "I told Oswald not to get involved over there." He shook his head. "The boy won't listen. Never has. Never will. Wants to inherit the business. But doesn't want to put in the work."

I nodded again.

"Kids want everything handed to them these days." He picked up his cleaver and started hacking away. "Thought the army would fix him." He scoffed.

"Might I ask—"

He ignored me and continued his rant. "Came home after a week. Injured. Finger blown off or some nonsense, and that worthless eye." He exhaled a hearty sigh. "Told him he had to save his money to marry a girl like that—"

"Yes, about that—"

"Silly girl got it into her head he was rich. Gold digger. That's what she is." He stopped slicing and stared at me. "He's better off without her."

"You didn't like—"

"Like?" He sneered. "Like. All high and mighty. Looking down on us like we were dirt, even though she thought we had money. Tricked him, she did."

"Tricked?" I asked.

He pointed at me with his knife. "Seduced. She is a *Hure*."

I didn't need a dictionary to get the gist of the word. The tone of his voice said it all. He loathed the girl. *Enough to kill her?* A butcher knife and not a tiny syringe seemed more his style. *But you never know the secrets of man.*

"If you don't mind me asking, where were you last night around eleven?" I held my notebook and pencil ready.

"In bed with my wife."

My cheeks burned.

"Your sister said you approved of the match between Elsie and your son.

175

That it would forge royal connections."

He thwacked the cleaver into the cutting board again. "Don't put your nose where it doesn't belong, or you may get it cut off." *As if his knife throwing wasn't menacing enough...*

"Just one more question." I touched my nose "Do you know who might have wanted the poor girl dead?"

"Look lady, if you ask me one more damned question, I'll throw you out on your ear."

"I see." To say he wasn't forthcoming was an understatement. Maybe I could get more out of his son, Oswald. I touched my ear. But did I dare ask to speak to him? "Is your son working today?"

"Oswald?" He scoffed again. "He's in bed crying his eyes out. *Kleine Schisser.*"

Little sissy. That wasn't a nice way for a father to talk about his grieving son.

"Papa, is someone looking for me?" A young man with a mop of curly reddish-brown hair and puffy dark eyes appeared from the back room. "Did you know my fiancée?" He practically choked on *fiancée.*

His father gave him a stern look. "Pull yourself together, man." Since he said it in English, I can only assume it was for my benefit.

"Yes, I knew Elsie, poor girl." I dropped my notebook back into my handbag. No need to scare the fellow. "I'm so sorry for your loss."

He nodded and wiped his eyes with the backs of his hands.

"Might I buy you a cuppa... a cup of tea to calm your nerves? I'm staying at the hotel up the street." I pointed.

"I'm not much for tea." Oswald's heavy eyes were glazed over.

"Perhaps something stronger then? They have a jolly nice bar....you could tell me about Elsie." It was morning, but as Clifford had shown, here in Vienna, people drank at all hours.

Oswald gave his father a questioning look.

"Oh, all right. Go on then." Herr Fuchs waved the butcher knife in the direction of the door. "You're useless today anyway."

Oswald scooted out from behind the butcher counter and scurried out the door like a boy just released from detention.

"Elsie was a very sweet girl," I said, trying to make conversation as we walked toward the hotel.

"The sweetest." Oswald stared down at his feet as he walked.

"Intelligent too—"

"The smartest."

"And pretty—"

"Beautiful," he said forcefully.

"Yes, the very best of girls." I dare not say anything else.

I got the impression that he'd had to defend Elsie to his father and his aunt too often.

"The very best of girls," he repeated. "We were getting married next month."

"Next month?" I remembered that Elsie said she'd been here two months. "But you'd only known her for a month or two."

"It was love at first sight. Elsie agreed when I'd saved enough money."

"You saved what you earn at the butcher shop? Very wise."

He quickened his pace considerably, and I had to rush to keep up.

"Elsie made money a condition for marriage?" I asked. I was really beginning to wonder about that girl.

"Aunt Anna and father also wanted us to wait. Otherwise, we'd already be..." His voice broke. He stopped and buried his face in the crook of his arm. "If only Aunt Anna would have given her blessing."

So it was his aunt, Frau Sacher, who had prevented him from marrying Elsie? I should have known she was the matriarch of the family. Still, did Frau Sacher have more power over the boy than his own father? Perhaps she was the oldest. She was decidedly the richest. And where there was money, there was power. "Now, now. Let's get you some fortification." I led him inside the hotel and straight to the bar.

After a few sips of brandy and more than a few sniffles, he finally pulled himself together. *Obviously, the Viennese don't abide by the stiff upper lip of the British.*

Once he'd calmed down, I resumed my gentle questioning. "Tell me about

Elsie."

"What is there to say. I loved her." He ran his hand through his hair. "And now she's gone."

"Did she ever ask you for money?" I asked. I hated to pressure him, but something just wasn't right.

Oswald tightened his lips. "I was happy to give her what I could."

Max interrupted us to deliver a note from the palace. I quickly scanned the message:

> *Dearest Mrs. Douglas,*
>
> *I regret that I won't have time to meet you today. Given the events of last night, we are packing for a family retreat to the mountains. We leave this afternoon. Might I be so bold as to ask you to come along as a companion for the children and myself? They took a liking to you. And they love your English Mr. Sherlock Holmes. I feel foolish asking. But I hope by some miracle, you will accept. If so, I will send a carriage for you and your husband. —Zita.*

So Fredricks was telling the truth. I smiled. Now I wouldn't have to go with the beastly man. I could go at the invitation of the empress herself. *Imagine.* The empress of Austria-Hungary was inviting me to join a family trip. Of course, I would go, even if it meant giving English lessons to the children. I would send a response accepting her invitation along with Clifford's regrets... as soon as I finished questioning Oswald.

Glancing up, I saw Max still standing there. *Right.* I took my coin purse from my handbag and offered him a few coins. My fingers brushed against Elsie's hair ribbon. I'd nearly forgotten about the bookmark doubling as hair ribbon. I pulled it out of my purse.

"Where did you get that?" Oswald's face turned the color of curdled milk. He snatched it from my fingers. "I gave that to Elsie."

So, Oswald is the notebook thief. Perhaps he was blackmailing Albert Einstein to afford to get married, ransoming off the notebook. And would that mean he was also the dognapper? "It's lovely. She was wearing it when she… May I ask where you got it?"

His brow wrinkled. "A boy dropped it on the sidewalk." He caressed the ribbon. "When I called out to him, he ran away." Oswald gulped his brandy. "I didn't steal it, if that's what you're getting at."

"Of course not." *Then Oswald is not the notebook thief—or so he says. If Oswald is telling the truth, this other boy is the thief, which explains why the lad ran away.* But why was he hanging around the butcher shop? *Seems like a convenient coincidence.* "Can you describe the boy?"

"Small. Maybe six or seven. Haircut like yours." He pointed at me. *A boy with bobbed hair.* I'd seen a boy with bobbed hair lately. But where?

What children had I seen around the hotel? The cook's two children, a girl and a boy. One of the other guests had three boys. I'd seen them playing chase in the lobby. I'd seen several children enjoying the cook's sugar biscuits in the kitchen. Given my inability to have children, I noticed them unduly, like picking at a wound.

"At first I thought he was a girl." He shook his head. "I didn't really get a good look at him. I was making a delivery, heading around to the back entrance, when he ran out. The ribbon fell out of a book he was carrying. I picked it up and shouted. But he ran. I would have followed him, but I had a cart full of meat to deliver." He drained the last drop from his glass.

"Back entrance?"

"Of the Sacher Hotel."

"So the boy was coming out of the hotel?" Aha. Maybe the boy had just stolen the notebook and was on the run.

He nodded.

"When was this?"

"Two days before Elsie died." Tears welled in his eyes. "She was so pleased with the ribbon that she wrapped it in her hair."

That matched up with when Mrs. Einstein discovered the missing notebook.

"Do you know someone called Oscar Fuchs?" I asked. Yes, I'd already asked him. But it didn't hurt to try again.

"Oscar?" He wiped his eyes with the backs of his hands. "I told you before,

I've never heard of him."

If this Oscar Fuchs was a relation, everyone denied it. And if Oswald really was Oscar, he was jolly good at hiding it. He didn't flinch when I mentioned the name. *No. Oscar Fuchs the British agent is proving deuced elusive.*

I ordered a second brandy for Oswald and an *Einspanner* for myself. *I could use a sweet, caffeinated pick me up. Perhaps a piece of Sacher Torte to go with it? That reminds me.* I ventured a little fib. "Elsie told me you brought her sweets and treats."

"She loved chocolate." He smiled wistfully.

"And Sacher Torte from the hotel?"

"Yes." In a daze, he stared down at his hands.

"Does your aunt know?"

He jerked his head as if suddenly waking from a stupor. "My aunt gave it to me. And bonbons too. I didn't steal them if that's what you're suggesting." *The lad doth protest too much.*

I patted his hand to reassure him. "You were telling me how you'd saved enough to get married."

"Thirty thousand kroner." He nodded.

"And your aunt gave her blessing—"

"Blessing," he burst out. "Blessing!" He pounded the bar with his fist. "She practically made me perform the seven feats of Hercules before she'd allow us to set the date."

Seven feats of Hercules. The boy was well-read. I thought of Fredricks and the statute of Omphale at the palace. I wondered if acting as Omphale's sex slave counted as one of the seven feats.

"It's her fault we aren't already married." His face was red.

"You're too young to be a widower." Just like all the war widows... too young to know such sorrow. I thought of the poor injured maid. She was a war widow just trying to make ends meet by delivering clandestine messages. "Did you push that poor woman in front of the trolley to distract us from the ransom pickup?" *Why keep beating around the bushes.*

"I didn't know she'd be hit by the trolley." Oswald paled. "I didn't mean to hurt anyone."

"You didn't mean to, but you did." Sigh. "Our brains continue to develop from the time we are born until we fall in love," I said under my breath.

The pebbles. He must have strewn them on the street, knowing the poor maid passed by there every day on her way to work. "You put the pebbles on the street?"

He stared down at his hands, tears streaming down his face.

Sacher Torte, Mozart Bonbons, thirty thousand kroner, a grudge against his aunt. Yes. I had found our dognapper.

Chapter Nineteen

Villa Wartholz

Thanks to the carriage the palace had sent for me, I arrived early to the railway station. The *Hofpavillon* was on the grounds of Schönbrunn Palace. And according to my guidebook, it had been built by Emperor Franz Joseph not long before he was assassinated. With its ornately trimmed dome and whitewashed exterior, the pavilion looked like an adorable wedding cake. *Must be nice to have your own private railway station.*

I dropped my case on the platform. It was deuced heavy. Not knowing what to expect from a getaway in the mountains with the royal family, I packed everything from my best evening gown to a practical split skirt and boots for hiking—nearly every piece of clothing I'd brought to Austria. My stomach growled as I paced back and forth in front of the pavilion, waiting for the royal party. Blimey. I realized I'd barely eaten all day. No wonder I was running on fumes. I should have accepted Fredricks's lunch invitation.

Poor Clifford must have wondered where I'd gone. I'd slid a note under the adjoining door before I left. By some miracle, I'd managed to avoid him all morning. Poor chap would have to amuse himself with Frau Sacher and the dogs. Of course, he could continue the murder investigation. I cringed, remembering his deerstalker cap and Inverness cape. *I'm sure we'll both have stories to tell upon our reunion.*

I stopped pacing and sat on the edge of my suitcase. Even in the shade of the pavilion, it was too warm for me. I fanned myself with my clutch, which was jolly worthless.

Next time I travel to Austria in August, I must remember to bring a proper fan. "Fiona, *ma chérie.*"

Of course, I knew that voice. I craned my neck to see him. The Great White Hunter strode up the platform in his jodhpurs, black knee boots, and open-collared white shirt, carrying his riding stick in one hand and a small leather case in the other. The muscular Ivan followed behind him carrying a large trunk as if it were a handbag.

How on earth did Fredricks pull off that outfit? Pull it off he did. I had to admit, he was almost handsome in his hunting kit with his thick black curls and long lashes. I could see how *some* women found him attractive.

"Mr. Fredricks." I stood up.

"Call me Apollo," he said, kissing my cheek.

I scoffed. Even if we were bosom friends, I would never call him Apollo. *Another appellation he had given himself, the arrogant cad.*

"After all we've been through, I think we can drop the formality." He set his case down next to mine. "Don't you?"

"Apparently not."

"Your indignation is adorable." He laughed and then pointed to my oversized suitcase. "What have you got in there? Dr. Vogel? Harold the bellboy? Or Sister Margaret?"

I tightened my lips. He was as bad as Captain Hall, mocking my disguises.

"Or perhaps someone even more alluring?" He raised his eyebrows.

I glared at him. He didn't even seem bothered that I'd stood him up at the hotel. Who knew he'd been planning to drive us to this railway station?

"Cheer up." He chuckled. "The sun is glorious. And we're traveling in luxury to one of the most beautiful spots in the Alps. What more could you want?"

"To be left alone." I knew I should take any opportunity to talk to him, see if I could garner any information that could be useful to the War Office, but the man bothered me too much to be practical. I removed a hanky from my skirt pocket and dapped my forehead.

"I bet you wouldn't say that to your daredevil Lieutenant Somersby…if he's still alive."

"Has something happened to Archie?" I blurted out, and then felt my cheeks flush. I wished I'd restrained myself. What was Archie Somersby to me? I'd probably never see him again even if he was still alive. A pang stung my heart. *Calm down, old girl. He's just having you on.*

"Archie, is it?" He smirked. "Awfully informal, now aren't we Miss Figg? Or should I say, Mrs. Douglas?"

Insufferable man. Why did he always have to wind me up?

"Sorry we're late." The empress was coming toward us, her entourage in tow. An elderly woman carried the baby. A ruddy footman with a slight limp held the hand of the toddler. And a porter pushed a trolly laden with luggage.

Young Otto ran up to me. "Tell me about your friend Mr. Holmes," he said in a small but excited voice.

"Otto," his mother said. "Be a good boy and help the steward with the luggage." She winked at me. "Watch out for him, will you?" she said to the steward, obviously just trying to get the boy out of her hair. *Still, I doubt English princes were ever asked to help the steward with luggage.*

"Yes, Mamma," the boy said and trotted off with the steward.

"I'm so glad you came," the empress said. "Both of you."

"Your Majesty." Fredricks clicked his heels and gave a little bow. "At your service, as always."

"Where is Mr. Douglas?" the empress asked.

"Clifford isn't feeling well."

"He does have a delicate constitution." Fredricks smirked.

I scowled at him and then turned to the empress and made my best attempt at a proper curtsy. "Thank you for inviting me."

"Totally selfish on my part," she said. "Otto wants to practice his English with a *lady friend* of Sherlock Holmes." A twinkle enlivened her pretty dark eyes. "He insisted we invite you. And with his nanny gone…" Behind her smile, I sensed trepidation. Her hand trembled as she fanned herself with a lovely pearl-inset fan. "After the tragedy, my little loves need some

184

consolation."

Two railway cars pulled by a steam engine screeched to a stop on the tracks in front of the platform. The royals had their own private steam engine. *Why am I surprised?*

"Shall we?" The empress gestured toward the vestibule.

Ivan loaded Fredricks's trunk, saluted his master, and then took off at a trot.

"He's bringing the car to Rax," Fredricks said. "I prefer to accompany you ladies."

"Isn't His Majesty joining us?" I asked the empress.

"He went ahead last night to meet my brothers," the empress whispered in French. *Ah, the joys of hearing a language I fully understand.*

So, the emperor left his own birthday party to travel to Rax. The trip was not a spontaneous reaction to Elsie's death.

"They have important business...." Her voice broke off. *Why is she whispering and why is she speaking French?* Jolly odd behavior.

I glanced at Fredricks, who gave me a knowing smile. I knew that this trip was more than a retreat from death and the city. But what was it really? What was I walking into?

With its gilt chandeliers and burgundy satin divans, the royal railway car was as ostentatious as the palace. The children and servants occupied one car and the empress, Fredricks, and I the other.

After our bags were loaded and we were settled, the footman delivered a pitcher of water and a tray of coffees in gold-rimmed demitasse cups on small saucers accompanied by tiny silver spoons. He offered sugar but no milk.

I heaped four demitasse spoonfuls into the black sludge, hoping that would make it drinkable. I'd just gotten used to Viennese coffee with plenty of warm milk. But I'd never tried this new Italian style they called "espresso."

The railway car jostled into motion, and I watched out the window as the pavilion receded into the horizon.

"I just can't stop thinking about that poor girl." Empress Zita put her hand to her forehead. "It's my fault she died."

"Don't blame yourself," I said. "How could you know she would be murdered?" It occurred to me that she had known someone might try to kill her, and that's why she had Elsie go to the ball in her place. "You didn't poison her." *I wonder if Elsie knew the risk.* "Do you know who might have wanted her—"

"No one." The empress shook her head. "She'd only been with us for a couple of months. And she kept very much to herself. She was a fine girl."

"She got along well with the rest of the staff?" I asked.

"Perfectly well."

"Had she... stood in for you before?"

"Thank God it wasn't you, Your Majesty." Fredricks interrupted. His tone seemed a tad exaggerated. Like everything about him.

"Yes, I suppose..." The empress turned her face toward the window and stared out as if looking into a void.

Far from void, the farther we got away from the city, the more verdant and rugged the landscape became.

"Who else will be in Rax?" I asked, changing the subject from the gruesome murder.

The empress looked startled. "Sixtus and Xavier."

"Your brothers?" I hesitantly took a sip from the demitasse and quickly regretted it. Even with three spoonfuls of sugar, it was utterly undrinkable.

"Two of ten brothers."

"Ten brothers," I blurted out. *Any girl with ten brothers has to be tough.*

"The two princes are fighting with the Belgian army against Austria," Fredricks added. "And Princes Elias, Felix, and René are fighting for Austria, isn't that right, Your Majesty?"

"Yes, my brothers are on opposite sides." She wrung her hands. "The belligerents have agreed to keep them out of skirmishes at the borders lest they be forced to shoot each other."

"How thoughtful," I said.

"Italy, the country of your birth, is also at war with Austria," Fredricks said. "It must be very difficult for you. Your family fighting on opposite sides."

186

"Yes, it vexes me considerably. At least my brothers will be kept from the Italian front," the empress said thoughtfully. "I haven't seen Sixtus and Xavier since their last visit to Villa Wartholz over a year ago."

I couldn't imagine the battle of loyalties raging in Zita's heart. How could she sleep knowing that her own husband could give orders resulting in her brothers' deaths? She must be torn apart by this bloody war. Yet she bore it as well as any Englishwoman. Stiff upper lip and all that rot.

"Charles and I met at Villa Wartholz," the empress said wistfully. "We were just children." She smiled. "I think we're as much in love with the place as we are with each other."

"Villa Wartholz is your palace in Rax?" Come to think of it, I had no idea where we were going.

"It's a very special place." The empress folded her hands in her lap. "I hope we can find peace there."

* * *

Villa Wartholz was indeed a special place. I couldn't help but let out a little gasp as our carriage made its way around a lovely man-made lake. We pulled up in front of a pink-and-white castle, complete with a bell tower and several other towers with steeply sloping roofs that looked like pointed hats sitting on regal heads.

"I'm eager to explore the grounds again," Fredricks said. "Fancy a stroll before tea, Miss... Mrs. Douglas?"

"That would be lovely." I took his arm. *Keep your friends close and your enemies closer,* as my father would say.

The grounds were lush and green but not artificially manicured like English gardens. A thick assortment of conifers and evergreens surrounded the lake and the palace. In the distance, rugged mountains blushed violet in the afternoon haze. "Marvelous." Smitten, I clapped my hands together. "Breathtaking."

"It is wonderful, isn't it?" The empress smiled. As she walked across the driveway toward the house, she looked as if the weight of the world had been lifted off her narrow shoulders. Her little wirehaired terrier ran out to greet her. The dog must have come out early with the emperor.

I thought of Frau Sacher's bulldogs. She'd recovered her puppies but not her money. *When I get back to Vienna, I'm going to expose the dognapper. How would I break it to Frau Sacher that her own nephew was the culprit?*

One of the staff at the villa showed me to my room. Every detail was absolutely perfect. From the linen towels with green embroidered stags, to the rustic carved wooden headboard. I even had my own electric teapot and the cutest little teacups with wildlife portraits painted on them. *Golly.* The private washroom was as roomy as the sleeping chamber and sported a clawfoot tub big enough for two. Not that I'd ever allow anyone else in the bath with me.

My room was on the top floor, up in the pitched eves, which made it extra cozy, like my own little nest in the treetops. I had a private balcony with a spectacular view down the valley.

The whole place had the feel of an alpine Swiss chalet. *Of course, I've never been to Switzerland, but in my imagination, this is how it looks.* Or a cross between a chalet and a hunting lodge, surrounded by forest and fauna. *I suppose the royal family do use it for hunting.* The dry pine scent was heavenly. I was beginning to see why people enjoyed getting out of the city. Fresh air, unsullied by coal smoke, was such a delight.

Perhaps that's why the Great White Hunter knew the grounds so well. He'd probably killed as many animals in those woods as Noah had gathered on the ark.

I was heading out to find Fredricks and explore the gorgeous grounds when little Otto caught up to me. He insisted that I read "the latest Sherlock Holmes story" from *The Strand Magazine.* "You can tutor me in English," he said in perfect English.

Looking around for Fredricks, I tried to demur, but Otto stuck to me like a deer tick. I couldn't shake the little fellow. He held open the magazine to the story he wanted me to read.

Turns out, the story, "The Prisoner's Defense," came out over a year ago. I remember buying it at the newsstand on my way to Charing Cross Hospital.

I read it to the injured soldiers. So many times, in fact, I knew it by heart. If I set my mind to it, I could conjure the pages before my mind's eye without even opening the magazine. "You know, Otto, it's not actually a Sherlock Holmes story."

"It is!"

"It's Arthur Conan Doyle, but not Sherlock Holmes."

He knitted his little brow. "Who?"

"The author of the story is Arthur Conan Doyle. It's a crime story, but not Sherlock Holmes."

"Can we read it anyway?"

"Of course."

Keeping an eye out for Fredricks, I allowed Otto to take my hand. He led me across the lawn and down to the lake. There we sat on a bench and began to read aloud. After recent events, the story struck a little too close to home.

In the story, Captain John Fowler was accused of murdering his beloved Miss Ena Gamier—the nanny and French teacher to three children. He discovered she was a spy for the Germans about to deliver secret information that could change the course of the war. But the captain could not defend himself at his trial without divulging the military secret. So, he allowed the jury to think it was a crime of passion. After killing his lover, he took the sentence and went to prison rather than reveal the military secret.

When I finished reading, Otto looked at me thoughtfully. "Like Count Czernin and Elsie."

"Count Czernin?" *My sainted aunt.* Was Otto suggesting that Count Czernin, his father's foreign minister, murdered Elsie? "What do you mean?"

"Elsie came to teach us French just like the lady in the story." He pointed at an illustration of Captain Fowler. "And he's a soldier like Count Czernin."

"Were Elsie and Count Czernin... *friends?*" I asked tentatively. Of course, I knew the answer... they were more than friends. But I wanted to see what else the boy knew. Did Elsie and the count merely look like the pictures in the magazine to the mind of this little boy? Or was there something more sinister linking this story of love, betrayal, and murder to the nanny and his father's minister?

"Oh yes," he said. "They played games together."

"What sort of games?" I was almost afraid to ask.

"She sat on his lap, and he fed her sweets." He smiled up at me innocently.

The nanny sat on the count's lap in front of the children? *Crikey. What would the count's wife think?* I thought of poor long-suffering Mrs. Einstein and her philandering husband. Seems we all had one. Not that Elsie was much better, apparently, cheating on Oswald.

Perhaps Elsie threatened to expose the count's little games to his wife. Blackmail was certainly motive enough for murder.

Chapter Twenty

The Sixtus Proposal

S porting nothing but my smalls, I stood in front of the open suitcase. *What in the world does one wear to a royal tea at an Alpine palace? Do they dress for tea?*

To be safe, I put on my second-best gown, a robin's-egg blue crepe number with black lace trim, and a string of pearls. I topped off the ensemble with my favorite ostrich plume hat and a pair of lace gloves. I changed out of my oxfords into my new evening slippers.

I'd worn them to the ball, and I was eager to wear them again. The gorgeous camel Mary Janes had tiny beads sprinkled on four buttoned straps across the vamp and a flared Louis heel. My reflection in the looking glass gave me a nod of approval, and off I went.

After picking my way down four flights of stairs, muscles tense, I wasn't quite so fond of my new shoes. They pinched. And their soles were deuced slick.

Relieved I'd made it to the bottom without breaking my neck, I let out an audible sigh of relief.

"Are you quite well?" Fredricks hadn't dressed for tea. He was still wearing his hunting outfit. Then again, he was always wearing that absurd getup. At least, I hoped he was underdressed because it was too late for me to change.

"Of course I am. Why do you ask?" I lifted the hem of my gown an inch off the floor so as not to tread on it.

"May I escort you into the sitting room?" he asked with a slight bow.

"That would be lovely." I forced a smile.

"Apologies for my clothes," he said, taking my elbow. "I've just come from a stroll around the grounds. They have the most magnificent game in this part of Austria. Red stags, alpine ibex, mouflon ram, chamois, capercaillie—"

"And you plan to kill one of each, no doubt," I huffed.

"Just a few black grouse if our hosts fancy an early morning hunt."

"The Black Panther. Always ready to pounce."

"How well you know me." He led me through the foyer and into the dining room.

We were the last to arrive. Everyone else in the royal party was already seated on divans and upholstered chairs around a low table. *Golly. Did I get the time wrong?* When they all stood up to bid us welcome and make introductions, I saw it was not only the time I'd gotten wrong.

They all looked as if they'd just come from a hunt or a hike through the woods. I was the only one all spammed up. Face on fire with embarrassment, I apologized for being late and overdressed and took my seat. I glanced at Fredricks. He grinned at me, clearly amused.

The informal tea was spread out on a side table, buffet style, and consisted of various cold cuts and cheeses, along with a hearty brown bread. Thankfully, Fredricks delivered a plate for me, so I didn't have to stand up and show off my finery.

Staring down at my lap, out of the corner of my eye, I saw a footman fill my glass with claret from a decanter. I slid the glass off the table and took quick sips to avoid having to make conversation. I wanted to run back up the stairs and throw myself on the bed like a jilted schoolgirl.

When I got over my chagrin, I realized that the party was speaking in French and not German. *Hallelujah.* They were speaking their mother tongue. Finally, a language I could fully understand.

I lifted my gaze just enough to glance around the room. If I hadn't been so mortified, I might have remembered the introductions. Luckily, it was a small party.

The emperor and empress were seated at opposite sides of the circle. The rest of the party consisted of me, Fredricks, and Zita's two brothers, Sixtus and Xavier. *But which was which?*

One was a rather nice-looking chap with close-set eyes, slicked-back hair, full lips, a chevron mustache, and soft eyes like his sister's. The other had a thin face, thick black brows, and a piercing gaze that made him look a bit mad. The way he deferred to his brother made me think he must be Xavier, the younger of the two. So, the attractive one must be Sixtus, the oldest.

"What can we do about Czernin?" the older brother asked in a hushed tone.

"I can handle Czernin," the emperor said.

What does he mean "handle Czernin"? Does the emperor know about Czernin's affair with Elsie? Does he suspect Czernin killed the girl? I nibbled on a corner of buttered bread and strained to hear what they were saying.

"The restoration to France of Alsace-Lorraine is critical," Sixtus said. "Without it, Clemenceau will never agree."

"Impossible!" The emperor said. "Anyway, how do you know Clemenceau will succeed in taking over France?"

Clemenceau? The newspaperman who published Émile Zola's letter *"J'Accuse...!"*? As I recalled, he defended Alfred Dreyfus against the anti-Semitism that was responsible for getting him convicted of treason. Clemenceau was a powerful man in France, but what did he have to do with the emperor and his brothers-in-law?

"He is poised to become the next prime minister," Sixtus said.

"I have it on good authority that he will," Fredricks said. "But we also have to please the Kaiser."

Really? How does he know that? Politics was never my strong suit. I thought of something my father said. *We hang the petty thieves and appoint the great ones to public office.* Whatever else it was about, this bloody war was about territory—protecting the stolen loot from the last war and stealing more.

"And Clemenceau insists on the return of Alsace—" Xavier said.

"Not going to happen. Germany will never agree." Fredricks took a bite of his sandwich.

"And I could never sell it to the people," the emperor said. "I'm in a precarious position here. Austria is rife with factions who want to depose me. I'm caught between a rock and a hard place."

"We must have an open mind," Zita said. "After all, world peace hangs in the balance. France has never forgiven Germany for taking Alsace in the last war. And the Germans still hold a grudge against the French for Napoleon. Perhaps they each can find a way to compromise. And if the people realize that peace requires compromise, they might go along."

"I suppose you are right." The emperor wiped his mustache with his serviette. "As always."

More than a family reunion, this tea was a political coup.

What is happening here? I kept my mouth shut and my ears open. I didn't understand all the political talk. In fact, truth be told, I never understood why we were at war in the first place. Zita made it sound like the war was the consequence of old grudges. Perhaps it was.

In any case, I had to commit to memory every word that was said so I could report it to the War Office. I had lucked into the perfect situation for espionage. Finally, something to impress Captain Hall. He would be keen on hearing about this meeting between the emperor of Austria-Hungary and two Belgian officers.

Were Sixtus and Xavier representatives of the French government? And why was Fredricks here? *More to the point, why am I here?*

As if reading my mind, Fredricks leaned over and whispered in my ear. "What would the British brass think of the Sixtus proposal?"

The Sixtus proposal? I shrugged. *What in blazes is the Sixtus proposal?*

"You are going to report back to your commanders, *n'est-ce pas?*" Fredricks asked.

I furrowed my brows. *Did he invite me along as a witness to some sort of political negotiation?* At least if he needed me to report back to headquarters, he wasn't planning on doing away with me any time soon. *Where is Clifford when I may need to swap a poisonous drink?*

"And the restoration of Belgian independence," Sixtus said. "Germany must give up Belgium."

I knew that Belgium and France were allies and that Sixtus and Xavier were fighting for the Belgian army. It was deuced confusing. The brothers were born in Italy, but were fighting in the Belgium army, and consider themselves French, and therefore allies of England. It was no wonder the people of Austria, not to mention the German Kaiser, didn't trust the empress.

"And what will France give up?" The emperor asked.

"We need a compromise solution," Fredricks said. "Both sides have to give up something or we will never achieve our goal of peace."

I drained my glass of wine. *Blimey.* The realization hit me like the blade of a guillotine. *They're secretly negotiating terms to end the war.*

* * *

After lunch, I dashed back to my room to change out of my ridiculous clothes. Sitting at my dressing table, I made a few notes about what I'd overheard at lunch. *How can I get word to the War Office from the middle of the mountains? And how can I find out more about what this Alpine family reunion is really about?* Perhaps there is a telephone about that I can use to call Alice Dubois.

But what exactly would I tell her? I wished I'd paid more attention in history class back at North London Collegiate School. Then I might understand what was going on here.

I traded my finery for some sturdy boots, a split skirt, a plain cotton blouse, and a wide-brimmed straw boater. Neither a hunter nor a hiker, at least now I wouldn't stand out like a misfiled folder.

So far, I'd gotten more out of little Otto than the rest of the household. *Does he know what's up?* Perhaps I should seek him out and bribe him with more Conan Doyle stories. *What am I thinking? He's a little boy for heaven's sake.*

I shuddered to think of what those little eyes had seen in that nursery. Elsie and Count Czernin should be ashamed of themselves. Then again, adultery in itself wasn't a capital offense. I cringed. The image of my own Andrew in the arms of his secretary came flooding back.

195

Oh, Andrew. How could you? Why did you have to be unfaithful? Why did you have to die? I shook the macabre thoughts from my mind.

I stared out the window into the gardens below. The deep blue of the sky was a tonic for my soul, and the rugged mountains made my heart sing. I may not be an outdoorsman, but I could appreciate a gorgeous view...from the comfort of a nice indoor vantage.

Wait. Where is he going? Fredricks was crossing the lawn toward the lake. If I hurried, I might be able to catch him up, or at least follow him and see where he was going. Throwing on my hat, I dashed out of my room and down the stairs.

The air outside was fresh. And while it wasn't exactly cool, it was pleasant, unlike in the city. I followed the path I'd seen Fredricks take toward the lake. Drat. He was nowhere to be seen. What was he up to? Where was the empress? I hoped she was safely back in the palace.

I sat down on a bench by the lake wondering what to do next. Should I head out on my own into the forest in search of Fredricks? Or wait here until he came back? Fredricks had known the emperor was planning secret peace talks. And he'd invited me here to report back to the War Office. He wanted the British brass to know that Austria would use its power to push France and Germany to end the war. Was that how I could help the peace process? By reporting what I'd heard here?

Watching a bonded pair of mallard ducks dabbling in the lake, I lost track of time. The male's gray body was sandwiched between an iridescent green head with a bright-yellow bill and a blunt black rear. When it spread its wings, a blue speculum appeared, its secret lure. It was completely devoted to its smaller, plainer mate. *What men could learn from these simple creatures....* Again, I thought of poor Mrs. Einstein, protecting her unfaithful husband's reputation in exchange for money to support their children.

"May I join you?" Dressed in drab country day clothes, the empress stood holding a book.

"Of course." I scooted to one end of the bench. I was relieved to see her... still alive. I still didn't know if she was Fredricks's target, but I wouldn't put anything past that man.

"I apologize for the conversation at luncheon." She took a seat. "You must have found it very boring."

"Not at all." *In fact, I found it deuced interesting.*

"The emperor and I want peace more than anything." She troubled the corner of her book. "My brothers have agreed to help bring it about."

"Admirable," I said.

"As long as the Germans don't find out." She looked at me with worry in her eyes. "We could be tried for treason. Holding secret peace talks with our enemies."

"But they are your brothers. Certainly—"

"Yes, and officers in the Belgian army and agents of the French government." She stared down at the book in her lap.

I wondered where the British fit in and why they weren't at the secret peace talks. With over twenty siblings spread across the monarchies of Europe, surely one must belong to the British royal family. *Dare I ask?* "I'm sure the British would be eager for peace too."

"Do you think so?" she asked hopefully. "We will find out this evening."

"How?" *What happens this evening?*

"Representatives from Britain and America will be joining us."

"I see." But I didn't see. If someone from the government was joining the party, why was Fredricks so eager for me to report back to the War Office?

"I trust you'll keep our secret." It was more of a command than a question. "Fredricks assures us you are trustworthy. And if he trusts you, so do I. It's funny. He told me just the other day that he's engaged to a woman named Fiona."

I'd nearly forgotten that lie he'd told at lunch when I was dressed as Charlie Chaplin, trying to get a rile out of me. "It's a popular name."

She nodded. So Fredricks really was a good friend of the family. He was nothing if not an expert manipulator. "And how do you know Mr. Fredricks?" I knew the answer from that lunch, but I wanted an opening.

"He's an old friend of my husband and he's been very good to me...to us."

"And you trust him?"

"What an odd question." She cocked her head and gave me a queer look.

"I trust him with my life."

Either Fredricks has some redeeming qualities or Empress Zita is not a very good judge of character. Since I'd started into dangerous territory, why not continue?

"Do you think perhaps the poison that killed Elsie might have been meant for you?" I asked tentatively.

"I'm sure it was." Her lashes fluttered. "That's why we decided to leave the city. I feel much safer out here."

Out here with the suspected murderer in tow? "Who would want to...to... want you gone?" I shifted uneasily on the bench.

She laughed. "Any number of people. The Germans think I'm a spy for the French. The French think I'm a traitor. The Austrians think I'm suspicious because I'm a foreigner. The list goes on."

"It must be difficult fearing for your life all the time," I said more to myself than to her.

Her countenance turned serious. "Less difficult than killing and being killed on the battlefield."

I suppose she has a point.

The empress sat staring out over the lake. After a few seconds, she looked over at me. "I should oversee preparations for dinner. Do you mind reading to Otto for a while? He's been asking for you."

We'd just had lunch and already she was thinking about dinner. *Golly. That must be what it's like to be a mother.* "I'd love to." Maybe I could get more information out of the little tike.

Watching her walk away, her skirts flowing in the breeze, I got the impression that she was the gale-force behind these peace talks.

* * *

Not one to make the same mistake twice, I didn't change into my best gown—or even my second-best. Obviously, the rules of dress in the country palace were different from those in the city palace. *Even royals need to relax sometimes.*

Instead, I chose a simple cotton frock, sprinkled with pretty little yellow roses, sporting a matching wide belt, a sailor's collar, and oversized pockets. I admired my new beaded Mary Janes but passed over them for my sensible oxfords. *Now what hat should I wear?* I didn't own a yellow hat. It wasn't really my color. Yellow was fine for a tiny rose here or there, but not a head covering. Especially not with auburn hair... even if it was someone else's hair.

I had only three hats with me. The ostrich plume I'd worn to luncheon, my straw boater, and a close-fitting lilac cloche. Obviously, the first two wouldn't do. I tugged the cloche down over my bobbed wig. A glance in the mirror convinced me to add a dab of rouge, a smudge of kohl, and a hint of lipstick. *Much better...better being a relative term.*

Speaking of relative. While we were reading Sherlock Holmes a couple of hours ago, little Otto told me about Elsie's brother Kurt. According to Otto, they played a game where Kurt was a ghost and no one else could see him except for Elsie and the children. Kurt was especially invisible to Count Czernin, who was not to know about his existence under any circumstances.

Amazing what people say in front of children. The little tikes ken more than we know.

Even more interesting than his status as a ghost was Kurt's fraternity with Mr. Holmes, hailing as he did from the same country. Otto once slipped up and told his father, who apparently found his story so compelling that he took it upon himself to summon the apparition. After that, Kurt came around more often, but always through a secret passageway in the palace.

A knock on the door made me smear my lipstick. *Dash it.* I tidied up my face with a hanky and then opened the door.

Fredrick Fredricks stood in all his splendor, wearing a black evening suit, starched white collar, silk shirt, waistcoat, and black spats. His mustache was waxed into two perfect curls. Now he'd be the one all spammed up. Served him right, arrogant rake.

He looked me up and down and smiled. "Lovely as always, *ma chérie.*" He held out his elbow and I took it. *Why does he always look like he's about to burst out laughing?* Either he found my company jolly amusing, or he was a complete scoundrel.

We arrived to find the dining room entirely transformed from luncheon. The table was laid with delicate linens, fine china, and silver cutlery. And flickering candlelight made the pretty scene even more romantic.

We were the first to arrive, which was all a bit awkward. I glanced around the charming room. *What is the appropriate thing to do when one arrives before one's hosts?* As usual, Fredricks was at ease and was making small talk with one of the footmen. I stood fiddling with the latch on my clutch purse.

Finally, the footman suggested we take a seat. He led us to the same seats we'd had at luncheon... except the table was set for more diners. Perhaps the government men the empress had mentioned to me earlier.

"Would you care for a cocktail before dinner, ma'am?" the footman asked.

Not being much of a drinker, the first cocktail that popped into my head was one of Andrew's favorites. "Cream gin fizz, please."

Fredricks ordered a Black Cat martini.

Figures. Even his drink order is cheeky.

"I think you'll enjoy this evening," Fredricks said with a smirk.

"And why is that?"

"I have a surprise for you." His eyes lit up.

"Oh dear." I'd suffered through too many of his surprises in the past. *The Black Panther insignia stamped into the wax from a poisoned bottle of spirits. Or his miraculous recovery from paralysis and theft of my nun's costume. And then the invitation to join him in Vienna for the royal ball.* The man was plummy with surprises. Surprises that left me holding the wrong end of the stick.

"You are going to love it," he said with a sly tone. "I promise."

"Your promise is as empty as a quill."

The footman reappeared with two cocktails on a tray. As soon as he set one in front of me, I snatched it up and took a gulp. *Utterly foul.* Cream gin hit the tongue like a heavy vanilla flower concealing a wasp. *I didn't see why Andrew liked this foul swill.*

"If I'm a quill, you're my ink," Fredricks said with that rakish glint in his eyes.

Unable to think of a quick-witted reply, I ignored him and forced another drink of the foul cocktail.

The royal party began filing into the dining room, starting with the emperor and empress. *Good grief.* The emperor wore full military regalia. And Empress Zita's bejeweled gown must have been a national treasure.

I wanted to slide under the table.

Sixtus and Xavier followed, bedecked in fine black evening suits. *Dash it.* I looked like a fishmonger by comparison. No wonder Fredricks laughed at me earlier. *Why didn't the dirty dog warn me?* Completely mortified, I sank deeper in my chair.

Behind the brothers, a tall handsome figure appeared in the doorway.

Oh, my sainted aunt. What's he doing here? And he's with a woman.

"Surprised?" Fredricks asked.

My cheeks caught fire. I reached for my cream gin and drained the glass. The fire spread to my throat.

The man smiled as he approached me. With that wavy chestnut lock tumbling down his forehead and those dancing green eyes, he was even more beautiful than I'd remembered.

"Miss Figg. Good to see you again." He bent down and kissed my cheek. "Where's your mustache?" he whispered in my ear.

The warmth of his breath on my neck sent shivers up my spine.

"Archie," I gasped. It's true. The last time I'd seen him, I'd been wearing a mustache.

Chapter Twenty-One

Vanilla Hiccups

Throughout the dinner, whenever I glanced at Lieutenant Archie Somersby, he was staring at me from the other end of the table. *Bloody unnerving.* Either Archie was more important to the War Office than I'd imagined. Or something was amiss.

Fredricks had warned me that Archie was a double agent. Could he be Fredricks's target? There was certainly no love lost between them. Then again, if Archie was a double agent, that meant he and Fredricks were on the same side. I didn't know who to believe. Espionage was a deuced unsettling business.

I pretended to eat, but I'd quite lost my appetite. I could barely swallow a morsel. In fact, cream gin fizz turned out to be the only appealing part of the meal. The footman had just delivered my third when Fredricks leaned closer... too close.

"Pace yourself, *ma chérie*," he whispered. "The evening is about to get interesting."

Archie was seated at the other end of the table, next to Sixtus. I was dying to talk to him. And I was keen to find out what they were discussing. *Is Archie the British government representative? He must be. Why else would he be here?* But who was the woman?

I knew Archie worked for the intelligence service. But I never really knew what he did. Of course, I would never have guessed he was a spy when I met him last winter at Charing Cross Hospital, where he had been recovering from a war injury. Even then, he had an air of mystery mixed with playfulness that I found irresistible.

If Fredricks was telling the truth, and Lieutenant Archie Somersby was really a double agent working for the Germans, then maybe he was here as a representative for the Kaiser. I must keep my eyes and ears open.

After everyone had finished the main course, the tenor of the party changed as suddenly as a summer thunderstorm overtakes a pleasant afternoon.

Fredricks stood up and started making introductions.

Fredricks! Why is he suddenly in charge?

I already knew everyone except the woman with Archie.

When it was her turn, Fredricks introduced her as "My good friend, Miss Jane Addams from America."

Good heavens. Jane Addams. The woman I'd walked across Vienna trying to find. *Gracious me.* That meant that everyone on Fredricks's list was here at Villa Wartholz. The list I'd found in his pocket was a list of participants in these clandestine peace talks.

Fredricks said my name and I stood up. *Why on earth, I don't know.* I felt like a schoolgirl caught out by the headmaster for not doing her homework.

I must have looked faint. Archie dashed over and held out my chair for me. "Why don't you sit back down?"

I didn't need to be convinced. My head was spinning.

As gracefully as I could muster, I slid onto the chair. Holding on to the seat with both hands, I steadied myself. *Get a grip, Fiona.*

Turns out, Jane Addams was the leader of the Women's Peace Party, which counseled the American President, Woodrow Wilson not to enter the war.

Bloody good thing they did. As frivolous as they are, the Allies need the bloody doughboys. I felt like giving her a piece of my mind. If only the room would stop tilting.

Dressed in a dowdy navy suit, Jane Addams was matronly, no-nonsense, and spoke her mind. She had a stern but kindly demeanor and talked like a book. Jolly impressive really.

"A lack of imagination is responsible for our inability to weigh the burdens of others," Jane Addams said. "The good we secure for ourselves is precarious and fleeting until it is guaranteed for all."

A vanilla hiccup ambushed me. I held my handkerchief to my mouth until the attack subsided. Fredricks and Archie exchanged glances. Two cats squaring off. If Fredricks was the Black Panther, Archie was a white tiger.

Yes, I suppose I am more of a cat person than a dog person. Not like Frau Sacher, a commanding presence. Dogs need a firm hand.

The footman brought me a fourth cream gin... or was it a fifth? *Am I seeing double?* They were jolly tasty. *But why do I feel like I'm on a sailing ship?* The room was ebbing and flowing, the conversation carried along by a tide of good cheer.

By the cheese course, the party had split into two. The emperor and his brothers-in-law at one end of the table, heads together, very serious. And the empress, Fredricks, and I at the other, not so serious. Archie and Jane Addams were a sort of bridge between continents, sometimes toasting with our end and other times conspiring with theirs.

We lost Archie to the other end of the table when their conversation turned to Russia, which was all to the good since now I could look at him without the risk of meeting his gaze. He was completely absorbed in a debate about Constantinople.

"The Triple Entente promised Constantinople to Russia if we win the war," Archie said. "In a secret agreement. That's why Russia agreed to fight on our side."

Triple Entente. Yes. That's our side. England, France, and Russia... and now America. We're making secret deals with the enemy? I thought of Jane Addams. *The cure for the ills of democracy is more democracy.*

"Yes, but if the damn Bolsheviks take over, Russia will be out of the war or worse," Xavier said.

"Or worse?" the emperor asked.

"Social progress depends as much upon the method through which it is secured as the end result," Jane Addams said. The men ignored her.

"They'll throw in with the Germans," Sixtus said. "That's why you must hand over Constantinople to the Russians." He pounded the table with his fist. "Alsace-Lorraine returned to France. Belgian independence. And the handover of Constantinople. That is the cost of peace."

"Why hand over Constantinople today if the Russians are going to drop out of the war tomorrow?" Fredricks asked. And I thought he wasn't listening to what was happening at the other end of the table.

These men talked about the exchange of cities and entire countries as if they were pawns in a game of chess. I wondered how Constantinople felt about that.

Constantinople. Hand over Constantinople. Every time one of them said Constantinople, I started to giggle. I couldn't help it. The word sounded so funny. Constantinople. *Snort.*

Whoa. My chair seemed to be tipping sideways, and I felt as though I might fall off.

"Are you quite all right, *ma chérie?*" Fredricks asked.

"Never better." My words boomeranged through an echo chamber and arrived back at my ears distorted.

"What-ho," Archie said, jumping up from his chair. "She's sozzled."

Before I knew it, Archie had ahold of one my elbows and Fredricks the other.

Straining to hear what the men were saying at the other end of the table, I nearly fell on my ear. All I heard was Jane Addams. "The cure for the ills of democracy is more democracy."

"I'll call for one of the servants," the empress said.

"I'm fine." I tried to free myself. But it was no use. My limbs refused to obey the commands from my brain. And I couldn't stop giggling.

"I'd better take her to her room," Fredricks said.

"Oh no you don't." Archie tightened his grip on my arm. "Fiona is not one of your conquests. If it's all the same, I'll take her to her room."

"You've got me all wrong," Fredricks said. "And why should I trust you?"

"My maid can take her upstairs," the empress said.

"Where's the fun in that?" I asked.

The two men glared at each other. They pulled me this way and that like a rag in tug-of-war.

"A duel at dawn," I suggested playfully.

"Even up the pole, she's a brick," Archie said with a chuckle.

"Quite." Fredricks pulled at my elbow. "Let's get her to bed before she collapses."

"*Ménage a trois.*" The giggles were back...and so were the bloody hiccups. "Good idea." *Hiccup.* "Safer." *Hiccup.* "than a duel." *Hiccup.*

"I doubt that," Archie said, a wicked smile spreading across his face.

"You can always count on Fiona for diversion," Fredricks said.

"She is quite a girl." Being held so close by Archie produced a strange sensation, simultaneously electrifying and calming. It was good to see him again. If only there weren't two of him bobbing back and forth. *Why doesn't he hold still?* All the jostling was making me deuced dizzy.

"She's a bit peaked," Fredricks said.

"I hope she's not going to chunder."

I really wish Archie hadn't said that. Just the thought of vomiting made me feel unwell. I let out an involuntary moan. *Why is the bloody hallway spinning?*

"Let me carry her up the stairs," Fredricks said. "It will be easier."

"If anyone is going to carry her, it's me." Archie swept me up into his arms. I draped my hands around his neck and leaned my head into his shoulder. "Gosh, you smell good." *Cinnamon and peat.* "Like my grandfather."

"Gee thanks." Archie held me tighter to his torso.

"Gosh, you're strong."

"And you're sloshed," he said.

"My being sloshed doesn't make it any less true." *Hiccup.*

On the second flight of stairs, I saw Fredricks following us.

"What are you doing here?" I raised my head. "Haven't you heard, three's a crowd."

"Consider me your chaperone," he said. "I invited you here, and I'm responsible for your safety."

"You don't think I'm safe?"

"In some respects, no."

"I'll safeguard Miss Figg," Archie said.

Jolly chivalrous of him and all. But I can take care of myself. I tried to tell him so, but it was just too much effort. I laid my head back down on his shoulder and closed my eyes. *Big mistake.* The spinning got worse. I opened my eyes again and clung to Archie like a June beetle to a blade of grass.

"I'm not sure you're up to it, lad," Fredricks said. "She's a handful."

"Yes, well, she's my handful at the moment." Archie shifted my weight and I clung even tighter.

Archie stopped... but somehow the movement continued.

"Wrong door, *mon ami,*" Fredricks said. "Her room is down here."

"And how do you know the location of Miss Figg's room?"

"She's my guest. And our hosts are my dear friends."

"You know, Fredricks, you're so full of rubbish—"

"Stop it," I interrupted. "You sound like naughty schoolboys."

Eyes locked on each other, I really thought they might come to blows.

"Put me down, if you please." Although I was enjoying the snuggle, I'd best get into my room and lie down as soon as possible. "I'm feeling a bit grotty."

"I'm not surprised after four and a half cream gins." Archie set me on my feet.

"Counting, were you?" I steadied myself against the doorframe. "It actually was six. Or was it seven?"

Archie turned to Fredricks. "And you were feeding them to her," he said accusingly.

"How did I know she can't hold her liquor?" Fredricks tugged on his waistcoat. "She's a grown woman, after all. No one forced her to drink—"

"Why, I'd just as soon punch you as look at you." Archie balled up his fist.

"That won't be necessary," Fredricks said, retreating a couple of steps. "Are you alright?" he asked me.

"I'm fine." I nodded. "I'm a big girl. I can take care of myself."

"I don't doubt it." Fredricks gave a little bow. "I'll bid you good night then, *ma chérie.*" He turned to Archie. "I trust we're both men of honor." He turned on his heels. After a few steps, he spun around.

Blimey. Does he have a gun? Is he going to shoot us?

"Somersby." Fredricks menaced us with his riding stick, waving it about. "Remember what I'm capable of."

"A duel at dawn is sounding more appealing by the minute," Archie said under his breath. "Too bad the War Office wants him alive."

"Why?" I gazed up into his sea-green eyes, which were not gazing back at me.

"Upper brass thinks he will lead us to a hornet's nest of spies." He watched Fredricks walk away.

"But you'd like to pluck his stinger now?"

"Something like that." He looked down at me and then moved a strand of hair out of my eyes. Someone else's hair, but nonetheless, it was sweet. "You'd better get to bed before you pass out."

The stimulation of being so close to him would most certainly keep me from losing consciousness. "You're like smelling salts."

He looked perplexed.

Golly. That came out wrong. "You're stronger than Austrian coffee."

He furrowed his brows.

Third time's a charm. "More stimulating than Dr. Freud's cocaine?"

He laughed and wrapped his arms around my waist. I put my hands on his shoulders. We stood like that for a moment, speechless, eyes locked. I stood on my tiptoes and kissed him. *Not very ladylike. My mother is probably turning over in her grave.*

He kissed me back. *Crikey.* Knees weak, I melted into the warmth of his lips. He pulled me closer. I ran my fingers through his thick hair. *Soft as mulberry silk.* "I like it better without the mustache," he whispered in my ear.

"Me too." Delirious, I melted into the combination of gin and kisses. Something hard pressed against my thigh. *Goodness. Is Archie carrying a gun?*

He pulled out of the embrace. "You should go inside before..." He was half-panting. "As much as I'd like to continue our *conversation*, you're not sober and I'm not a cad." He took my hand and kissed it. "Good night, Miss Figg."

"Such passion in your kisses and formality in your voice." I gave his hand a good shake. "Good night, Lieutenant Somersby," I said with exaggerated formality.

"You really are a brick."

"You mean I have a brick in my hat, don't you?" *Speaking of hat... where is mine?* I touched my head. It must have fallen off when Archie whisked me off my feet.

"That too. Which is exactly the reason I must leave you now." He kissed my hand again. "You will be all right, won't you?"

"Right as rain." I resisted the urge to kiss him again. "If you'll fetch my hat."

"At your service." He clicked his heels together and gave me a salute.

I heard a noise at the end of the hall. A door opened. Lest they see me alone with Archie, I ducked into my room. "Thank you," I said before closing the door.

Breathless. I leaned against the door. Hands pressed against my chest. To still my pounding heart.

Archie's kisses were more intoxicating than cream gin fizz.

Chapter Twenty-Two

The Hunt

The morning came too early. The sun streaming through the window was harsh. Right outside, crows cackled like witches. My tongue was swollen, dry, and stuck to the roof of my mouth. And my brain was too big for my skull.

Too bright. Too loud. Too big.

Wait. Why am I on top of the bed covers? Without opening my puffy eyes, I patted my side. Wide belt. Deep pockets. *Good grief.* I was still wearing the frock from last night.

Nothing was as it should be. I was decidedly unwell.

I put my arm over my eyes and groaned. I must have caught something. A summer influenza? Cholera? Pox? Typhus? My head hurt. My stomach roiled. I was feverish. Food poisoning? *What did I eat?*

Yes. I remember. The royal dinner. Cream gin fizz. Kisses in the hallway.

My eyes flew open, and I sat up in bed.

Oh, good heavens. Archie. What had I done? Whatever it was, God was surely punishing me for it. I fell back against the pillow. *My blooming head.* I pressed my hands into my temples. My head felt like it might explode.

The Women's Temperance Association was right. "Where there's drink, there's danger." *After I return to London, I will have to don a white ribbon and join Lady Henry's Colony for Women Inebriates.*

Unfortunately, the damage was done. I needed to see my way clear of this brain fog and drag myself to breakfast. It was too late to build a lighthouse. I needed a lifeboat.

I rolled over and tried to suffocate myself with the pillow. A knock at the door interrupted my self-pity. I groaned.

The assailant must have taken it as an invitation. "Coffee, ma'am?" The maid entered without ceremony and left a tray on the bed table. *I would kill for a good cup of tea.*

Even if my body could make it down to breakfast, my mind wanted to crawl into a hole and never come out. What I did remember from last night made me cringe. I could never face Archie—or the royal family—again.

And then there was Fredricks. *I'm not sure how, but he arranged this whole sordid affair.* The invitation. The surprise. The cocktails. He knew "the dashing Lieutenant Somersby" would be here all along. *The scoundrel.*

I had a fuzzy sense that Archie and Fredricks almost came to blows last night... over me? Or over their past history? Whatever that was.

I rolled over and stared at the tray on the bed table. The thought of consuming anything was repulsive. But I couldn't stay in bed all day. *Stiff upper lip and all that.*

I stretched my limbs, preparing to sit up. *Ouch. My lip isn't the only thing stiff. Did I take a tumble last night?* My whole body hurt.

I propped myself up on my elbows and examined what was on offer. A silver pot—presumably filled with strong coffee—a tiny pitcher of warm milk, a lovely porcelain cup and saucer, and a semmel, the Austrians' favorite bread roll.

Too bad I had a devilish headache and no appetite. Unlike the usual war rations, the light bread looked heavenly. Maybe the coffee would help clear my head.

Sigh. I took a deep breath and sat up again. If only the blooming room would quit spinning. *Come on. Concentrate, Fiona.* I prepared a cup of coffee with half milk and then forced it down in gulps. The dark brown taste of coffee had replaced the bitter bile of last night's improprieties. If it stayed down, I'd know I'd won the first battle. But the war wasn't over yet.

Carefully, I slid my legs over the side of the bed. I sat for a few moments holding onto the bedcovers with both fists. I never wanted to see a cream gin fizz again in my life.

Another knock at the door. *Is the blooming maid back again?* "Come in." Even the sound of my own voice reverberating in my head caused me distress.

The door opened and Archie appeared at the threshold, hands behind his back. "Fiona. We have to talk." He entered the room and then shut the door. "Do you mind?"

I shook my head and immediately regretted it. Hands shaking, I poured myself another cup of coffee. "About last night…" Since I remembered only bits and pieces, I didn't know quite what to say.

"You were a beautiful mess." Archie smiled.

"Quite." I stared at my lap. "I'm so embarrassed."

"You're wonderful even with a brick under your hat." He held out my hat. "As requested." He walked across the room and sat it on my dressing table. He came back and opened his palm to reveal two white tablets. "I brought you some aspirin."

"Why ever would you think—"

"Just take it."

I snatched the pills off his palm. When he handed me the glass of water off the tea tray, our hands touched. He flinched ever so slightly, and then went back and took a seat in front of the dressing table. "We've got to talk."

I remembered some kisses, but I was beginning to fear something more had happened last night. "Did I? Did we?" I felt tears sprouting in my eyes. Surely, I'd remember if we had…wouldn't I? "We didn't…I didn't…"

"You're always a lady." He chuckled. "Except when you're not."

I wiped my eyes with the backs of my hands. "That's not very helpful," I said, sipping my coffee. I seemed to remember he had no qualms about kissing me back in Paris when I was disguised as Harold the helpful bellboy.

He must have read my mind. "While debating the virtues of kissing a girl with or without a mustache is always of interest, I have something more important to discuss."

What could be more important than kissing? "I'm listening." I choked down more of the milky brew.

"Emperor Charles is negotiating for peace. His brothers-in-law are here on behalf of France. And I'm here on behalf of England."

"So I gathered. And what about Fredricks?" I asked. "Is he here on behalf of Germany?"

"The Kaiser must not find out or he'll have the emperor's head and all hopes for peace will be dashed." Archie stood up and started pacing the room. "If the Germans find out their allies are discussing giving up territory, who knows what they'll do. They already suspect the worst from their Austrian allies. And the emperor is in a very precarious position at home."

"I suppose it doesn't help that Empress Zita is an Italian princess raised in France and Britain. The Kaiser must already be suspicious of her." Tentatively, I took a small bite of the breakfast roll.

"Exactly." Archie stopped pacing and turned back toward me. "The Germans must not find out about these talks, or all is lost. That's why I have to bring in Fredricks now. I will take him back to London for questioning."

"Bring in Fredricks?" I dropped the roll back onto the plate. "Captain Hall has made it clear. I'm to follow Fredricks. Learn what he's up to and report back. You said so yourself."

"The playing field has changed. These talks are essential." He started pacing again. "That's why I'm going to town this morning. To contact Captain Hall and persuade him to let me bring in Fredricks now."

"Golly." Archie was definitely much higher up in the ranks of British espionage than I. He had direct access to Captain Hall. "What do you mean, bring him in? Surely you can't arrest him?"

"I'm going to take him back to England, if I have to bind and gag him. I'll not let him muck up the chance of peace…or worse."

"Golly." *I must sound as daft as a brush. "Golly." Come on. Get a grip.*

If Fredricks reports back to the Kaiser, the peace talks will fail." He sucked in air as if in pain. "And the emperor's and empress's lives will be in danger. Now, I must go."

"When will you be back?"

"Tonight." He approached the bed. And then went down on one knee.

Golly. My breath caught.

He took my hand and gazed up into my eyes. "Be careful." He kissed my hand. "Fredricks is very dangerous."

When I nodded a wad of hair fell into my eyes. *Bother. Is my wig on straight?* I must look a sight. And I hated to think how I smelled.

Archie certainly had seen me at my worst. I first met him back at Charing Cross Hospital, crying my eyes out right after Andrew died. Last night, I was drunk as a skunk. And this morning, my head was full of cotton wool. What would be next?

"I have to go now." Archie stood up and made for the door. Before he left, he turned back and blew me a kiss. "Goodbye, beautiful. Until tonight."

"Tonight," I repeated.

After he left, I tucked into the bread roll like a squirrel in a hazelnut tree at harvest time. I washed the roll down with the last of the coffee. I had to get down to breakfast and keep my eye on Fredricks. Maybe a hearty Austrian breakfast would be just the ticket after all.

Archie's visit had acted as a tonic for my swollen head. *Do I have the courage to face the rest of the party?* If I was to keep an eye on Fredricks, I'd best get cleaned up and down to the dining room *tout de suite*.

I'd known from the moment I met him that Lieutenant Archie Somersby was an important player in British Intelligence. Although his position was still a mystery to me, his pull with Captain Hall and the War Office proved me right.

Still, Archie needed the element of surprise. If the Black Panther knew he was bound for the net, he would surely run. I had to make sure he didn't suspect the net was closing in on him. A cornered cat was jolly dangerous.

I had to get downstairs and keep the cat amused until Archie returned. Archie was right. Playing cat and mouse with Fredricks was a dangerous game. He'd killed before and he would kill again. All the more reason for Archie to bring him in now.

If Fredricks had intended to kill the empress but accidentally killed Elsie, then he could have his sights on Zita at this very minute. Fredricks may appear to be an important part of these peace talks, but his plan could be to scuttle them all together and dispose of the Austrian monarchy in the process.

I stripped off my floral frock. Wanting to avoid its recriminations—given it was a witness to my indignities—I wadded it up and threw it in my suitcase.

As much as I needed to hurry, I needed a bath more. I simply couldn't face anyone, let alone the empress or Fredricks, in my present stale state. I may not have been able to wash away my sins. But my trepidation about showing my face had circled the drain and disappeared with the bathwater.

I applied an extra bit of makeup to camouflage any remaining traces of my indiscretion. At the last minute, I snatched up my clutch…just in case I found myself in need of a mirror lipstick, lockpick set, or miniature pistol.

When I arrived at the dining room, the entire party—*sans* Archie of course—was starting breakfast. Fredricks and the empress had just come from shooting birds… thank goodness the empress wasn't one of them. And the others were already deep into politics.

The east-facing windows made the breakfast room light and cheery. The conversation, on the other hand, was deadly serious.

As usual, the empress pretended to be otherwise engaged, chatting with me, but was astutely listening to the peace talks and occasionally interjecting her opinion, which was generally highly esteemed by her husband and her brothers. In fact, after what I'd observed of the negotiations so far, if I were a gambler, I would have wagered that Empress Zita was the mastermind of the entire plan.

Little Otto ran into the breakfast room. He'd escaped from the maid again, who was trailing behind. "Miss Fiona," he said, coming to my side. "Can we read together when you finish?"

"Of course." I pulled him onto my lap. I really was becoming quite fond of the little rascal. And he was proving jolly useful for getting information. Still, with my attention divided, I was worried about Fredricks. The empress invited me along to keep little Otto company. But I also needed to keep an eye on Fredricks.

I spent the rest of the morning reading to little Otto with one eye and watching out for Fredricks with the other.

After luncheon, the empress insisted I sit with her in the corner of the morning room while the men continued their negotiations.

Miss Jane Addams had left to go back to America via London, where she hoped to start another house for wayward women and children like one she'd founded back home. *Given how little mind the men paid to what she had to say, it's no wonder Jane Addams left.*

Ostensibly, the empress and I were knitting. Luckily, when she wasn't picking sheep ticks off my person, my granny had taught me knitting during the summers I stayed at my grandparents' farm.

We'd been at it for at least three hours. And so had the men.

Even though I was an experienced knitter, I was much slower than the empress. Hoping to catch up, I tried to hurry through the masses of boring stockinette stitches required to finish this sweater for the troops. Unlike the empress, I purl much slower than I knit. I'd be lucky to finish this sweater before the end of the war, let alone the end of our holiday.

Zita's lacework was especially impressive. More impressive was the way she nonchalantly commented from the corner of the room and made the men prick up their ears.

"The Bolsheviks will take over Russia before Christmas," she said, knitting needles ticking away. "Mark my words."

Speaking of words. If only my photographic memory extended to the auditory. I'd been trying to memorize everything said so I could report back to the War Office. If only I could write it down... or knit it into this sweater like other clever women spies had done.

"Zita is right," Fredricks said. "Then they will drop out of the war and Constantinople will be a moot point."

I cringed just hearing the word Constantinople. I had a vague memory of that word leading to my downfall last night. My cheeks burned just thinking about what a fool I'd made of myself.

The men nodded in agreement. Even Fredricks seemed beholden to Empress Zita's opinions. *Yes, Empress Zita is definitely the mastermind behind these secret peace talks.*

I kept my ears open and my mouth shut. It helped that my hands were busy with the yarn. *Drat.* I'd dropped a stitch. Five bloody rows back. *To tink or frog, that is the question. Try to hide it or tear it out and start over?* My good old dad used to say, "Never try to hide your mistakes. Learn from them." *Frog it is.* I ripped the yarn from the needles.

"Let's take a break for refreshments," the empress said, laying her needles and yarn back into her knitting basket.

Yes, she was clearly running the meeting.

"Afterward, would anyone like to join me for an evening hunt before supper?" she asked. "I saw some beautiful roebuck in the meadow this morning."

"Sounds delightful," Fredricks said.

"Yes, delightful." Truth be told, I abhorred blood sports. But I had to keep an eye on Fredricks... especially when firearms were involved.

Then again, he'd had plenty of chances to kill the empress, or me. *Maybe he truly wants peace.* I'd like to believe that. *Can a leopard change its spots? How about a panther?*

* * *

Evening in the Alpine countryside was divine, especially compared to the infernal heat of the city. The empress, Fredricks, his valet, and I headed out to the meadow to the east end of the house, a favorite hunting spot of the royals. The hike afforded panoramic views of snowcapped mountains in the distance. Lovely rampions dotted the lush green grass. I rarely saw the light-purple flower back home, but they grew all over Austria and France.

I inhaled the scent of juniper and cedar on the warm breeze. The sun disappeared behind the gorgeous peaks, creating a kaleidoscope of purples and a blaze of orange across the soft blue sky. The tranquility of the pastoral scene was *almost* enough to turn me from an inveterate city girl into a naturalist.

To my surprise, the empress carried her own rifle slung over a shoulder instead of having one of the servants carry it for her. She was dressed for hunting in an earth-tone brown shirt and matching jacket. I was not dressed for hunting... unless we happened into a field of poppies. Then I'd be well camouflaged.

The strapping young Ivan carried a large basket, two rifles, and a seat cushion. Fredricks carried only himself in his usual proud manner.

I followed behind them with my clutch purse, wishing I had sturdier boots. What the streets of London deemed sturdy, the bogs and mudholes of Reichenau an der Rax could reduce to soggy tatters.

Picking my way along the path, I strained to hear the conversation between the empress and the Great White Hunter. They laughed and cavorted like best mates. Once again, I wondered if I was wrong about Fredricks. Perhaps he was telling the truth when he said he just wanted peace.

Then again, my father always warned me, "Sometimes what looks like sugar is really salt." It wouldn't be the first time Fredricks had used sweetness to camouflage poison.

Trying not to twist my ankle and break my blooming neck, I rushed to catch up. How could I keep an eye on the empress if I tripped and fell on my face?

Two viewing platforms fifteen feet up in the trees welcomed us to the forest entrance. They had wooden railings and looked to fit a couple of people each. They were on either side of a forest path, camouflaged by tree cover, but providing an open view into the meadow below.

When I finally caught up to Fredricks and Zita at the base of the tree stands, the empress was inviting the Great White Hunter to visit in May when the gorgeous blue-headed capercaillie grouse were in rut. Ivan was already up in one of the stands laying out a picnic.

"The males sit on low branches singing their uncanny knife-grinding, cork-popping song," she said. "It's magnificent."

"Of course, I would love to shoot with you anytime." Fredricks flashed his canines.

"Why don't you two take the stands," the empress said. "I'd like to do a bit of solitary walking. The forest acts as a balm for my restlessness." She disappeared into the trees. Blast it. How could I keep an eye on her if she went off wandering like that? All the more reason to watch Fredricks.

I stared up at the platform. *Did she really expect me to climb that rope ladder? I'm a bloody spy, not a trapeze artist.* My two-week crash course in espionage had not prepared me for dangling twenty feet off the ground by the heel of one of my sodden boots.

"Too bad there isn't room for you in my stand. Otherwise, I'd love to share it with you, *ma chérie.*" Fredricks smiled. He leaned closer and whispered. "High above the rest of the world, we could negotiate our own peace, you and I."

"Yes. Too bad." I would have preferred to keep the blackguard within arm's reach. Luckily, the second stand was just across the path from the first. I would have a jolly good view of Fredricks and the entire meadow from up there. I tucked my purse under my arm, mounted the rope ladder, and braved the climb.

"Do you need help?" he asked, putting his hands around my waist.

I twisted my head around and glared at him. "Unhand me."

"Have it your way." He let go of me. "You always do."

Halfway up the ladder, I glanced over at Fredricks. He was already in the tree stand, sitting comfortably on a canvas chair smoking his pipe. And Ivan was serving him a glass of wine. With his hacking jacket, waistcoat, light-colored breeches, tall boots, stock tie, and bowler hat, Fredricks looked like a member of the aristocracy himself.

I didn't dare look down. The higher I got, the faster my heart raced. I held my breath as I lifted my foot onto the penultimate rung of the ladder. At least I'd worn my split skirt.

Dash it. My heel caught as I was trying to hoist myself onto the platform. Clinging for dear life, I wriggled onto the bloody tree stand. Not very ladylike, but at least I arrived at the top unscathed.

"Would you like me to send Ivan over with a glass of wine?" Fredricks chuckled. "A bit of the hair of the dog? Or would you prefer a cream gin fizz?"

"No, thank you." Just the mention of that foul cocktail turned my stomach. I flopped into a canvas chair and waited to catch my breath. Mopping my brow with a hanky, I surveyed the meadow. The view from up high was stunning. The tree cover provided wonderful shade. Indeed, it was almost chilly.

After getting my bearings, I finally relaxed enough to enjoy the fresh air and gorgeous scenery. Lush evergreen trees danced in the breeze. Their grace reminded me of Archie.

Sitting on his cushion, nibbling on cheese, and sipping wine, Fredricks was ostensibly watching for wildlife. And I was watching Fredricks.

A twig cracked below me. Leaves rustled.

Fredricks handed his glass to Ivan, wiped his mustache with a serviette, and slowly picked up one of the rifles.

I cocked my head to listen. More rustling.

A roebuck? A capercaillie grouse? Some other poor innocent forest creature risking its life crossing under the hunting platforms?

A shadow emerged from the forest. Fredricks quietly raised his rifle and took aim.

I peered over the edge of the platform. What poor beast was going to sacrifice itself for our dinner?

Not a roebuck. I sighed in relief. Empress Zita stepped out into the meadow. Thank heavens. I wouldn't have to watch a fellow creature being shot before my eyes.

Fredricks cocked his rifle. *What in Hades is he doing? Crikey. He's aiming for the empress.*

"No," I shouted. I fumbled with my purse and withdrew Mata Hari's little pistol. "Fredricks. Stop." I pointed the gun at him. "Put your rifle down or I'll shoot."

Fredricks jerked his gun, and a crack echoed through the valley. I fired the gun. Fredricks grunted. Instinctively, I fired again. He moaned. Hands clasped to his chest, he collapsed onto the platform.

Oh my God. What have I done?

Chapter Twenty-Three

The Accident

The empress stood in the meadow, her hand shielding her wide eyes. "What's going on? What's happened?"

"Fredricks shot at you..." I dropped the gun. "He was aiming right at you." *Wasn't he?* A tremor ran through my body. I was paralyzed with disbelief. *Had I just killed Fredrick Fredricks?* I'd seen plenty of men die back at Charing Cross Hospital, but I'd never killed one myself. "Fredricks shot at the empress." I stared across the space between platforms. "Isn't that right, Ivan?"

Ivan shook his head. "No, ma'am!" He was kneeling down over Fredricks, inspecting the wound. He pointed out to the meadow. "He shot a wild boar," he said with a thick Russian accent. "Go look. It was charging at Her Highness." His voice cracked. "He saved her life and you shot him dead." He ran his hands through his hair and looked like he might start wailing.

No. That can't be right. He was shooting at the empress. I saw him take aim. He planned to assassinate her. "No." My voice trembled. I fell to my knees and let out a great wail. *How could I?* I'd taken a man's life. And not just any man... a respected enemy so wily he was almost a friend. Yes. He'd done bad things. But he wasn't all bad.

It was easy to think the enemy was all bad, but in reality, people were complicated, and war was complicated. What if I was wrong about him? And now I'd killed him.

What would Captain Hall say? I'd be sacked for sure. And Archie? He was going to take Fredricks tonight. The War Office was counting on information from Fredricks. I'd ruined everything. I might have lost us the war.

"I'll go get help," the empress said.

"It may be too late, Your Highness." Ivan gathered his master in his arms and cradled him like a sleeping child. "He's gone."

"Gone?" I was shaking like a wet dog.

"Unconscious and bleeding very bad," Ivan said.

"We need help getting him back to the house." The empress dropped her rifle and sprinted toward the palace.

I buried my face in my hands. *What if I killed him?*

Grunting and huffing sounds made me look up. With Fredricks slung over one shoulder, Ivan was descending the rope ladder.

"What are you doing, man?" I asked. "Don't move him." If he was bleeding, jostling him would only make it worse. And if he died...if he died, this was a murder scene. And I was the murderer.

"I'm not going to leave him out here for the buzzards," Ivan said.

"No, quite." *Come on Fiona. Do something.* "Let me help. I'm a nurse." A volunteer nurse.

"I've got him."

"We need to stop the bleeding." I gathered up my purse—and the possible murder weapon—and crawled to the edge of the platform.

"Bleeding very bad," Ivan repeated.

Clutch tucked under my arm and palms gripping the flooring, I dangled one leg over the edge. Slowly, I lowered myself onto the rope ladder. The ladder swayed back and forth as I made my way down. Queasy from the movement of the ladder... and the fact that I may have just killed a man, I took a deep breath and stood for a moment at the bottom.

Ivan strode across the meadow, carrying Fredricks in his arms like a baby. All I could see were Fredricks's feet dangling and his head nestled against Ivan's broad chest. None of it seemed real. It was like a strange nightmare. I wished I'd wake up.

Glad to be on solid ground again, I hurried to catch up, stopping only to collect Empress Zita's rifle. *What would the royal party think? A possible murderess arriving with a gun in each hand?*

With his long legs and powerful stride, Ivan was too fast for me. By the time I'd reached the midway point, he'd disappeared.

When I reached the front gate, a footman ran past me and nearly knocked me over. On my own, with no one to greet me, I let myself in and closed the oversized wooden door behind me.

Inside, maids scurried up and down the stairs, and people spoke in hushed voices.

I found everyone gathered in the morning room. Fredricks was laid out on a chesterfield, covered in a white sheet. A blossom of red spread across it. Feet apart and arms crossed, Ivan stood guard over Fredricks. Loyal even in death, the bodyguard would not let anyone touch him.

"I called for the ambulance," the empress said. "It will take a while for it to get up the mountain roads."

I rushed over to the sofa. "We must stop the bleeding."

"Fiona, is that you?" Fredricks asked weakly, not opening his eyes. He groaned.

"Thank God. You're still alive." I tried to slip past Ivan, but he stepped in front of me.

"You care." A weak smile formed on Fredricks's pale lips.

"Let me see the wound," I demanded. "I've got to stop the bleeding."

"I will take him to the hospital," Ivan said. "We cannot wait for the ambulance."

"I concur." I reached for the sheet, but Ivan stopped me. "Let me at least wrap the sheet around the wound."

"Lady, you have done enough damage." Ivan put his hands together in prayer. "God will save him just as he saved me."

Did he mean God or Fredricks had saved him?

Ivan looked up at the ceiling or perhaps to the heavens. "Tobias is bringing the car around now."

Tobias. That must be the footman who nearly mowed me down.

The one and the same footman rushed into the room, panting. "Your automobile is ready, sir." He went to help Ivan with Fredricks, but Ivan refused.

"I will carry him," the big man said. He gathered Fredricks up and, cradling him, carried him out to the car.

The rest of the party trailed behind. I watched in awe as Ivan carefully laid Fredricks on the backseat. He lovingly wrapped the sheet around him as if he were tucking in a child.

I dashed to the motorcar. "I'll come with you."

"No, lady," Ivan said. "Thanks to you, my master could die." He held up his hand. "No, don't come any closer. You shot him."

I stopped in my tracks. *He is right. Why should he let me go with them?*

"I'll go," the empress said.

"Darling, please." The emperor came to her side. "I think you've had enough of a shock. Think of the baby." He put his hand on her stomach. "You need to rest."

Aha. She's pregnant.

"Tobias," the empress said. "Would you be so kind as to accompany Mr. Ivan? Please call as soon as you arrive at the hospital?"

"Yes, Your Majesty." Tobias bowed and then sprinted to the car.

We all stood watching as Ivan drove away.

For the next hour, everyone was restless. The men smoked and drank whiskey. The empress sat quietly knitting. And I paced back and forth in front of the window.

At least we'd moved to the library and out of the morning room, which seemed positively haunted. Every time I passed by the threshold, I imagined the blood-soaked sheet lying motionless on the sofa.

I was waiting for someone to ask me about the shooting. For the empress to ask why I thought her friend would try to kill her. But no one did. As if a man being shot in a tree stand were a regular occurrence. Perhaps they were just being polite, biding their time. For all I knew, the police were on their way at this very minute to haul me off to jail.

I'd been in jail for murder before. I didn't care for it, not one stinking bit.

Of course, this time I was actually guilty. I had the weapon tucked under my arm in my clutch purse. *Please, Fredricks, don't die. You're strong. You've got to pull through.*

I put my hands together in prayer, and like Ivan looked up to the heavens. "Please, God," I whispered. "Please let him live, and I promise I'll do whatever you ask of me."

When the telephone rang, everyone froze. The emperor held a glass halfway to his lips. Prince Sixtus stopped in the middle of lighting a cigarette. Empress Zita's knitting needles stilled. Prince Xavier looked up from his book. And I stopped pacing and stared into the hallway, waiting for one of the footmen to arrive with news.

"Excuse me, Your Majesties, Your Highnesses, ma'am." The footman nodded at each of us in turn, a grim look on his face. "Tobias called from the hospital." He cleared his throat. "I'm sorry to report, the gentleman is dead."

No. No. No. The news was like a dagger through the heart. I stood paralyzed, tears flowing down my cheeks. *Fredricks is dead. And I am a murderer.*

"Tobias is asking if we might send a carriage for him." The footman's face reddened, and he looked at his boots.

"He can't ride with Mr. Ivan when he returns?" The empress asked.

"Ivan refuses to leave the body, Your Majesty."

"I see." She dropped her knitting into a basket. "Very well. Order the carriage to pick up Tobias from the hospital."

"Yes, Your Majesty." The footman bowed.

"And please tell Mr. Ivan that he is welcome to stay here with us for as long as he likes."

The footman nodded and then turned on his heels and disappeared.

"Ivan is a loyal friend," I said. *But he will have to leave his master behind eventually. Unless like an Indian widow he commits sati and throws himself on the funeral pyre. What a terrible thought.*

"Now that we've heard the dreadful news from Tobias," the emperor said. "Might we hear from Mrs. Douglas?" he asked in a hardened tone.

I started. The moment I'd feared was upon me. I would have to answer for my crime.

The empress stood up and stretched her back. "Why don't we have our supper first." She pulled on a cord. "There will be time enough to question Mrs. Douglas after."

A few moments later, a petite maid appeared in the doorway.

"Ursula, please tell Cook that we're ready for supper now," the empress said.

The girl curtsied and practically ran from the room.

Over dinner, I recounted what happened. Not very appetizing conversation. Indeed, I couldn't eat a bite. I simply moved the food around on my plate. I wasn't even tempted by the offer of a dreaded cream gin fizz. I needed something to calm my nerves and clear my head.

"Why on earth would Fredrick try to kill Zita?" the emperor asked.

"Perhaps he thought she was too close to the French?" I ventured.

"But Fredrick is a family friend," the empress said. "We've known him for years."

"Keep your friends close and your enemies closer." At least that's what my dear departed dad used to say. "Fredricks is not what he seems."

"Why do you say that?" The emperor's tone was brusk. "I thought you were good friends."

"True," I said. Although of course, it was not true. The few months I'd known Fredricks were enough to tell me that he couldn't be trusted. "Not all of my friends are trustworthy."

The emperor waved his hand as if shooing a fly. "I don't mean to be disagreeable Mrs. Douglas, but you did shoot the man."

"Also true." Maybe the emperor was right. Maybe Fredricks really had been aiming for a wild boar. "Do you have a torch I could borrow?"

"Why do you need a torch?" the empress asked.

"To find the wild boar." I bit my lip. "If Fredricks is as good a hunter as they say, then he should have shot and killed the beast, in which case, its body should still be out there."

"You can't go wandering around alone at night," the empress said. "The wild boars can be quite dangerous. And what if you twist an ankle or get lost out there?"

"What's all this about getting lost?" a familiar voice asked from the doorway.

"Archie!" I was never happier to see anyone in my life. Archie would know what to do. *Crikey.* I would have to tell him that I'd killed Fredricks before he could bring him in. *Blast and dash it.*

Archie took a seat next to me at the table. "Where's Fredricks?"

I grimaced. "I'm afraid there has been an accident." It was no accident. I'd quite intentionally shot Fredricks... although I'm not sure if my intention was to kill him.

"An accident?" Archie glanced around the table.

"I shot Fredricks," I confessed and then explained what happened.

Archie looked at me with a mixture of awe and incredulity. "I'll be..." He shook his head. "Well, let's go look for that wild boar, shall we?"

I knew he would help.

After supper, the empress asked a footman to bring us each a torch and some walking sticks. Archie and I excused ourselves, and then headed out to the meadow in search of the phantom beast.

I didn't know if I wanted to find it or not. If we found it, then I was guilty of murder. If we didn't find it, then it would be clear that Fredricks had been sent to assassinate the empress, and someone else would be coming in his place. As she'd said herself, the Germans didn't trust her because her family was French, and her own people didn't trust her because she was foreign.

The dew, still a heavy mist, hadn't yet settled on the grass. Crickets droned in the background, while nightingales serenaded us with a flutelike melody. A thick crescent moon hung low in the sky.

What you don't see is as important as what you do.

I gripped my torch and followed Archie down the garden path. Once we were outside the gates, a dark solitude shrouded us. At that moment, we could have been the only two people on earth.

"Watch for roots on the trail," Archie said. "They're sneaky buggers."

"Indeed."

Yet despite my paying attention, Archie had to scrape me off the ground more than once on the way to the hunting platforms.

As we got closer to the forest, the nighttime chorus of owls, nightjar, and other nocturnal creatures grew louder. Every time the bushes rustled, my heart leapt. A crashing noise sent me flying into Archie's arms.

"We should go boar hunting more often," he said with a laugh.

"Let's find the blasted thing and get it over with." Not that I wasn't enjoying the warmth of his embrace. "We really should separate so we can cover more ground."

"I don't think that's a good idea," he said, holding me closer.

If I stayed any longer in his embrace, I'd never want to leave. I pulled away. "Well let's get to it then." Pity we were in the midst of a bloody war. Why couldn't we just fall in love and enjoy life instead of tiptoeing around death and tragedy at every turn?

Side by side, we thrashed through the meadow with our walking sticks for another ten minutes.

A rustling from the forest stopped us in our tracks. "What is that?" I asked.

"Shhhh," Archie said, drawing the handgun from a holster usually hidden by his jacket. I knew I'd felt a gun the night he kissed me.

More rustling behind me, sent Archie spinning around. Now the gun was pointed at me. Good heavens. I held my breath. *Is Archie going to shoot me? Is he really a double agent?* My eyes fill with tears. I hoped to heaven there wasn't going to be another *hunting accident.*

Archie took a few steps toward me and then stopped.

I listened in the darkness for the sound of a wild animal...or Archie's gun going off. My heart was racing. Silence.

Archie holstered his gun. "I thought I heard someone."

I let out a huge sigh of relief. My imagination was playing tricks on me. Of course, Archie wasn't working for the Germans. I ventured farther into the meadow. "If we don't find the animal, then most certainly Empress Zita's life is in danger. The Germans will send someone else."

Archie lagged behind.

I heard a buzzing noise off to my left. I followed the sound.

Rustling behind me indicated that Archie was rushing to catch up.

"Did you find something?" he asked.

I jumped back. *Thud. Ouch.* I'd tripped and fallen. *Bloody hell.* I landed right next to a great bloody stinking beast.

My heart sunk. "Fredricks was telling the truth."

Chapter Twenty-Four

The Code

I'd twisted my ankle when I jumped back from the beast. Archie had to carry me back to the palace. If it weren't for the throbbing pain in my foot, I might have enjoyed the proximity. As it was, every time he jolted or jerked, my injured foot screamed in agony.

First, I'd killed a man. And now, I'd broken my bloody foot.

When the empress learned of my mishap, she sent one of the chambermaids to help me to bed.

The maid insisted I soak my foot in magnesium salts. She prepared a poultice of herbs and creams and then she wrapped my ankle and foot in a tight cloth bandage.

"Comfrey. Otherwise known as bone-knit," she said in broken English. She helped me change and get into bed. Before she left, she slid two pillows under my ankle. "Keep your foot above your heart," she said. "You'll be fixed up in no time. Just like poor Elise."

I sat up. "Elsie?"

"She was always wandering in the forest. Every free minute, she was getting off someplace. You'd think she had a secret lover." The maid laughed. "God rest her soul." Her tone turned somber again and she crossed herself.

"How well did you know Elsie?" *A secret lover? Was she meeting Count Czernin in the woods? Or someone else?*

"I bandaged her twisted ankles and scratched up hands more than once."

The maid rolled the unused bandages and gathered up her herbs. "Very secretive that one." She screwed the top back onto the jar of cream. "But a nice girl, she was."

"Do you know anyone who would want to harm her?"

She tilted her head. "Why would someone want to harm her? She was a good girl." With her hands full of healing, she headed for the door. "Good night, Mrs."

"Thank you. You've been very helpful." *And not just with my injured foot.*

* * *

The next morning, I woke early due to the pain. Not the pain in my foot, mind you, but in my heart. Fredricks was dead. The reality began sinking in.

I owed my new life as a spy to Fredricks. He was my first assignment...my only assignment. I'd met him at Ravenswick Abbey, followed him to Paris, visited him in prison, eaten strawberries with him... Even if I didn't go to prison for murder—or get hanged—I'd surely go back to being an ordinary file clerk. Either way, my espionage days were over.

I'm going to miss him. Yes, he was a scoundrel and a complete blackguard, but he wasn't without his charms. And he did have his reasons for the things he did. I could even understand some of them.

Hang it all. Today I'd have to get word to the War Office and then turn myself in. I rolled over and buried my head in the pillow. *Ouch.* My foot. It hurt.

Tentatively, I withdrew my leg from under the sheets. I unwrapped the bandage and brought it as close as I could to my face then examined it. My ankle was swollen and purple. The sight of it made my stomach churn.

Sigh. Here goes. Gingerly, I laid my foot on the floor. I placed both feet next to each other. With great concentration and intention, I stood up. Adjusting my weight to determine whether the leg could support me, slowly, I took a step. I was limping, but at least I could walk.

Surely, this means it's not broken. Either that or I've suffered nerve damage and can't feel the excruciating pain.

A knock on the door sent me flying for my robe. *Probably Archie come to check on me.* Modesty trumped agony, and I reached the closet in seconds.

"Morning, ma'am." *Only the blooming maid.*

The maid entered carrying a tea tray. To add insult to injury, there was no tea. Only coffee. Thank goodness for warm milk.

At least I'd proven that I could move in a hurry if necessary. Wrapped in my robe, I sat on the edge of the bed and nibbled on the soft bread, and sipped the milky coffee. I could get used to having coffee delivered in bed. Although tea would be better. Back in my flat in London, I was lucky to have anything in the cupboards at all, let alone fresh baked bread.

Another knock. *Here we go again.* "Come in."

This time it was Archie...looking deuced handsome in his linen suit. "I'm off to Graz." He fiddled with his hat. "How are you getting on?"

"Fine." I put the cup down on its saucer. "What's in Graz?" *Surely, Archie isn't going to fetch the police, is he?*

"The morgue," he said grimly. "I'm going to see the body for myself."

"I'll come with you," I said, standing up. My grimace must have spoken volumes.

"You stay put and rest that ankle." He crossed the room. "I'll be back soon." He kissed me on the cheek.

"What about the police?" I stuttered. "I did shoot a man after all."

"We'll get everything sorted when I get back."

"Are you going to call Alice Dubois?" I asked.

Archie furrowed his brows. "I have a contact with direct telegraph access to Captain Hall."

"Don't let him give me the sack."

Archie chuckled. But I could see the worry behind his laugh. "We'll get it sorted."

"Promise?"

"I promise." He kissed my cheek again, then turned on his heel and was off.

* * *

Limping to breakfast, I overheard voices in the morning room. I stopped just outside the door and listened. Not to eavesdrop. But because I heard my name—or at least, my assumed name.

"*Frau Fiona Douglas ist unser Gast.*" I recognized the voice as belonging to the empress. Even though my German was appalling, I was pretty sure she'd said, "Mrs. Fiona Douglas is our guest."

Golly. Is she talking to the police? I rapped on the door and then entered. "Apologies," I said. "But I couldn't help but hear my name."

The empress was sitting on an upholstered divan and a man was standing over her. Sunlight bathed the room, which would have been jolly cheerful had it not been for the pall of yesterday's shooting hanging over it.

The man was holding a small notebook and taking notes. *Blast it.* He must be a detective here to investigate Fredricks's murder. He narrowed his eyes and looked me up and down appraisingly. With his protruding ears and sagging jowls, he reminded me of one of Frau Sacher's bulldogs.

Thankfully, the empress switched to English. "I was telling Detective Hammer that you are our guest and Mr. Fredricks's death was the result of a hunting accident." She waved her hand. "Apparently, one of the servants called it in early this morning."

Not the maid bringing me my coffee, I hope. Or the one who helped me with my foot—which was much better but still not tiptop. I took a seat and rubbed my ankle. "And so she should."

The empress frowned.

"Where is the dead man now?" Detective Hammer asked.

"At the hospital in Graz," the empress said. "In their morgue."

"I heard there was also an accident at the Hofburg Palace." The detective smirked. "A woman at the royal ball. With all due respect, Your Majesty, the imperial family seems to be accident-prone these days."

"The Vienna police are investigating," the empress said, frowning again. "I assure you, the imperial family is cooperating fully."

"I'm sure." The detective stood up. "Mrs. Douglas, can you tell me what

233

happened? Why did you fire at Mr. Fredricks?"

I bit my lip. Heavens. Should I tell him that Fredricks was a spy and the empress was his target? How could I explain that Fredricks was a loyal footman in the Kaiser's army who set out to murder the empress of a country that was one of the Kaiser's allies? It was deuced confusing. And confessing would surely cost me my head. I grimaced. "It was an accident. A hunting accident."

"Yes, so I understand. But can you please tell me how it happened?" The detective held his pen over the notepad and looked at me expectantly. "Take your time."

"Surely that isn't necessary." The empress raised her voice. "I told you it was an accident. Or don't you believe me?"

"Just doing my job, Your Highness."

"I saw it with my own eyes." The empress used her imperial voice. "Do you doubt my word?"

He scowled. "No, Your Majesty, but I need to question the suspect." He stared at me, his beady eyes full of expectation.

The empress rang for a servant. "There will be time for that later." It was clear that his interview was over.

"Yes, ma'am. Then I'll take my leave." He made no bow or any attempt to show the empress the respect her position demanded. "Mrs. Douglas, please don't leave the country. I will send someone to collect your passport." Mopping his sweaty brow as he went, the man seemed quite put upon as he slouched out of the morning room.

"I'm sorry you had to go through that." The empress said after he'd left. "Odious man."

"He's right. He's just doing his job."

"Bosch." She waved her hand in front of her face like she'd smelled something foul. "Every time we're here that man comes around bringing trouble. He's a loyalist who resents my husband for marrying a foreigner." She looked at me with those intelligent amber eyes. "Many people do, you know."

The maid arrived. The empress asked her to bring us a breakfast tray.

234

"Since it is late, we can have a light breakfast and coffee here. If that suits you, Mrs. Douglas?"

"That would be lovely." My stomach growled in agreement. The slice of bread I had upstairs was nice but not filling.

"Mamma." Young Otto ran into the room, a magazine clutched in his little fist, and his aging governance trailing behind him.

"Apologies, ma'am." The stout elderly woman grabbed him by his collar. "Hard to keep up with this one," she said, clearly out of breath. "At my age, I shouldn't be chasing naughty boys."

"It's okay, Helga," the empress said. "He can stay."

"Bad habits die hard." The governess shook her head. "He's a very—"

"That will be all, Helga," the empress interrupted. "Thank you. You may leave him with me."

"I'm here to see Frau Douglas." He ran over to me, waving his magazine. "My favorite Sherlock Holmes story. We can read it together, *ja?*"

"Apologies for Otto." The empress patted the arm of her chair. "Come to Mamma now and quit bothering Mrs. Douglas."

"It's no bother." I reached out and ruffled the boy's curly locks. "I'd love to read your favorite story."

The boy climbed into my lap. A pang stitched my heart. Andrew and I were never able to have children. But he had a son with Nancy, proving that the inadequacy was all on my side.

The maid returned with a tray and set out bread rolls and coffee. She handed me a cup of the dark brew. Too bad she didn't leave more room for milk.

"See," little Otto said. "'The Adventure of Silver Blaze.' It's about a horse. They paint his forehead." He opened the magazine and pointed to a picture of the horse, sans silver blaze. "The man doesn't want Silver Blaze to win the race. But he does!" He shoved the magazine under my nose.

"Ah, yes. Silver Blaze. Hidden in plain sight." I took the magazine from him. "An oldie but goodie... same age as me."

"You're not old." Otto fidgeted in my lap. "Papa is old."

The empress laughed and so did I. "Your papa—His Majesty—just turned thirty. That's not so old."

"I'm almost five." Otto held up the fingers on one hand. "How old are you?"

"Otto, darling," the empress said. "It's not polite to ask a lady her age."

He pouted.

"Twenty-five." I ran my hand over the magazine. *Curious.* It had deep indentations all over its front. I examined it. "Someone's been using this as a blotter pad."

Otto got a very serious look on his little face. "I didn't think she'd mind since she's in heaven."

"In heaven?" I sipped the dark coffee and then grimaced. Quickly, I plucked a bread roll from the tray and took a bite.

"Miss Elsie."

"This magazine belonged to Miss Elsie?" I perked up.

Otto nodded his head vigorously, his golden locks bobbing up and down. "I got it from her bedstand. Blaze was her favorite too."

"May I borrow it for a bit?" I wanted to see what Miss Elsie had been writing.

Otto's little head kept bobbing up and down like a duck's. "When can we read the story?"

"Otto dear." The empress looked up from her yarn. "Don't bother Mrs. Douglas."

"No bother," I said. "How about right now?"

He was nodding so furiously, I thought he might fall off my lap.

As I read, Otto stabbed the illustrations with his pudgy little finger. I suspected that's why he loved these stories, for the pictures. After all, Sherlock Holmes's methods would tax even the cleverest adult, let alone a four-year-old child.

"Gregory: 'Is there any other point to which you would wish to draw my attention?'" I read for a second time. "Holmes: 'To the curious incident of the dog in the night-time.' Gregory: 'The dog did nothing in the night-time.' Holmes: 'That was the curious incident.'"

"You already read that." Otto squirmed.

"But it's my favorite part."

"Otto, let's take you back to the nursery." The empress had been silently knitting. "And give poor Mrs. Douglas some rest."

The empress rang a little bell. A few seconds later, a young maid appeared at the entrance to the morning room. "Mary, please take Otto back to the nursery."

"Yes, ma'am." She curtsied. "Come on, little prince. Let's get you back upstairs."

Otto jumped off my lap and ran across the room. He grabbed the maid around the legs. "Mary, guess what?"

Mary took him by the hand and off they went.

"Your Majesty, if you'll excuse me," I said. "I think I'll go rest before luncheon." I wasn't at all tired. But I wanted to inspect the magazine's cover in the privacy of my own room.

"Of course. I'll see you at luncheon." The empress laid her knitting aside and went to the piano.

Her melancholy tune trailed me up the stairs as I limped back to my room. Such an accomplished woman. She could hunt, knit, and play piano with the best of them, all while running an empire from behind the scenes.

Behind closed doors, I set out my tools. Pencil, paper, and a flat surface. I set the magazine on the dressing table, smoothed out the cover, and laid the paper over it. Carefully, I rubbed the pencil over the surface of the paper. As I did, numbers began to appear.

- 1-5-5
- 5-14-1
- 3-3-6
- 1-11-5
- 1-3-2
- 2-13-4.

- 3-14-4
- 2-13-4
- 1-3-2
- 1-7-7
- 3-4-6
- 1:6:16
- 1:6:20
- 2:1:2
- 2:1:1
- 1:1:4
- 1:1:3
- 1:2:4
- 3:1:2
- 2:2:19
- 1:1:2
- 1:3:4
- 4:8:3
- 2:7:9
- 1:3:3
- 1:1:6
- 1:1:4
- 3:4:1
- 3:2:1
- 3:2:2
- 3:1:2
- 3:1:5
- 2:1:1
- 2:5:4.

- 1:1:7
- 2:3:2

- **2:4:12**
- **2:1:2**
- **2:5:3**
- **3:3:17**
- **3:3:17**
- **1:1:9**
- **1:1:3**
- **1:1:5**
- **3:7:3?**

Crikey. It was in code. A simple number-to-letter or -word code. I'd seen many of these in Room 40 at the War Office. The code breakers loved them because once you had the key, they were a breeze. But there was no way I could decipher it without the master text. Why was Elsie using code? What master text did she use to write this? And who was the recipient?

A thought spread across my mind like the bloodstain across Fredricks's fresh white shirt. Elsie was using code because she was a spy. If Elsie was a spy, she may have been the murderer's intended victim all along.

In that case, Empress Zita's life had never been in danger. And the notion that Fredricks would try to kill her was my own fantasy.

I buried my face my in hands. *A deadly fantasy.*

A knock at the door interrupted my remorse. When I opened the door, I was glad to see Archie. "How was your trip to the morgue?"

"Bloody enlightening." Archie leaned against the doorframe.

"How do you mean?" I gestured for him to enter.

"There was no body." He crossed the threshold and I shut the door.

"What happened to it?"

"I went to every hospital from here to Vienna." He shook his head. "There never was a body."

What the...? I stood there blinking. "Either Ivan took the body elsewhere or—" *Could it be? But I shot him.*

Archie ran his hand through his hair. "Or Fredricks is still alive."

Chapter Twenty-Five

Breaking the Code

After luncheon, Archie and I retired to the library. After all, my bedroom was no place to entertain a man alone.

The library was my favorite room at the palace. One wall sported three gigantic stained-glass windows, giving the room a sense of reverence. The greens and reds in the glass threw off an eerie glow, making the whole scene otherworldly.

The other three walls had floor-to-ceiling bookshelves loaded with leatherbound books. A table in the center of the room was laid out with recent newspapers and magazines. I thought of Mrs. Einstein's missing notebook...and Elsie's magazine. Oswald saw whoever took the notebook... unless of course, Oswald took it himself. But why would he? *And the magazine is a clue to Elsie's murder.* But what about Fredrick Fredricks?

"If Fredricks is still alive, then obviously I didn't kill him." I poured myself a cup of coffee from the silver pot. I'd given up on getting a good cuppa. I poured a second cup of coffee for Archie.

"He's a slippery fish," Archie said, taking the cup and saucer from my hand.

"But I shot at him. And I saw the blood." Could I have hit him, but he didn't die?

"With your penchant for the theater, you must know how to stage a murder scene." Archie raised his eyebrows.

"Fake blood. Maybe I didn't hit him." I took a sip of my coffee and then added more milk to my cup. A lot more milk. "Fredricks must have known you were going to try to haul him in."

"And he faked the death scene to escape."

"Exactly." I hoped in my heart it was true. Had he truly orchestrated the whole scene? "But how did he know I would shoot at him? How could he be sure I wouldn't actually kill him?"

"Could he have gotten to your rifle?" Archie asked.

"I wasn't hunting. I didn't have a rifle." I grimaced. "I used Mata Hari's tiny pistol."

He narrowed his eyes. "Where is the gun now?"

I pointed to the desk. "In my purse."

He went to the desk, fetched the purse, and withdrew the gun. "A Webley four-hundred-fifty-caliber Bulldog." He glanced over at me. "Cute little thing." He opened the gun and spun the chambers. Something I'd never done. In fact, I'd never even checked that it was loaded. Some spy I was. "Two empty casings."

"I shot at him twice." I stared at my bare feet. The swelling in my injured ankle had gone down considerably, and the angry purple bruise was mellowing into a sickly yellow.

He shook the remaining bullets from the revolver. "Look." Palm open, he came to my side. He held out the remaining bullets.

"Three left." I plucked one from his palm. "What is that crimping on the tip? Is that normal?"

"Proof that you didn't kill Fredricks." Archie grinned.

"What? You mean they're not real bullets?"

"They're blanks. That's why the tips of the casings are crimped."

"I didn't actually have live bullets?"

Archie nodded. "Right."

I knew Mata Hari didn't use blanks. Clifford had incapacitated a murderer in Paris with that very gun. So Fredricks had orchestrated the scene down to replacing the live bullets with blanks. My head was reeling. *Thank God.* I couldn't bear the burden of having killed a man, even if that man was the infamous Black Panther. "Why do you think they call him the Black

Panther?" *He's as sneaky as a cat and just as clever.*

"The arrogant so-and-so calls *himself* the Black Panther." Archie rolled his eyes. "Something to do with hunting panthers in Africa, no doubt."

"The Great White Hunter and all that rot."

"Exactly." Archie drained his cup, set it on its saucer, and then leaned forward. "I have to go after him." He pulled two passports from the pocket of his jacket. "You need to leave the country immediately."

"But the police inspector said not to leave—"

"All the more reason to get out now. If the Austrian police start digging around, they'll undoubtedly discover your true identity." He grimaced. "Then you'd be in a real pickle." He held out the passports. "When I told Captain Hall what had happened, he arranged for these."

"New passports?" I took them and opened one. "You've got to be joking. Upton Snodsbury? Was that your idea?" *Upton Snodsbury is a town in Worcestershire near North Piddle, for heaven's sake.*

"It seems apt for your *husband*, Clifford Douglas, don't you think?"

"Very funny. I'm to be Mrs. Snodsbury?" I opened the second passport. *Blimey.*

Archie smiled. "I know how you love to dress up like a boy."

It's true. I did love a good disguise. What self-respecting British spy doesn't? "Barton Snodsbury?"

"Upton's little brother." He was grinning from ear to ear. "You'll make such a cute little lad."

I took a closer look at the picture. *A bloody crumb catcher mustache, and a straggly one at that.* "Captain Hall doesn't approve—"

"He did this time. You need a cover to get out." A cloud of worry fell over Archie's face. "Seriously, Fiona. It's dangerous for you to be here. You've got to get home as quickly as possible. Don't dally. The Austrian police will be looking for you."

I nodded. *But not before I tie up a few loose ends back in Vienna. Elsie's death. Mrs. Einstein's notebook. And of course, Frau Sacher's ransom.* I nodded. *Barton Snodsbury.* My mustache would come in handy after all. I clapped my hands together. I missed the smell of spirit glue.

"Tell Upton Snodsbury he'd better get you back to England safe and sound or I'll—"

"*I can get myself back safe and sound.*" *If Archie thinks I need Clifford to get me home safe, he has another think coming.*

Archie sighed. "Yes. I'm sure you can." He stood up. "Goodbye, beautiful."

"You're leaving right this minute?" My urgent tone took me quite by surprise. The cup clattered as I put it on its saucer. "Shouldn't you at least stay for dinner? What about the peace talks?"

Archie came over to my side. He bent down and kissed me. On the lips. In full view of anyone who happened to be passing by the library. *Golly.* He straightened. "They already know my thoughts on all the proposals. And it's best to follow fresh tracks before they go stale. Until next time, my love."

My love. He called me "my love." I smiled, admiring his backside as he walked across the room. At the threshold, he turned and blew me a kiss.

"When?" I asked. "When is next time?"

He shrugged. "Soon, I hope." He disappeared around the corner.

A stabbing pain in my chest forced my eyes shut. *Oh dear.* I pressed my hands to my heart. I must have eaten too much schnitzel for luncheon.

Archie's head popped back around the corner. "Lay low until you get back to London. No snooping around playing Sherlock Holmes."

"I don't—" He was gone.

* * *

After Archie left, I limped back to my bedroom, where I'd left the magazine. I still had to break that blasted code. I was part of Room 40 after all, the best code breakers in the world. Last year, I'd provided the clue that enabled the men to break the Zimmerman telegram, which persuaded the Americans to join the war. Surely, I could figure out how to break the nanny's secret code.

What is the master text? I sat at my dressing table, fanning myself with Elsie's magazine.

What would Sherlock Holmes do in this situation? Use deductive reasoning and his powers of observation. Elsie had to have kept the master text close by in order to write the coded letter. No one—except me—could do that by memory. I needed to get back to the Schönbrunn Palace nursery and search for the key text.

If she was writing in code, she had something to hide. But she also had a confidant who knew the code. Was the letter delivered? Presumably, it wasn't with the magazine when the child picked it up. In any case, if Elsie had a secret, surely she would have hidden the letter until it could be delivered.

Luckily for me, Otto, the little thief, had taken the magazine with her letter etched into its cover. *The purloined letter.* I sat staring at the magazine cover, trying to hone my powers of ratiocination. But it wasn't Sherlock Holmes who came to my aid.

No. It was C. Auguste Dupin, my first fictional crush, and the creation of the American author Edgar Allan Poe. I remembered his short story called "The Purloined Letter."

In the story, a minister had stolen an incriminating letter from the queen's secret lover and had threatened to expose her to the king.

Another story of infidelity. My word. Is that all detectives do? Track down murderous lovers and blackmailers?

Although the police had made a thorough search, they did not find the letter anywhere in the minister's rooms. The prefect of police came to Dupin for help. A month later, the letter still had not been found and the queen offered a sizable reward for its return.

Dupin had the prefect produce the reward, after which, the detective produced the letter. While the police had been looking under cushions and behind wallpaper, Dupin had looked in the letter rack. Like the horse Silver Blaze, the letter was hidden in plain sight.

I examined the magazine again. *"It's her favorite story too,"* the child's voice echoed through my head. *Could it be?* I opened it to the beginning of "The Adventures of Silver Blaze."

Let's see. The code is made up of lines of three numbers each. *Of course!* Page-line-word.

Gathering up my pencil and paper, I quickly counted pages, lines, and words, until I'd decoded the letter. It took a while. So many letters. Eventually, I cracked the code. I stabbed the air with my pencil. "Yes!" I was jolly pleased with myself.

He is on to me. Take me back to England before I am hung for treason. Can Figg help?

The last line was especially troubling. So, Elsie did know I was working for the British. But how? Had the War Office gotten word to her?

At least the code proved that Elsie was a spy. I thought of the money she'd taken from Count Czernin. She was afraid of being hung for treason. Was she working for the Germans, too? If so, that made her a double agent. No wonder she needed out of Austria fast. She knew she was in danger. *Surely, someone at the War Office knew she was now working for us. Why didn't Captain Hall tell me they had an agent in the palace?* It would have saved me a lot of anguish…and possibly saved that poor girl's life. Sometimes their lack of faith in me was deuced annoying.

"He is on to me." *Who is he?* Fredrick Fredricks? Or Count Czernin? Or someone else entirely?

Had Fredricks killed Elsie because she had turned and was now spying for Britain? This letter proved she was the target after all. Not the empress. And whoever killed her knew she was posing as the empress the night of the ball.

An inside job. Her lover Count Czernin perhaps.

Elsie must have been using the count to get Austrian military secrets. That would explain why such a pretty young woman would have a liaison with an older married man. And it would give the count a motive to murder her.

And, as Frau Sacher told it, Elsie was bedding other military officers and government officials. Was she getting information out of them? Did one of them find out she was a spy and dispose of her?

I still hadn't ruled out Oswald. If he'd gotten wind of her affair with the count, that would be motive enough for him, the jilted fiancé. Elsie attended the ball in costume. Maybe Oswald did too.

I should make a list of the things I need to do before leaving Vienna. I flipped over the sheet of paper with the decoded letter and then picked up my pencil.

1. Determine who killed Elsie. She is a fallen sister British spy after all. I owe it to her.
2. Find Mrs. Einstein's notebook.
3. Persuade Oswald to return his aunt's money and confess to kidnapping her bulldogs.
4. Transform Clifford into Upton Snodsbury and myself into his younger brother, Barton.

I snorted. *Upton and Barton Snodsbury.* Archie had a sense of humor. I'd give him that.

I reviewed my list. Number one. Find out who killed Elsie. I needed more information about her background. I folded the list and tucked it into my purse. *No time like the present.*

After a quick wig adjustment and lipstick touch-up, I limped back downstairs to ask the empress about her deceased nanny... and her husband's foreign minister.

I found Empress Zita still seated at the piano in the morning room. She was playing a cheerful waltz. The kind that makes swaying to the music irresistible. I did love to dance. I thought of the royal ball. Too bad my first—and most likely my last—ended in murder.

I tiptoed into the room, trying not to interrupt her playing. When she saw me, the empress smiled. Distracted by the music, I nearly sat on the chesterfield where Fredricks's body had lain covered with a blood-soaked sheet.

How could he do it? How could he let me think I'd killed him? I moved to an upholstered chair next to the sofa. *If I ever catch up to Fredricks, I really will kill him next time.* I really should tell the empress that Fredricks is still alive. She was so upset by the accident. And they are friends after all. Then again, Fredricks manipulated us. Made us think he was dead. And fooled us all.

The empress finished the waltz and closed the lid to the piano. "Have you heard the strange news?" she asked. "Fredrick's body has disappeared from the morgue."

Thank goodness. She knows. I didn't have to break the news that Fredricks had fooled us both. "If it ever made it to the morgue," I replied.

"Archie thinks Fredricks staged the scene to escape the country."

"Why do you think Fredricks would need to escape?" I played dumb. Perhaps she knew more than she let on.

She furrowed her brows. "He's always been a good friend to Austria."

"And a better friend to Germany?"

"Germany is our ally," she said defensively.

I couldn't very well say what I was thinking: *Perhaps he didn't like your husband engaging in clandestine peace talks with your enemies. Some might see that as treason.* "What if your ally discovers the true nature of our holiday in Rax?"

The color drained from her face. "Yes, I see what you mean."

If Fredricks reported the secret talks to the Kaiser, it could mean the end of the alliance between Austria and Germany. Indeed, it would make the emperor and the empress traitors. Perhaps Fredricks wasn't such a good friend to Austria after all. Or to the empress herself.

He'd seemed truthful when he said that he hoped he and I could change history and end the war, but that must have been an act. He was a skilled actor; I'd give him that.

I thought it best to change the subject. "Do you mind if I ask you about Elsie?"

"What do you want to know?" The empress left the piano and joined me in the sitting area. She didn't mind sitting in the spot where Fredricks performed the final act of his little drama.

"Anything you can tell me. For starters, how well did you know her?"

"Elsie was a friend of my younger sister. They met at St. Cecilia's Abbey on the Isle of Wight in England." The empress wrung her hands. "When the poor girl's parents died in a boating accident a couple months ago, she came to us."

"She was English?"

"Swiss. But like all students at St. Cecilia's, myself included, she studied English, French, and German."

Yes, it really was no wonder the Germans didn't trust Empress Zita. She was a French-speaking Italian Princess who went to school in England.

"And no one on the staff might have resented her position or disliked her?"

The empress shook her head. "No. Elsie had her own suite attached to the nursery. She had no reason to interact with the rest of the staff. And as far as I know, she didn't."

"Do you know of anyone else in Vienna who might have disliked her?"

"She hardly knew anyone." The empress stared down at her hands. "Poor girl."

Boy, was she in the dark. "What about Count Czernin?"

"Czernin?" The empress looked startled. "What about him?"

"He's your husband's foreign minister... and friend."

"Foreign minister." Empress Zita's voice was hard.

"Do you trust him?" My cheeks were burning. *I really should learn to be more diplomatic and less straightforward.*

The empress stood up. "Apologies." She circled around the chesterfield and pulled on the cord to call her maid. "I just remembered I have to tell cook what time we want dinner."

That was all the answer I needed.

Chapter Twenty-Six

The General

The next afternoon, after the royal carriage dropped me off at the Sacher Hotel, I left my bags in my room and immediately went looking for Clifford. We needed to pack up and get out of town before I was sent to prison...or worse. He was probably beside himself with worry.

Still, he'd be jolly interested in what I'd learned on the trip home. Although I could have managed to return to Vienna without the emperor and empress, it was helpful they decided to return to Vienna today too.

While the empress and I were alone, she had admitted that she didn't trust Count Czernin, and she suspected there was something going on between the count and Elsie. I rubbed my hands together.

Most importantly, she had confirmed my suspicions that Elsie often appeared in her stead at public gatherings. I was now more certain than ever that Elsie was the assassin's target all along.

I'd seen a large sum of German banknotes hidden in her lav. And Count Czernin delivered another envelope of banknotes, which suggests that she was working for the Germans. But I now knew that she was also working for the Allies. Presumably, she'd turned and become a double agent. And that made her a target for Fredricks, who probably wanted to dispose of her before she gave up too much information.

And my blurting out that Kurt Müller was Elsie's brother alerted Fredricks.

249

If only I'd kept my mouth shut, Elsie might still be alive. Fredricks may not have discovered that Elsie was a double agent.

I also suspected that Elsie's brother Kurt was working for the Allies. Given that Elsie knew her life was in danger, surely she warned Kurt to leave the country. Sadly, she didn't get out in time.

I would have to wait to confirm that the War Office had a female agent in the Austrian palace. I planned to ask Captain Hall why in blazes they didn't tell me. If they had, then I might have been able to save her... Just because I didn't have high enough clearance. Captain Hall's zipped lips in the name of protecting Elsie ended up costing her life.

Where in the blazes is Clifford? Wait until I tell Clifford—not everything, mind. Although I'd have to swear him to secrecy, if that was possible.

I found him in the library smoking cigars and laughing with Frau Sacher. So much for gnashing his teeth and despairing my absence.

The hotel's library was much smaller than the library at Villa Wartholz back in Rax. It was a cozy room filled with the scent of musty books and cigar smoke. Right now, the foul smoke was winning out. The bookshelves were crammed with old books, memorabilia, and knickknacks.

Clifford and Frau Sacher were installed in a snug sitting area in front of a stone fireplace, which was cold and dark now but must be delightful in the wintertime. A radio was broadcasting an impassioned speech in German.

"There you are, old girl," Clifford said. "Jolly inconsiderate to run off to Rax like that without me." He tried to look hurt. But it was obvious he'd been having too good a time to bother about me. He didn't even rise to greet me. "Anna introduced me to this lovely coffee called *Kaisermelange*. You should try it." He lifted his cup. "It's made with raw egg yolk and brandy."

Anna. They're using Christian names now, are they? Huff. And drinking before noon. It must have been the trip from Rax... or perhaps the need for an urgent departure? For some reason, I felt rather put out. *Raw eggs in coffee? Appalling.* I didn't want to talk about coffee. I wanted to finish my mission and get back home to London before the Austrian police discovered my true identity.

"Have you seen your nephew recently?" I asked Frau Sacher.

"Oswald?" She laid her cigar on the edge of an ashtray. "Such a good boy. With the war, we're so short-staffed, and Oswald has offered to help out by walking my babies."

Wait until I tell her that her darling nephew extorted money from her and stole her beloved bulldogs. "He hasn't found himself a new fiancée already, has he?" I dropped into a cushioned chair across from the new best mates. "Saving up for her dowery, is he?"

"Dowery?" Frau Sacher squinted at me. "Whatever do you mean?"

"Never mind." Had Oswald lied to me? So, it was her future daughter-in-law who'd demanded the large dowery.

Poor Oswald. He was wracked with guilt over the dognapping and the fallen maid. Then again, he had brought flowers to the hospital. And she couldn't remember what happened. Maybe they could find happiness together. There have been worse starts to happy lives.

Frau Sacher gasped and twisted her head toward the radio, which was sitting on the fireplace mantel. "Did you hear that?" she asked, turning back to us. "The foreign minister is insulting the French president." She reached over and turned up the radio.

"The foreign minister," I repeated. "You mean Count Czernin?"

"He's attacking him personally and blaming him for the impossibility of any peace treaty."

Is it a coincidence that just days after Emperor Charles began meeting with Prince Sixtus to negotiate peace, Count Czernin makes a fiery speech insulting the French president and proclaiming the impossibility of peace? Is he publicly trying to undermine what the emperor is doing in secret?

"He doesn't mince words," Clifford said. "Inflammatory even for enemies."

"We will win the war," Frau Sacher said. "Never fear."

Clifford got a sour look on his face.

"Can we talk?" I asked him and then glanced at Frau Sacher. "In private?"

"I say." Clifford set his drink on the side table. "Has something happened?" Sputtering, Clifford excused himself and bid goodbye to Frau Sacher.

For all I knew, I'd interrupted another of Clifford's marriage proposals. Frau Sacher wasn't exactly his usual young damsel in distress.

251

Back in our suite, I brought Clifford up to speed on all that had happened in Rax. Well, not all. I left out the parts where Archie kissed me and called me "my love." My cheeks warmed just thinking about Archie.

"Good Lord," Clifford said, staring at me as if he'd never seen me before. "You can't be serious. We're going home using fake names? I'm supposed to call myself Upton Snodsbury?"

After everything I told him, that's what has him shocked? "Indeed I am." I lifted my suitcase onto the bed and opened it. "We need to pack and leave as soon as possible." *Right after I find out whether Fredricks or Czernin killed Elsie, retrieve Mrs. Einstein's notebook, and persuade Oswald to return his aunt's money.* Golly. I had a lot to accomplish in the next few hours. I'd better hop to it.

Good thing I had time to map out a plan on the trip from Rax this morning. Even better, the comfrey poultice had worked wonders on my swollen ankle. It was almost as good as new, which was a jolly good thing since there would be a lot of running around in the next few hours.

I knew Oswald was the dognapper. I just had to get him to confess and return the money to his aunt. And given Oswald's description of the boy who ran out of the hotel with the notebook, and the only children who might know its value, I had a suspect—or should I say two—in mind. I should have realized it earlier. I just had to figure out how to get my suspect to lead me to the notebook. Unlike with Oswald, if I was right, then a confession wasn't going to be the most efficacious means of finding the notebook.

As for Elsie's murderer... If the empress had been the true target, then it could have been anyone who didn't like the fact that she was a foreigner. However, since I now knew that Elsie was indeed a double agent working for the British while accepting money from the Germans, I was convinced she was the target all along. Knowing that, narrowed the list of suspects considerably.

After all, who would want a royal nanny killed? She had only arrived two months ago and didn't know any of the other staff. It was unlikely anyone had a personal motive to kill her. Much more likely, she was murdered for being a double agent.

The most likely suspects were Fredricks and Czernin. Fredricks because he was known to dispatch double agents, and Czernin because he had given her that envelope of money and therefore must have been her contact for the Germans.

Since Fredricks had flown the coop, and I couldn't very well confront Czernin, pinning it on one or the other of them was going to be difficult.

"But...but...but." Clifford stammered. "Why do we have to leave right away?" Anguish did not become his long face. "Let's at least wait until tomorrow and get a fresh start."

"Because you've been drinking?" I took a skirt from the wardrobe, folded it, and laid it in my case.

"I'm perfectly capable—"

"Yes. I know, Clifford dear." I went to him and patted his hand.

Archie's warning came back to me. *You've got to get home as quickly as possible. Don't dally. The Austrian police will be looking for you.*

"Tomorrow morning before dawn then." *I did have a lot to accomplish between now and then, including perfecting my disguise. Hopefully staying just a few extra hours won't be the death of me, literally.* "Speaking of disguises," I said. "I haven't told you the best part."

"Disguises? We weren't speaking of disguises." Clifford got a worried look on his face. "Not again, Fiona."

I pulled out a small case from the bottom of the wardrobe and took it over to my dressing table. I opened it. Pursing my lips, I surveyed the mustaches and beards on offer. "Upton Snodsbury." Trying to match the look to the passport photo, I chose a sandy-colored handlebar and matching short beard. "Come here."

Like a scolded puppy, Clifford obeyed.

I held the furry beasts up to his face. "Perfect."

"I say. Stop it." He batted away the fake facial hair. "You don't actually expect me to wear those things?"

"Indeed, I do." I fetched a wig from the bottom of the case where I kept my men's wigs hidden. "And this too." I reached up and tugged it onto his wagging head.

253

Clifford just stood there scowling.

"The orders came from Captain Hall." I adjusted his wig. "As I said, you're to be Upton Snodsbury and I'm your younger brother, Barton."

"Good Lord," Clifford said, rolling his eyes.

I trotted over to my purse and pulled out the passports. "See?" I opened his to the picture.

He snatched the passport out of my hand. "Stone the crows." He stared down at it. The wig slid down his forehead and he looked like a werewolf.

I clapped my hand over my mouth and stifled the cackle rising up in my throat. *Stone the crows, indeed.*

* * *

After I bustled Clifford into his own room, I tidied up and then set off to Fuchs Butcher Shop.

The sun was high in the sky and harsh on my eyes and my face. I certainly would not miss the brightness or heat of Austria in August. The mountains had been cooler. Vienna was a lovely city, but too hot for my London blood. Luckily, the butcher shop was only a couple of blocks from the hotel.

I stopped short of the shop and stared across the street at the opera house. I could have sworn I recognized the muscular silhouette of Fredrick Fredricks. The figure disappeared behind a column. I must be imagining things. Surely the bounder wouldn't be so brazen as to return to Vienna after that charade in Rax. I took a deep breath and continued to the butcher shop.

The shop was empty except for Oswald, who was wearing a bloodstained apron and hacking away at some animal's ribs. *What a gruesome job.*

The brutal spectacle was enough to turn me into a vegetarian. Or as Clifford calls them, vegetable-eaters. What the war made a necessity could become a principle.

"I don't want to talk about it," Oswald said, looking up from the carcass. *No hello or good day?*

"Talk about what?" I asked.

"I'm not answering any more of your questions." He went back to butchering the pig. At least, as I looked closer, I think it was a pig. *Someone is in a foul humor.*

I took a few paces around the shop, pretending to admire... the meat. After volunteering at Charing Cross Hospital, the smell and the sight of dressed carcasses hanging from meat hooks unnerved me. Some of the poor boys arrived there in not much better shape.

"Actually, I want to ask you to do something for me." In reality, I came to give him an ultimatum.

He glanced up from his work. "For you?"

"And for yourself." I stopped directly in front of the counter. "And for your aunt."

"My aunt?"

Time to quit beating around the bush. "I know you kidnapped Frau Sacher's bulldogs and then demanded ransom."

He quit chopping and stared at me, mouth open.

"And I know you did it so you could marry Elsie."

His dark eyes welled up and he wiped them with the backs of his hands. When he did, he nearly took off an ear with the knife.

"And you had an accomplice, the woman who delivered the ransom note."

He jerked his head to one side. "What woman?"

"The woman dressed as a war widow. Witnesses saw her at the hotel."

"I don't know what you're talking about." His face paled.

"I think you do. Who is she?"

He shrugged and went back to work.

"I want you to return the money." I gave him a stern, but compassionate look. "And tell her what you did and why."

"If I do, she'll never speak to me again." His voice cracked.

"If you *don't,* she'll never speak to you again."

"She hated Elsie. It's her fault we couldn't marry."

"Even so, you must return the money."

From what I'd gathered, Frau Sacher had good reason to be suspicious of Elsie. My hunch was that Elsie was leading the poor boy on. Why else would a double agent who cavorted with high-ranking military men want to marry a butcher's son?

Oswald Fuchs. Oscar Fuchs. Aha. Like me, Elsie may have been trying to make contact with Oscar Fuchs and mistook Oswald for Oscar. Or thought Oswald would lead her to Oscar.

Then again, perhaps Elsie really was in love with Oswald. But then why demand he save money...or give her money?

I thought of Mata Hari. She had any man she wanted. And every man wanted her. Yet, the man she chose was a homely little Russian soldier. *Every great love is followed by paralyzing grief or murderous revenge.*

"You might as well tell me who helped you," I said gently. "If you return the money, then perhaps your aunt will forgive you both."

"She won't. She'll sack him."

"Sack who?"

"Werner. I paid him to deliver the note."

"Werner, the waiter?" *Aha.* So that's why Werner always seemed so suspicious. The war widow was probably really just a war widow. There were so many of them after all.

Geez. I was glad I never got a chance to ask Werner if he was a British spy. No self-respecting British agent would get involved in a dognapping scheme.

"I don't want him to lose his job." Oswald turned around and gave me his back. "I really didn't mean anything." His voice cracked. *He doesn't want me to see him cry, poor lad.* "I just wanted to marry Elsie. I loved her."

That's when I saw it. Another one of Mrs. Einstein's ribbon bookmarks wrapped around Oswald's ponytail. "What's that in your hair?"

"One of those ribbons."

"Where did you get it?"

He whipped around to face me again. "The boy said I could have it."

"What boy?"

"The little boy who dropped it."

"You talked to him?"

"He came into the shop to ask for a glass of water. He saw it in my hair and said it belonged to his mother, but I could keep it."

"His mother?" Just as I suspected. "What did this mother look like?" With her flat face and lace collars, Mrs. Einstein was distinctive looking.

"I guess she was sort of short. Not exactly kindly."

"Can you describe her?"

"Dark hair and eyes. I don't know."

Some people were deuced unobservant. I decided to try another tack. "What was she wearing?"

"Maybe a blue dress with white stuff around the collar?"

Blasted fellow couldn't give a description to save his life. "You mean lace?"

"Yes. That's it."

"Did she have any other children with her?"

"Yes, an older boy."

Good enough. It had to be Mrs. Einstein and her sons. One was a teenager and hardly a little boy. So, it must have been the younger boy who came into the shop for water.

The pieces were falling into place. It all made sense now. I had no time to waste. I had to get back to the hotel and question Mrs. Einstein and her son Eduard.

"It reminds me of Elsie...." Oswald's voice trailed off.

"Of course it does." *Poor chap.* I took a deep breath, which I immediately regretted. The butcher shop was raw with fresh meat. "I'm sorry, Oswald. I really am." I fiddled with the latch on my purse. "But if you don't tell your aunt, I will."

"You wouldn't." He glared at me.

"Don't test me." I turned on my heels and marched to the door. "Tell her this afternoon or I'll tell her this evening." With that, I left the shop.

When I arrived back at the hotel, the place was aflutter with activity. Frau Sacher, cigar in one hand and bulldog in the other, flitted from room to room, barking orders.

"What's going on?" I asked, finally catching up.

"Paul von Hindenburg." She took a nervous puff and then blew a cloud into my face. "He's arriving momentarily."

"Who is Paul von Hindenburg?" The name was vaguely familiar.

She eyed me suspiciously. "How can you not know that?"

Crikey. My mind was racing, trying to place von Hindenburg. If I didn't remember soon, I'd blow my cover.

"Paul Ludwig Hans Anton von Beneckendorff und von Hindenburg, the general of the German Imperial Army, and Kaiser Wilhelm's right-hand man."

"What a name." Mark Twain came to mind. *Whenever a German dives into a sentence, you won't see him again until he emerges on the other side of the Atlantic with the verb in his mouth.*

"He's the one running this war." She shifted the dog from one arm to the other. "Now, if you'll excuse me, I have to check on the kitchen staff." Still shaking her head, she clamped the cigar between her teeth. "Oh, before I forget, a police officer was asking for you. He said he'd come back this evening." With that, she took off toward the kitchen.

A police officer. Blast it. Archie was right. Clifford and I had better get out of town as soon as possible or my goose was cooked.

I'd better warn the empress. *Is it merely a coincidence that the commander of the German army shows up immediately after the secret peace talks? I jolly well hope so.* Otherwise, Emperor Charles and Empress Zita could be tried for treason. I shuddered at the thought. They may represent the enemy, but they clearly were good people who were trying to stop the war.

In the distance, the *Pummerin* bell wailed its baleful lament.

I stood fixed in the lobby like a potted plant. I'd rushed back to find Eduard and his mother, Mrs. Einstein. *Should I change course and warn the empress?*

Surely the emperor and empress knew that the general was in town. They had to. In fact, why would he come to Vienna except to meet with the emperor? Maybe the emperor thought he could persuade the general to accept the terms Prince Sixtus proposed. That must be why he and the empress returned to Vienna today.

Arriving at the palace in a panic to warn the empress about the leader of the German army hardly counted as "laying low." Anyway, Austria and Germany were allies. *Really Fiona, what are you thinking? You know nothing about politics.*

A commotion at the front doors alerted me to the general's arrival. Paul von Hindenburg was here. The hotel staff was abuzz with anticipation. I moved into a remote corner of the lobby to watch the spectacle.

Werner held the door open while Max carried a large suitcase in each hand. A man with a high-collared uniform dripping with metals walked through the door, his bristled head held high. *That must be him.* His entourage trailed behind him.

The general's stern eyes were being swallowed up by the flesh of his face. His handlebar mustache stood at attention at each side of this mouth. And he sniffed the air as though he'd smelled something bad. He had an ominous presence that made me want to run away.

Frau Sacher checked him into the hotel herself. It was the first time I'd seen her without either a cigar or a dog or both. Whatever the general said, she responded *"Ja, Ja."* Smiling and fawning, her lashes fluttering, she was giving the general the royal treatment. If I didn't know better, I'd think they were having a liaison. Come to think of it...I didn't know better.

A dark thought crossed my mind. *What if Frau Sacher reported me and the general is here to string me up in the public square? Or perhaps that police officer told the military that I am a British spy.*

I ducked behind a column and watched as Frau Sacher led the general up the stairs. I followed at a safe distance. Peeking around the wall at the top of the stairs, I saw Frau Sacher open the door to one of the private rooms where the well-heeled Viennese carried out their secret affairs. *Does the general have a tryst this afternoon?*

Good heavens. Frau Sacher was heading my way. I dashed back down the stairs and across the lobby. Trying to look nonchalant, I picked up a newspaper from the front desk.

"Practicing your German?" Frau Sacher asked when she spotted me.

"Ja," I replied.

"Sehr gut." She smiled and then leaned closer. "It's such an honor to have General von Hindenburg staying with us. No doubt the emperor will pay us a visit now too. The hotel is back to its glory days." As if realizing she'd

forgotten something, Frau Sacher got a startled look on her face. "I really must go and get everything ready. We're having another royal visit."

"Might I have a word with you later?" I asked. If Oswald didn't tell her about the dognapping, I would.

"Later," she said and took off toward the kitchen.

If I go to Mrs. Einstein's room now, I will miss whoever was coming to meet with the general. I was dying to know who it was. *Not because I'm nosey, mind. Finding out could be an important bit of information to pass on to the War Office.*

Max sat behind the front desk. I asked if I could use the house phone. As usual, he looked at me like I was speaking Greek, but passed me the phone anyway. The operator rang Mrs. Einstein's room, but there was no answer. Just as well.

"The police were looking for you," Max said.

"Ja. I know." I glanced at my watch. *Blimey.* It had already gone one o'clock. No wonder I was so hungry. As my good old dad would say, "I could eat a scabby donkey between two backyard gates."

I would order lunch and then eat it in the lobby while I waited for the general's tryst to arrive. I just might catch Mrs. Einstein and her sons that way too. Two birds with one stone.

Given my status behind enemy lines with the coppers on my tail, it could be my last meal.

Chapter Twenty-Seven

The Stake-Out

I sat at one of the café tables along the far wall of the lobby. A small row of flowerpots separated the rest of the lobby from the eating area. Along with the peace lilies, large ferns and lanterns made it almost feel as if I was sitting outside at a sidewalk café.

Not taking my eyes off the entrance, I tucked into my schnitzel and potatoes. I was definitely going to miss the food. Suet pudding was no match for Sacher Torte. Even before the bloody war, I'd rarely eaten as well as I had in Austria.

I heard footsteps behind me. They seemed to be coming from the hallway that led to the kitchen. I didn't dare take my eyes off the front entrance. If only I had eyes in the back of my head. *Aha. The lipstick.* Quickly, I snapped open my purse and withdrew the spy lipstick. Finally, a chance to use it.

Pretending to apply some, I positioned the mirror so I could see the back hallway and the lower landing of the stairs. Muffled voices were getting louder. An elbow and a bulldog came into view, followed by the rest of Frau Sacher.

Who is she talking to? The dog? Not unless the dog was talking back. I heard another voice, a man's voice. I could see his uniform, but not his face. *The emperor?* Why would he have entered through the kitchen?

I followed their movements with the mirror. I couldn't get a good look at his face. *Dash it.* Frau Sacher's hair was always in the way. When they reached the landing, I finally got a look at him. *Good heavens. It's Count Czernin.*

Frau Sacher must have let him in through the kitchen. Now she was escorting him up the stairs. *To the private room where General von Hindenburg is waiting?* And she said her secrets weren't dangerous. *Horsefeathers.*

So that's who the general is meeting. Count Czernin, the emperor's foreign minister. *But why aren't they meeting at the palace? Why are they sneaking around, meeting in secret?*

Then it dawned on me. They were keeping their meeting a secret from the emperor. If I was right, this was bad. Very bad. Dangerous secrets indeed.

Count Czernin had refused to deliver the emperor's letter to Prince Sixtus in France. Now I knew why. The emperor's letter was arranging for the secret peace talks. Czernin must have wanted nothing to do with peace talks. *Blimey.* If the count told the general about the emperor's secret meeting in Rax—a meeting with the enemy to negotiate peace—the emperor and empress would be run out of town on a rail... or worse.

Forget about Mrs. Einstein, I had to warn them. I gathered my things and prepared to go. A commotion at the entrance made me freeze.

Mrs. Einstein's two sons burst through the door, laughing and tugging at each other's sailor shirts. Mrs. Einstein followed on their heels, grabbing at Eduard's ear. "*Stopp,*" she said sharply. A torrent of Slavic words surged from her depths. Her red face looked like it was about to explode.

The boys ignored her and chased each other around the lobby, dodging the columns and ferns. Scenes like this made me glad I didn't have children.

"Mrs. Einstein." I raised my voice to be heard over the children's shouting. "Mrs. Einstein. Boys." I waved. "Boys. Would you like some Sacher Torte?"

The younger boy stopped in his tracks and stared at me. The older one rammed right into him, knocking his brother to the floor. Eduard started to wail. Mrs. Einstein marched over to him and picked him up by the ear.

"Mrs. Einstein." I scooted out from behind my table and rushed over to them. "Would you and the boys like to join me for some cake and coffee?"

"Yes, please," the oldest said.

The younger boy stopped bawling. "*Kuchen?*" He looked up at me with tears in his eyes.

"*Ja. Kuchen und Kaffee,*" I said.

For some reason, this made the boys giggle. *What's so funny? My accent?*

"You can have cake with the kind lady," Mrs. Einstein said, still grasping Eduard's ear. "But only if you both promise to behave like proper gentlemen. Mrs. Douglas, my sons, Hans Albert and little Eduard."

The older held out his hand and I shook it. He must be Hans Albert.

"Yes, Mama," little Eduard said, pulling out of her grip.

Mrs. Einstein looked to Hans Albert.

"Yes, Mama," he said.

Given the scene they'd just made, and my true purpose in proposing cake, I decided it best to ask Werner to deliver Sacher Torte and coffee to the library. The conversation I needed to have with Eduard and his mother should be conducted in private.

I only hoped I could conclude my chat with the Einsteins before Count Czernin concluded his meeting with the general.

Without any windows, the library was dark. But it was also cooler than the lobby. Being surrounded by books was always reassuring, even if some of them looked like they'd never been opened. An odd mishmash of local history, continental travel, and popular fiction, the available books made for light reading.

The Einsteins followed me to a cozy sitting area in the middle of the room. The thick burgundy rug added to the effect of everything being wrapped in a blanket. "Shall we sit here?" I whispered. It was that kind of space, the kind that makes you whisper for no reason.

Once we were settled—and Max delivered our cake, coffees, and milk—I broached the subject of the notebook. I wanted to see Eduard's reaction to the mention of the purloined book. Given that the lad never sat still, it was difficult to tell if his fidgeting increased as we discussed the missing notebook.

I didn't think it right to accuse the boy, so I recounted how I'd found some of Mrs. Einstein's bookmarks, which were doubling as fine hair ribbons. Mrs. Einstein was on the edge of her seat, listening intently to my story.

Both boys were completely captivated by their Sacher Tortes. Except, in between bites, Eduard kept craning his head as if he expected someone to sneak up behind him. I followed his movements and realized he was looking back at the bookcase. With each turn of his head, he became increasingly agitated.

A pattern emerged. The boy took a bite of cake, stared back at the bookcase, and then gulped his milk as if he'd just crossed the Sahara Desert. *What in heaven's name is he doing?*

After another couple minutes of this game—which accelerated whenever I mentioned the notebook—I got up and went over to the bookcase to investigate.

"Eduard." Mrs. Einstein stared at her son in disbelief. "What's going on?"

I knew I was getting warm. Every time I approached the far end of the bookcase, little Eduard began to squeak. His high-pitched noises put me in mind of William Baxter and the kick to his shin I delivered that day my mother saw me at the bus stop.

I wouldn't let up until little Eduard's squealing and carrying on pointed the way to the notebook. *In a battle of wills, I always win.*

I ran my hands over the books one by one. *Aha!* Wedged between *Letters from Niš Regarding Harems* and *The Cruise of the Snark*, I found the thin black notebook. I slid it out. *Just like Dupin's purloined letter. Hidden in plain sight.*

"No," Eduard shouted.

"My notebook." Mrs. Einstein's face lit up and then it darkened again. "Eduard, did you take my notebook?"

The boy's lips tightened.

"Hans Albert." She turned to the older boy. "You were supposed to be watching your brother."

"But, Mama, I was studying for my exams."

She grabbed Eduard's arm. "Tell me. Did you take my notebook?" Mrs. Einstein demanded. "Papa will be very unhappy with you."

"I hate him!" Eduard bawled.

Perhaps my inability to have children was a blessing in disguise.

"Eduard. Don't say such a thing." Mrs. Einstein looked mortified. "Your father is a good man, a brilliant man."

I couldn't believe she was defending the man who left her for a younger, prettier woman. His cousin no less. I didn't even know him and already I hated him. *Only those who give no ground for jealousy are worthy of it.*

Mrs. Einstein didn't appear to be jealous. But she was obviously a broken woman.

I handed the notebook to a very appreciative Mrs. Einstein.

She clutched it to her chest. "Thank God." Her entire body seemed to soften.

"Now Papa will never come back," Eduard said.

Mrs. Einstein gave the boy a quizzical look. "My notebook is not the reason Papa is away." She glanced up at me. "It's a matter of the heart and not the mind. When you're older you will understand."

Eduard balled up his fists and started hitting himself in the face.

Oh dear. The boy believes his father is gone because of the notebook. That the notebook has substituted his beloved papa. My heart ached for him. Poor boy. He couldn't know that he actually might have saved the notebook from falling into the wrong hands. Eduard may very well have kept Fredricks from getting his hands on it.

Mrs. Einstein knelt in front of Eduard. Murmured something in her Slavic native tongue, she put her arms around his small waist and pulled him close.

If Eduard took the notebook and hid it in the library, then how did the bookmarks and letters end up in the butcher's stairwell? "Eduard," I said in a soft tone. I moved closer to him. "Did you take the notebook outside the hotel?"

He looked up at me with tears in his eyes. "I had to get away from Hans Albert. I ran through the kitchen and out the back door. When a man started chasing me, I hid down some stairs. After the coast was clear, I came back."

"With the notebook?" That explains how the bookmarks and letters ended up in the stairwell. Oswald must have scared young Eduard, so he ran around the hotel, down the block, and then hid in the stairwell.

He nodded. "I didn't know where else to put it. A book belongs in a library."

I didn't think mamma would find it here."

"Good thinking. Books do belong in the library." And certainly not in the hands of a dangerous criminal

Speaking of dangerous criminals, I heard footsteps in the hallway. Count Czernin? Or perhaps the general was expecting another visitor? "Excuse me."

Mrs. Einstein looked up at me with tears in her eyes.

I smiled sympathetically. "I'm leaving tomorrow. I really should go pack."

"Thank you," she said softly.

"You're most welcome."

I left the family alone in the library. Once I reached the threshold, I poked my head out toward the lobby. *Right.* Count Czernin had used the back door. I turned on my heels and trotted down the hallway toward the kitchen. I peeked through the glass in the door just in time to see Count Czernin depart through the back door.

I dashed back to the front entrance, went outside, and installed myself at the corner of the building.

No sooner had the count popped onto the sidewalk than one of the general's entourage flew past me and caught him. They were standing no more than four feet from me. I pressed myself up against the building and hoped I was invisible, just another insignificant woman loitering. *Goodness. I hope they don't think I am a lady of the night—in the afternoon.*

The general's emissary handed the count a folded piece of paper. They were speaking German, of course. Even so, I heard them both repeat "Sixtus Affäre" several times.

Affäre. A cognate of affair? Sixtus Affair. The peace talks with Prince Sixtus.

"Blimey," I said under my breath.

The general knew about the clandestine peace talks. The emperor and empress were in trouble. The time had come. I must warn them.

Chapter Twenty-Eight

The Traitor

Despite my wide-brimmed hat, the late afternoon sun scorched my cheeks. Moving as fast as my legs would carry me without breaking into a run, I sped past the opera house, coffee shops, and greengrocers. My light cotton blouse was wet with perspiration by the time I reached the Hofburg Palace.

Hopefully, the emperor and empress were still there and hadn't left for Schönbrunn already.

Panting, I waited in the foyer while one of the footmen notified the empress of my arrival. *Funny how when you're anxious, everything except your heart seems to move in slow motion.* After a few minutes—which seemed like an eternity— the footman returned.

"Her Majesty will see you in the morning room," he said in German. *At least that's what I hoped he'd said.*

In any case, I followed him across the grand entrance, down a long hallway, around a corner, and into the last room on the west side of the corridor.

The morning room was a cheerful space with pale-yellow wallpaper, a baby grand piano, a writing desk, and, of course, a lovely sitting area.

The empress was seated at the piano, playing a lively, almost violent, classical piece. With the last furious crescendo, she pounded the keys and bobbed up and down until her hair came loose from its chignon. I'd never seen her so passionate.

After she finished, she smoothed her hair. Like a switch had flipped, she went from fervid fury to gentle serenity. "To what do I owe the pleasure of your visit so soon after our farewell?"

"I'm not sure how to say this." I bit my lip.

The empress stood up from the piano and rushed to my side. "What is it? You're flushed." She took my elbow and led me to the sitting area. "I'll call for coffee. Or would you prefer tea?"

"Tea would be lovely." I folded my hands in my lap to compose myself. "And perhaps a glass of water too, please."

"Of course." The empress rang for service.

While we waited for tea, I tried to catch my breath and calm down.

After a few sips of water, I felt much better. A couple of sips of tea for good measure, and I dove in. "Around one this afternoon, General Paul von Hindenburg arrived at the Sacher Hotel. About thirty minutes later, he met with Count Czernin in one of the private suites." I took a biscuit from the tea tray.

Empress Zita's face paled. She sat staring at me, confusion in her eyes.

"I thought you should know." I nibbled on the biscuit to calm my nerves.

"Quite right," she said finally. "Czernin didn't tell us the general was in town." She squinted intently, as if doing long division in her head.

"Is it possible that the count told the general about your meeting in Rax?" I took a quick sip of water to wash down the very idea of the count's betrayal.

Emperor Charles burst into the room waving a newspaper. "Darling, look what's in the evening papers," he said in French in a worried tone. Surprised to see me, he stopped and stood there gaping. "Apologies. I didn't know you had company."

"It's just Fredrick's good friend, Mrs. Douglas," the empress said.

Fredricks's good friend. Horsefeathers.

"Right. Well, look at this." The emperor strode across the room to Empress Zita's side. He handed her the newspaper.

I glanced over at the headline. *Good heavens.*

The front page had a cartoon of Emperor Charles wearing a French beret. And, if I wasn't mistaken, the headline read: *Whose side is he on?*

"In response to Czernin's harsh speech, the French president got offended and went to the press with my letter to Sixtus." The emperor's tone indicated that the situation was urgent.

Wasn't the letter just an invitation to Rax? What's so odd about inviting your brother-in-law for a country holiday?

The empress gasped. "The newspapers have your letter?"

"Unfortunately, yes." The emperor paced the room. "And no doubt Czernin told Kaiser Wilhelm too."

"Count Czernin met with General von Hindenburg earlier today at the Sacher Hotel," I said. I may not have understood the full import of the situation, but I knew Count Czernin was untrustworthy.

The emperor stopped pacing, closed his eyes, and exhaled. "Czernin has betrayed us. If General von Hindenburg knows about the Rax meeting, then the Kaiser does too. Now the Germans are our enemies."

"If the Kaiser knows, then our lives are in danger," the empress said.

Golly. What was in that letter?

"Germany could invade Austria if they see us as conspiring with the French." The emperor ran his fingers through his hair. "We have to leave the country. That's the only way to save it."

The letter must have been more than an invitation to the mountains. But would an invitation to peace talks really be viewed as conspiring with the French? And then I realized—the letter must have set out terms for Austria leaving the war... perhaps even joining the Allies? I didn't hear anything about that while I was in Rax, but I was very drunk that first night so it could have been discussed and I simply don't remember, or maybe after Archie carried me to my room.

"Let's not rush into anything," the empress said. "Dearest, let's think through our options."

"What options?" His voice sounded desperate.

If the Germans had found out the emperor was negotiating with the enemy, then he had good reason to be worried. He was caught between the devil and the deep blue sea, as my father would say. If he denied writing the letters, then he gave up any possibility of negotiating peace with France. But if he admitted writing it, then Germany would dethrone him one way or another. The Pummerin bells came to mind.

"They can't blame us for trying to negotiate peace." The empress joined the emperor at the window.

I wondered what they were looking at. Perhaps they were surveying their kingdom to say goodbye.

"They can and they will," the emperor said. "Why did I have to become emperor? Why did my cousin have to marry a commoner?"

"He married for love like we did. You can't fault him that."

"Couldn't he have just as easily married an aristocrat for love?"

Every great love is followed by paralyzing grief or murderous revenge. That same can be said of war.

The empress frowned.

"If only my uncle hadn't been assassinated—"

"We can't change the past." The empress interrupted. "What's done is done," she said thoughtfully. "If we leave and Czernin has free reign, peace is even less likely." She sat on the windowsill and stared out. "It's not just our lives and those of our children, but the Austrian empire at stake. We must stay and clear our reputation."

"How will we do that?" the emperor asked.

"Deny it," the empress said. "Deny that you wrote the letters. Tell the Kaiser it is French propaganda. It will be the word of an ally against the word of an enemy."

"That would mean lying." The emperor put his hand on her shoulder. "I don't want to lie."

"Do you want to go into exile, or prison...or worse?" Her eyes flashed as she looked up at him. "What happened to the Romanovs in Russia could happen to us. We may have to go into hiding. Think of the children."

They both seemed to have forgotten about me. Like a fly on the wall, I had become nearly invisible. I quietly sipped my tea and listened intently to their conversation.

"We must deny it immediately." She turned to me. "Mrs. Douglas, is General von Hindenburg still at the hotel?"

"As far as I know."

"Good." She stood up. "We must go see him at once."

The emperor nodded. "I trust your judgment, dearest."

"Mrs. Douglas, can we give you a ride back to the hotel?" the empress asked. She rang for her maid.

Less than thirty minutes later, we were bundled in the carriage trotting off to the hotel. Good thing I went along. I learned that Count Czernin's days as foreign minister were numbered. The emperor would ask for his resignation effective immediately.

Blimey. The next in line for the job was none other than Oscar Fuchs. If he was working for the British and had managed to infiltrate the highest level of the Austrian government, Mr. Oscar Fuchs was a good spy indeed. Especially since he'd seemed bloody invisible. He must be more than a low-level operative as I was led to believe. Either that, or he'd gotten a promotion since the War Office gave me that list.

Exhausted, as soon as we arrived at the hotel, I retired to my room. I couldn't very well accompany the emperor and empress to see the general, after all. Anyway, I still had to finish packing and hurry Clifford along too.

Clifford must have heard me come in. For, no sooner had I entered my room than a knock came from the interior door that separated my bedroom from his.

"Where have you been all afternoon?" he asked. Rather pouty too. "What have you been up to?"

"Let's see." As I spoke, I busied myself taking clothes from the wardrobe, folding them neatly, and placing them in my suitcase. "I found Mrs. Einstein's missing notebook."

"Really? Where?"

"Hidden in plain sight in the library." I placed a blouse in the case. "Little Eduard took it thinking if he did his father would come back. Poor little mite."

"How did you figure out the thief was little Eduard?"

"Oswald saw him and gave me a description of the boy."

"Oswald?"

"Frau Sacher's nephew."

"Speaking of Anna's nephew," Clifford said with excitement. "You'll never guess what happened this afternoon while you were out. The nephew, this Oswald chap, came and confessed—"

"That he'd kidnapped Frau Sacher's bulldogs and collected the ransom." I folded my linen skirt. Not that it would do any good. Linen was so temperamental.

"How on earth did you know?" He put his hand to his cheek as if he'd just been slapped.

"Ratiocination, dear Watson." I smiled as I shut my case. How did I manage to end up with more than I brought? I couldn't get the blasted thing shut.

"Let me help you." Clifford came to the rescue.

"I discovered in my interview with Oswald that he was angry with his aunt because she wouldn't allow him to marry Elsie. And, get this, Elsie demanded that he'e saved enough money." I sat down on the edge of the bed. "Thirty thousand kroner, to be exact."

"The amount Frau Sacher paid in ransom," he exclaimed. He sat down next to me.

"Exactly."

"But why did you suspect the nephew in the first place?"

"He was Elsie's fiancé. She had a stash of bonbons and cake from the hotel. I found the toast and cake at the scene of the crime." I jabbed the air with my finger for emphasis. "Elementary, dear Watson."

"I say. Jolly clever of you." He smiled. "You've had quite a busy afternoon."

"I haven't told you the most interesting part. The Sixtus Affair."

"I say. What is the Sixtus Affair?" He was practically bubbling over with excitement. "Didn't you say earlier one of the empress's brothers is named Sixtus?"

Nodding, I leaned closer and whispered, "The president of France published the emperor's letter to Prince Sixtus to arrange the peace talks."

"And the Germans know about this?"

"They do now."

Clifford whistled. "Good thing we're leaving before dawn. This place is a powder keg."

"And it's about to explode."

Chapter Twenty-Nine

The Ticket

The next morning, well before daybreak, I reprised my woolen suit from the Dr. Vogel disguise I'd used at Ravenswick Abbey. Although it was liberating to wear trousers, it was also broiling. *However do men manage to wear so many clothes in the heat of the summer?*

Brown trousers, cotton shirt, and tweed jacket. Unlike other animal species, human males were plain by comparison. Still, I enjoyed the anonymity of blending in with the scenery. And for once, I didn't have to stand at my wardrobe for twenty minutes trying to decide what color frock to wear or which of my dozen hats to choose.

Now, the most important question was which mustache to wear. I opened my case and fingered my selection of crumb catchers. I settled on a thin pencil number.

As I applied my mustache, the familiar smell of spirit glue tickled my nose. All I needed now was the right wig. Given that I only had two men's hairstyles—Dr. Vogel and Harold the helpful bellboy—and I'd given one to Clifford, I was left with Dr. Vogel and his chestnut side part. I tugged on the wig and admired myself in the looking glass.

Very nice. I added a pair of spectacles for good measure. *Yes.* I made a passable young man.

All packed and ready to cross enemy territory as Barton Snodsbury, I knocked on Clifford's door.

He opened it and then took a step backward. "Good Lord. I didn't recognize you at first." He chuckled. "I say, you make a jolly attractive boy."

"And so will you." I looked him up and down. As usual, he wasn't ready. He was still in stocking feet and sans jacket. It seemed I'd interrupted him in the process of dressing. "We have a long way to go. Hurry up or the blasted war will be over by the time you're ready." I pushed him back into his bedroom.

Sometimes I felt like I spent half my life waiting for Clifford. *Sigh.* I remembered what my father used to say. "You want to go fast, go alone. You want to go far, go together." Whatever his faults, I was glad to have Clifford by my side.

"With you in a sec." He disappeared back into his room and then reappeared a minute later wearing shoes and a jacket.

"That's better." I bustled him into my room and led him to the dressing table. "Sit down."

He did as he was told.

"Did you settle the bill last night so we can leave before daylight?"

"I did."

"And you're all packed so we can sneak out before Frau Sacher is up?"

"Yes. Although I don't know why we have to sneak."

"Hold still," I barked. Blasted man kept wiggling and giggling.

"It tickles."

"We have to sneak because our lives are in danger. Have you forgotten where we are?" After painting his upper lip with spirit glue, I carefully pressed on the full handlebar crumb catcher. I followed it with a matching beard.

"That stuff smells gawd awful." He wrinkled his nose.

"And now for the eyebrows."

"What?"

"Hold still!"

Clifford scowled.

I applied big bushy brows and then stood back to admire him. I clapped

275

my hands together. "Excellent. Now for the wig." I tugged my Harold the helpful bellboy wig over Clifford's sandy hair. Then I stepped back again to admire my handwork. "Not bad." I handed him the looking glass. "Meet Upton Snodsbury." He didn't look exactly like the photograph in the passport, but close enough.

"Good Lord! I look like the bloody czar."

"All you need is a cigar, and you could pass as Dr. Freud."

"After what you've told me about his theories, I'll stick with the czar."

"You mean his notion that all desires are based on sexual instincts."

Clifford blushed. "I say, Fiona. You say the darndest things."

I laughed. I really did enjoy winding him up.

A knock at the outer door to my room made Clifford and I stare at each other, mouths hanging open.

Who in the world would be knocking at this hour? I hate to think. The police come to cart me off? The military come to drag me off to St. Stephen's square?

"Should we answer it?" Clifford whispered.

I put my finger to my lips and shook my head. We would be more suspicious for answering the door in the dark than we would for not answering. Whoever it was must expect us to be asleep at this hour.

An envelope appeared under the door. I stood paralyzed, staring at it. Neither Clifford nor I moved for what seemed like ages. I listened for footfall. Silence. Whoever had been knocking must have left after they slid the note under the door.

Like a stealthy cat, I moved slowly toward the door and bent down to retrieve the envelope. I couldn't believe it. The envelope was sealed with Fredricks's black panther insignia. Was the bounder back in Vienna? Was it him I saw yesterday across the street? I figured he'd be halfway around the world by now.

I opened the door and glanced down the hall in both directions. No one. Had Fredricks delivered it himself or hired the maid to do it?

I dashed to the window and looked out. Maybe I'd see someone leaving the hotel.

"I say." Clifford followed me. "What's going on? Who is it from?"

"Your dear friend Fredrick Fredricks."

"Good Lord. What does he say?"

I ripped open the envelop, dropped it on the floor, and read the letter.

> **Fiona, ma chérie. I trust I'll see you again soon. If you value your pretty little neck, please be careful. All my love, Fredrick.**

Why, the cheeky cad. Pretty or not, I did value my neck. "We'd better get a move on." I grabbed my suitcase and headed for the door. "The enemy is upon us."

* * *

Clifford's good humor and my quick wits got us out of more than a few sticky wickets crossing through enemy territory between Vienna and London. Clifford only slipped up and called me Fiona once during the three-day trip. Otherwise, we slapped each other on the back and played practical jokes on each other like two regular brothers. Clifford was a good sort.

One crotchety old innkeeper kept giving us the evil eye. I thought for sure he was on to us. Turned out the old bird had cataracts and always went around squinting at his dinner guests.

The trip through Germany was especially nerve-racking. We passed several caravans of lorries carrying armed soldiers.

Simple farmers, the Snodsbury brothers were for the most part left alone.

Once we'd left enemy territory, we gave up our disguises and changed back into our regular clothes. To be safe, we ditched the false passports and costumes under a log in a forest along the roadway.

After a long three days on the road, we made it back to London in one piece… safe and sound, just as Archie had ordered. I only chundered once on the ferryboat, which was my least favorite part of the trip. Even the trip across enemy territory didn't roil my stomach like the sea did. *Hopefully, I won't have to get on another boat ever.*

At last, we pulled up in front of my flat on Warwick Avenue. Covered in dust from the journey, and longing for a bath, I bid Clifford farewell. My brain knew it was sunup, but my body didn't know if it was morning or night. As I climbed the stairs to my flat, my suitcase banged against the stairs. Completely knackered, I didn't have the wherewithal to lift it any higher.

Once inside, I dropped my case, went straight to the tub, and turned on the faucet. It groaned and complained, but eventually produced a stream of warm water. I couldn't wait. I hadn't bathed since we left Austria.

Clifford had driven such long days, I arrived at our stopping place so completely knackered that I'd fall into bed with my clothes on. Since Clifford and I shared a room, I thought it better that way. Always a gentleman, poor Clifford spent the nights sleeping on the floor.

As I ran the bath, I stripped off my filthy clothes. Already I felt ten pounds lighter. I stepped into the bath, and my worries began to melt away. I slid down into the water. As my body relaxed, so did my mind. What a trip it had been.

Dognapping. Stolen notebooks filled with incriminating equations. I hoped that someday I would meet this Mr. Albert Einstein. I would surely give him a piece of my mind.

Yesterday, I'd learned that the Kaiser believed that the letter was French propaganda. The empress was right, as usual. Her plan worked to appease the Germans and keep them from invading Austria.

My only regret was not preventing the murder of Elsie Müller…and of course allowing her killer to get away. Although I might not be able to prove to a court of law that Fredricks was the murderer, the gnawing in the pit of my stomach convinced me it was true.

I felt especially bad because it was my fault that Fredricks figured out Elsie was working for us. If only I hadn't blurted out that she was Kurt Müller's sister, she might still be alive. All the more reason I had to find Fredricks and bring him to justice at last.

Archie was right. He was a slippery fish. He'd slipped the hook yet again.

It was going to take a special lure to catch him. And I had a hunch that I was going to have to be the bait.

After a good long soak and scrub, I emerged from the bath as wrinkled as a prune but content. It was good to be home.

My favorite plush robe hung from the familiar hook on the back of the bathroom door. I wrapped myself in it and then wrapped a towel around my stubby head. *Sigh. Yes, it is good to be home.*

The light streaming through the windows of my second-floor flat told me it was morning. Although I'd hardly slept in days, I was in a hurry to report to the War Office. Captain Hall would be pleased with all the information I'd gathered... even if the slippery Black Panther had gotten away again.

Already the flat was heating up. It was going to be a warm August day. I went to my wardrobe. *Dash it.* All my summer frocks were packed in my suitcase.

I dragged the blooming thing into the sitting room and unlocked it. Kneeling next to it on the floor, I took out my clutch and unloaded it. One by one, I put the contents on the coffee table. Spy lipstick, lockpick kit, and Mata Hari's pocket revolver. What did Archie call it? A Webley .450 Bulldog? I still couldn't believe Fredricks had replaced the live bullets with blanks. Had he done that when I was sound asleep from whatever he slipped in my drink that night at the hotel? That would explain why he'd drugged me. The thought of him creeping into my room while I was sleeping. I shivered.

Where is he now? He claimed he wanted peace, but his actions said otherwise. *Sigh.* The Great White Hunter had eluded me again.

I carefully lifted my blouses, skirts, and frocks from the suitcase. *Ah.* I held up the cotton frock with the pretty little yellow roses and oversized pockets, the one I was wearing when Archie kissed me...or had I kissed him?

Wait. What in the world? There was something in one of the pockets.

I reached in and pulled out a folded piece of heavy card stock. On the outside was written in bold letters, **To Omphale, from Hercules**.

Omphale. That was the statue at Schönbrunn Palace. The one Fredricks teased me about. *Omphale*. After her husband was gored by a bull, she took over his reign and then made Hercules her sex slave. I blushed just remembering the story.

When I sniffed the card, a familiar juniper cologne assaulted my nose. I jerked my head away. Fredrick Fredricks. *Of course*. I should have known.

I opened the card, and a ticket fell out onto the floor. I reached over and picked it up. **Anna Case, Soprano, Sunday, October 14th, 1917, at 3 p.m. Main Hall. Presented by Metropolitan Music Bureau. Dress Circle. Row FF seat 107. Carnegie Hall.**

Carnegie Hall? I fell back onto my bum and sat there on the floor staring at the ticket.

Screwing up my courage, I opened the card. My breath caught. The Black Panther insignia was stamped in dark ink on the thick card stock. The cheeky devil had written a note in elegant black strokes. I read it out loud.

"*Ma chérie*, sorry about Elsie. But Czernin thought it for the best. I hope you understand. As they say, all is fair in love and war."

I knew it! Fredricks was involved in Elsie's death. He and Czernin must have planned it together. *Love and war, indeed.*

If a great love ends in grief or revenge, then what of a great war? Sure to end in both, I had to have faith that end it would, eventually. After all, it couldn't go on forever.

I turned the card over. In bold black letters, **Meet me in New York. You won't regret it.**

Good heavens. The ticket. The cad wants me to meet him at Carnegie Hall. Paralyzed, I just sat there staring down at the note, the concert ticket, and my trembling hand.

Should I tell Captain Hall? If I did, would he order me to follow Fredrick Fredricks all the way to New York?

I'd never been to America. It could be deuced exciting.

Argg. My stomach groaned. If the boat ride across the channel made me seasick, how would I survive a week on a steamboat crossing the Atlantic? *Fredricks, you blackguard. I'm already regretting it.*

In my slippers and robe, I padded into the kitchen and put on the kettle.

Finally, I would get a good proper English cuppa. If only I had some milk.

Down the street from my flat, the Whitechapel bells of St. Saviour's rang out, calling parishioners to solemn mass… and, hopefully, not inviting the enemy to attack. The bells of Big Ben may have gone silent to protect Parliament, but the grace of God would have to protect the faithful.

I dropped into my very own chair, leaned my elbows on my very own table, and surveyed my own cozy kitchen. Indeed, it was good to be home.

Author's Note

Many of the characters in this novel were based on real people: Fredrick Fredricks, Frau Anna Sacher, Emperor Charles and Empress Zita and her brothers, Mileva Einstein, and Jane Addams. I have changed the timeline and some of the events for the sake of the plot.

Fredrick Fredricks really was a spy for the Germans in World War I (and in WWII). His real name was Fredrick "Fritz" Duquesne. The aliases mentioned in the novel were ones he really used. Reportedly, he was one of the most brazen spies in history. He really did work for a newspaper in New York. And he did go shooting with Theodore Roosevelt.

Frau Anna Sacher was widowed young and took over the Sacher hotel, which was known for its private rooms and discrete liaisons... and, of course, the famous Sacher Torte. Frau Sacher was rarely ever seen without a cigar in one hand and a French Bulldog in the other.

Emperor Charles of Austria-Hungary was called "the prince of peace," and beatified by the Catholic Church for his attempts at peace. Some historians say Empress Zita was a strong influence on her husband and his politics. The "Sixtus Affair" was a threat to Emperor Charles's reign. In 1917, the secret peace talks did take place with Empress Zita's brothers, but not in Austria, but rather in Switzerland. And the infamous letter was delivered by Zita's mother. Charles and Zita really did meet and fall in love at Villa Wartholz in Rax.

Mileva Einstein was from the former Austrian-Hungarian Empire, what is now Serbia. She did collaborate with her husband, Albert, when they were both young physicists. And she did receive the Nobel prize money. Letters indicate that she was more important in Einstein's early theories, including relativity, than she has been given credit for.

Jane Addams was an American peace activist. Although she made several trips to Europe, she was not actually part of the secret peace talks held by the Emperor of Austria. You will see her again in the next Fiona Figg Mystery set in New York.

A Note from the Author

If you enjoyed *Villainy in Vienna,* please consider leaving a review on Amazon or Goodreads. Those reviews mean a lot to indie authors like me.

Acknowledgements

Thanks to my various editors, Lisa Walsh, Barb Goffman, Verena Rose, and Shawn Reilly Simmons. As always, I'm grateful for my companions, my hubby, Benigno, and my three demanding felines, Mischief, Mayhem, and Mr. Flan.

About the Author

Kelly Oliver is the author of three award-winning and bestselling mystery series: The Fiona Figg Mysteries, The Jessica James Mysteries, and The Pet Detective Mysteries.

When she's not writing mysteries, she is a distinguished professor of philosophy at Vanderbilt University. She is the author of sixteen nonfiction books and over one hundred scholarly articles. She lives in Nashville, Tennessee with her husband and three demanding felines.

SOCIAL MEDIA HANDLES:

AMAZON AUTHOR PAGE
https://www.amazon.com/Kelly-Oliver/e/B001HN3HCM/ref=dbs_p _ebk_rwt_abau

Kelly Oliver Author FACEBOOK
https://www.facebook.com/kellyoliverauthor/

BookBub
https://www.bookbub.com/authors/kelly-oliver

twitter
@kellyoliverbook

pinterest
https://www.pinterest.com/jessicajamesmysteries/

INSTAGRAM
@kellyoliverbooks

Goodreads: https://www.goodreads.com/author/show/15643052.Kelly
_Oliver?from_search=true

LinkedIn

TikTok
Kellyoliverbooks

AUTHOR WEBSITE:
Kellyoliverbooks.com

Also by Kelly Oliver

Fiona Figg Mysteries
  Betrayal at Ravenswick
  High Treason at the Grand Hotel

Jessica James Mysteries
  Wolf
  Coyote
  Fox
  Jackal
  Viper
  Cottonmouth
  Cobra

Pet Detective Mysteries
  Cub Reporter
  Treasure Hunter
  Geocacher

Sixteen nonfiction books

CPSIA information can be obtained
at www.ICGtesting.com
Printed in the USA
LVHW030710120722
723226LV00003B/286